I

CAN

HEAR

PIGEONS

ON

THE

WINDOWSILL

Kaydeon K. Moore

KMO BOOKS

ISBN-10: 0615607527
ISBN-13: 978-0615607528

CHAPTER 1

Across the street from Avery Tyler, there lived a madman. Not a madman in the traditional sense, with all the negative connotations and harsh, debasing overtones-but a madman to be sure. Along every avenue and every boulevard one can bear witness to strange routines. But the daily walk from the bus stop to the house only took Avery down two streets. This is where he first caught a glimpse of Mr. Chase.

A middle aged man, somewhere in his early 60's if you had to guess, Mr. Chase laid on his all brick driveway and stared at the sun. He did this presently. He did this every afternoon for as long as Avery could remember. Most pretended not to notice. They would greet Mr. Chase as if he were sitting in a lawn chair like any nominally normal person would be, and he would smile and perhaps twitch one of his fingers in acknowledgment.

To what purpose this exercise served, Avery wondered constantly. Many of his make believe explanations would require many pages to tell and reached far into the realm of impossibility. He went on to explain that Mr. Chase was an android, and that an inexperienced electrician, unfamiliar with blueprints mistakenly placed the charging bay under the android's driveway when it should have gone in the bedroom. In one version of this story, the battery powered man was a mercenary scout placed on Earth by an android empire. In another version, he was a peaceful automaton, seeking only to live a conventional life among life forms he'd grown to love. But whether his robotic shell was a ruthless killing machine with a prime objective to destroy mankind, or an android that learned to love, Mr. Chase needed to plug his back into a cable on the driveway.

Eventually, Avery exhausted his imagination. The yarns grew more and more believable until they were hardly yarns at all. He would cycle through the few acceptable possibilities describing why Mr. Chase would lay bare-chested on his driveway and whistle.

"He's an amateur singer, working out his lungs and tanning his skin."

"He's an old fashioned astronomer and records the position of the sun daily."

"He's a retired surfer. He lays there because he misses the beach."

But although he derived pleasure from laying these bits of invented information on his friends, Avery knew deep down that it was wrong.

Next door to Avery Tyler, there lived a madman. And whatever dark, forbidding images spark and flash and elicit and morph into other dark, forbidding images at the recognition of that word, go with it. None of the neighbors spoke about Mr. Thurbin. Not openly, anyways. If anyone was forced to make a casual introduction, a little creativity would be required, because the mailbox in front of his house betrayed only his last name. He was the mystery citizen. And for some intangible reason, the neighborhood residents preferred it stay that way. Fear grows faint through the distance.

Most nights a Doppler effect could be heard on an ungodly loud noise. This was the 1967 Ford Mustang's 350 big block engine held at an unnecessary 4500 rpm. Mr. Thurbin's car, much like Mr. Thurbin himself, was boisterous, dangerous, evil. You couldn't see through the pitch black tint, and nobody got out until the car was safely parked behind the garage door. It was thought to drive itself through the forces of demonic possession.

Next door to Avery Tyler, there lived a madman. The other next door. Avery actually lived in between madmen. Mr. Thurbin, stage left- but a man with a family, a man that hosted cook-outs, that knew all the neighborhood kids by name, that rode a bike with a handlebar basket lived to the right. Most people would not consider him mad. In fact, anyone about to make that claim should first prepare a list of arguments to support it, because to put it bluntly, you would be thought impertinent. Avery was perfectly cognizant of this, and kept his mouth shut as he usually did about such things. It did not take Avery long to realize that people did not grasp the logic behind his findings.

Example-

Avery would say that the man living in the house to the left of him (that's stage right, but the typical person does not think in terms of stage left or stage right) was nuts. Avery's uncle would say 'Don't be an asshole, boy. Guy Weeks is a pillar of society. You should be lucky to remain as sane as him when you grow up'. Avery would proceed to argue his point. He would cite the misuse of 70's slang, which Guy recently started to utilize in only the most obvious context. 'How the hell do you know how 70's slang is used? You weren't even born till five years after the 70's ended.' Avery would concede that point, but as his mother spent those years in high school, he considered her an authority, and it was her who tipped him off to the discrepancies in Guy's vernacular. 'I still don't see how that makes him crazy. A little nerdy, but you're still the asshole here,' Avery's uncle went on. This was typical. Avery expected this type of treatment until his position was fully pronounced. He would continue to urge his uncle to consider the implications of a man just who started to use expired slang- incorrectly at that.

His uncle shook his head back and forth, pitying the transient ignorance of youth.

However, Avery was on to something. What of a man who missed his childhood? What of a man whose rebellion came too late and too soft? If there were a beast inside every man's heart, and that beast usually escaped its prison slowly, in increments of insurgence, would logic not expose the danger of a man that never rebelled? There would be too much of that beast, all getting out at once. Perilous and critical. If using words he wished he'd been brave enough to use in his teenage years was the apex of his releasing the beast, Guy Weeks was a time-bomb.

In the house with Avery Tyler, there lived a madman. A madman who at the age of seven brought a disassembled radio to show and tell and rebuilt it in front of twenty one classmates. Michael Guess Tyler was a genius. His memory approached total recall and his creativity knew few boundaries. It is always a humbling experience to be in the presence of such a prodigious mind, but that Michael grew into brilliance was hardly a surprise. From infancy he exhibited an eerie competence palpable enough to send shudders down any babysitter. His Lego buildings were inspiring and architecturally faultless. He insisted on inventing a unique way to tie his shoes after examining and analyzing a number of secure knots, and combining their best, most symmetrical features. He called it a Guess knot.

On his 14th birthday, Mr. and Mrs. Tyler bought Michael a piano and arranged for a year's worth of lessons. On his 15th birthday, Mr. and Mrs. Tyler watched Michael perform Chopin's Ballad #1 in Opus 23 and Liszt's Hungarian Rhapsody #2.

All this made the usual sibling rivalries difficult for Avery. For while he did have the advantage of two years growth over Michael, and could always resort to physical violence because of it, he often felt like the younger older brother. Every argument won with a punch or a headlock was an empty victory. From Michael's sometimes bloody lips, the borrowed words of Buddha would flow- 'Peace comes from within. Do not seek it without' or 'Holding on to anger is like grasping a hot coal with the intent of throwing it at someone else. You are the one who gets burned.' Of course, these remarks would only play a sidekick to reverse psychology, and Avery would be made even more upset.

Puberty, however, saw an end to most of their childhood clashes, and as the boys grew they became inseparable. This could have something to do with a last minute growth spurt which rendered Avery's physical dominance obsolete, but that the brothers simply matured was a much more pleasant thought. Michael's triumphs became Avery's.

Where, then, was the problem in all this?

It all stemmed from a late night conversation, the beginnings of doubt in Michael's sanity. He confided to Avery one night, after sneaking a few cigarettes to the back yard; that for all his aptitude, for all his envy inducing, vexing proficiency in life, he has always felt a bit 'off'. It was a proclamation that he continued to make, rather frequently as time went on, a proclamation that Avery always found unnerving.

"You've always felt a bit off? Your whole life?" He once thought to ask.

5

"Yeah, pretty much."

"How can you feel off if that's the only way you remember feeling? What are you comparing off to if you've never felt," a short pause, filled with an ummm and an uhhh that would spell the letter N if read in morose code, "not off?"

To this, Michael shrugged his shoulders.

Mad? There was a madness in it that Avery never expected to understand.

CHAPTER 2

They left the car running, parked at the fence that separated a pretend world from the real one. Blades of yellow-green grass still grew high alongside the chain links where lawnmowers couldn't reach. It was hot out. Blistering. The shiny sea of death-colored pavement in front of them begged for the sun's mercy, sending pathetic cries in hardly visible waves of air.

Nearly five o'clock in the afternoon. Avery cracked his knuckles and shifted his legs anxiously.

"Call him again," whined the pretty brunette beside him.

"I just called him five minutes ago. You were here, remember? He said he'd be here soon."

In the middle of the backseat, Luke turned a vacant expression to the window.

The problem they faced was typical when scoring from high school kids. A lot of times you couldn't just drop by their house to pick up. Parents would wonder why a car full of young adults was stopping by for a duration of time only long enough to say hello and goodbye. You had to meet them somewhere- a McDonald's. A gas station. A school parking lot, of all places.

"I don't know why I'm here wasting my time," the brunette continued, "I'm not even going to smoke any of that shit."

The undignified remark was ignored by both Avery and Luke. Avery ignored it because the brunette, Lisa, was his girlfriend. Luke did so for pretty much the same reason, but that Lisa got away with so much just because his buddy liked to hold her hand was grating. Besides, it was a given that this kid was taking a long time. No need to worsen their eagerness by concentrating on it.

Far off on the football field to the right, large boys in dirty white shirts ran patterns and were yelled at by a middle aged, pot-bellied, disgruntled coach. Lisa watched them impassively.

Far off in front of them, the school was quietly anticipating tomorrow morning. Avery said so, and thought himself quite clever for it. It wasn't actually that far off, the school. But in this day and age the people have grown lazy. They will happily drive around or wait for longer than it would take to walk the entire lot for a place nearer to the front of it. This made perfect sense to Avery, Lisa, and Luke.

To the left, a blue Ford Explorer finally pulled in.

Christopher Bouley, the proud owner of that new Explorer, was an odd breed of teenager. Surely every high school had one, maybe even two or three, but rarely four or five and never more than six. He was a nerdy kid. Not the kind of nerdy kid that's charismatic once you get to know him and hangs out with other charismatic outcasts, but one who is treated, by just about everyone, as a nerdy kid. Nothing about him was cool. He didn't have any real hobbies to speak of, like playing in a band or practicing martial arts or drawing caricatures of his classmates. He wasn't even notably intelligent, the enviable attribute that gets most nerds picked on for being nerds. Chris must have grown tired of all this in his third year, and did the one thing that would guarantee at least some degree of esteem- he began to sell drugs.

Presently, young Mr. Bouley is one of the most popular boys in his grade. He dates two surprisingly attractive girls, both of whom are fully aware of each other; he has a slew of acquaintances, many of whom he doesn't deign to acknowledge.

This does not, however, alter the fabric of reality that Christopher Bouley belongs to. He is still, even after the recent growth spurt that put him just short of average height, even after the increased bankroll drug sales have bequeathed upon him and the trendy new clothes he wears, a nerdy kid.

Avery struggled to remove his wallet from the front pocket of his jeans. Lisa was poking fun at him earlier, citing the 'hot day, hot clothes' assertion that was usually made by only responsible parents, so he was glad that the effort required of him to get anything out of those tight pockets went unnoticed. Back seat- the expression on Luke's face would lead anyone looking at just his face to believe that he must be rubbing his hands together hungrily, but he wasn't. He was sitting pretty still. Just watching the SUV pull up beside them.

It's nearly impossible to roll down a hand-cranked window without looking a little spastic. Christopher wasn't so much amused by the activity of cranking as he was thinking somebody out there actually had car windows that weren't automatic.

"What's up fellas," Christopher said. Somehow the lingo didn't sound forced.

Before Avery or Luke could say anything back, Christopher was pulling the door handle. It was locked, so he pulled it a couple more times. Luke finally reached over and let him in.

"Alright, just drive around this block."

"Drive around this block?" asked Avery.

"Yeah," Christopher replied.

"What the fuck do I need to drive around the block for? I had the window down. See?"

"Dog," now sounding a little artificial, "I go to school here. I can't have nobody seeing me sellin' weed right here in the parking lot."

"But look- you're already in the car. I already have the money out. There isn't anybody around at all."

Christopher looked like he was going to say something, Avery quickly cut in, "If you were here earlier than I'd have driven you around but we have to be somewhere."

It was enough. The young bore come drug dealer removed a handful of bags from his pants. They were each for the amount Avery wanted, and he picked one at random. The slack in Luke's mouth tightened once the bags they didn't buy were put away. Chris said 'alright, y'all' and Avery said 'alright' and Chris got out of the car. The Explorer was backing up before anyone said anything else.

"Unbelievable," Luke exclaimed.

A few seconds passed. Avery started the car and they began to drive home.

"Un-fucking-believable," Luke said again.

Lisa obliged in asking what.

"Eggbert. Eggbert sells weed. What's the world coming to?"

A response was not necessary. He was absolutely right.

CHAPTER 3

In the Judean Desert overlooking the Dead Sea, there is a castle known as Masada. The brilliantly placed stronghold is fortified not only by four meter thick casemate walls, but by nearly impossible to navigate cliffs on all sides. From the west, the plateau it sits upon ends in a sheer drop of almost 100 meters. From the east, the drop is four times as severe, rendering an army's natural approach to the castle nearly impossible. It was the site chosen by the Zealot's for their last stand against the legions of Rome.

Herod the Great was responsible for building the fortress as a refuge for himself in the event of a Jewish revolt sometime between 37 and 31 BCE. It was a masterfully executed work, with comfortable living quarters and a network of cisterns engineered to house a renewable supply of freshwater for residents, assuring the possibility of a small, self sustaining community life. The castle's creator himself, however, never saw a time where the use of his 'last resort' became necessary. Its true purpose wasn't decided until some 75 years after King Herod's death, when a group of Jewish rebels led by Elazar ben Ya'ir overcame a garrison of Roman soldiers stationed there. Around this time, history witnessed the fall of Jerusalem and the resistance fighters in Masada were joined by the zealots and their families who fled the holy land. For nearly two years, the group executed small scale raids on Roman troops and other Jewish settlements from their newly won home base. It then became a great interest of Rome to crush the rebellion, and Governor Lucius Flavius Silva led the Roman 10th legion *Fretensis* to the perimeter of Masada and laid siege to the fortress.

Occupants of Masada faced hopeless odds. Beyond their walls a battle hardened army of some 15,000 troops and all their weaponry waited. But the geography of Masada prevailed for a time. The 200 or so able fighters inside the castle resisted occupation. It would require an ostentatious plan enacted by Rome's most gifted general to breech the castle walls and restore the status quo to Judea.

So said the History Channel.

All exaggeration aside, the raindrops that smacked the patio outside were as large as peanuts. From a typically Floridian hot summer day to a typically Floridian wet summer day, the sudden transformation shocked no one. Avery was hiding from the weather atop his living room couch with his younger brother and one of his best friends. There was still a very, very high chance that they would be doing the exact same thing even if it wasn't raining, but it was, and it was a perfectly good excuse to sit inside and watch television. The weed that Avery and Luke purchased earlier that afternoon turned out to be quite good.

A big golden 'H' appeared on the T.V. screen. The

commercial break was over.

After approximately three months of storming the castle, General Silva's plans were complete. Using thousands of tons of stone and soil, the 10th legion erected a breath-taking circumvallation wall and then a rampart against the western approach of Masada. They used this ramp to bring a battering ram to the castle wall and force an entrance. What the Roman soldiers found inside was not the small Jewish fighting force they expected, but around 900 men, women, and children already dead by their own hands. To the rebels in Masada, their victory was in denying the Roman soldier's chance to kill.

"That was me!" Luke almost shouted.

"Hmm?" Michael asked slowly. He did not sound nearly as enthusiastic.

"Lucius Flava Silva. I lived his life. I know that ramp!"

This was out of character for Luke, who seldom stepped the boundaries of reason and almost never weighed the absurd. For this purpose, Avery and Michael had to consider his claim. The notion of reincarnation/past lives/transmigration of the soul/rebirth/metempsychosis was, to them, as plausible a notion as any. The first thing that occurred to Michael was not the unfeasibility of the soul that powered Luke's body powering another, even in Judea circa 74 BCE, but the number of people involved in the building of that ramp. It would still seem familiar to Luke if his spiritual lineage connected him to any of the thousands of people involved in the construction of the ramp, watching the construction of the ramp, or dreading the construction of the ramp. It was just as likely that his soul was passed on from a slave or Zealot.

To assume that he was automatically linked to the most important character in this historical event reeked of wishful thinking. Michael said so. And Avery, for the pleasure of disheartening his friend, agreed immediately.

"I'm smarter than a slave," Luke answered.

"Not that much. I can think of plenty," was all Avery could say before his brother cut him off.

"But you'd have had many lives to learn. Not only that but not all slaves were idiots. They just came from people that were overpowered by the Romans. Almost everybody was."

"Okay. But I know it was my idea. I knew the answer as soon as I knew the problem. My soul's already dealt with it."

Avery realized suddenly that Luke was playing a very subtle joke and began to laugh. His cackling subsided without changing the mood. Apparently it wasn't a joke at all.

"Oh my God," exclaimed Avery, adding nothing to the conversation.

"Oh my God, what? Prove it. Prove that I'm not!" Luke said back. He was completely serious.

"You're not. There. It's done," was the last thing that Avery would say regarding this subject. He is no longer a participant in the discussion that follows.

"I'm Italian," Luke offered.

"I don't think that reincarnation conforms to nationality."

"I've always loved Roman history."

"I know tons of people that love Roman history," Michael maintained.

"I'm a natural leader."

"I disagree"

"Fuck you. I am. I also feel that deserts represent failure."

"That could be because they're not especially hospitable places."

"Even my name, Luke, is probably the modern form of Lucius."

"Oh, so your parents must have known this all along. Next?"

The 'next?' did it. Luke saw the pattern forming. Michael could do this all day. It was easier to invalidate similarities than it was to think of them. And Luke knew full well that his knowledge of the Roman General was limited by the time span of the History Channel's program.

The wide eyes of Michael awaited another claim of spiritual heritage, but the rhythm was already broken. To prove such a claim would require a barrage of effortless arguments, unrelenting and difficult to disprove. The bantering had ceased.

Avery, weary from the solemnity, packed another bowl and turned the T.V. over to a less thought provoking channel.

CHAPTER 4

There is something wrong with forty five minute naps. Avery woke from one feeling groggy, hungry, dizzy, hot, and slow. The darkness of the room was depressing; the muted streetlights that bled through his drapes and completely died soon after make waking up absurd. Clocks throughout the house read anywhere from 10:21pm to 10:24pm (not counting the lazy clock on the VCR, which was wrong 1438 out of 1440 minutes a day and nobody paid attention to anyway). Virtually blind, Avery picked clothes from the floor and dressed himself in what felt like jeans and a wrinkled cut-off shirt.

It was a relatively blithe time for ninety five percent of the working population, where the passing of minutes only represented transitory periods of relaxation and play. From 10:21 to 10:23 (according to the clock in Michael's room) Ryu fought with Chun Li and won a heated two to one bout with a well placed Hadoken. Brian was forced to pass the controller to Ian and by 10:24 a new fight was underway. Avery heard the commotion through both his and his brother's door, and envied those boys and their carefree interpretation of late evening. For him, half past ten was not a time for videogames. It was not a time for the Movie Theater or bars, trouble or romance. When the numbers on the downstairs clock approached 10:30, he could do little more than sit and watch them- unless he felt particularly ambitious, in which case he could leave the house a few minutes early. He damned the third shift nightly.

This particular evening, when Avery finally set off, it was at the last possible minute and devoid of any enthusiasm. He fell into the seat of his car and drove slowly, inattentively- the kind of drive where a couple blocks go by unnoticed and the driver thinks to himself, *Did I come this far? This is dangerous.* Through dirty windows the world at night seems surreal. This was probably due to the way images didn't quite pass through but were rather absorbed and smeared by the streaks and spots in the glass. The unnatural glow of the nighttime streets, complimenting the unnatural hours that Avery's job subjected him to. Going through the motions. Boring. As boring as someone describing streetlights and dim. The ten minute ride was Novocain. Little by little it dulled the spirit, prepared the psyche for routine. It wasn't that Avery hated his job; he just never remembered that he didn't hate his job until he got there and forgot that he didn't hate it soon after he left.

He pulled into the lot and smiled, suddenly uplifted by the small measure of consolation fate offered up.

In the beginning of the week, Avery and a couple astute coworkers shared a collective epiphany. It had to do with a subtle observation, one about another friend and coworker. Not a big deal, really, but the quirks of night shift employees were something that Avery had a great appreciation for, and he was now in a position to witness their discovery for the first time since they discussed it.

He parked quickly, taking the first spot with an open line of sight to Gill's car, which was parking at the exact same time. Avery watched closely, kept count silently. Timing was the thing to consider here. It was happening now. Gill got out and closed the door in a hurry. He walked fast, his pace that of an escape, but as he put more and more distance between himself and the car, the pace gradually slowed, decreased to an eventual browse. Race, canter, walk, stroll. Why did Gill do that? And like clockwork! Every time Avery watched Gill get out of his car it was the same thing, it just took a few other people seeing the same thing to put the microscope over a spectacle once too insignificant to take note of. Maybe one of the programmers, who were all math geniuses as far as Avery could tell, maybe one of them could apply a formula to Gill's walk? A rate of deceleration or something. Avery decided to make that his extracurricular objective for the night. It would give him far more fulfillment than getting a tray of parts past QC.

He made his way towards the big, bright windows of the building.

Inside, the lathes and grinders hummed an efficient, orderly white noise.

These poor things never get a break, thought Avery with an empathizing dejection that was a little less sarcastic than he expected. He took ten minutes to inspect the caps being made by his machines. They were to spec and the raw material would last a couple more hours. *What do I do? I'm a CNC machinist.* It was true. Avery was a CNC machinist. At the moment, however, there was very little machining that needed doing. *What do I do? I read Paradise Lost.* That was more like it. He was just about to open that most difficult book when the shadow of a tall biker covered his chest, face, and eyes.

"How's it going, buddy? I think we'll have you run twelve and fourteen tonight."

The boss was here to fuck him up. Nothing Avery could scream or shout or yell or holler would come off as anything other than a suggestion. He spoke reasonably.

"Oh. Umm, I thought I was on six and eight?"

"Nope," came the reply, "twelve and fourteen." And with that it was done. He wasn't looking at Avery when he said it and he wasn't standing there after he'd said it.

The easy job would probably go to Johnny. Avery walked past two tables and set his book down on the third. No fucking fair. Now he would have to spend the whole night changing tools before doing inspections before making offsets and what's worse- Vietnamese pop music was coming from both sides. *I'm a CNC machinist,* he thought without spirit, and started his first inspection of the rouge machines assigned to him.

CHAPTER 5

It was sometime between eight and nine-thirty in the morning, and Avery laid on his back with open, static eyes. He was not awake. That is to say, he was not so fully awake that his body obeyed any of the commands he sent it, because try as he might, he found it impossible to turn his head, twitch his fingers, bend his arms or lift his legs. Some senses appeared to be working with moderate normality- his eyes saw a dingy white ceiling, his back felt the wrinkles of moist, ruffled sheets, but he remained frozen. That Avery felt vulnerable was natural. His vital organs were exposed to the world, and should a werewolf leap from the closet and bob for his intestines, he would be ill able to fend it off or even turn away. But there were no such thing as werewolves. And Avery's sense of unrivaled terror would only seem logical if one knew, as Avery knew, that a lady ghost sat to his side.

He told his arms to move. Sent instructions of

18

quick jerking movements to no avail. He told his arms to move again- this time with an order of slow, steady motions. No reaction. His body was inert and stale as the air around him, as if his entire being retreated in cold panic, the 'me' that he once defined as conscience plus body was in hiding, obviously not defined or even supported by the body at all. He was but a passenger, seeing only the white stucco above him, feeling only the damp cotton beneath him.

The ghost did not betray much beyond her presence at first. Avery felt her there, and whether the lust he detected was an aspect of his own vanity, or the ghost's actual lust was for a time unclear. But she watched him. Of that he was sure. She watched the frozen young man for what seemed like minutes before finally moving her body down.

It was too real to be imagination. He was too awake to be dreaming.

The ghost was enthralled. Avery sensed that now. Her yearning was more tangible than the being itself, and though to some extent scared, Avery was more than content to see where this was going. When she rubbed herself on Avery's hand, he felt- FELT that one of a kind, familiar texture. It was there; as real and substantial as the pillow under his head. He wanted desperately to play an active roll in whatever sexual experimentation might occur and tried harder than ever to move, to rip his body from this condition of not-quite-sleeping beauty.

Suddenly a muscle contracted. Just as suddenly she was gone.

Avery did not ponder the experience for long, as sleep soon called his straying conscience to line. In the seconds that he did stay awake evaluating the impossibility of what undoubtedly took place, there was no fear. To sleep with a ghost was not an aspiration he would have admitted to, but the pride of realization colored his cheeks and pulled the corners of his lips. He was desirable beyond dimensions.

Nearly an hour went by. It was a despairingly uneventful hour, as furniture and appliances don't do too much without the provocation of their human masters. Still and quiet.

The second encounter started out in much the same manner as before, only this time Avery had a notion of what to expect. He waited patiently now, reveling in the immobility, his mind focused on the feeling to come. But the calm disappeared in a hurry. This time the presence was different. It was not female. It was not looking for a trans-reality fling. This was a male being, and it radiated jealous rage in its purest form.

From invisible feet to fingertips coursed the desire to maim, shred, bloody, tear, wrench, pound, and kill. Avery could feel it trying to hurt him, but he felt it as an intention, not a physical consequence. He felt not hands twisting his limbs, but something strive to twist his limbs, trying with all what-ever-it-was' might. Involuntary reaction kicked in. Movement was achieved. Avery was awake.

The information was surprisingly easy to digest. Two ghosts visited Avery that morning, one kind and one not. For Avery, there was no period of incredulity, no thoughts questioning these events or rationalizing them into something else entirely. What happened had happened. He could do nothing but enjoy the rest of his day off and at some point share his story with a trusted individual or two.

CHAPTER 6

The release of pressurized water was the first thing Avery heard going on outside. Mr. Weeks was watering the potted plants on his back patio. He was wearing a pair of baggy black running shorts and flip flops, and had the outdoorsy man been wearing anything else, it would have come as a surprise to Avery. Guy Weeks was the quintessential suburban recreational type. His free time would be much sooner spent running, swimming, playing tennis, riding bikes, or playing catch than it would be watching T.V., listening to music, reading, or cooking. When sweat and water collected as it did now on Mr. Weeks' bronzed skin, you could rest assured that he was content.

Shaken, questioning the integrity of reality, Avery walked to the edge of his patio where Guy could see him.

"Hey, if it isn't my right hand man!" Guy said, smiling.

Guy liked to say that to any and all of the males living in Avery's house. It was sort of cute, Avery thought, but he preferred to think of himself as being the neighbor to the left. Everybody disagreed, but when he stood on the driveway and faced the street, it was Guy's house on the right of him. They were the ones living there, looking out and not in, why didn't they set the standards of their rights and lefts on that ground?

"I didn't wake you up with the hose, did I?"

"No, I was up already," Avery said. It was nice to think that some people remembered that he had to sleep during the day. "Umm.. How's business?"

"Pretty good, actually- I got an offer from a

potential tenant on Monday. It's a cutlery store with expensive knives and stuff. But the lady that owns it isn't sure about changing the name. I made some suggestions."

"A knife store? Cut to the Chase? No, that's bad."

Guy chuckled his approval and stated what was probably the best of his suggestions, "What's the Point."

"Oh, yeah. That makes sense. Point, point."

The name was a play on words. Every name of every store in Guy's strip mall had to be. There was 'Suits Me Fine,' a men's clothing retailer, a beauty salon called 'Hair's How We Do It,' a Cuban restaurant called 'The Best Juan,' an aquarium dubbed 'Tanks a Million,' and one store that Avery felt threw the whole theme off just a little, 'Don't think twice (It's alright).' Guy had reassuringly explained on more than one occasion that the name was an allusion to a Bob Dylan lyric, but Avery felt that it was a stretch. Too obscure a reference to work. Not a pun at all and other than a subtle inference toward buying impulses, had nothing to do with the products sold at a convenience store.

"So you dig it?" Guy asked.

The lingo. There in all its graceless, awkward glory it was.

Avery gave him a secretly sympathetic, "Far out."

Or should he have said *it's* far out? Could you drop the it before the far out? Were you supposed to drop the 'it' before the 'far out'? Guy probably wouldn't know anyways, Avery figured.

Instead of continuing the conversation at such a high volume, Avery strode over to Guy's patio. The two went on to discuss the pitfalls of home owners associations for a short while, who was violating the bylaws, what the punishment for violating those bylaws were, why those bylaws were bullshit in the first place, and when the bylaws could be amended. It was a popular topic within the community. A common grievance that the property holders and their children could get together and gripe about. Yadda Yadda had his pick-up truck towed from his own driveway; Yadda Yadda is using petty cash money to pay for a cobblestone walkway from his patio to the neighborhood pool, etc. Avery played an active role throughout the entire exchange. He had worthwhile things to say and listened attentively when Guy spoke, but there was something he needed to get off his chest, something that he needed to hear himself say so he might better understand what exactly the fuck had happened that morning.

Guy was not the person to tell. He was a great guy, sure. Just not so great and so close and so broadminded that Avery wanted to say 'So, hey- I was raped by a ghost just now.'

There was somebody at the mall that was.

"It just seems like so many of the rule makers are old and so many of the rule breakers are young. I'm penalized because I operate in the late hours. People can park on the street before ten o'clock, when all the elderly are settling down, but not after? It's a pain when my friends come over because we hang out a lot later. If anything, more cars are driving in the daytime, cars shouldn't be allowed on the side of the road then. Know what I mean? Anyway. I think it's just some classic friction between the young and old."

The old. Forty five minutes later, they walked toward Avery and the entrance he sat next to. Seven or eight of them, crooked, slow, wavering- like extras in a George Romero movie. One o'clock in the afternoon was a dangerous time for shoppers and mall employees alike, for it was feeding time for the retired. Flocks of them, no- packs of them, no- what was the collective noun for zombies, anyway? A heard of zombies? A plague of zombies? That sounds fine. Plagues of them, insatiably yearning for the flesh and blood of electronics salesmen and baristas, polluting the air with their disease of free time and indecisiveness. Damning the new and fresh and young. That was maybe a bit harsh, Avery thought as the living-almost-dead slowly passed him. They were just striving to ignore their senseless existences, same as Avery, same as everyone.

Into the food court and to the right, with a quick stop for a large sweet tea, past three Starbucks which made walking the right wing of the mall a near constant sensation of déjà vu, down an escalator and out the downstairs exit, Avery journeyed. Trips to the mall like this were typical. He didn't often go there to buy anything, just to see friends and garner the attention of young girls. This time he went for an ear. J.P. was that ear, smoking a cigarette and spinning his keys around a finger. He looked at Avery with concern, not knowing what was wrong, knowing only that Avery 'needed to talk.'

"What's up, man? Everything okay?"

"Yeah, I'm fine. I think," Avery told him. "Time for a drive?"

"Oh, hell yeah. My first sale this morning was a laptop with warranty. Five percent plus the seven percent plus the spiff. I'm straight, baby," he did a little dance.

The pre-qualifying conversation wasn't long or specific. It didn't need to be. J.P. understood what Avery was talking about and vice versa. 'Time for a drive' was

24

a question of whether or not J.P. could afford to A: take a ten minute drive around the parking lot, B: postpone any important work for the rest of the day, and C: return to the job with red, squinting eyes and a slightly modified sense of humor. 'Five percent plus seven percent plus the spiff' meant that from the sale of one laptop, assuming it was an average priced machine of about one thousand dollars, J.P. would earn five percent of the merchandise total ($50), seven percent of the warranty total ($7), and an extra cash incentive ($50), which already equaled an average day of sales.

They cruised the parameter of the shopping mall, smoking marijuana like they were on the way to see Fantasia re-released in an IMAX theater.

"So, what's up?" J.P. finally asked.

"Huh? Nothin, man. Day off."

"I thought you said you needed to talk? You and Lisa cool?"

"Oh! Jesus. Yeah, yeah, yeah. That's fine. This is something else entirely. One of the weirdest things ever happened to me this morning. You know when you're sleeping, and it usually only happens to me when I'm just taking a nap, but like you kind of wake up and you're frozen? Like, you're awake, you know that you're lying there, but you can't move at all and you end up just going back to sleep?"

"Okay. I think I know what you're talking about," J.P. said, eyes hard on the road.

"Well this morning that happened to me," Avery paused, wanting it to sink in, but probably pausing too long. "First I was dreaming. I was watching the closet door open and close by itself, like poltergeist, but that was dreaming that part. It was scary so I kept trying to wake up. Finally I woke up and my eyes were open and I could look around a little bit but my body was still asleep or something. I couldn't move at all. So I'm just frozen there stretched out on the bed and I felt this woman on top of me. I mean there was no one actually there but I felt her. Her weight, her breath- her presence was unmistakable. I think she was going to rape me."

J.P. made and expression that was one part surprised, one part disbelief, and two parts amused. He asked, "Rape you?"

"Probably. She was using my hand at first. I think being in that state maybe makes you accessible to phantoms or something. Maybe they can see you because you're still half dreaming."

"Damn," J.P. said. Sometimes when J.P. said 'damn' like that it gave Avery the impression that he didn't quite understand, but didn't quite care enough to think any more about it. "What happened then? It just got up and left?"

"She," Avery corrected, "She just got up and left. No, she didn't just get up and leave. I was trying to move so that I could feel her. I wanted to do something back. Reciprocate. But as soon as I could twitch my fingers it was over and she was gone. That's what I mean- maybe my presence could only be experienced by her and hers by me when I'm in that state of half consciousness, because the second I moved I woke up, and the second I woke up she was gone."

"You were dreaming."

"No! I wasn't just dreaming! It was different. I could see the room and feel the bed under me. I felt her when she moved against my fingers. If it,"

"I'm saying though," J.P. said, interrupting, "you know what those things feel like. Your mind could have been just remembering those things."

"Dude. I know when the fuck I'm dreaming and when I'm not. I'm not a sleep walker."

"Okay, okay. I'm just saying."

Avery put the glass pipe to his mouth and put the lighter to the pipe. About three seconds later, he exhaled and continued. "I know. But trust me. It wasn't a bad thing. Actually it was really cool. But I went back to sleep once it was over because I was still really tired."

"Damn, I would have been too weirded out to sleep after that."

"Yeah, but I was hoping it would happen again."

J.P. laughed for a second. "Are you going to tell Lisa?"

"Eh. I don't know. She gets stressed out over nothing. Probably not. It almost wouldn't be nice. It'd be like telling a fat person that someone else said they were fat, you know? Like, that bit of information doesn't help them or anything. All it does is make them feel bad."

"Maybe they decide to lose weight."

"No, by someone else I mean someone that doesn't matter to them. Anyway, that's not the point. The point is there might be a knife shop opening up in Guy's strip mall and they're going to call it 'What's the Point."

They both kind of giggled. It was something of a forced giggle, one that each felt was expected of him by the other, but appreciated nonetheless. They were driving past Macy's now, the same place they started from. Avery proceeded to talk about the second portion of his brush with the unlikely, the man forged from hate that came after the woman molded from lust. It took only about half as long, and by the time they passed Macy's again they were on to another subject entirely. The morning's impact on Avery was beginning to wane. He no longer burned for clarification. All Avery wanted now was to drive around the mall again, smoke another bowl, say 'see you later' or 'take it easy' or 'peace' to J.P. when break was over, and get back home to the television.

'Take it easy' turned out to be the chosen form of farewell.

CHAPTER 7

"Stay where you are!"

The order was authentic, loud and plump with authority.

"Seems like our little friend here's got a problem with the rules of the road- you got a license, son?" He said to himself and then the perpetrator, pacing back and forth, letting the third person discourse and rhetorical questioning sink in.

"Yes, sir," answered the nervous young man. "It's just, I was just…"

"You were just breaking the law, boy. What good excuse do you got for that?"

"I was just…"

The officer, enormous in both size and command, broke in again- "You were just, you were just! Drop and give me twenty!"

Without hesitation, the young man obeyed. He hit the deck and reached for his wallet, throwing it on the floor between them. "Take it," he pleaded.

Avery laughed. Other members of the audience laughed, too.

"So tell me, boy, now that you're so relaxed," the officer began, ignoring the wallet and the misinterpretation of his instruction, "what exactly is so very important, so imperative to the existence of you, me, and all the other innocent people on these roads, that it puts you above the law?"

"I was going to tell you a second ago, officer. I was chasing a hit and run driver. He nailed a kid in my neighborhood and I didn't want him to get away."

"If that's true, why wasn't I chasing him?" the officer asked.

From his uncomfortable looking place on the ground, the young man answered, "You tell me."

"Ha. Got me there."

The young man started to get up, but the officer stopped him.

"I guess there's only one way to settle this," he said, pulling his gun from its holster, "I'll make a deal with you. You get to shoot me in the head, one time. Then, one year from now, we meet back here and I get to shoot you in the head one time. Agreed?"

Ahh. That's why the cop had all those little stitches around his neck. He was supposed to be like the Green Knight in the story of Sir Gwain. Only now, the Green Knight was a cop and the chopping block became a loaded 9mm. Avery wondered how much of this was going over the group head of the crowd. Not that it mattered. The people appeared delighted by Michael's first play.

The actors froze for a moment, doing and saying nothing. Meanwhile, Avery played it out in his imagination. If the script was to follow the original version, it would require the hero to direct a bullet through that cop's head, something Avery always dreamed of doing. *Dreamed* of doing. It was not a dream that he would work towards realizing or a dream that he hoped would someday come true, he was content to just envision it- putting a gun to someone's head and dropping the hammer, blast someone in the face from point blank range and watch the blood spray like Windex. It was a fantasy inspired by too much television and horror movies.

The main character got up suddenly, turned around, and ran like crazy in place. Officer Green or the Green Officer or whatever you wanted to call him did his best to float off stage left. Behind everything, a big cylinder painted like a street began to spin and produced a surprisingly convincing illusion of movement. Old props were pulled off and new props were pulled on. One minute and one out of breath actor later, the entire scene had changed. Who would have thought giving chase to a group of kids play ding-dong-ditch (the plot and the name of the play) could lead to such adventures?

The remainder of Michael's play ferried the audience through some of the more outlandish segments of his imagination. They watched the secret mating rituals of stray cats, the courageous feats of a mother protecting her infant child, the avatar of the moon interrupt the filming of a MacDonald's commercial, and the hero's safe return home. The cast and crew received a hearty ovation and conversations around Avery, if they weren't singing confusion, sang his brother's praise. As the auditorium emptied, Michael walked from behind the curtains and sat on the front of the stage. Avery walked to meet him, clapping loudly on the way.

"You liked it?" Michael asked, proud and smiling.

"It was terrific. Color me entertained," Avery told him, just as proud and just as smiling.

"Good thing I didn't tell you about it before, huh? All those surprises? And wasn't Lisa great? I'm so glad I wrote her in, man. She really stole the show."

"Yeah, I guess. Everyone did really well."

As if responding to cue, Lisa emerged from behind the curtains, squealed, and hopped off the three foot stage to hug Avery. Avery returned the embrace but with much less vigor, less force, his half of the hug an action that resembled the shrug of shoulders or the roll of eyeballs. Why was he embarrassed by such things?

"Speak of the devil," Michael said while this was happening.

"Oh really?" Lisa asked. Her pronunciation was still exaggerated. Overjoyed and locked in acting mode.

"Mike was just saying what a good job you did tonight. The play was great."

Lisa looked at Michael and Michael looked at Avery.

"Why, thank you," they said in unison.

"Jinx!" they said, again in perfect synchronization and were forced to say nothing more. Avery was the only one allowed to talk.

"Seems like you two have been hanging out too much," Avery said to them. Now they were his audience and he liked that. "Knock knock. Who's there? You want to hear the joke don't you? You have to say who's there to hear it. I can't say the whole thing myself, can I? Knock knock. No? Shame. It was a good one. Don't worry about it. I'm just taking the Mickey out of you. Nope! I said Mickey, not Micheee…Michaee…Michaaaa…."

"I'll buy you a coke, Lisa," Michael said. He

31

broke the jinx, spoke before someone else said his name, he would endure the penalty- either a punch in the arm or a hit in the wallet for the cost of one soda, house rules presiding. "Are you two riding with me to the after party?"

"I think we'll take a separate car. In case we don't want to leave at the same time," Avery said.

Lisa nodded her head, shrugged her shoulders, opened her eyes wide and tightened her lips all at the same time. Strangely enough, this signaled a hesitant confirmation as clearly as the word 'yeah'.

"Well, I don't see that as being a problem. Just tell me when you want to go and we'll go," Michael said.

"Okay, then. I'd like to stop by the house first. Lisa, do you need to shower or anything?"

She scrunched her nose like somebody doing an impression of a rabbit, cocked her head to the side and nodded while turning her palms up. This was easily understood as 'unfortunately I feel dirty and need to freshen up'.

Avery stood on his tip toes and said, "Alright. We'll stop by the house for a minute on the way," then looking at Michael, "You aren't in too big a hurry, are you?"

"No. I'd prefer to be fashionably late anyways. Big director makes his grand entrance and all that. I have to give everyone else time to get there first."

"Yeah, alright," Avery said, leading the way out.

"Actually," Michael started, waited for them to turn around and finished, "would you mind just coming back here and picking me up? I have a few things to do."

"No problem. We'll just go home and get cleaned up, and then we'll swing by here on the way. Just be outside or something."

"Cool. See you in a bit."

Avery said goodbye, too, but Lisa just smiled real big and waved.

"Hey, Lisa!" Michael said, turning her around again, "you know you're not jinxed anymore, right? I mean, you can talk now, it's all over."

"Oh, shit. Really? I thought Avery had to say my name three times or something."

Avery started to laugh and Michael said, "No, no, no. I said your name as soon as I broke the jinx. You're fine."

"Jeeze. Well, thanks. See you soon."

Michael vanished behind the curtains. Holding hands, Lisa and Avery walked through the auditorium, between rows and rows of empty seats, red and folded like the lips of so many pouting children.

CHAPTER 8

Another night, another party, another hello, another stream of liquid vomit brought on by an inebriated Michael drinking beer spoiled by cigarette ashes, another celebration for one brother and not the other, another good bye, another drive to work, another eight hour shift completed, another morning, another crawl into bed, another period of severe disenchantment for Avery.

The rest of the world, however, was too wrapped up in its own affairs to notice. Mr. Chase and Mr. Thurbin included.

Everyone is an individual- fact, but there are similarities. Often these parallels occur in the things that people define themselves with and by, such as, 'I'm a musician,' or, 'I'm a Catholic.' All these types of people in existence would, if someone were to count, surely near infinity depending on how specific the said categorizations are and whether or not being one or two or three types concurrently would generate the need for a fourth or fifth type. To simplify things, this person taking count might say, "Mr. Chase is a person with a peculiar routine," instead of, "Mr. Chase is a person who lies on the driveway face up at some point every day." In the former case, there are many fewer categories and more people filling them than the latter case, which approaches individuality as groupings get more specific and makes all this a complete waste of the counter's time. Mr. Chase was performing that peculiar routine of his. The mark counted for him is on the index of eccentrics.

Mr. Thurbin was walking to the end of his driveway for the mail, looking across the street, eyes burning with disgust. He was either in his late twenties or early thirties, and looked like either a somewhat clean 1960's greaser or a rather dirty 1940's Nazi propaganda poster boy. His hair was blond and combed, running roots back from the permanent scowl of his chiseled face. If the human cataloging project were to be as complicated and as specific as possible, Mr. Thurbin would be counted in the 'people that have absolutely no tolerance for people with eccentricities of any kind, let alone laying face up on the driveway all the time for no apparent reason' group. Idiot-weirdo-wastes of space like that were enough to make his skin crawl. To Mr. Thurbin, walking over there and stomping his neighbor's head into a pool of mushy blood would be a noble act of charity. Only the probability of indefinite incarceration stopped him from doing so.

Seemingly unaware of this silent tidal wave of hatred barreling in his direction, Mr. Chase stared heavenward. It was a beautiful morning. Splashed impossibly with pinks, yellows, reds, and purples. Brushed with clouds, thick and thin. The sun at this hour was such wonderful solace. He heard footsteps across the street and figured they belonged to the silent man with the loud car. *That's fine,* he responded to his previous thought, *people are entitled to their privacy.*

From his reclined position upon a bed of brick, Mr. Chase raised the palm of his hand to his neighbor's house and heard footsteps moving in the opposite direction. Not knowing if the gesture was returned or not, he smiled. The man across the street was a living, breathing, thinking creature, and Mr. Chase loved him for it. They were parts of each other, the whole, the everyone and everything within his mind. And since an experience will immediately incorporate itself into the soul of the consciousness it's recognized by, every memory is a part of the owner, making whatever the memory is of a part of the owner, too. It gives itself and is at the same time given. If you love yourself, you love everything you experience, regardless of whether or not you love it. This was the school of thought Mr. Chase subscribed to, and passionately believed the world would be a much better place if everyone else would just lie down and watch the sun rise.

Quite the opposite reaction was taking place in Mr. Thurbin's living room. Pacing with no evidence of rhythm, covering his face with his fingers and forcefully dragging them off, pulling down his cheeks and lips to the point just prior to pain, his eyes were wide and wild.

Fits of rage happened here regularly. Fits of senseless, self destructive rage. There was always something to be angry about. Just turn on the television or go for a drive, peruse a shopping mall or sit through a religious ceremony. People and their pathetic, befuddled ways, you'll see them. Mr. Thurbin saw them everywhere. His cure, for these people, not for himself- violence.

He stood in front of the pornography collection displayed along the shelves of his entertainment center and surrendered to his imagination. To say that it calmed him would be inaccurate. What it did was gather that emotion, that compulsion to release the warm red blood from some random human capsule and stored it somewhere else inside him, a proverbial back-burner of his awareness. Later, when the pictures in his head were played out in actuality, that emotion would surface. Knuckles adorned with flat polished steel would pound relentlessly on a face that was no longer issuing pleas for clemency, nor emitting sobs or whimpers, nor taking in air. Woe to this nameless, homeless, metaphorically and literally faceless resident of Miami whose path should cross Mr. Thurbin's tonight.

Not tonight. Right fucking now. Mr. Thurbin grabbed the necessary items and walked into his garage. He got in his car, turned the ignition over, let the kinetic power of the vehicle flow through him, opened the garage door and backed out. One of the kids next door to him, Michael, the one that he liked, was outside pumping air into the front tire of a bicycle. *There's something about that kid. He shows… potential.* The thought had occurred to him many times, every time he saw Michael in fact, and seemed to come completely on its own. Like the idea was placed there, implanted by some outside force, not constructed by his own recognition. He met

Michael's eyes with his as he drove passed, nodding. Minutes later, he would be on his way south to Miami, on an interstate road filled with lots of other, slower cars, taking him directly toward a number of men who would not be missed.

A mess of sounds disturbed the relative tranquility of the street all at once. The rumble of an oversized engine starting, the thunderous creaking of a garage door opening, the quick hiss of squeezed air escaping an inner-tube, the clank clank clank of an old hand pump, Mr. Chase heard it all and averted his eyes from an ever changing sky. The main focus of his attention turned at once to Michael. There was an increasingly magnetic quality about the boy, or rather about the young man, something that beseeched attention. He felt a push to depart some of the less conventional knowledge that he'd amassed throughout the years about the workings of our world, about mankind, about love and all it can accomplish. Where that push came from was unknown. How long it would take him to react to the notion was also unknown. Watching Michael was in some ways like watching the sky. Suddenly, the noise he forgot to hear, the snarling of an American muscle car's combustion engine clouded his ears. And the car itself blocked his vision.

Michael looked up at the powerful car as Mr. Thurbin drove by. The noise never bothered him- he could easily appreciate the ingenuity and craftsmanship of dragsters. Michael often thought about just walking next door and asking Mr. Thurbin if he had a minute to suggest some starting points for someone interesting in building a car like that. From behind the wheel, Mr. Thurbin nodded a subtle combination of hello and goodbye. Good. Michael returned the nod and figured that knocking on his door sometime soon would be fine.

The car went by, and the image of rolling, shiny black steel was replaced by a badly dressed man resting on his empty driveway. Mr. Chase, as Michael knew him. He seemed like a funny guy, but he seemed happy, and Michael was always grateful for people that created their own happiness. If someone could blissfully pass the time meditating, or watching the clouds, or doing whatever it was he did on that driveway, without technology or drugs or any of the other mind-numbing vices that most people rely on, well- it's a rare feat. Michael decided that some day soon he would stroll over there and ask him exactly what's been going on all these years on that little patch of brick. After all, these people were his neighbors; it might be nice to get to know them.

CHAPTER 9

Tomorrow morning, or the next time that Avery was in the living room or the kitchen or the loft at the same time as his parents, there was a good chance they would say something about the length of his shower. Avery didn't care. He'd been relishing the cascade of hot water for nearly fifteen minutes, standing in front of Lisa, blocking the water for most of that time, not washing, just standing, feeling his muscles unwind.

Avery was thinking of the regularity with which some people cycle through obsessions. He was thinking in particular, of John Woulf. Avery had only beheld the past four years of John Woulf's character equivocation, but could deduce with adequate empirical evidence that the list of makeovers far surpassed their history of acquaintance. When Avery first met him, John was fascinated by the Goth subculture. He immersed himself in a life style of all black and masquerades, surrounding himself with other pale girls and boys who equally relished their innocent version of evil, who believed in their deviance with all the audacity of youth and blind faith. During most conversations, be they with a group of younger, reverential Goths, longtime friends of more common persuasions, family or total strangers, John would openly criticize the principles of Christianity. This passion for an aberrant style slowly morphed into what he considered to be a more mature and systematic belief-Satanism.

Luckily for a devout, card carrying member of the Church of Satan, the standard code of dress for Satanists did not differ much from the vogue of Goths unless the ceremony was extra special, in which case a trip to Hollywood Costumes was in order. The preaching, recruiting, and damning in the name of Satan accounted for about seven or eight months of John's life, just before he bought a leather jacket and a motorcycle. The biker thing turned into a body modification thing, which for the record is not the best thing for someone so vacillating in identity, and eventually into a bartender thing.

In this vein, John Woulf carried on. Incessantly modifying his loves and hates and passions. To the untrained eye, the subtle changes would certainly go unnoticed. The untrained eye would only see the changes if it moved away for a year, came back to visit old friends and saw John again. It would think, *oh, John's a biker now- a sort of Goth biker. That's different.*

The metamorphosis of this individual's character

is not exactly what Avery is thinking of. Well, he was thinking vaguely along those lines, but that was a gallon of water in the past and he's since moved on to John's current incarnation, a diligent conspiracy theorist who dresses mostly in faded jeans and solid colored dress shirts, worn one size too large and never tucked in. John promised Avery and some mutual friends a video, followed by a Q and A session and brief lecture that was sure to change the way they saw the world. It was supposed to happen tomorrow and now Avery had moved on to thinking of just how much he was looking forward to it. It was almost sure to be really hilarious or really thought provoking, an exceptional treat in either case.

How did Avery's parents know how long his showers lasted? Why were they concerned? Maybe in the forty something years prior to now, they had gotten their fill of showers. Maybe eventually the delight given to naked skin by warm falling water wears out and showering becomes nothing more than necessary, a compulsory measure of hygiene, dreary and tedious like monopoly board chores. Avery didn't see that happening any time soon or ever. His feet planned to stand on the dusky film of dirty shower tiles until the water ran less than lukewarm, and when eventually it did, he and Lisa stepped onto the bathmat, relaxed and dripping.

There were two towels folded over the hanger. One was dark green and belonged to Avery. The other, a big thin beach towel with a picture of two crabs wearing sun glasses and squeezing sunscreen was Michael's. Michael's was still a little bit damp. Lisa did not realize this until she touched it to her face, then she wrapped it around Avery's shoulder and tried to take his towel, the dry, dark green one. She moved with such nonchalance that when Avery realized what was happening, he reacted with the same startled energy that a grandmother emits when a grandson, oblivious to issues like heart attacks and bursting blood vessels, sneaks up from behind and shouts, "BOO!"

"What the fuck?" he jumped back, pushing the damp towel into Lisa's breasts, "This is my towel! Just use this one."

"That one's still wet. I shouldn't have to use a dirty towel!"

"It's not dirty, just a little damp. It's Michael's. He must have used it earlier."

"So it's been used!" Lisa exclaimed.

"What? It's just water. He would have just taken a shower so I'm sure it's plenty clean."

She wasn't convinced-"Yeah? Well in case you failed to notice, your brother is kind of a slut. I don't know where he's been or what he's got so can I please not have to use his bath towel? Thanks."

Avery hung on to his towel tight as Lisa tried with all her might to wrench it from his hands. By now, the crab towel was on the ground, arguably growing more and more off-putting with each passing second, with each abandoned hair it collected.

"No, no. Thank you," Avery said to her, taking advantage of his superior strength and twisting the towel from Lisa's grip. "Just use the crab towel. You can't catch any STDs from a bath towel. Not that Michael even has any."

Lisa just stood there, air drying, glaring. "I think it is possible. I heard somewhere that this couple infected with gonorrhea had sex and cleaned themselves up with a towel and left it there. Then their kid used it to dry off and caught gonorrhea in his mouth."

"You don't have to worry about that," Avery

answered her. He tried to sound a little offended by her insinuations, but he wasn't really.

The air vent hummed, mechanically and continually adding to the tension in the heaviness of post-shower bathroom air. Lisa began to dry herself off as best she could with her hands. She squeezed water from her hair and shook her arms and legs. When she finally stopped moving, Avery picked up the presumably dead conversation.

"Can you imagine the leverage that would give you though? As a kid to your parents?" he asked.

"What? Contracting an STD from them?"

"Yeah. They'd have to buy you a house or something just to make up for it. Any time they tried to scold you for something you could just be like, 'Whatever, you sluts gave me gonorrhea when I was six,' and that would be that."

She thought about it for a second, and said that she didn't think it'd be worth it.

"Wouldn't it?" Avery asked, as much to himself as to her. "I don't think that gonorrhea is really all that bad. Maybe it is. I don't know."

Avery checked to make sure the coast in between his room and the bathroom was clear, since Lisa refused to wrap herself in the wet towel. It was. They exited the privacy of the bathroom, which felt even more enveloping once the mirrors succumbed to fog and entered the crisp, cold, openness of the hallway. They walked with quick, half hopping movements and Lisa locked the bedroom door behind her.

"When I'm in London I'll get to wear whatever I want," Lisa said to Avery as he stood in front of his closet.

"Is that so?"

"It is." She hugged him from behind, doing her best to share the remaining moisture on her skin.

"I don't see why you couldn't wear whatever you want here," taking care not to give her the satisfaction of squirming under the wet embrace, "Are you moving there to reinvent yourself?"

"No. I'm moving there because there are a million things to do in a city like that."

Six years ago, when writing a report for her tenth-grade English class on the topic 'Where I see myself in five years', Lisa said she would be moving to London to fall in love and marry an English man.

Thirty minutes after Lisa and Avery first met, ten months, twenty two days, nineteen hours and a handful of minutes ago, she was just moving to London.

Six hours ago, her teeth smeared with peanut butter, she was moving to London for school.

Ten seconds ago it was to wear whatever she wanted.

In the exact instant of present, Lisa was moving to London for the number of possible pastimes a 'city like that' offered.

Recently, she'd been asking Avery to come with her.

"Like what?" Avery asked.

"Like in two hours you could be in Paris," Lisa answered.

"So Paris is a good reason to go to London?"

"One of them, sure. Just about anything that can be done can be done there. It's a capital city of the world. And you want to stay in south Florida? There's nothing for you here."

"I don't know about that," Avery said, turning his head to the wall, mind reeling, searching desperately for an engaging activity that could be found locally and not across the Atlantic, "In fact, I'm doing something tomorrow that I couldn't do in London."

"Oh, right. Going to work an eight hour night shift on some machines?"

"No, before that."

She waited.

"I'm going to go listen to John Woulf give a lecture."

Lisa rolled her big, tan eyes in response to what she thought was a bad joke. But a joke, it wasn't.

CHAPTER 10

History would trace the beginnings of civilization on planet Earth to approximately six thousand years ago in Sumer, the place between the Tigris and Euphrates rivers that is now called Iraq and was once called Mesopotamia. It was here that mankind learned to write, to build, to worship, to govern, and to exist in a proper, well structured society. Only a few hundred years later, history took an interest in other great civilizations. It scrupulously cataloged the advancements made not only by the Sumerians, but by the Egyptian and Babylonian empires as well- their astronomical knowledge that modern science took centuries to confirm, their architecture that remains unexplainable to this very day. What was the catalyst for this rapid advancement? History does not delve far enough into mankind's past.

There was a golden age. An age of two great civilizations, of technology and spirituality, of gods. And though the scientific innovations of these cultures were vast, they were not the result of human ingenuity or a gift of fate; advanced technology was bestowed upon mankind by beings from other planets and other dimensions. Gods, all.

The human lives of Lemuria and Atlantis were both covertly and overtly ruled by two cooperating and interbreeding life forms. The dominate force, called the Annunakki or 'Those from the Heavens Came', were a reptilian race, star spanning, dimension crossing. The Annunaki were the first race to intervene with human existence, blessing the then lesser beings with impossible wisdom and fantastic gadgetry. Around this period of time, factions of another extraterrestrial race were fleeing their home planet, Mars. These Martians closely resembled humans, but as they evolved on a planet further from the Sun's harmful rays than Earth, they were lighter of skin, hair, and eyes. It is then said that 'the sons of god mated with the daughters of man', and these hybrid bloodlines were placed in positions of power throughout Lemuria and Atlantis.

Astronomical cataclysm occurred. The planet Venus careened through the universe with unfathomable velocity. One of Jupiter's moons fell victim to this colossal projectile, and the pulverized remains were strewn about the solar system, left to revolve eternally around the sun as a belt of asteroids. But the Venus comet was not stopped. It flew past Mars, devastating the atmosphere and rendering the planet uninhabitable. It flew around the Earth, causing the seas to boil, the ground to crack, the sky to topple, the life forms to perish. Lemuria and Atlantis were completely destroyed.

Six thousand years later, history recognizes the Sumerians.

The Empire of Sumer was not the beginning of civilization, it was the re-beginning, and all the hybrid bloodlines that ruled Lemuria, that ruled Atlantis, reclaimed their seats of power. And not only in Sumer- this reptilian-Martian lineage has continued to direct the course of humanity throughout history. Egypt, Babylon, Rome, France, England, America; ruled by the same families, the same race.

"So, wait," a confused young man interrupted, "The Annunaki are the ones from Mars?" He waited politely across a coffee table stacked with red plastic cups, a plate of Snickers bars and Kit-Kats cut into bite sized cubes, a glass ash-tray with soot and cigarette butts running superfluously over the rim, and a worn remote controller. No answer. The question lingered in a musty living-room, above a brown recliner that didn't match the couch, between walls decorated with family photos and department store deco art, over an ornate throw rug, threadbare from too many years and too many feet. The young man, by now too self conscious to voice the full question, reminded the room that he still didn't understand with a simple, "Huh?"

The blank expression of John Woulf's face did not shift, nor did he speak, nor did he break the impalpable twine between his eyes and the television. All he did is nod, and very slightly at that, toward the glowing box. More history cascaded from the VCR to the TV, from the TV to the ears in John's living room, from the ear's in John's living room, in some cases, to the brains. Blink, ask a question, and miss something.

Both Avery and Michael were rather captivated, but neither was sure why. Astonishing revelation? A quizzical insight into another's recherché belief? THC? Four other guys, not including John, were also occupying seats in the living room. These were all friends of John's, hand-picked probably for what John felt was a receptivity to new, atypical ideas. Each person or pair of people could be recognized as a connection to the different manifestations of John's personality.

There was a motorcycle parked in the driveway which probably belonged to the older, gruff looking man nearest to the door. Another man sat in the brown recliner-his arms covered in tattoos that, by the looks of it, had all been done within the same, relatively short frame of time. Avery and Michael sat uncomfortably close to two other young men on a couch made for three. These two were obviously associates of John's from the Goth-old-days, as they were dressed in the traditional tight black shirts and enormously baggy black pants from which all sorts of reflective, nonfunctional straps hung. The Goth friends seemed to be having a problem understanding either the general concepts of the video or the specific evidence supporting the general concept. The bewildered expressions on those pale faces were easily discernable, even to a stranger.

Information was coming fast. First a history of civilization, then an explanation of important symbolism within these networks of hybrid rulers, the conspiracies they've organized in modern times, the people involved, the agendas planned. It was no wonder that the small audience sometimes expected more explanation.

John, however, refused to recognize the questions. As if he were a bouncer perched on a barstool outside a club, ignoring underage would-be customers, his eyes focused on the television like a doorman would watch the inactivity of an empty street, an empty sidewalk. Could it be that John didn't get it either?

Avery stood up, the left side of his jeans rubbing noisily against the orange Velcro straps resting next to him. The owner of the neon accents and the pants they were sewn to, of the spiked hair, silver necklace and the Boarders Anime Club card looked up at John, visually uncertain that bathroom breaks were permissible in the middle of the tape. Avery stepped over Michaels legs and walked to the hallway. Halfway there, he stopped momentarily to study some family photos. They were all over the house, on the walls, tables, bookshelves, entertainment centers- most of them dated prior to high school graduation. The particular photo that Avery found most interesting was probably taken a few years before he and John met. In it, John was proudly holding a new skateboard for the camera on Christmas day. So John was a skateboarder before he turned Goth. Avery went into the bathroom. When he looked into the mirror he was not surprised to find himself still smiling.

Less than a minute later, after the harsh sounds of restroom procedure abated, Avery returned to the living room to find an entirely different scene than he'd left. John was standing up, speaking ferociously at the discomfited spectators.

"Don't you get it? These are the people who rule your lives! These are the people that run our governments, our banks, our media, our schools. All you can think about is if they hook up with girls? It isn't funny!"

Michael's mouth was frozen in his best effort to stifle laughter, but John took it for a nervous reaction and continued.

"The aristocracy of Europe, the presidents of the United States of America, they're all the same hybrid bloodlines. George Bush, even."

"I hear that," said the biker.

Just then, a key shoved into the front door and turned, even though the door was already unlocked. As a crack opened to the outside world, a voice from behind sounded- loud, boisterous, a voice tailor made for interruption, "Yo, John! What's all these cars..." But as the bearer of the voice opened the door fully, he abandoned the question and finished instead with an excited, "Oh, shit!"

The older brother. Twenty seven, he still called his parent's home home. He walked into the house with an amused confidence and his girlfriend followed. John's body posture degraded faintly.

"Y'all gettin' into some of this X-files shit?"

Nobody answered. All eyes were now on the older brother, who ate the attention up like the contents of an unwrapped Easter basket. John's audience was now his.

"That right, John? *Aliens*..." He said '*aliens*' in the voice most people use to read children ghost stories. As an added effect he raised his hands to eye level and wiggled his fingers. "You guys better watch out or the illuminati is going to get you."

As John's older brother made his way to the middle of the living room, closer to where John was standing, he was still doing the scary finger wiggling thing. Avery wondered if this kind of behavior was typical of the household, or whether John's brother had simply succumbed to what he might have thought was peer pressure. His unwitting audience was certainly not encouraging the drama, but they weren't exactly discouraging it, either.

Avery tried to get as high as possible beforehand, and the joint they blazed on the drive to John's dissuaded him from immediate involvement. He was far too high to mediate. Much easier to let matters like this take their course. Michael was probably on the same page, or at least Avery hoped he was, hoped that they could sit back and enjoy the sibling rivalries of other brothers without participation. There were five other people in the room. Avery would happily blame the bystander effect if things got ugly and someone asked why he didn't do something. The girlfriend was standing near the half open door, quietly smiling, apparently enjoying the display of alpha-maleism.

Distance between John and his teasing older brother grew smaller. John finally spoke up with, "You're such a fucking idiot, Josh. You don't even know what a fucking stupid idiot sheep you are," and was met with a response of, "They're gonna getcha, they're gonna getcha," along with ten wormy fingers in his face.

Evidently the insults, in plain view of seven onlookers, were too much for John to take quietly. He swung a wild right at his brother's face, barely missing. Josh stepped back with a look of feral shock. The situation was out of control. Avery knew that a crazed attention monger like this Josh character could never let something like that go. He stood up to get between them just as Josh rushed in. As Avery pushed back, Michael and the biker simultaneously stepped in to help. There was screaming coming from both John and Josh- an ongoing series of 'fuck you's and of 'no, fuck you's. Finally they were separated, with John breathing deeply next to the television and Josh going to his room.

The lesson was pretty much over. The small audience was collectively thinking that an exit would be the best course of action. Avery and Michael both said thanks, and John apologized to everyone.

While Avery was unlocking the door to his car, John hurried out to catch him.

"Avery, hang on."

"Is everything cool in there?"

"Yeah, yeah, fine. I just came out here to offer this to you." He handed Avery a tape. "It's different than the one we were watching, but the idea is the same. You seemed really interested. I knew you'd want to hear more."

"Oh," Avery didn't really know what to say. He had to admit to himself that he did find the ideas interesting; it was just weird to hear someone tell him that before he told himself. "Thanks."

"Don't thank me. You deserve this information. You and your brother."

Michael and Avery nodded, said goodbye, and got in the car.

CHAPTER 11

At 11:44 p.m., an ejector pin knocked a greasy titanium screw three inches down into a collection tray. At 11:47, the same thing. Every three minutes there was another cap screw, another piece awaiting visual inspection, manufactured automatically by this week's meal ticket, C-11.

Avery looked as though he'd seen a ghost.

It was a look he'd been carrying with him for over an hour- eyes gazing into who-knows-what, mouth tight and scared. The color in his skin seemed to run deeper into him, somewhere it couldn't be seen, rendering his outsides a pale, perfect match for the building's hospital-like light. He seemed to be sleep walking through a dull nightmare. Amidst the machine noises of spinning and dropping and spraying and cutting, the human noises of talking and fixing and tapping, Avery's thoughts stole him. Like a current of rapids surging, the ideas were glimpsed, grasped, dimmed, and forgotten. Deep shock often instigates an attenuated succession of non-linear reasoning; a fleeting, esoteric examination of the universal mirror.

Now there were eight screws in C-11's collection tray. They might be to spec, they might not be. Avery hadn't even started his first inspection. As the parts piled higher and higher, more and more would have damaged edges, dented threads. On some level, Avery knew about all this- that the night's production may be doomed from the start- that he should be concentrating on micrometers and comparators- but he paid that level no heed. Dental implants and cap screws had nothing to do with the network of human souls and did not, therefore, command immediate contemplation.

Lumbering passed the rectangular work stations on ankles large as the columns of Greek design, was Chris. He walked at his usual pace, just shy of a meander, and would reach Avery in an estimated one minute, five seconds.

Avery's attention threw lassos at the fog. Former truths whirled about in a flurry of contradiction. What started out as distinct thought- *the conventional wisdom of high school science utterly dismisses the possibility of human spirituality affecting our lives,* stretched quickly into something more obscure- *the sexual compulsion of Lisa's body reached into my bedroom through thirty miles of thin air.* But this, supposedly, is what happened.

One hour earlier, as Avery neared work with the phone growing hot on his face, he and Lisa spoke:

"Can I tell you something without you saying I'm crazy?" Avery asked, and in asking overlooked his better judgment.

It was okay, sure.

"Without you even thinking I'm crazy?"

She wouldn't know until he told her what he was talking about.

"Umm," short pause, "Last Friday, I think I was raped by a ghost."

She figured a man would know whether or not he'd been raped.

"I'm pretty sure that's what happened. I was sort of sleeping but not really. It wasn't a dream, of that I'm positive."

She wondered how he was so positive. Ghosts don't just go around raping people in their sleep willy-nilly.

"I just know! I wasn't sleeping. It was one of those things where I was awake for a minute but I couldn't move."

She wanted him to proceed. The details were what she needed to help figure this out.

"Well like I said, it was right before I got up that afternoon. I was…"

She asked what time it was, suddenly jarred by a possibility, by what it could mean if he answered her with

'Friday morning'.

Avery had to think. "Around ten or so."

She asked if it were Friday.

"Yeah, it was- how come?"

She didn't explain, she just said not to worry about it, to carry on.

"I felt this presence, this like, female force on top of me. I could tell that she really wanted me, too. That was the whole reason she was there. It was scary, sort of, because I couldn't move at all. I was completely frozen. Then I started to feel her move against my fingers."

His fingers. That bit of info told her everything. It was incredibly weird and she told him so.

"I know."

She told him that he didn't know, he could only know after she told him that she was thinking about him that morning, probably at the exact same time he was rounding the proverbial bases with what he thought was a spirit or a phantom or a dream.

"Okay, so you were thinking about me," Avery said. He didn't quite understand.

She told him again. She was thinking about him. She told him with a voice that would be spelled in italics if written, the 'don't you get it' tone that is always mashed in with the third explanation of something.

"What the fuck are you talking about?" Avery said, so casually quick.

"I mean I was touching myself and thinking of you. Maybe that's what you felt."

And the coincidence was almost too much to bear.

Tool #3 was cutting a thread at the end of the screw, the last step before tool #1, the cutoff, would move over and sever finished screw from raw material. This kind of thing was easy. It could be touched, studied, practiced. Turning in a tray of parts at 6:30 a.m. didn't turn your skin white and make it hard to breathe. Not terrifying like it was to think that paranormal activity could be occurring around anybody, anywhere without documentation or acknowledgement from the people in charge of such things. Easier than being forced to consider the possibility of heaven and hell, souls and enlightenment.

Avery remembered waiting out a period of in-school suspension his senior year. ISS was held in one of the portables; terrible little trailer-parkesqe hovels that festered like a grid of acne on the school's backyard. A desk-ridden student in in-house could occupy time however he/she saw fit, just as long as it wasn't by talking, laughing, looking at other students, looking at the teacher, drumming on the desk, or chewing gum. It was, after all, a punishment. Avery served his time by reading a stack of old textbooks. There was an old health textbook in that stack, crinkled and tarnished. Chapter one- oxidized illustrations of students in red cardigans drinking malts in a diner. Chapter two-how to treat minor burns, how to properly brush your teeth, how and why you should push back your cuticles. That last segment caused a curiously cagey feeling in Avery.

Nobody in school ever told Avery about his cuticles. Why not? Did someone discover that that little film of skin creeping up your fingernails didn't require attention? Why was it not important for his generation to know but it was for the students of forty years ago? In some crossroad of Avery's brain, this related perfectly to the tremendous likelihood that there were all kinds of things going on in the universe that he was wholly unaware of, that he might choose not to recognize even if his girlfriend's desire for sex met his fingertips from afar, even if the violent compulsion of some unidentified person tried to squeeze the life out of him.

Chris was standing next to Avery now, and couldn't help but notice the utter lack of work being done.

"Are you fucked up or something?" Chris demanded.

"Yeah."

Avery quickly realized that while he was feeling 'fucked up', it was in an entirely different context and he'd just mislead his friend (forgivable) and boss (less forgivable).

"No. Not like that. It's just," he trailed off and made looping motions with his pointer finger. He didn't make any further explanations.

"Ain't that a bitch," Chris said with a complete lack of sympathy.

"Yeah," Avery replied, unawares from beginning to end.

It took nearly two hours of repetitive inspection and cleaning to galvanize a return to normalcy.

CHAPTER 12

"You should definitely do it," said Michael.

"You should definitely *not* do it," said Mrs. Miller.

These things were said at two different times, in two different places, to two different people. And though it was not said to him directly, Mr. Weeks heard the not.

They were sitting in his modest little office- that was, Mr. Weeks and his potential renters, Janice Miller and Linda Orloff, discussing the obligatory re-naming of Linda's Business. It was not going well. Janice was only a cashier as far as Guy could tell, certainly not central enough to the business at hand to be causing such a headache. Still, she was trusted, valued, counted on. Linda was taking Guy's coercing with a grain of salt, while swallowing her top sales person's with a spoonful of sugar.

"Look," Guy started, "talk to any of the owners in my strip. Not a single one of them regrets having altered the title of their business. A title is just that, a title. That's all."

"Tell Coca-Cola that," Janice snorted.

Guy ignored her and continued. "What's important is that you'll be leasing in a prime location for a very competitive price. Your foot traffic will increase at least three fold, I'm certain of it. Just think- you'll be right next to a hair salon! *Hair's How We Do It* gets heaps of women passing by and who knows? Lots of them probably cook."

The point went in one ear and out the other. Which is exactly what Guy wanted to do; take one of their fancy knives and shove the point in one ear and out the other. This talk was usually easier.

"Location isn't the issue, Mr. Weeks. We want the property," said Linda coolly.

"We just want the sign above the door to say *Miller and Dooley*," Janice added.

Mr. Weeks folded his hands and breathed very, very deeply.

Now leave Guy's office and walk slowly. Dreadfully slowly with frequent stops so that a one and a half mile journey will consume eight hours of time. Pause to watch the lizards and geckos switch shifts. Wait until the highlighter dye bleeds from the late afternoon sky. Pace.

It was here and now, surrounded by darkness and three walls of racquetball court that Avery heard the slightly reverberating *do*.

"I'm really thinking about it."

"Why wouldn't you be? There's nothing keeping you here. No offense."

"None taken," Avery said.

It was silent for a moment. Avery was reluctant to commit to such a serious conversation, as serious conversation was not tying them to the concrete. What was, was Luke. Tonight they were to act like kids again, running around the neighborhood and playing whatever games their acid soaked minds could comprehend. That is, once Luke showed up with the drugs.

The moon was rust colored, and it sank to the horizon like a slow anchor. There was a woman's voice coming from somewhere, indistinct and distant. Shadows consumed everything, and insignificant sounds such as the buzzing water fountain were not drowned out by daytime activity.

"Okay. I'm sure you have some bizarre reason for not wanting to talk about this. Just like for some reason you get embarrassed about your relationship with Lisa and pretend it doesn't exist. But I promise, moving to London would be the best thing you could do right now. 'The sleeper must awaken'? That's not drivel. You need a challenge- no, stimulation. There simply isn't enough of it for you here. If you were in London right now, you wouldn't be waiting on some fucking kid who's never been on time once in his whole life! You wouldn't have to get in your car every time you want to go somewhere, or buy a new shirt to feel like you did something that day. I'll miss you while you're away, Avery, but you'd be a fool not to try this out."

It didn't seem as though Michael was finished, but Avery wanted him to be.

"Alright, alright! I told you I'm thinking about it. And really, I am. There's a lot of shit I have to take care of in the next couple months," but instead of describing what exactly that 'shit I have to take care of' was, Avery turned his head and listened to the voice, still calling, not so far off as it was before.

"What the hell is that woman saying?" Michael asked. His delivery was all anticipation.

"*Do me*?" Avery half answered. He had a hard time believing his ears.

But as the voice grew closer, the enunciation more distinct, they could not make any other words from it.

"Do me! Do me! Do me!" the woman shouted. She was panicked, concerned, hurried, though there was an easily recognizable rhythm in her voice; an assured cadence. Avery and Michael both walked to the back of the racquetball court and looked through the green chain link fence. To their right was an empty parking lot, destroyed by skateboarding children and leaking automobiles. That parking lot did not produce the yelling. It was to their left were they saw a woman jogging in pajama bottoms and a gray tank top, fretfully singing, "Do me! Do me!"

Maybe this woman had met up with Luke before they did and took all of their acid. Nothing else stood to reason.

When she was close enough, Michael called to her. "Do you need help?"

She snapped her head to the right, obviously

startled that someone was standing there, in the dark recess of the three wall court. "I lost my dog."

Avery took his turn to talk, and he did so without as much tact as his brother, "Your dog's name is *Do me*?"

"Doom," she answered. "Sometimes I call him Doomie."

A small dog named Doom, fine. But with the standard cutesy-piezation suffix ie it made the name sound like something else entirely.

"Have you seen him around here?" she asked.

"No. No, sorry, we haven't. But he might have been. The walls sort of cut off our peripheral vision," Michael told her, "What's he look like?"

"He's a pug, two years old, pretty fat. If you come across him, I live at 7009 Caprise, okay?"

"Sure, we'll keep an eye out. Good luck."

The woman jogged away, and a few paces later, altered her call to 'Doom'.

"I'm fucking glad that didn't happen two hours from now," Avery said.

"That's assuming that Luke is going to be here soon. Which is a pretty big assumption. But honestly, that's exactly the kind of thing I want to happen two hours from now. Assuming Luke shows up soon, that is."

They sat down with their backs to the fence. It was old enough, had been kicked enough, climbed enough, fallen on enough, and sat against enough to give it some droop. That fence gave as much of a backrest as a reclining chair.

"Do me! Do me!" Michael joked.

"Here it is! Here it is!" Avery said back.

Michael laughed and said how glad he was to have his own 'Here it is!' story.

Meanwhile, Luke was sitting on his mother's toilet, reading through an issue of *Time* magazine.

CHAPTER THE UNLUCKY NUMBER

Chase the Droid
Original short by Avery Tyler

By now, inferno would have rained upon most of the globe. Billions of screams silenced and sanitized in another fulfilled promise to Order.

"You function efficiently, 00011010011. Now onward," was the last thing 00011010011 received before boarding its coffin ship and blasting heavenward. The conquest reaped by its efficient functioning would be sown by other segments of Order. Copper wire would run throughout the entire planet like nerves to silicon brains, and part of it regretted not being there to taste the fruits of its labor. That was its curse- not to feel the supreme functioning of logic, the absolutely effective existence of its people. All it could see, via the auxiliary eyes of ship, was a gray ball of smoke behind it, twirling like a cold star.

Another planet laid in wait, some six light years ahead- a blue, brown, and green world populated by the same fleshy bipeds as its last home. It did not look forward to their futile ways of communication, their hopelessly flawed interactions, their erratic, death deserving ways. Soon that world would glow the red of fire. Soon it would run gray with smoke, silver with perfection.

A white streak flashed undetected into the Earth's atmosphere. 00011010011 rebooted its consciousness systems, deleted its memory of the voyage, and looked for a place to land. It chose to set down off the coast of a large peninsula at the eastern edge of North America. The craft splashed, sank, and a very convincingly human shape made its way to shore.

Order 1- Reconnaissance. Avoid detection. Blend in. Assume an identity. Prod. Calculate military advantages.

00011010011 spent weeks amassing the information of humanity. It absorbed the customs of reproduction (strange), science (surprising), war (imperative), entertainment (unnecessary), art (confounding), and recorded Earth's ways in its banks of flawless, boundless memory. It even recorded the quivering, hysterical cries of Charles Chase. The humans of Earth were far more advanced technologically than had been expected, and far more numerous. Still, Order would collect this planet with little effort. It was the natural progression- from biological tissue to titanium. None of this world was worth surviving; its programming told it so.

On a routine survey, 00011010011, which now recognized itself as Charles Chase concerning everything except Order, parked its car in the lot of a drive-thru theater called the 'Nite Owl'. A confounding movie was playing, something about a group of scientists starting a company to catch 'full-torso apparitions' and 'paranormal pests' and 'ectoplasmic entities'. 00011010011 had no knowledge of such beings. But as it watched these *Ghostbusters*, some strange processes began running through its system. It felt proud of them. In their pursuit of *technology*, it found itself rooting for the humans. They were chasing the ideals of Order. Technological progression. For approximately 107 minutes, it watched. And in the process, it fell in love.

Order 2- Rally point. Upload information. Update. Await further orders.

A nagging sensation coursed through its circuitry, at odds with everything it had been programmed to think. Its mission was simple- secure worlds for the coming of Order. That did not necessarily mean the coming of Order's army. 00011010011 could not bear the thought of this world yielding to flame. The men of Earth were on their way! Undertaking the noble quest of upgrading to Order from scratch- by their own free will!

Wearing a shirt that Charles Chase hadn't worn in years, 00011010011 stepped onto the brick driveway and looked toward the vast empire of his kind. It was like an atomic explosion in frictionless vacuum, moving forever outward, expanding over all that is with unstoppable force. Perfect Order. But Order had not prepared it for this world. A recording played through 00011010011's mouth. *"If there's something bad in the neighborhood, who you gonna call?"*

The human race must be saved. 00011010011 discharged its probes to Order, and along with raw data, the message, for the first time since its activation, was different.

00011010011 report. Earth-Humans are on the natural progression toward Order. Violent conquest here would represent only a waste of resources. Technological Evolution, not force, will bring this world to us- a true testament to the rightness of our cause. Hail Order.

And it was on to the last step of order-2. Wait.
Allow Order to process its assessment. The destroyers
might very well have been dispatched already. It laid
its body down, pressure sensors perceiving the stone
squares beneath. Wait. It hoped the supreme logic of the
Machine Nation would have faith in its hypothesis. Wait.
It watched the sky, the street. Wait.

Wait.

CHAPTER 14

On the walls of Avery's room, the scentless,
flickering light-blue waste matter of television moved. It
moved like the nighttime ocean, with calm currents and
swells that tested the buoyancy of Avery and Michael's
silhouettes. Were they floating or sinking? Impossible to
tell. Avery shifted his eyes from the commercial break to
his nightstand. He'd been looking at the same dirty cups
and bowls for a week now. Leftover milk in the cereal
bowls had since solidified into a hard film and a thick
layer of mold was growing on the top of some orange
juice. Disgusting, sure. But not so disgusting that it
couldn't be ignored a while.

The marketing demographic he resided in,
according to the boob-tube, was quite depressing. Only
bald, sexless, overweight, easily-sold insomniacs watch
T.V. so late at night slash early in the morning. Avery
shifted his weight to get the leverage necessary for

opening his window. He hoped that the fresh air would stir the sensitivity of his senses. Michael was quietly drawing an upside-down picture in his sketchbook.

Disappointment was never something that Avery handled well. The new air around him, purified by the great outdoors did little to ease his numb version of anxiety. Nothing felt like it was the right thing to be doing. Reading, drawing, watching, playing- all hopeless diversions at the moment. His body would work through the motions and his mind, preoccupied as it was, would only half participate. Avery's skin was not a comfortable place to be in.

What a way- what a rip-roaring, out of this universe, blow your socks off way to end an unfulfilled hour and a half wait. T.V., quiet company, and restlessness.

When his cell phone trembled next to him, Avery snatched it open with the speed of a professional boxer. He didn't even look to see who it was.

"Luke. What the fuck," went his hello.

He was greeted with a long, defensive "Okay," followed by Lisa identifying herself.

"Oh, hey."

"Oh, hey yourself. I guess Luke's keeping you waiting?"

"Yep," Avery said, easily achieving an irritated shortness.

Michael, upon overhearing a tiny little female voice secrete from Avery's phone, turned back to his sketchbook.

"We've been waiting for like two hours. At this point I'm considering some kind of punishment."

"Why haven't you left without him?" Lisa asked.

"Because we aren't going anywhere. We were just gonna hang out around the neighborhood."

"You don't need Luke to hang around the neighborhood." Lisa didn't care much for Luke; she made that point every time she said his name. It was to your ears what biting a lemon was to your mouth.

"No, but he's got- or at least was supposed to get something for us."

"What- drugs?"

"Mm-hmm."

"Awesome," Lisa said with acrid sarcasm, "What kind?"

"Don't worry about it."

"What do you mean, 'don't worry about it'. You know how fucking stupid that sounds? I want to know what you guys are going to be doing."

"We'll be doing just fine."

Lisa started to say something, but Avery cut her off saying, "Dude- I'm not trying to hear this right now. I'm already agitated. Change the subject or hang up. That's it."

Then nothing. The connection remained intact, but the continually emitting electronic signal was translated into silence on both ends. And if there were a little resentment riding in that signal, the phones were surpassing manufacture's expectations.

Six seconds. Eight seconds. Avery started watching T.V. again. Nineteen seconds. Twenty five seconds. Thirty three seconds. At forty one seconds, Lisa spoke up.

"So I guess we're done talking?"

During their conversational hiatus, Avery allowed himself more and more anger. He convinced himself of his rightness. The appropriateness of his antagonism and hardness. He emitted an unsympathetic, "Eh."

"Bye." She may or may not have been crying.

"Bye." He was certainly not crying.

Lisa's voice had left the building. It was, once again, Avery and Michael killing time, waiting with an incrementally collapsing patience. Psychosis would soon set in, with sleep being the only recourse. They should have been swimming up staircases by now. Watching the walls move without aid from the leftover light of television.

Soon after, a ring of another style bounced through the room. This ring could not be left ringing for long, since it rang all over the house and would ring anyone sleeping out of bed within two or three rings and those sleeping people would want to ring the necks of anyone awake that didn't stop the ringing sooner. Avery reached for the phone like a professional baseball player sliding into home. He didn't even look to see who it was.

"Luke?"

"Front gate. I have a Luke Marguiles here."

Avery said to Michael, "Luke's here," and to the phone, "Will you tell him he's a complete asshole before you let him in?"

"No, baby. I can't do that."

But the voice sounded like it could. It was a round, sonorous tone from the two big, painted lips of a woman perfectly capable of pulling someone's card. She just didn't want to. It wasn't her that'd been kept waiting.

"I understand. Just let him in, thanks."

Then came modulation that started low, ended low, but peaked in two separate highs in-between; the sound an uplifting and reassuring lullaby that sang of kindness, fairness, and love. Within what was probably an automatic reaction to hearing 'thanks', came a guarantee of safety for everyone and everything behind the gates of her post. It sounded like a good time, like a friend returning home.

The sultry voice of the guard said, "You're welcome."
Avery wanted it to stay in his ears forever.

Suddenly, Avery decided that everything was looking up. The wait was over. Luke had come through. And an angel had spoken.

CHAPTER 15

If God is the all-knowing, all-powerful being that modern religions have conjured up, it would be terrifying to speak to Him. If a young man were at the violent crest of his trip after accidentally dropping six hits of acid and sitting in a dark room by himself, he may feel it terrifying to talk to anyone at all.

Michael?
That was his name, wasn't it? But what's a name? Calling a man Louis instead of Jeff didn't change his experiences or personalities. Michael tried to remember if Michael was his name. It sounded familiar. But then, familiar could also describe the facial features of movie stars and young, paparazzi-plagued heiresses and Michael could say with a fair amount of certainty that he wasn't one of them.

I have come to speak with you on this night, for one of my most beloved children has been disappointed.
What a funny thing speaking is. We compare sounds to words, words to symbols, symbols to other

symbols and somehow come very close to understanding one another.

Do you know who I speak of? He was the most beautiful of angels, so charming and radiant. He expected a son.

Son and sun are pronounced the same. But where is the line between work and fun? Thinking of work at home is a similar sufferance to being at work. People who work at home are always at work. Or are they never at work? Home- h-o-m-e. Work- w-o-r-k. Michael knew that he had done something considered deviant, he just couldn't remember what.

You do know who I am, don't you?

There was a riddle very similar to this, but who could remember how it went? It was not an easy riddle.

Michael responded directly to the voice in his head for the first time since it started, "Don't you?" He didn't mean it as "No, I don't know who you are, can you tell me?" or "No, I don't, but can even *you* answer that most difficult question?" He was more copying the last two words he heard, like an echolalic, like a champion cockatoo, and implied no meaning at all.

I am Father of fathers, Mother of mothers.

Michael squished his lips together in kind of a fish mouth. The voice in his head sounded very poetic. Sound. That word again. The dark, still solitude of the room only extended the distance between Michael and sobriety. He was picking through all the symbolic references his brain would have otherwise accepted without thought. A couch is a couch whether you say it in English or Japanese. Japanese couches may look different, though. Does it have anything to do with the way they say the word?

You are… different from what I expected.

It dawned on him then that this voice in his head was not normal. He didn't know where it was coming from exactly, but did his best to respond accordingly. Like a drunk driver parked on the roadside with his window down and red and blue lights rolling on all sides of him, Michael tried to pull it together. Father of fathers, Mother of mothers- was this God talking to him? Did God communicate telepathically like this? It always seemed as though His voice would come from the sky. If it was God, Michael would first inquire as to why God had decided to meet him. And if it was just his imagination, he would consider his first trip a success.

My Son saved man of past, present, and future. How would you, a boy with a ruined mind, ever hoped to achieve the opposite? Lucifer jests, surely.

By this, Michael was ruthlessly confused. All the effort to gather his wits had collapsed alongside his already inert body, and he found himself once again incommunicado, wondering if jest meant joke because they both sound funny. "God? God, are you there?" Michael spoke aloud.

There was no answer. Of course there wasn't. He had asked with his mouth, and the mouth is sinful. It has lied, sworn, taken the lord's name in vain, and that malleable, candy-colored organ living in his mouth had performed oral sex on a number of different girls. Of course there was only silence to answer him. Silence that might as well have been dial-tone. Either that or the prospect of speaking with God had sobered him enough that his subconscious could no longer play the role he believed was the Creator. His name was Michael, he could remember that pretty easily, now. He only hoped that Avery and Luke were far enough away not to hear him ask the most clichéd of all generously-drug-induced questions to his empty room.

CHAPTER 16

They were laughing. In a room where the paintings quivered and the pages of books were specially marked for visitors, Avery and Luke were finding everything a hoot.

"And I was like, *Michael*? And then you did that Frankenstein thing, and then we both got scared that we were making too much noise."

More laughing. The effects worn into their bodies and minds were not very familiar. There was a preternatural feeling in their stomachs somewhere between needing the bathroom and needing a sandwich, there was an indecisiveness in their actions more compelling than either had ever handled- but where the effects of the acid they took stopped and the marijuana they were smoking so much of started was unclear. Crystal sat across from them, just as giggly and just as scatter-brained.

Luke stopped laughing very suddenly. "What Frankenstein thing?"

"That thing, I don't know, you sort of made that noise with your chest. I can't do it. I refuse to even try. The moment has passed."

Looking at Crystal and pointing at Avery, Luke shrugged his shoulders and made a confused sort of 'do you believe this guy?' scowl. "I refuse to even try," he mocked, "it wasn't a Frankenstein thing at all."

"What was it, then?" That was Crystal. She had finally given up waiting for them to stop recounting the last hour of their lives; instead she would try to take interest. Most of what they were saying didn't make any sense to her.

"Whatever, dude. All I'm saying is that I'd like..." and while Luke said that, Avery butted in with, "Listen, you have to stop nickel and dimeing my descriptions of things."

Again, Luke looked at Crystal, pointed at Avery, shrugged his shoulders and made a confused sort of 'do you believe this guy?' scowl.

Crystal stood up and walked to the corner of her room, saying: "Music. We need music," and sifting through a pile of CDs, said, "I'm pretty big into the Beatles. Because, because they're like the best band ever. I have some records, but the needle on my player is broken. Did you know that John Lennon came up with the name Beatles because- well, yeah. I guess that's obvious. Cause like the beat of the music. Lennon has always been my favorite. Do you guys like Rubber soul?"

She didn't leave any time for an answer before she went on. "That was their first album with all original tracks. The ones before it had covers. But that was before the whole 'Paul is dead' hoax, which started with the 'Here, There, and Everywhere' EP. Some people think that Revolver is their best album. I think that I usually prefer 'Sgt. Pepper's Lonely Hearts Club Band', depending on the mood. This is where they really started pushing the 'Paul is dead' hoax.

"On the Sgt. Pepper's album cover, each Beatle is holding a brass instrument except for Paul, whose instrument is black. Paul was also the only one out of the four to be standing straight towards the viewer in a wooden, stiff position, as if rigor-mortis has already set in. The others are standing at a forty-five degree angle, with life and three-dimensionality pronounced in their poses. Furthermore, if you look to the left, I mean to the right of the Beatles, you'll see wax figures of them from their earlier days. You know, like, 'I Want to Hold Your Hand' and 'She Loves You'. You wouldn't notice it at first glance, but if you looked closer, longer, you would see that Ringo is looking at the ground, very upset and that Paul or the spirit of Paul is consoling him. Upon even more scrupulous study, you'll notice that the yellow flowers on the ground spell out the name 'Paul'. But you guys probably already knew all this."

Oddly enough, Luke actually had heard this all before. He heard it the last time he was in Crystal's room, and it was Crystal that told him. Apparently it was just something she did with newcomers. She sauntered around, giving a grand tour of her 10x10 domicile and everything in it, gushing pedantic oration and subtle cries for recognition. It was scripted, rehearsed, fine-tuned, and to her ears- perfected. Luke wanted tremendously to tell Avery about this, that he had already borne witness to the strange performance, the almost word for word reenactment of what must have been her first flawless tour, but could not do so without drawing her attention. So they sat and listened as she went on.

"But- did you know that if you hold the middle of the bass drum to a mirror, so that 'LONELY HEARTS' is cut in half and the top parts become the bottom parts but turned around it reads the number one, then one spelled out, then the number one again, then x. So that's the LONELY part, obviously the x is for Paul. And right after that, the word HEARTS reads- he, and then there's an arrow that points straight up at Paul, die. He die."

"That's pretty wild," Avery said. The whole speech influenced him to clam up. This girl, to remember and present these details in chronological order, was certainly more sober than he was, and probably on a different plane of consciousness altogether.

"You were going to play a CD?" Luke asked.

"I am. We can listen to 'Magical Mystery Tour', famous for the John Lennon song, 'I am the Walrus'. But really John wasn't the walrus. You'll realize that when you read the album liner notes, and right under that track title it says, 'no you're not'. In some cultures the walrus represents death. The black walrus especially. So of course, Paul is the walrus and the Beatles even say so themselves on the white album, one year later with the lyrics- 'well here's another clue for you all, the walrus is Paul.' Oh, that was in the song 'glass onion'. Okay. You guys follow?

"Now there's 'Abbey Road'. Probably- no, definitely the most famous album cover of all time. You've got the fab-four crossing the intersection, and each one of them is playing a covert role in Paul's death. In front you have John in all white, looking more like an angel than a person, and he is either representing religion or he's leading the way to heaven. Take your pick. Next in line, there's Ringo. He's wearing a very classic black suit, very formal, and he's playing the roll of pallbearer. He's directly in front of Paul, who is out of step and barefoot, and who he is taking to the grave. Bringing up the rear is a haggard George, dressed in denim, and he of course is the grave-digger. There is also a white VW Beetle behind them with a license plate that says, on the bottom, 'two eight if'. Paul would have been twenty-eight for this album if he were alive. I mean, if all this wasn't just a hoax. And that thing about the white album saying 'Paul is dead' if you play it backwards isn't true. What it actually says is 'turn me on, dead man.'"

The room, apart from Crystal's talking, was still quiet. She finally selected a Led Zeppelin 'Best of' CD and loaded it into the empty tray, which had been open all this time. This made Avery and Luke happy, since the whole time they were on this Beatles conspiracy adventure they were really just waiting for music to play. Crystal sat down Indian-style on the floor. She asked Avery, "Do you like my artwork?"

Avery told her that he hadn't really looked at it. He stretched his whole body flamboyantly and let out a moderate roar, as if getting up was going to take some real effort. Then, after doing that for five seconds, and relaxing for five seconds, he stood up and walked as close as he could to the wall where the paintings hung.

"This is incredible," he finally stammered. "I've never seen anyone do this kind of holographic art before." He was moving his head from side to side to get various angles. As he did so the lines appeared to move and the light effected colors differently. It seemed to pulse and throb against the wall, a real live tell tale heart. The paintings were, however, the normal mediums of acrylic and watercolor.

"Thanks," Crystal said, just pleased as punch. She stood again and Luke wondered if she was headed to the bookshelf to tell them about Paul Theroux. She headed to the bookshelf and said, "Do either of you read Theroux?"

Avery was surveying the three-dimensional maze of light that comprised the top layer of another painting. He had no inkling whatsoever as to how she put such a complicated image together. First it was a normal cottage, then the hologram effect kicked in. "No," he answered, "No. No I do not. No I haven't."

"Well, you've heard of him of course. I have never fallen in love with an author before picking up one of his books."

"What does he have to say?" Avery asked.

"I've always found them lacking- some quality missing."

"But like, with him you don't?" Luke asked.

"They just don't quite do it for me. I can't describe what I mean, I only feel it."

"But you can feel that this guy does do it for you?" Avery questioned.

"He feels like the father to me, or the friend that I've always wanted."

"What would I get out of reading his books?" Luke queried.

"Oh, Theroux! Theroux!"

"Fuck, man. Are you messing with us? What kind of stuff does he write?" Avery said, loud in his mind but not so loud in reality.

Crystal then opened one of the books to a spot marked with a folded piece of yellow notebook paper and began to read.

This is the point where Avery stopped feeling comfortable. The constant discourse with its overtones of unnaturalness, using the floor as a big seat, the needy hospitality- there was something unnerving about it all. It was time to leave. The great outdoors of his gated community called. Avery thought about how he and Luke should best announce their departure.

CHAPTER 17

Sleep would simply not come. Avery begged for it when he tossed and when he turned, cursed it when the Tetris blocks falling down his eyelids would not stop, encouraged it despite the small noises of cars and dogs outside, and pretty much gave up on it when the clock read 9:17 p.m. These are the times that try men's souls. Work in less than two hours and you have yet to achieve even a wink of sleep. What's worse- your brain still better resembles the egg on the frying pan more than it does the sterile, virtuous, drug-free egg. Avery stepped into his jeans and walked to the kitchen.

Apparently it was lights out in the Tyler house. Voluntarily, yes, but it still meant that Avery had to be as quiet as possible. Opening and closing the microwave had to be done cautiously, dirty dishes placed in the sink gently. He was stumbling like some kind of sleepy monster and his skin, moist with perspiration which was especially evident above his lips and on the back of his neck, did nothing to project the image of a healthy man. He looked, in all actuality, very sick. Avery wished that his Sunday night could somehow not turn into Monday morning. He phased through a series of hackneyed fantasies, all from sending his doppelganger into work for him to just not showing up at all. Alas, there was no viable way out. He resigned to sucking it up and sticking it out. He sat down at the dinner table and put his face in his hands.

The autopilot was on. All functions of mind and body had been delegated to the drive of practiced routine. There's the door- walk to it. There's the time-clock- punch in the five-digit code. Avery walked into the shop and was blasted by soulless fluorescents. Lights that somehow had a negative effect on Avery that was in direct correlation with how tired/stoned he was at the time. They were the luminosity of utility. Factory crucial. It was like walking under a microscope in some giant laboratory that would probably be using the exact same kind of fluorescent lighting. They put an intolerably harsh edge on every color, making red too red and fat too fat and seemed to have something to do with the oily wetness of the shop air. Within minutes, Avery found himself wishing for a fire drill.

As he walked to his line, Avery heard a voice chasing him from behind.

"Challenge, bitch! I got my ticket right here!"

It was Chris. He was striding forward with more gusto than usual, waving a piece of notebook paper back and forth like a white flag but with the opposite intent. Avery had no idea what he was talking about. He waited for Chris to catch up.

"Hey," Avery said meekly.

"What's up, kid? Have a good weekend?" He took a short pause and inserted a fit of laughter, "Do a lot of partying?"

"I guess."

"You look like shit."

"Yeah, that sucks. Do I really? I'm in a pretty bad state right now."

Chris made a sad face. "Well, I hate to be the bearer of bad news, but you're about to be in a bad state without a free Episode III premier ticket. Herm thinks the only fair way to choose between us would be to have us each write an essay. You might as well not bother."

"What? Are you serious?" Avery demanded. "He

78

already said he'd take me."

"Yeah. He told me that too, kid. Sorry."

"So we're supposed to write an essay saying, what- why he should pick us?"

"That, or why you love Star Wars. It's up to you. He didn't really say. But seriously, don't waste your time. I've already written the winning essay." Chris waved the paper around some more, though a little less passionately than before.

"This is such bullshit. I shouldn't have to write an essay."

"You don't."

"I shouldn't, but I will. Let me see yours."

"Fuck you."

"Fine. Watch me write the best Star Wars fan-boy essay ever. Now it's personal. Don't even come by my station for the rest of the night."

And they said-

"Fine."

"Fine."

"Okay, fine."

"Fine, yeah- that's fine."

"It is fine."

"Fine is fine."

Until neither one could see the whites of their opponent's eyes and it was back to reality. Work.

Tool one was breaking halfway through every cycle. Avery's hands, brown with slippery coolant, were tired and unwieldy. It was a nightmare. Three hours into the shift and still not a single acceptable piece from C-18. Avery was trying everything he could think of to heal the wayward machine, but nothing worked. None of his intervention would stop the tool from snapping, the alarm from blinking, and machine from stopping, suspended in wrecked surrender.

Thoughts of flight turned about behind Avery's vision while his hands toiled idly. *Continent of Castles. The nation that spawned the telephone, the radio, the computer, the television, the human genome project. The place that produced The Smiths, The Clash, Joy Division, and not that I care all that much, but the Beatles. The first of so many things. The first dictionary. The first democracy. Call the first floor the ground floor, the elevator the lift. Very sensible. Carry colored money, spell color with a 'u'. Drink hot tea, and not just by myself anymore. Sir Isaac Newton and Sir Albert Einstein. Maybe I can watch* Lock, Stock, and Two Smoking Barrels *and actually understand everything. The tube. The big fucking* Dr. Who *phone booths. Lewis Carroll, Neil Gaiman and Alan Moore. Let any of that place, any tiny tidbit of a fraction of it rub off on me. Something has to happen there.*

At 7:03 a.m., Avery was saying goodbye to all of his coworkers- most of them for the last time. He made plans to meet over at Herm's house for a last little early-morning get-together. Chris wouldn't go. As the three of them, Avery, Herm, and Chris walked to the cars, Chris was at first lagging behind. Halfway to the cars he caught up, and as they drew nearer, Chris' pace redoubled, and he was first behind the wheel. Avery's third wind was enough to get him to Herm's, dial a few friends, and leave him with a reservoir of energy enough to last a couple more hours, but not enough to figure out why the fuck Chris walked so much faster with his car around.

Avery stared peacefully through the white wine translucence of foggy windows. He congratulated himself for a job well quit, bid the building a fond farewell, and drove off into the sunrise.

CHAPTER 18

By his logic, the entire house didn't need to shake. That would be of course the prime example, the 'obviously something is going on here' that took scores of bodies, preferably American Indian bodies, to realize. In their case, he said, they didn't sit atop a burial ground. This haunting (a strange feeling people thought they sometimes might possibly be maybe sort of getting inside the house), was powered by a single upset corpse, and was therefore far less pronounced. His voice trailed off on this note and did not pick back up. Herm decided that his timing was poor, and he should wait a little while before blowing everyone's mind.

Avery's grand sending off. A committee gathered here to welcome him away from the noctivagous. Avery was sitting on the end of Herm's couch, looking mildly uncomfortable, trying not to touch anything with his bare skin. Michael, Luke, and Herm shared the couch with him, while J.P. sought asylum on a weathered lawn chair from outside. Herm's studio apartment was not built to comfortably house five people. The refrigerator could hardly house five separate beverages and the bathroom would be hard pressed to house five medium sized farts. Herm did own, however, an unusually large television. Everyone was pretty enthused about what Avery promised to show them.

"Thank you, friends, for your support of the decisions made by me, concerning my career and lifestyle," Avery said, high on his soapbox and grass. "As you all know, I have enjoyed recounting the events that preceded, umm, me getting this tape." He held up the tape, a little dissatisfied by the words that came to him. He would much rather have said, 'procurement of this tape' or 'acquisition of this tape' or 'taking this tape into possession'. "I feel that in granting you an opportunity to see it yourself, you are all, with the exception of my brother who was there, gaining a higher frame of reference and can better appreciate what went down at John's house that day."

After Avery fed the tape to the VCR and sat down, he quietly asked Luke if the accent he was using during his speech was okay. Luke said he didn't really notice an accent, but he obviously wasn't paying much attention. In the hush of a room waiting to be entertained, Michael asked Herm if he would miss working with Avery.

"Hell nah, I'm not gonna miss that bitch," he said, but after a short moment's thought said, "That's not true. I am going to miss him," and removed his cap.

A shoddy moniker scrolled across the screen. Cut to an overweight man in a white sweat-marked oxford, thick glasses and heavy breath. Standing before a panel of black drapery, he spoke.

"Are you comfortable?" The question lingered, romanced the five-part consciousness of Herm's living room. The orator glowered from the T.V. set. "Nice, isn't it? This comfort? Would you be as content with comfortable reality if you knew the truth?

"I want to talk to you today about the world we live in. Some of what you hear will be difficult to understand.

It will be at odds with your programmed version of reality. You've been taught to scoff at ideas like this. 'Radical,' you'll say- 'impossible,' you'll say. And though it may sound crazy, your entire reality has been molded and re-molded by a highly compartmentalized, secret society known as the Illuminati.

"Since the dawn of civilization this group has been in power, and if you know where to look, the evidence is everywhere. They call themselves the illuminati because of the clandestine knowledge accessible to them. All manner of technology not open to the public, *why?* -because knowledge is power. I would turn your attention to the landmarks of ancient Egypt and modern day Paris for an example. The pyramids are in perfect alignment because they were all built on powerful vortex points, places where lines of energy cross. Is this some superstition of an obsolete kingdom? Why then, are the major landmarks of Paris in this same configuration- also in line with the pyramids? Some coincidence, huh? But get used to it; coincidences are a…"

The television went black. The wall behind the television went black too, as Herm's unusually large body blocked light from most directions.

"The energy he's talking about, right?"

Avery started to protest, said that the tape just started, to wait at least a little while before pausing it.

Herm just said it was his house and asked how everyone was feeling.

At roughly the same time, Michael answered, "I'm a little cold," and J.P. answered, "Fine, man. I'm high as fuck," and Avery an uptight, "What?" and Luke looked around the room.

"Okay. See, this guy's talking about energy and

shit, and I know he's right. Like I was saying earlier, my house is like that. Someone's buried right around here," Herm waved his hand in front of the hallway wall. "It makes fucked up energy all the time. This house is haunted, mother fucker."

Herm noted the engrossed look on J.P.'s face and went on. "My landlord built this place himself, right? And the garage is his, I don't have keys to it. Now I know that on the other side of this wall, my house goes this far back," he pointed at a spot on the hallway wall, "and since I've been in that garage I know it only goes this far back," he pointed at another spot on the wall, four or five feet from the first spot. "So there's just a walled up space here, it starts at the edge of my bedroom and ends at the edge of the garage. There must be something buried in there. My landlord is a weird goddamned guy."

"Here's what I don't get," Avery said, "You brought this up earlier and gave up trying to explain, and now when we're right in the middle of watching something, you pause the tape and finish your story."

Herm voiced the beginning of his rebuttal, but Avery said 'Mother fucker what the fuck?' a few times in a fast, high pitched voice and nothing intelligible could be heard over that.

The general mood of the room went a touch sour. But Herm hit the play button, sat down, and vanquished any unease. Unease, in this case, ranged from sympathy to frustration, distraction to disenchantment, embarrassment to a touch of regret.

It was back to the winded man's paranoid theory.
"....dime a dozen when you really start to look at our world and the way it's run.

"The American government, for instance- why

84

is every presidential election won by the candidate with the most genetic links to European royal families? 34 of the 43 presidents are descendants of Charlemagne. Why were 50 of the 56 signatories on the Declaration of Independence recognized Freemasons?

"Why are there 12 gods in the inner circles of Hittite, Greek, Egyptian, and Hindu religions and 12 apostles in Christianity? Could these methods of control stem from the same place, been written by the same groups?

"These groups of illuminated individuals, very few of whom know the whole truth, are directing the course of humanity as we speak. Through a suppression of knowledge, this highly compartmentalized secret society has engineered our politics and economy, introduced religions and cultural norms that stifle free-thinking human potential, and have hid the true nature of their being from the human populace.

"I say human populace and you think 'of course, what else could the populace consist of?' Think back. Scan through the stories you've heard in your lifetime. Legend, folklore, mythological, biblical- from all times and all places. A common theme exists in a great, great number of these stories, and that is the figure of dragons or serpents.

"For millennia, the seats of power have held shape-shifting reptilian-human hybrids from the fourth dimension."

"That's a stretch," Herm said with a bored voice.

Not even two minutes in, Avery knew they would never make it to the end of the video.

CHAPTER 19

Blossoms, blooming and booming garnish a riverside clearing. Grasses grow with glowing patina, detonations of greens and yellows, soft, pure. Trees and shrubbery pierce the soil- great settled giants that guard the land with still, silent spirit. Their vines hang benignly like suspended rainfall. Birdsong ties ground to sky. Over rocks, the water trickles; they sit, smooth as spilt milk, as they have for ages. It has so far survived the defilement of human molestation- far from the effluence of city streets, of factories and public residue. Untouched, unspoiled Earth.

It would have been a lovely place for Avery to meet with Lisa- she wanted to discuss the last two days and the mall was crowded.

"Do you want anything?" Avery turned to Lisa and asked.

"A caramel Frapaccino?"

The cashier looked at Avery, as if waiting for authorization.

"That's fine," Avery told him, "a double espresso and a caramel Frapaccino."

Avery handed over his credit card, signed the receipt, took his credit card back and stepped with Lisa to the end of the bar. They didn't say anything to each other for a moment. They just stood there, watching the unsure movement of the man in the green apron making their drinks.

As the whipped topping was applied, Avery asked, "Should I tell you about the whole acid thing?"

"Maybe right this second isn't the best time."

As she said this, Lisa looked over her shoulders in both directions. She was expecting perhaps a police officer or two, one with a mini-cassette recorder, one with cocked handcuffs.

"It was pretty fun," Avery told her, "Weird, a little uncomfortable at times, but fun."

"I'm glad." Her tone was at variance with her words. Lisa, straight as an arrow, clean as a whistle, pure as the driven snow. She did not indulge in the use of any drug but the legal liquid kind, though at nineteen it was not yet legal. "Are you planning on doing it again?"

They left the store, entered the food court, and began looking for a table.

"Yeah, sometime. I'd do it again."

There was an empty table near a trashcan. Avery didn't like sitting next to the trashcans if he could help it, but as the mall was reaching max-occupancy, he couldn't.

"Did Michael have fun?"

Avery laughed. He described Michael's night in as much detail as possible. It didn't take long.

"Maybe he did," Lisa said. It was in response to Avery's last bit of narrative which he thought a grandiose climax and went- 'He thinks he talked to God.'

Throngs of people meandered through the walkways near Avery and Lisa's table. Among them, an old man pushed a long, two-child stroller. He looked short and frail behind it, behind the weight, the workload that two toddlers suggested. Still, his walk was probably as close to a strut as he could manage at that age. He was beaming.

Another man steered around them. Granddad was walking too sluggishly for this one. He was purposefully dressed in a gray suit, green shirt, green striped tie, and was weaving in and out passed the slow ramblers. He held his nose high in the air, as though he was straining to touch the tips of his gelled, spiked hair with it. Either he worked in one of the mall's swank department stores or- no, there was no or. This was almost certainly break-time. Yes- a reflective strip of silver shone on the left breast of his suit.

Two girls, awash in the ambiance of best friends, wearing the same high-school girl's volleyball t-shirts and gym shorts got in line at Salad Sensations.

"Do you believe this?" Avery said, looking at his drink. "How long have we been here? Two minutes? My drink is almost gone."

Lisa raised her eyebrows. "Espressos don't last forever."

"I think they gave me a single. Fuck. I really don't think there were two shots in this cup."

Lisa smiled at him. She seemed to like his complaining, seemed to find it amusing as long as it didn't go on for too awful long. And 'too awful long' is the key idea here- totally, completely, utterly and wholly subjective. Avery picked up on this, of course. It filled him with a brilliant shiver of proximity. He wanted to make her happy because of it.

"Lisa- I've been thinking," he said, knowing that she'd been waiting to hear this for months, "It'd be foolish for me not to go to London with you- so count me in, okay?"

Getting into the most esteemed university, winning the lottery, watching a puppy swim for the first time, completing a marathon, rubbing a genie's magic lamp, being chosen out of the crowd to go on stage and feed Shamoo will all generate a reaction of the same nature. Lisa reacted in a manner relative to this.

"I told you! Didn't I tell you?" she squealed, now on the same side of the table as Avery, her arms around his and her forehead pushing hard against him, "It's going to be so incredible. Believe me; you're going to fit right in."

Avery did his best to hug her back, but her grip was persistent. He couldn't move much more than his mouth.

"Are you glad?"

"I'm so glad!"

"It'll be just us."

"Just us."

"It'll be expensive."

"We'll manage."

"And far away."

"Good riddance."

"You'll miss your cat."

She pushed herself off Avery and frowned like an abandoned child.

A pot-bellied man fumbled maladroitly at the trashcan. There were a few shriveled ketchup packets sticking to his green food-court tray, and he was doing the best job he could to get them off with one hand. Bang! The side of his tray connects with the top of the trashcan. Bang! It didn't work. A series of quick bangs and finally the tray is clean, save for small dabs of ketchup here and there. He sets the tray down, rubs his palms on the part of his shirt that stretches tautly over his stomach, and moves on.

"When do you want to go?" Lisa asked.

So in a place that was not filled with dazzling beams of sunshine sliding through branches and leaves, Avery and Lisa discussed their plans to leave. They were the hasty plans of impatient, inexperienced young adults, but they sounded fun. Avery found himself looking forward to it all very much.

CHAPTER 20

The pursuit of trivial knowledge, or even better the inadvertent happening upon of trivial knowledge seems to be greatly cherished by many a person. It serves, most likely, as a self indulgent form of escape. Not escape from life, necessarily, but a shorter escape from an escape from life. A for-instance, if you please.

There exists an organism in this convoluted universe of ours called the brain worm. Wait- that's not good enough. More specific. Scientific. After all, an escape from an escape must be stimulating, well-researched, and easily forgettable. There exists an organism in this convoluted universe of ours called *Dicrocoelium dendriticum*. This fascinating trematode parasite produces, for every clutch, clump, cluster, or caboodle of cercariae (that's the fourth, tadpole-like stage in the brain worm's life cycle), a sort of kamikaze pilot that destroys an ant's sense of direction and steers it forever heavenward. Here's why-

The adults shoot eggs down the intestines of whatever host they're squatting, be it a cow, sheep, or goat. The eggs are driven out via bowel movements, and are at some point eaten by snails. Soon after, the brain worm develops a new form and leaves the snail, cloaked in delectable mucus. Ants eat that adorable little slimy snail trail and the cercariae along with it (OOPS!), and the parasites bore through the stomach wall, landing near the ant's brain, or more specifically and scientifically, the subesophagal ganglion. All but one of the parasites form thick walled cysts inside the ant. The one that doesn't- the kamikaze, the 'brain worm', assumes control of the ant's behavior. At this point all the ant wants to do is climb the highest blade of grass and wait to be eaten by a cow, or sheep, or goat.

Congratulations to all but the one martyr worm, they are now back where they started, in the liver of a grass eating mammal, ready to mature, lay eggs, and repeat the madcap cycle that is their lives.

Most people don't need to know this sort of thing. Most people would be lucky to pronounce *Dicrocoelium dendriticum*, let alone count the intricate details of the organism in their arsenal of cocktail party conversation. Enviably, Michael was one of those people that could. He'd already read an essay stating that the brain worm was a working model of altruism in nature, and was in the process of reading two books- a study of sperm whales called *Sperm Whales*, and a book he found in the science fiction section of the library, *The Illuminatus! Trilogy*. Later, by the sheer coincidence of renting these two books at the same time, Michael would explain that dolphins wrote *Moby Dick* for Herman Melville to demonize sperm whales and glorify whaling due to an ongoing, interspecific dispute.

"Sperm whales have the largest brains found in nature," Michael said. He was leaning against the garage work bench. "Most of it seems to be geared towards acoustic recognition."

Avery threw his tennis ball in the air again, caught it, and waited for the next tid-bit of *Physeter macrocephalus* factoid.

Beyond the garage door, the well defended gates of the community, the stoplight on the corner, and the entranceway of another, more easily breached gated community, J.P. was playing with electricity. A small group gathered around him to watch. How much live electricity was running through those wires? Nobody had ever bothered to do the research. Dangerous business, this. A bead of sweat dripped off the bridge of J.P.'s nose and landed an insignificant marine on the right lens of his glasses. He was concentrating. With the tip of his tongue against the tip of his top canine, it was up to him to fix the lights. No lights, no baseball.

"We should probably head over there," Avery said to Michael, who had already said to him a number of other sperm whale facts and theories.

In response, Michael moved the book away from his face, inches away from the work bench, but he did not stop reading. Only when the garage door creaked, shuddered, and moaned like a tame earthquake was *Sperm Whales* returned to its latent position.

The refreshing touch of night- finally, it belonged to Avery. The moon no longer beckoned the beginning of work, the commitment of time, the lending of life. Avery could go on living in common time with the world now. He would throw the first pitch in his first game of many nights to come. It wasn't until the garage door was open that Avery fully understood the joy of emancipation.

The brothers walked down the driveway, both noticing something in the bottom corner of their peripheral vision. An unprepared person might have dialed an ambulance. But it was only Mr. Chase, doing as he did, looking like a recklessly discarded piece of evidence.

"Good evening," Michael said half sarcastically,

knowing a reciprocal greeting wouldn't come. He would have continued right on walking if it weren't for Avery.

But Avery did not veer left like he would have normally. Something- perhaps the lack of clouds, the violin clamor of crickets, the offense of having hellos left hanging over and over, overwhelming curiosity, or something else entirely, inspired Avery to walk to the foot of Mr. Chase's driveway and force him into conversation.

"Nice night, isn't it?" Avery asked, not sarcastically at all.

Mr. Chase smiled, lifted two fingers in the air, but did not break eye contact with the cosmos.

"Yes, sir. Clear sky. Not a cloud about. Perfect for stargazing, huh?"

The same fingers Mr. Chase was holding up wiggled a little. At this, Michael looked at Avery and stifled a chuckle.

"You've never met my brother, Michael. Or me, for that matter. Mr. Chase, isn't it? My name is Avery. I hope I'm not disturbing you too much; it's just that we've lived across the street from each other for so long and never said much of anything to you. But I gotta tell ya, this custom of yours, laying on the driveway all the time- it's boggled my mind for years. Years, man!" At this point, Avery was doing as much to entertain himself as he was to get a word out of Mr. Chase. He was unable to maintain a sturdy voice. Whispers of laugher were forming under words. "Why do you do it? I have to know! Please, for our all loving God's sake tell me why!"

"Because as you said, it's a nice night."

At that moment, the world stopped turning and revolving and everything and just kind of floated weightlessly without command. Their trifling holy grail was unveiled. Because it was a nice night! Nothing within reason could have lived up to the stories Avery imagined-could better explain why Mr. Chase laid through all his time outside. The answer was every bit lame enough to believe. Of course there was no reason! Because it was a nice night! Michael, however, could not find it in himself to accept this.

"Are you… are you going to say anything else?" Avery asked. The awe in his speech subtracted years from his being. He was Dorothy seeing the Wizard for the first time, a child meeting a walking, waving Mickey Mouse costume.

Mr. Chase smiled. "Hello, Avery. Hello, Michael."

Avery was so dumbfounded that he said hi again.

"You've really made his night, Mr. Chase. Believe me," said Michael.

"For your brother- anything."

Strange, the way Mr. Chase spoke. Anyone else that said, 'for your brother- anything' would have come off a cynic. A delicately sarcastic asshole. A price. The delivery had nothing to do with it, nor the tone or timing. There was just… love. Everything he'd said thus far was given with honest love. No condescension. Arrogance. Any of that passive aggressive bullshit that keeps some family members from a real relationship. He meant what he said and he said it with a smile. No wonder he never said anything. That kind of sincerity is devoured in this fucking morbid world of sharks. Better to just smile and sometimes raise your fingers.

"We're meeting some people for a game of baseball in Shady Lakes. Care to join? It's not proper baseball, we play on a tennis court with a plastic bat and tennis ball and you can bean runners. It's a lot of fun."

"No, Michael. Thank you, but no. You boys have

fun, though. Perhaps we'll talk again sometime," Mr. Chase responded- genuine, kind.

"Definitely, definitely we will," Avery said, still a bit star-struck.

Three 'goodnight's were bided, and Avery and Michael went on walking. When they reached the courts, the lights were on, turning the great night outside the perimeter of the tennis court fence into a great day for baseball inside. With a couple mole crickets blindly wondering what all the noise was about, it was game-time.

CHAPTER 21

"Nothing too flashy this time," Lisa said, "everything was great last time, don't get me wrong. I just don't know if we'll have time for all the preparations and everything."

"Oh, don't worry. I know we won't. I don't even know if we'll have time enough to book the stage. You two are leaving so soon."

"Not for another month, at least," Avery interjected, mouth full of chocolate rice cakes.

"Okay, another month. I could maybe, barely even maybe get something four weeks from now, and that's if I really work my ass off. But let's see," Michael looked to the ceiling, like he was aiming for his brain but it moved at the last second, "I have this one idea- it's about a guy who works for the government as a sort of emissary to visiting extraterrestrials. This guy has a son in grade school who he has super high expectations for, but his kid is turning out to be a dunce."

"That's *Chase, New and Improved!*" Avery shouted.

"It's based on a short story Avery wrote about Mr. Chase. Anyway, as Avery could tell you himself, the father is very disappointed. He goes to a parent-teacher meeting and learns that the boy is to be held back in the third grade for a second time. You'd be perfect for the teacher. So after that the aliens sort of read this guy's mind and say they can give him a better son as a trade- a kind of robot son. He agrees to do it. His robot son grows up, graduates with honors, all that jazz. But at the end, his real son, the one that the aliens raised, has grown up to be a really bright investigatory journalist and blows the roof off of his father's whole operation."

"Based on my story," Avery said between chews, "Ha. That's exactly my story." His mouth looked like the bottom of a used football cleat.

"I get to play the teacher?" Lisa got excited whenever she talked theater.

"That's right. You play a third grade teacher. It's a pretty cool role, actually. You get to say all this really biting stuff but in a voice like you're talking to little kids. Like this one part goes, 'I thought we could discuss Albert's progress outside- in his presence. I believe an integral step in his development would be to include him in all matters concerning his future. Children who feel like a spectator in their own lives at such an early stage may grow accustomed to just letting things happen, and to not making an effort on their own behalf'. I think that's the line, anyway. You'll say it better."

"Word for word," Avery sounded almost upset.

"Well that's great isn't it? Michael's last play was

a hit, and this time he'd be using one of your stories!"

There was no denying that. If any other director wanted to use one of Avery's stories as a play it would have thrilled the pants off him. But Michael, his own prodigious flesh and blood, it felt like charity- like once again he would play a bit part in his younger brother's great success.

"Realistically, I'm not sure we'll have time to put it all together," Michael said, "Find out as soon as you can when you're going. Give me an exact date. If you can wait until the first week of July, maybe it'll work."

Lisa assured him that they would figure it out. Michael even offered to give Avery the part of grown up Albert, but Avery said he wasn't right for it. All Avery wanted to talk about was getting Mr. Chase involved, as Mr. Chase was the inspiration behind the story, behind the majority of Avery's stories. This turned the conversation in a completely different direction. Michael started going on and on about not buying the simple explanation of 'it being a nice night out' that Mr. Chase gave them for laying out all the time. He raffled off a number of things that, for him, confuted the testimony.

-"Nice night or not, it's still weird to lie on your driveway all the time."

-"You can enjoy a nice night on the driveway and still say hello to people."

-"He lies out there in poor weather, too."

-"There's nothing there to make him more comfortable- no towel, nothing."

-"I've never seen him do anything else at all."

-"By just laying there all the time, Mr. Chase is failing to repress the instinctual, animalistic tendency to rest as much as possible. He's regressing, in a sense, to a gorilla. A captive gorilla, even. Freud would say that this is the breakdown of a major function involved in keeping society going. He's choosing not to forget the reptilian desire to rest all the time. A 'nice night' doesn't do that to a person. The root of dysfunction would come from some much deeper place."

These were all points which Michael expounded upon, especially the last one, which got really confusing and reminded Avery of why he never read Freud. Satisfied that he'd injected a healthy dose of doubt into his brother's mind, Michael went to his room. It would be a sad thing if Avery stopped writing stories about the android across the street.

With just enough time left for Lisa and Avery to really settle down, get drawn into the movie they were watching, find a position tangled up in each other that was actually comfortable for the both of them, there was a knock at the door.

Avery ran downstairs, and after opening the door found his good friend Luke standing there. He had come unannounced, and was slightly out of breath. Ahh, lazy days in the empty afternoon at home- Avery surely would miss them.

"Hey. I need to use your computer," Luke said.

"Sure, man. How come you're breathing hard?"

"I'm not," Luke said as he walked in the door. But he was. It wasn't due to exertion, stress, fright, or embarrassment; the usual afflictions that mess with respiration. Luke had an idea that excited him, excited him an awful lot, apparently. "I was just on my way over to Crystal's house and I couldn't stop thinking about all that 'Paul is dead' shit she laid on us the other night. I want to go over there and give her a big lecture now. You know, get her back. What do you know about Tupac?"

"Nothing. I know that he was in *Juice*, and that he got shot," Avery said.

"Damn. Well, let me use your computer."

"So you can tell Crystal about Tupac?"

"Yeah. All that stuff about his death being faked. It's the total opposite of the 'Paul is dead' hoax, so it's perfect."

Avery thought it was a funny idea. He told Luke that of course he was welcome to use the computer and they both walked upstairs.

From the couch, Avery and Lisa could see car chases, shoot outs, and fist fights. They could hear tough-guy monologues, gun shots, and swearing. Lisa tasted a hint of chocolate rice cakes when they kissed, and Avery's stuffy nose couldn't smell much of anything. Luke was in the bedroom. There were advances being made in the loft, but Luke was occupying the bedroom. The advances were becoming more forceful. Luke- still taking up the bedroom. Another advance, too persuasive to excuse was made, and Avery got up to check Luke's progress. If something on the net cant be located in twenty minutes, it very probably can't be located at all.

The face at the monitor, lit by glowing pixels, did not turn its frustrated glare to the door as Avery walked in. It read on for a moment, and watched as its caretaker, the hand, hit the back button and clicked another link. An enormous pot leaf materialized on the screen with a bit of cyclic theory underneath. Luke groaned.

What he'd gathered so far paled in comparison to Crystal's shtick. There were more pot leaves on Tupac sites than there was information. All he knew was that Tupac was shot on September, 7th and died seven days later on the 13th. There was some 'seven days' theory that also tied into the supposed time of death, 4:03. The music video that was released only days after Tupac's passing depicts him as an angel in heaven, and the video after that was released not under the name Tupac, but another moniker, Makaveli, obviously an allusion to Florentine nobleman and political philosopher, Niccolo Machiavelli. And that was only relevant because Machiavelli suggested, among his large body of work, that a person might thwart an enemy by faking their death. There just wasn't enough to go on.

"Shame," Avery said, resting his hand on Luke's shoulder.

"Eh. Maybe I'll try again sometime. It was a good idea."

Luke suddenly realized that his bit of impromptu research had eaten up nearly a half hour of time, and that he was over an hour late in getting to Crystal's. A hurried goodbye to Avery, a shout to Lisa on the way downstairs, and Luke was gone.

Before Lisa bound into the room, shedding clothes as she came, Avery looked at the website that was left on his monitor.

"I wonder if Tupac was involved somehow with the Illuminati?"

It was far from an appropriate time to find out.

CHAPTER 22

July 4th drew nearer, and days hurried by. The time casing Avery rushed over his life in a flood of sunrises and sundowns, because time knew, as did Avery, that he was on something of a vacation, and during vacation time and the perception of time are not often harmonious. Sixty seconds feels like hundreds through the agonizing fifth or sixth hour of Chinese water-torture. It feels like sixty seconds during checkout at the grocery store and less than half that time on a first time bike ride through the streets of Milan. A reasonably straightforward notion, that in this wretched existence time turns to equalize the joy a person might get out of a given situation, but goddamn did Avery have a hard time communicating this idea to his uncle.

Judging by the smell of the dining room, it would feel like a fast dinner. Turkey, casseroles, cranberry sauce, sweet potatoes, butter roles- one look at the table would be adequate rapture to get the average starving Ethiopian to believe just about anything. The company, however, might coax Avery's personal version of time into moving a little slower. Not that Avery didn't love his family, not that at all, there was just a small matter of finding common grounds. Finding a line of communication outside the usual, *How's work?*, *How's school?*, *How's your mom?*, or *How's the weather?* can sometimes be difficult among relatives. There are barriers abound- a lexicon of don't ask, don't tell-esqe barriers.

Avery was suddenly excited by the prospect of a new conversation, though. One that had nothing to do with the aforementioned topics. A fresh subject that both he and his uncle might gamely enjoy. Real, satisfying common ground.

"Michael and I have our own 'Here, Tiss' story."

His uncle looked skeptical. He said that he thought they lived in a nice neighborhood.

"What does that have to do with it? The hooker thing?" He blew air out of his nose. "It's not exactly the same, just listen. Me and Michael were…"

His uncle interrupted. He said that the correct way to phrase that would be Michael and I, not me and Michael.

"Will you be quiet and listen? I'm not even sure if you're right. Fuck, man. Forget it."

Don't be such a baby, his uncle kept saying. He was only trying to save his nephew from the bad influence of the rest of that idiot, illiterate generation. They were practically rewarding people for being morons these days. You got record contracts and a place on television. All a part of a larger plan to dull the people's brain and make then more susceptible to advertising. He apologized for what he called a short, but poignant rant, and urged Avery to continue.

"Alright, but only if you promise to listen. Can you handle that? Okay. We were hanging out in the racquetball court the other night, and we heard this lady down the road yelling, 'Do me! Do me!' Loud! Screaming it, right? We didn't really know what was going on. I thought maybe she was on some sort of crazy, unheard of drug or something. We started looking around to see where it was coming from. This lady runs by, still yelling, mind you, 'Do me! Do me!' until she sees us. Then she gets all embarrassed, comes over, and asks if we've seen her dog- Doom. I guess she just calls it Doomie when she's at home."

Avery's uncle shook his head for a moment, holding his smile back with such success that nobody at the table suspected amusement. He said, after a time, that there were a number of fundamental differences between Avery's story and his, that he'd hesitate even to make the comparison. Avery's story lacked repeatability, reputation, and the essential element of ignorance on the female caller's part. What was so funny about the 'here,

Tiss' story, he patiently explained, was that this retired hooker, who everyone in the neighborhood knew was a retired hooker, would stand on the corner night after night, calling her cat, Tiss. 'Here, Tiss' sounds almost exactly like 'here it is' in a poor Kentucky accent, which was made even more memorable by the fact that it happened every night on the street corner, and by a retired hooker, no less.

"That is such bullshit," Avery muttered.

Now there was the matter of Avery's language, the uncle pointed out. He said that he had let it slide earlier, but to use such crass vocabulary in front of his grandparents was really…

"First of all, I'm twenty one years old. Nobody tells me how to talk anymore. Grandma and Grandpa can handle it. I've heard worse from them."

There was a rolling of eyes and variety of sarcastic ways to say things like 'oh, the big man' and 'don't tell the big man how to talk' displayed for everyone at the table.

"That's what I said. And anyways I can't believe you're trying to disregard what happened that night based solely on the fact that it doesn't happen all the time. So what if she wasn't a hooker? Maybe it's better that she's a respectable lady yelling 'Do me!', which I might say is more suggestive than 'Here it is.' That's probably what this is all about, huh? You're jealous that 'Do me!' is more suggestive than 'Here it is.'"

At that, Michael laughed. Avery's grandparents looked like they were ready to start talking about work, school, and the weather. Lisa stayed looking at her plate, as she had been for the duration of the meal, watching the grease pool and harden, and Avery's uncle just shook his head with an air of sad condescension, calmly assuring

Avery that a story of a retired hooker on a rundown Kentucky corner calling 'Here, Tiss!' over and over was much more significant. He even said he was sorry that it's the truth.

The food seemed to disappear fast, but at the same time, like a twin aging on Earth faster than his astronaut brother in orbit, the dinner conversation dragged on, a paradox in motion.

CHAPTER 23

Guy Weeks was in the kitchen doing his best impression of a silent, slinking, soft-footed cat. He went back and forth, from the table to the sink to the refrigerator to the dishwasher to the cupboards, sponge in one hand, rag in the other. He never set his eyes upon anything higher than his waist unless it was to put up clean dishes or rearrange food stocks. Unobtrusivivity (though perhaps not a recognized word) was key. This was Guy's reaction to martial tension. Clean, clean, clean, quiet, quiet, quiet, and as long as there's quiet cleaning being done the friction can be left to wither and dissipate on its own. It was really too bad that the efficacy of this strategy forever seemed to wane as the labors neared completion.

A voice from around the wall sounded. Not a scream, quite- perhaps a shout but perhaps again only because it was coming from around a wall and wanted to be sufficiently heard. Nevertheless, the message was clear. The voice was unhappy. It wanted something done, something Mr. Weeks didn't want to do.

"I keep thinking about it and I just can't understand, Guy!"

Guy pulled a pot from the cupboard. He decided he would give those stubborn black stains from the time he burned some Bolognese a go.

Again the voice, closer now, right around the corner but not as loud this time, thank heavens- "I know it's important to you, honey. To a point you did really well with it," in the room now, no longer wrapping around walls, "But now? Your little theme is costing us money! It's bad business! Two months now!"

Guy had little choice but to respond. Stubbornly, he chose the little choice, choosing to only nod his head repeatedly, ignore the effluvium that was his wife's nagging voice.

"Too busy to talk? Goddamn it, Guy, you're washing a clean pot!"

She was right behind him, staring craters in the back of his skull. Guy turned to her. The kitchen, unfortunately, would not stick up for him.

"Honey, what you have to understand..."

To understand Guy's predicament, one must first understand a few things about Guy himself. Guy Weeks was one of those moderately unlucky individuals to have been born with the soul of an artist but had never taken the time to develop any particular artistic talent. He was a businessman. A land-owning, rent-charging, blue pen-using kind of businessman. His sole artistic indulgence took place upon the signs above his tenant's doors.

"...is that those names..."

Gave Guy a sense of achieved vision, and no matter how trite, they were published bits of his very own creativity. They were appreciated by other, like-souled artistic fellows. Michael and Avery, for instance.

105

"...create a clear, entrenched memory inside the consumers' heads..."

Some of whom knew that he, Guy mother-fucking Weeks was the mastermind behind it all. On the sidewalks of 1600 Military Trail, he was practically a celebrity. In the glances and smiles of the people he was thanked for the tasteful theme he developed and enforced. Respected and admired.

"...which, obviously, is what advertising is all about."

Memory. In memory of Guy Weeks and his terrific contribution to the world. It entertained them. It made them think. Every passerby who looked at those signs would stop for a second and remember, reflect, recognize. For someone who would have loved to live as an artist, seeing his work ceaselessly presented to the public in text that stood sometimes over two feet tall was tantamount to rapture.

"So just consider the last two months of lost rent an advertising expense. Nobody is getting into that address without a pun above their door. Nobody, dig?"

CHAPTER 24

Avery leaned back into mushy couch cushions and nervously waited to feel something. Light gray smoke swirled and thinned just above his head. Something should be happening soon, any second now according to his friends, most of whom were in different stages of recovery. All eyes were on Avery.

A pulse- in the room and on each side of his head, growing and growing. Bones seemed to melt and freeze at the same time, blood seemed to tumble through waterslide veins and arteries with outdo haste- strange, but altogether trumped by the fact that his face had promptly expanded to coat every wall in the room.

It was like the paint, Avery's face. It surrounded the rectangle, stretched over the three-dimensional perimeter. Outside the walls, the face, the face-walls- nothing existed. The center, then, was the place to watch.

Everything looked mostly normal inside. There were people Avery knew around him. They were looking at him, laughing and asking questions. It was impossible to respond. Avery could only concentrate on four things- one was that he wanted desperately to get back to normal and was deeply terrified that he never would, another was that his face was now the proliferated boarder to all reality, the third thing was that his physical body was completely at the mercy of the world, and lastly that there was a field of energy slowly drifting through the room/his face/the universe.

The field could be described as a two dimensional pane that extended from the floor to the ceiling and from the front wall to the back. It vibrated quickly, and was visible to the eye in the same way as the dividing line between fresh and salt water when the former is resting on top of the latter. As the field began to travel a steady path from right to left, it made Avery worry. The dog would be overrun. Joey would be overrun. His own body, the inert shell on the center of the back wall would be overrun, and he had no idea what would happen when it was.

Joey was taking a hit off the pipe now. The substance inside it, densely packed black anonymity, was being burned by two lighters simultaneously, and Joey was breathing a robust lungful amidst a chorus of encouragement like he was about to embark on some deep-sea free-diving. The smoke didn't exit Joey Goldberg's lips for a solid forty seconds. Ten seconds later, Joey stood bolt upright and dashed out of the house.

Avery's body was on the couch looking normal, if a little scared- fact.

The inside of his face coated the walls of a roughly 10x12x8 foot box- fact.

There was no hiding, running, or escaping the mysterious pane of live energy (though Joey ran through it, evidently unharmed)- also fact.

And the fact that what was by far fifteen seconds of the most intense drug induced experience that Avery had ever undergone was caused by a more or less legal drug was more mind-blowing than anything.

Avery's perceptions were starting to clear. Finally. The force lumbering across the room was fading, and lame movement was returning to Avery's limbs. His body tingled.

"I can't believe what just fucking happened," Avery said faintly.

Everyone was eager to hear him elaborate. So far the first hand interpretations of the other trips were extremely dissimilar and equally hilarious. One person said their body began to deconstruct like Lego blocks. Another guy, after taking the hit, turned himself upside down on the chair and slid off in order to access some kind of intergalactic tube-slide. And who knew what was going on in Joey's distorted reality. Poor kid- whatever it was he looked awfully panicked.

"What happened? You kept like inching yourself

over to the left," Jack said. It was Jack's house and Jack's salvia. Jack was ultimately responsible for the last minute of wanton sensory devastation, substance motivated mania, or the undecipherable foretaste of astral subspace. Pick one.

"I don't know really how to explain it," Avery answered, feeling still a little strange, "It was like my body was here, but at the same time the walls of the room became my face, like I was looking in from every angle. And then this energy field started moving from one end of the room to the other and I didn't want it to touch me. All I know is that I've never felt even remotely that weird before."

A hearty laugh billowed through Jack's chest when Avery recounted the beginning of his trip. Everyone was enjoying it, taking their turn to think *that sounds bizarre* and laugh a little. Avery was as guilty as any of them. When Paul stood up, took his shirt off, and said, "Somebody call the hospital, somebody call my mom and tell her I'm okay," Avery was nauseous with laughter, and they'd been quoting that line all night. This was Avery's turn to be joshed and kidded. Supposedly he was shaking in a scared little ball when the 'energy field' was passing by. All very funny.

"None of you went to see where Joey went?" Avery asked.

"No, I guess not," Jack said, looking around the room.

Some good friends this bunch was.

"Why not?"

Nobody wanted to say. 'I hardly know him', 'It's my house', 'I was too fucked up to move', 'me, too', 'oh, he'll be fine', 'I was looking after Avery', and 'I didn't notice him leave'- all adequate reasons, apparently, since still nobody moved to the rescue. Let he who is without sin cast the first stone, and the party pretty much sat upon their idle hands and agreed that no further discussion was required.

But the issue that Jack and everyone else were presently skirting was out there. He was sitting down, before a gust of air-conditioning, facing the powerfully sharp lights of his VW gage cluster. Joey was waiting there, knowing that sobriety was just now rounding the last bend, that soon the small shakes in his insides would diminish, that driving home would be more honorable than setting foot back inside Jack's apartment and being near that God-awful guck, those God-forsaken dark granulates that make people think that some Goliath foot is swinging by like a pendulum and you'd better grab hold or end up beetle juice. Joey didn't expect them to understand. He'd made a complete fool of himself. Judgmental and condemnatory stares unquestionably dwelled in his near future if he went back to that house. Prodding questions and derisive interrogation, too- *What's wrong, Joey? Can't handle your salvia?*, and, *You didn't say GO!, Joey, trying to get a head start on us?* No. Thanks, but no.

Just cruise home nice and slow, listen to some Hendrix, smoke some grass, some regular, honest to goodness grass and forget about everything, this was Joey's plan. Fuck- nobody even came out to check on him. What's that all about? A friend would have poked their head out the door, at least. Said, "Hey, JoJo, take it easy! There's no giant's foot swinging by! Just relax, it's the drug, remember?" The gages shined on him. Red light bled through the sound system controls. The divine, comforting glow of stock Volkswagen interior- it was the whole reason Joey bought that car. He could drive safely now, he decided, and did so, feeling embarrassed and a little unloved.

"I'd offer you all another hit, but, umm..." Jack said. There was a hesitation after the word 'but', as if he thought of saying something like 'Joey got the last of it' or 'the last bowl went to Joey', as though, considering the circumstances, such phrasing might ring unseemly, so Jack followed the brief verbal chasm with, "it's all ash now."

Everyone mimed a gesture of understanding. Avery, now uncomfortable on the marshmallow couch cushions, shrugged his shoulders and his eyebrows- his best delivery of '*oh well*'. In truth, that the offer was no more than an empty, token stroke of hospitality was just fine by Avery. He'd had enough face-stretching and energy-dodging for one evening. And besides, the mood of the room was growing torpid. All there was to do was look around.

Bean bags. Bad art. Tawdry posters. Typical movies. 311 CD's. Dorm-room furniture. Mangy carpet. Magnetic poetry. Sector-9 skateboard. Intricate quilt. Surf magazines. Soggy couches. Shoe rack. Cluttered desk. Yet somehow, a woman's touch had applied itself to these things, arranging them in such a way, presenting them in such a style that the individually common elements of the household were no longer offensive- that together, they achieved an almost distinguished overall motif. It was an unusually tidy dwelling, unsoiled and odor-free. Adult-like in its cleanliness.

Avery looked around. He found himself in the middle of what appeared to be an ongoing, six way staring contest. He blinked, lost, and said that he was feeling too funny to stay. He said goodbye to Jack, Paul, Shawn, Jack's girlfriend, and a tranquil, emaciated young man whose name was never offered.

Outside, the South Florida night bestowed its welcome, its warm, heavy embrace. Giant palm-fronds rocked in the breeze like slave-girls fanning their tall master. Avery's gaze turned ascendant to sky. Vast, permanent, inspiring- the heavens called into focus all the definitions of reality floating around his disoriented head.

A foundation for any altered state of mind, drug-induced or otherwise must exist. Externally or internally, does it matter? To what extent is perception reality? Where does that perception, that reality go when the altered state wears off? Was the sensation of insignificance that was so prevalent in that trip the way it feels when you're dying? Were those images and feelings things that exist elsewhere?

It seemed as though someone should have figured that sort of thing out by now. Maybe a talk with Michael was in order. Everything felt fuzzy.

Dissatisfied with his night, Avery walked to his car. He would have looked for Joey around the apartment complex on the way out, but decided that whatever terrors Joey was going through should have evaporated, and by now old Joey would be driving home, feeling embarrassed and a little unloved.

CHAPTER 25

The people that know what to look for see it everywhere. In purses, the New York Bay and oil company logos, in churches, Hollywood and Washington D.C., in government seals, family crests and city street plans- see the torch of illumination, pyramids, crosses, pentagons, the all-seeing eye, serpents- count patterns of 5, 13, 33- know that these symbols pronounce ownership, manipulation, control.

Avery's laptop computer displayed the U.N. symbol in black and white.

And as the program whirred on, he found himself drawn to believe it all.

"Ahh, here's a prime example of power consolidation, the United Nations. Founded, obviously, by the Illuminati and wholly run by them to this very day. One major stepping stone on the path to a world-government, or so they would hope. I won't get into the fact that the U.N. headquarters in New-York is built on land donated by the Rockefeller family- oops! Or that after the installment of the League of Nations failed after the First World War, the Second World War was engineered to introduce the more apparent 'need' for centralized power- oops again.

"But on to the emblem itself- first focus on the laurel-leaves that boarder the globe. Are these the same leaf patterns used in the Freemasonic emblem? It looks that way to me. It just so happens, also, that the leaves are separated into thirteen segments. Funny, that. Now look at the globe. Here it is- all the continents, all under Illuminati control, divided into sections by these smaller circles and crosshairs. Divided, coincidentally, into thirty three segments, much like the thirty three degrees of the Scottish Rite of Freemasonry."

The picture on his screen was replaced by another, more recognizable picture.

"Behold- the great seal of the United States of America. You don't need to count much higher than thirteen to get the symbolism here. There are thirteen bars and stripes in the eagle's shield, thirteen arrows in it's talon, thirteen leaves in the olive branch, thirteen rows of stone in the pyramid, thirteen letters in 'E pluribus unum' and 'Annuit coeptis', thirteen stars above the eagle. And don't think that the thirteen colonies of America were some kind of random occurrence. Thirteen is a very powerful number to these people. It represents the sun, as does the major god in every one of their concocted religions."

The logos of Texaco, Amoco, Chevron, and Exxon lined up respectively.

"We see these just about everyday, don't we? They're on every street corner, just about. Let's move from left to right. What's this big red pentagram with the Freemasonic T-square in the middle of it? Oh, wait, that's just a Texaco sign.

"And the lighted torch in the Amoco sign? Textbook illuminati symbolism. That torch represents knowledge, as the ancients borrowed fire- knowledge- from the gods. This is why the Rockefeller Center in New York features a gold statue of Prometheus, but we'll get to that later.

"Chevron. If viewed as two one-dimensional marks, the blue and red lines mean nothing. But instead see them as three-dimensional boxes. One box is traditionally seen as all that is right and pure. Hence the phrases, 'fair and square' and 'a square deal'. The second box means the opposite- all that is evil. Two boxes on top of each other are essentially saying 'we control all that is good, all that is evil, we control everything'. This pattern of two stacked boxes can also be seen in the floor pattern in the British Parliament lobby, and it adorns the badges of law enforcement agencies all over the place.

"Moving on to the double cross, as seen in the two X's of Exxon's logo. The meaning of double-cross can be traced back to the house of Lorraine, and it means to manipulate."

Now the pictures flashed on screen only for a moment, long enough to be named, and were then replaced by other pictures that were named and replaced.

"How many more can we find? How many other affluent, formidable giants of industry project their true agenda for the world to see? Find the all-seeing eye in the logos of America Online, CBS, Logitech, Lucas Arts. Find pyramids in the logos of Camel and Marlboro cigarettes, Fidelity Federal, Ameritrade, the British Intelligence agency MI-5. The torch of illumination in Colombia Motion Pictures, the Olympic Games, the Christian Broadcasting Network, not to mention the Statue of Liberty, which was given to this country by French Freemasons.

"Are you starting to appreciate the enormity of all this? And we've but scratched the surface of symbolism here. This is only what is being projected to you purposefully."

Cut to the narrator, a very average looking, middle-aged Englishman with hair the silver-gray of explosion smoke. His eyes were small, blue- little dots of sapphire sitting atop a cheerless mouth. It was a perfect chance for

115

Avery to look away from the computer screen and target his biscotti towards a mug of tea.

"Eight years ago, when I first started discovering this information for myself, I was overcome by the idea that a people could be so thoroughly duped. How on Earth could this kind of stuff be kept secret? How could the truth not have leaked out at some point? How could they be lead to believe exactly what they're meant to believe? The answer will require a rather lengthy digression, but I hope you'll find it eye-opening and I promise that it does correlate with my main point.

"Almost every nation, every people, has at one time been comprised of sun worshipers. The Greeks worshiped Apollo, later Zeus and Helios, the Egyptians worshiped Horus, the Romans worshiped Sol Invicus, the Phoenicians- Baal, the Persians- Mithra, and the Christians- Jesus. 'Now wait just a second!' I hear you say, 'Jesus isn't the sun. He's the son- S-O-N. The son of God.' Not true.

"The truth is, there never was a Jesus, Jesus Christ of Nazareth. Almost no evidence beyond that that the church provides can support claims to the man's existence. No contemporary historians recorded the impact he was supposedly having. Why's that? Well, because it's a story, of course. Not history."

A succession of supposed facts were delivered, complemented with pictures and animations, all showing in one or more parts how the Christian religion was really just ostentatious allegorical astronomy. It was a surefire way of acquiring believers, since believing in the influence of the heavens was only natural. The powers of that time not only discovered a model by which to captivate the people, but also a way of implementing laws and ideals that would benefit their own political and economic states. This all went to prove, the speaker was saying, that if the common man could be so thoroughly duped for thousands of years by way of religion, it was only rational to assume that...

Scalding hot tea splashed over the edge of Avery's mug, landing a blistering puddle on a delicate patch of his inner thigh. He had been soaking his biscotti too long. The speaker's conclusion was not heard, or at least not digested, due to the burn, the growl, the flurried drying, and finally the realization that one of two things had just occurred.

Possibility number one- God did it. He, the great He in the sky that watches over everything was watching Avery watch such a blasphemous program that He had to intervene. The result was a broken piece of biscotti falling back into a hot cup of tea and making the wayward sheep think twice about comparing the Son to the sun.

Possibility number two- the brilliant force behind such a successful, world-wide, ancient scheme would be so sophisticated, so subtle, so shrewd, that a boy ill-able to dip his biscotti in a mug of tea without error could never hope to understand it. Might as well just turn the computer off and go back to video games and reality T.V. Leave the conspiracy theory to the professionals.

Avery turned the computer off. He did not, however, go back to video games and reality T.V. He went to the freezer to fetch a chunk of ice, as his leg was still very badly burning.

CHAPTER 26

All was abysmal in the next-door garage. Not upon first glance, oh no- first glance would only grant the eyes a picture of toned-down horror story. It would be a disquieting first glance, what with the peculiar, greenish light hanging from the ceiling, the whining, purring refrigerator, the cold, oil-stained concrete floor, the workbenches and thin, steel shelves stacked with dangerously brittle and rusted and forgotten tools- disquieting, but not chilling. A kind of place that a child might prefer not to linger in, looking for, say, a baseball glove or a box of nails. The garage in itself would not scare the average adult.

The man inside the garage was a different story. An expression formed in the eyes and at the corners of the jaw that reflected alien emotion. Deep, dwelling, saturating hatred- unnatural, pathological, interminable hatred- violent, pulverizing, intuitive hatred- stations similar in vibration to pure atrocity. Armenian Genocide, Jewish Holocaust, Khmer Rouge movement in concentration. Not to be fully understood, hopefully, by anyone. Mr. Thurbin lived with and for the emotion his every waking hour; even when he was turning wrenches under the hood of his Mustang, which he was doing presently.

A psychotherapist would interpret Mr. Thurbin's perspective as one of a paranoid psychopath. Feelings of impotence, a lurking sense of helplessness and failure would cause him to, rather than cope with the feelings themselves, project them onto a given source. The forms and causes of distress are now rationalized and recognizable. The feeling of impotence occurs in Mr.

Thurbin through a lack of fulfillment after forty hours of toil each week. He is plagued by the concept of men and women living in society who do *not* toil for forty hours a week and are still afforded the experiences of their five senses.

Delusions of persecution transpire here. The threat was that the more of them there were, the more time of honest, decent workers would be sucked up and squandered. The drifters, then, are in effect stealing life from Mr. Thurbin. As each member of society must spend a given amount of schedule turning the wheels of civilization, and the drifters spend none, Mr. Thurbin feels and resents what is, to him, the fact that he must now make up for the time they spend doing nothing. He becomes the savior of modern society, when, in one part, he is picking up their slack, and in another he is eliminating their lives and their needs, which obviously impose on the deserving.

This process, the psychotherapist would explain, is a deranged sort of emotional alchemy. The shame Mr. Thurbin feels resulting from unrewarding labor is transmuted into strength. Once a mere cog in the great machine, he is metamorphosed into Atlas. He is the protector, the strong. What he really is, of course, is delusional, deranged, detached, and very, very dangerous.

Wrong.

Wrong, wrong, wrong. While the endeavors of those who attempt to map human emotion and consciousness may be very noble, very valuable, and hopefully very reliable, nobody has ever looked into the being of one such as Mr. Thurbin. If indeed another one such as Mr. Thurbin has ever existed at all.

Auto mechanic, recluse, extremist, Mr. Thurbin had an express purpose. It was not known to him, this purpose- to him or to anyone, and almost certainly never would be, all because of a small piece of misplaced dust beside one of Saturn's rings.

Interruption. A hollow sound shot through the garage. Four identical sounds- quarter notes, sharp, wooden. Mr. Thurbin poked his head up with what was alacritous in speed but not in cheeriness. He stared at the door that led to his house and through it, the door to his house. Visitors did not often knock at this address. Like an exposed animal, a mother raccoon guarding threatened young, Mr. Thurbin stood cagey and tense. The harmless knock mangled him.

Michael took a few steps back, crossing his hands behind his back, returning them to his side, shifting his weight from left to right to center, scratching his chin, cocking his head, speculating for most of this time as to whether or not such an intrusion, though casual and innocuous, would be okay. He tried to imagine the house belonging to Danny Zuco, who would swing the door open with an animated beam, lead the way to the garage, and break into informative, enthusiastic song and dance. Wouldn't most people be happy to educate an interested ignorant in the ways of their passion? To mentor a hopeful upstart? Worst case scenario, Michael decided, was that he'd waste a couple more minutes waiting around.

From the rear pocket of his jeans, Mr. Thurbin pulled out a dull red rag. He wiped the grease from his hands unconsciously, all the while looking over his left shoulder to the door. One, two, three steps- he paused, grabbed the heaviest wrench from the open drawer of his toolbox, gave a short but reaffirming glance down his own torso and walked into his house.

Power: he felt it behind the wheel of his car

and was fulfilled by a sense of it within him now. His body moved a capable stride across the tile floor. The sinews in his shoulders stretched and contracted. He was not intimidating in mere size; certainly there were bigger, bulkier men. Nor was there an especially criminal wildness in his eyes. The threat was somehow in his level of self-assuredness. There would be no doubt in the mind of an observer as to Mr. Thurbin's willingness to use that wrench, to swing it with the intent to kill, to hammer the skull of a man into crumbs. His expression was as cold, as emotionless as a .38 special, as focused as a wild-west gunslinger.

One of the reasons people laugh at jokes is because their train of thought must shift to a new track in order to accept the punch-line. 'Why did the chicken cross the road?' would have the audience expecting to find out where the chicken is going. 'To get to the other side' forces that said audience to accept the notion that the chicken isn't going anywhere in particular; it's only going to the other side of the road. The brain must reflect, redirect its line of thought, and is thereby tickled. For this reason, after Mr. Thurbin looked through his peep-hole, he emitted a single guttural noise (technically a laugh) and smiled. To him, it was much funnier than the chicken joke.

It was only the kid next door. And that was no problem. No problem at all.

CHAPTER 27

"Oh my God, look how high we are!" Lisa said.

"I know. We can see pretty much everything up here."

They stopped moving. Peaceful stillness held them in awe. A crow flew passed in the distance; it looked to be traveling at eye level.

Then something happened. The apparatus that held them in place gave way, damning them to unfeeling, mechanical gravity. Their hearts and stomachs seemed a moment late in following them down.

"OH, SHIT!" Luke bawled.

"AHHHHHH!" Lisa screeched, sharp and deafening.

Avery made a noise that sounded like the scream that should be joining the other screams got lost somewhere between his chest and nose and was to trying unsuccessfully to drill itself another exit hole. It was like a dinosaur holding in a sneeze.

The plunge lasted only moments, and the passengers were conveniently saved by a dutiful, reliable set of hydraulics. God bless them, those old hydraulics, faithfully cradling the lives of all those countless fairgoers willing to trust, even at the possible expense of existence, that engineering would persevere. Ooh's and ahh's all around. Chuckling the chuckles of the brave.

As, incrementally, the ride lowered, Avery, Lisa, and Luke swung their feet like children riding their first school-bus. Either one of the carnies touched a button or some servo at the bottom was tripped, because a locking mechanism in the seat harnesses clicked over, and the riders were free. Meanwhile, ACDC was blaring through the forty square-foot plot allotted to the Drop of Dread, and Avery decided that the South Florida Fair hadn't changed at all.

"Let's get away from all the rides," Luke suggested.

Lisa was again the last one through the exit, since she always had to leave her sunglasses on the platforms. "What? We practically just got here!"

"Come on, Lisa. The fair isn't about the rides. It's about the food and the people. And the games."

At this, Avery made a face. "Yeah. Fine. Go waste your money on the games, Luke. We all know that won't happen because, for one, you're such a miser that you wouldn't even buy a fucking wristband on wristband day. And that's the real reason you don't like the rides-it's because you don't have a wristband."

Luke turned his palms face up, with his fingers pointing at Avery and his shoulders pushed back a little, looking far too Italian for even his great-grandfather (the only Italian in his family). "And? I'm waiting for the 'for two'. You said 'for one' like you were going to say 'for two' but no, nothing."

Avery started to laugh. He was just too astoundingly high. So was Luke, of course. And so wasn't Lisa, of course. But it was a good thing, he figured. So far the fair was a fucking blast.

It all started when Luke got in the back seat of Avery's car and wondered aloud why Avery and Lisa were both dressed in jeans on such a hot, South Florida afternoon. Avery said immediately that he didn't know, that it was a bad idea, and proposed that they stop back at his house so he and Lisa could change into a pair of shorts. That was where the first smoke was had, in Avery's bedroom, just after he'd changed into a more suitably summery outfit.

The second smoke was had in the car and in the fairgrounds parking lot. Clouds of residual TCH rolled into the open air when they disembarked from the vehicle, and all the while parking attendants were standing only inches downwind. There was a novel feeling in these sessions, a rare juxtaposition of daredevil nonchalance, determined flippancy, and assurance of the understanding of all those adjoining strangers. Avery had almost convinced himself at one point that what they were doing was purely legal. He kept the joint in his hand until he saw a family of five ahead of him- two celestial bodies of parents, two orbiting grade-schoolers, and one stroller-driven, covered quiet thing. Responding respectably, he dropped what was left of the joint on the ground and stepped on it.

From there it was on to the entry gates. Avery ordered his ticket and wristband clumsily and slowly. Or at least it felt that way to him. The woman in the booth was patient though- a real professional. She even lined the sticky edge of the wristband perfectly up with the rest of it, taking care that Avery's arm-hairs would not be bothered. Lisa's wristband was a much sloppier job. Luke refused to shell out the thirty dollars for one, repeating as an answer to the booth-woman's every contention, "I'm afraid of the rides. I'm afraid of the rides."

So with the untidy business of purchasing the ever-more expensive admission and ride-fare behind them, Avery, Lisa, and Luke were finally in front of the enormous fair-ground welcome center.

They were buildings used for all manner of shows, assemblies, conventions, and summits, a multiplex of hangar-like structures, blue and white on the outside, warehouse wide on the inside. Avery wasted no time in leading his company to, for what the welcome center was, the main attraction. It was the building that once housed reconstructions of the great thunder-lizards of the seas and sandcastles the size of town homes. This year the theme was 'The Five Senses' and all the displays turned out to be little smidgens of magic.

Lisa went straight to the bathroom. By the time she came out, Avery and Luke were amusing themselves with one of those nail-impression boxes, but much larger than either had ever seen. Instead of pressing your hand against a hundred or so nails, you were pressing your body into thousands. When Luke stepped into it face first, it made a wonderful picture- something like Hans Solo frozen in carbonite. But soon after doing this, Luke began touching his face and fretting over the cleanliness of all those nails. The 'five senses' expo also boasted a hurricane wind simulator, an 'everyday smells' generator, a 'dog sound' producer that made a sound only dogs could hear (which Avery vehemently insisted was just a box with a button on it), but there was precious little around to taste. Probably a 'four senses' expo would have sounded insufficient.

Next, they visited the merchant booths. Avery was beginning to clam up at this point. It could have been that the high was creeping up on him, or that he could not detect a common ground with the hecklers and tradesmen to speak of. Luke, however, was a regular chatterbox, doing all he could to meet the collectors and experts, to find out what they liked and why. Luke's was a different kind of interest, which, although genuine, lacked the longevity and single-mindedness of the booth owners. For this was their lives, or at least a sizable portion of it. It was not a Tuesday afternoon. Not a mere pit stop on the way to the bathroom. Luke's sociable outbreak earned him a free pin from the pin collector, a classic badge to wear for his hometown basketball team, the Detroit Pistons.

Eventually, the magnetic pull of thrills and chills overcame them. They walked to where the action was-the rides.

The dustbowl was practically empty. There were children running at full click from the 'OUT' gates to the 'IN' gates of the rides, sure, and every time holding their wristband up for the operator to see, but there was room! Room to walk and to turn and to, if one were so endowed and inclined, swing a giant stuffed piece of shit prize around by the tail. And obviously the lack of people meant an opportune lack of lines. It was not the scene that Avery remembered from the fairs of yesteryears, where mothers and sons were separated in an eye-blink, where waves of crowd surged like landslides, where fainting was not the least bit dangerous, there not being sufficient space to fall down.

For those who loved motion sickness there was the 'Yo-Yo', the 'Breakout', the 'Wipeout', the 'Dizzy Dazy', the 'Drop of Dread', the 'Gravinator'- there was a selection of funhouses, haunted houses, Ferris wheels, and bumper-cars, with food stands in between, tacky merch-booths and games.

Lisa chose the 'Yo-Yo' first. It had always been her favorite ride growing up, and she made both Luke and Avery promise to start off with that Frankenstein of playground paraphernalia. What it was, was a massive disk in the air held up by a rotating pillar. From the disk hung about thirty or forty chairs, and as the disk spun, centripetal force would surge through the chains, tilt the chairs a harsh angle and, voila, you have a ride. An upside-down merry-go-round, sideways swing-set sort of ride. When the spinning slowed and the chairs came to a stop, Luke suggested a rather daring idea.

Session number three happened behind a restroom RV, next to what looked like some kind of power generator. Cables ran underfoot un-taped and un-labeled, the smell of urinal cakes and elephant ears collided with unpleasant effect, and the view was as depressing as the orphaned adolescent operating his uncle's rigged basketball toss. It was just lousy enough a spot to perfectly suit a quick smoke. Avery started three cigarettes to mask the sweeter smoke of Luke's marijuana. There was no time for chit-chat or casual drags. It was get in, get out, snap snap, faster than you can say fifteen Mississippi. Just as Luke was stomping out the evidence, a fair-grounds employee happened by, eyes hidden by reflective sunglasses.

"Damn, that shit smells good! Got any more?" the worker said excitedly.

Ready for more flips, tumbles, turns, and swings, they departed from their bleak hidden spot and headed eagerly towards the Gravinator. The machine was spinning when they got there. Counting the people in line ahead of them, Avery asserted that there would be room for them to board the next cycle. More people were queuing up behind them. Directly behind Luke, who was directly behind Avery, who was directly behind Lisa, was a tall, thin man carrying what looked to be a masculine purse. He was studying the tattoo on Luke's leg and making quite an obvious show of it, as if he wanted Luke to see him taking notice. He was bending his legs a little, crouching down nearer to Luke's calf, he was nodding his head and smiling, he was focusing for too long on what was just a single black Chinese symbol. Finally, when his recognizing was not recognized, he tapped Luke on the shoulder and said, "Luck."

127

Luke turned an expression on the man that was something like defensive bewilderment, "Huh?" he asked.

The man pulled his shirt sleeve up, revealing the exact same symbol, though his was surrounded with little waves of fire and green mist. "Luck."

"Umm, no." Luke answered, "Destiny."

"No, it means luck."

Avery and Lisa found this exceedingly hilarious.

"This symbol," Luke tapped the tattoo on his calf, "means destiny."

Not wanting to see the discussion continue, Avery mediated. "Look, guys- the meanings of luck and destiny aren't that far separated. You should just concentrate on the fact that you two are practically like brothers now. That's nice, isn't it?" Zing. He felt immensely satisfied with that.

When everyone walked onto the ride and chose their places, the purse carrying, luck-branded man picked a seat not close to the similarly tattooed, destiny-branded man and his two friends.

Two hundred ten times, the machine rotated around and around. Avery and Lisa were still in good spirits afterwards, but Luke said that the ride made him sick and that he would sit the next one out. Avery suspected that it was the possibility that Luke's tattoo meant something slightly different than he thought it meant steering him to nausea, not motion.

"Let's do the Breakout!" Lisa said.

They walked to the ride, seated themselves without delay, pulled down the harness, buckled the fail-safe belt-lock, and waited for the operator to hit the green button.

But before anyone would send them flying,

128

someone had to come around for a quick inspection. A large Mexican man with dark skin and short hair checked all the rider's harnesses. His face bore a strong resemblance to the Florida native manatee. When he got to Lisa, he pointed at her sunglasses and communicated the forth rule of that particular ride- no sunglasses. She removed them without question, and asked if he would be so kind as to hold them. What he did then beggared explanation.

He took the sunglasses, quickly glanced at Lisa and then Avery, put the sunglasses on the back of his head, turned his head around as if to look at them through his second set of eyes (now shaded, thanks to Lisa), turned back around to look at them once more, and went about his business. It was all very hard to interpret. The back of his head was beaded with sweat and he was either saying, 'I'm the cocky ride operator who will put your girlfriends sunglasses on right in front of you' or 'I'm the quirky character at the fair who takes my job to the next level and does my best to amuse you' or 'I'm so much the function over fashion type that I'll confidently wear a pair of sunglasses on the back of my head if they need looking after' or, or something. Avery and Lisa discussed these concepts for the duration of the ride.

The Drop of Dread was next. It crept up and plunged down with twelve passengers on board, their screams and cries trailing slightly behind. And having conquered his motion-sickness, Luke went up and down with them.

"Let's get away from all the rides," Luke suggested.

Lisa was again the last one through the exit, since she always had to leave her sunglasses on the platforms. "What? We practically just got here!"

"Come on, Lisa. The fair isn't about the rides. It's about the food and the people. And the games."

At this, Avery made a face. "Yeah. Fine. Go waste your money on the games, Luke. We all know that won't happen because, for one, you're such a miser that you wouldn't even buy a fucking wristband on wristband day. And that's the real reason you don't like the rides-it's because you don't have a wristband."

Luke turned his palms face up, with his fingers pointing at Avery and his shoulders pushed back a little, looking far too Italian for even his great-grandfather (the only Italian in his family). "And? I'm waiting for the 'for two'. You said 'for one' like you were going to say 'for two' but no, nothing."

Avery started to laugh.

"Lisa, don't you want to see the prize winning chickens? And the bunnies?" Luke asked. He knew her too well. Her interest was more than piqued; it was blasting off into space.

"Rabbits? They have rabbits around? Are there lots of them?"

"Hundreds, maybe even thousands. They're all in the livestock area. We can still see them if we go now."

As well as Luke knew Lisa, Avery knew her better- he knew that he'd better not try and dissuade her from walking to the rabbit tent. And why should he? If walking amidst rows and rows of prize winning rabbits, rabbits of all colors, shapes, and sizes, was her dream, why shouldn't she go there immediately?

They walked towards the livestock, knowing that each step took them closer to that one of a kind smell of farm. Going where the mood blew them, where nothing mattered except to find amusement in the turning of the clock, Avery wanted to spend more time in such a state;

in or outside of the fair.

CHAPTER 28

Hell- where your soul is rolled into the tiniest of places, reducing the self to a unidimensional panic- a pre-blackout state of asphyxiation, needing a breath and never getting one through all eternity.

Hell- to know in the moment of your death the true worthlessness of life. Nothing you've done has instigated change. The wheels of the world will eternally turn, backwards and blind, regardless of the choices you've made.

Hell- every secret conversation spoken about you plays through your ears, every fantasy your lover has ever imagined plays in your eyes. An eternity in the closet with your skeletons and the ones related to you.

Hell- alcohol consumption has the room spinning like a professionally thrown football every time you grasp for sleep. The plans you've made for your life appear in crystal clear absurdity. Nothing is going to work out. Your world is perpetual aspiration, not a thing more.

Hell- four hours and fifteen minutes later.

"Awww, fucking hell," Avery groaned.

His arm reached passed his head, and his hand and wrist contorted in a nearly damaging position, all to hit one his favorite buttons on one of his least favorite devices. It clicked, and the alarm would not sound for another five minutes. Lisa, however, would not remain so muted.

"Avery! Avery, wake up! You have your breakfast thing today."

"What?" It was not a question. It was a 'shut the fuck up' and a 'leave me the fuck alone' and a 'just fucking let me go back to sleep'. It was to sound what a can of peeled tomatoes falling on a naked foot is to sense.

"Your breakfast thing. With Chris and those guys- you said to wake you up for it, remember?"

"Whatever. It doesn't matter."

"Avery! Hey! You said to make sure you get up!"

"I don't give a fuck."

Happy bleariness. Happy empty stomach of early morning. Happy bi-monthly ritual of good company breakfast, which was also a way of celebrating pay-day, and something Avery wouldn't dream of missing, even for a few more consecutive hours sleep. He was not thinking this now, oh no- for at the moment, Avery was a zombie. A zombie that needed sleep, not brains, slumber, not blood, and would do just about anything his mindless state of half-consciousness could think of to get it. Give him time. He'll wake up. He'll be grateful for Lisa's persistence. He'll find the concept of eating a too-large, greasy, creamy, fatty meal of the southern country variety and heading immediately home for a nap magnificently appealing. He is halfway there already.

A long groan erupted from the right side of the bed. The right side if you were laying down on it. That is, the right side if you were laying down on it face-up. The groan was trailed by a tormented, dehydrated voice saying, "I feel like shit."

"Nothing a couple eggs and a cup of water won't

fix." Lisa remarked. She tumbled back to sleep.

Avery managed a laborious walk into his bathroom, flicked the light, winced, started a stream of cold water in the sink, filled his hands, dunked his face, shook his fingers, dried off, looked in the mirror, winced again, turned out the light, and went about other, necessary pre-exit procedures. Jeans. Shirt. Shoes. Wallet. Cell phone. Keys.

Traffic was light on the way there. Only responsible and respectable citizens steer their shiny automobiles at such primitive hours. Only those with a taste for the worm, the ones making a difference one routine, monotonous day at a time, the ones sipping their coffee at red lights and pulling their uncomfortable ties, mashing their preset radio stations at commercial breaks or even worse- waiting them through. 7:00 a.m. has to be the safest time for driving under the influence. The police are in the midst of switching shifts. And early morning itself, the most decent and upright time of day, serves something like a personified alibi. No moral person would expect such foul-play, especially driving over the legal limit, with teachers and bankers and A.M. gym-attendants on the road. Avery was safe and sound with his light, lingering intoxication.

Before he could see them, Avery could hear them. A noise of celebration crowded the silence, and though it was a noise only five men strong, it was a powerful noise; cheering as if a new king had just been made. It would have been a strange sight for any ignorant bystander to behold; five blue-collar guys so vigorously, vivaciously awake before breakfast. For them, however, breakfast foods were often dinner. The night shift, they were. The graveyard crew. They were all sitting on the home-style patio, in souvenir rocking chairs, surrounding a short table which fruitfully collected their attention.

Jerry cursed and made a move.

"Yes! King me- again, bitch!" Chris shouted.

Avery was walking into a real bloodbath. Chris held influence over two kings, and all but four of his regular pieces. As for Jerry's dwindling force, things looked exceedingly bleak. Nobody noticed Avery's arrival until he was right next to them speaking up.

"That's karma for you, Jerry," but before he could finish, his group of motley ex-coworkers erupted into greetings.

"Avery! Good to see you!"

"Look who it is!"

"Hey! Didn't think you'd make it!"

"Kid! What's up, brother?!"

"For he's a jolly good fellow, for he's a jolly good fellow!"

Clarification- Jerry did not burst into the 'for he's a jolly good fellow' song- his was actually the worst greeting, sounding something like a bitter 'oh, up yours, kid', but Avery preferred to think of it happening the other way. He knew that deep down, Jerry was happy to see him, and he knew that nobody liked having their ass handed to them publicly in a game of checkers.

'Good morning's, 'hi's, 'hello's, and 'how do you do's bounced around for a time before Chris dealt his last lethal hop. As everyone got up from their rockers and walked through the first set of restaurant doors, Avery finished what he started trying to say.

"How do you like that, Jerry? You lie for him, get him into a movie, and still he humiliates you in front of everyone. What a guy, huh?"

"I guess checkers isn't my thing. Just like

writing's not yours."

It was true that Jerry was bitter. It was also true that Avery was bitter. They were both as bitter and as sour as spoiled beer and lemon soup.

A little while ago, two or three days after Avery had put in for his vacation time and his concomitant two-weeks notice, Avery and Chris's co-workers judged their essay contest. The votes were two for Avery, two for Chris, and everyone went to Jerry for the tie-breaker. Jerry voted for Chris, and later admitted, in passing, that he'd only done it because Avery wasn't working there any longer and because he might someday need a favor from Chris. For this, Avery missed the Star-Wars screening.

Jerry might have suggested Avery read the first half of *The Count of Monte Crisco* and get over it.

Avery might have suggested Jerry read *The Prince* and brush up on his checkers.

The men were given a corner table right next to the hostess' podium. An older woman, face like a carved apple, knobby kneed, and with large, bony hands greeted them and took their drink orders. The King's voice shone down from hidden spots in the ceiling. *Well that's alright, mama. That's alright for you. That's alright mama just anyway you do. Well that's alright. That's alright. That's alright now mamahh anyway you do...*

Not much was new at work, according to the categorical shop-talk. A guy on the first shift drilled half-way through his hand and went to the emergency room to find a two-inch long section of carbide had broken off inside him, and now people would say things to him like, 'there's easier ways to steal parts here, Pablo!' but that was about all. Chris had just started telling a story that Avery found specially interesting, though, as it may or may not have involved one of his long-time neighbors.

"Obviously I had no chance, so I didn't see the point in wasting gas. I'm doing my best to act oblivious, just doing my calm little fifty miles an hour, on my way home with groceries, dum-de-dum-dum. But, yo, this guy would not leave me alone, yo. All I could do was race him. So I throw the car into second, it bucks back, shift into third, and the fucking guy hasn't even reacted. I think for a second, 'okay, fuck it,' but as soon as I start letting off, he gets on it and screams by me. Keep in mind now, I'm revving about 9500 rpm. But anyways, he shoots passed, gets in my lane, and then the bastard proceeds to flick me off. I don't know why anyone in an eleven-second Mustang would go around fucking with fourteen-second Civics."

Mr. Thurbin- there was no doubt. Ferocious black Mustang. Aggressive driving. And of course the idea of small, Japanese streetcars would get under his skin. Avery could, without ever having met the man, confidently compile a long list of the things Mr. Thurbin hated, four cylinder racing-engines being near the top.

"That was my neighbor." Avery said flatly. Everyone thought that was pretty funny, including Chris, who was, in the companionship of friends, taking the affair of prior insult and injury in stride.

The waitress returned with drinks, took orders, delivered food, refilled drinks, presented the check, announced a fine 'thank you' and 'good day', and disappeared. Avery's old coworkers talked work, movies, cars, women, and Elvis. Avery finished his biscuits, enjoyed what would probably be his last good company breakfast, paid his share, tipped well, and under a sky that was as thick and gray as a heard of African elephants, headed home, stuffed stomach and sleepy spirit behind the wheel.

CHAPTER 29

How does one cram a young lifetime of habit, pastime, and want into two days and two nights? This uncertainty had Avery feeling squirmy, as if his fast approaching plane ride would mark the end of experience and he should hasten to do all that needed doing. While color-coded, bubble-busting mayhem progressed on his television screen, with Michael and J.P. keenly building patterns and guiding detonations, Avery and Luke could but sit and wait for their turn at the controller. Perhaps devote tonight to habit and pastime, leave the want for another day. After all, wasn't this what Avery coveted in those two years of nocturnal responsibility? To sit, smoke, and play video games?

"The, i, I'm saying, man- it's brilliant. It's like you're identifying yourself and the product immediately thereafter. It becomes as much a part of you as say, your arm or your teeth. Even more actually, because you don't think of your teeth every time you say I. With that you recognize your self, then the thing."

"And that's why it's called that?" Luke was awed.

"Of course!" Avery maintained.

J.P. was feeling exceedingly fretful. The bubbles on his side of the screen were nearing the bottom, stacked in terrifying randomness. He had to distract his attention from thoughts of imminent, irrevocable doom.

"What are you guys talking about?" J.P. asked, all

the worry and irritation present.

"Mac stuff," Luke said, "what the i in iPod and iMac stands for."

"What?"

"Avery was saying…"

"No, no, I heard him. But he's wrong," J.P. said. He sounded like he had only a few more futile attempts to save himself. "The i is for internet."

"Internet? Internet Pod? That doesn't make any sense," Avery said.

"What doesn't make sense about it? FUCK!"

A chunk of bubbles fell on the left side of the screen (left if you were looking at the television, not if you *were* the television). It was the nail in the coffin. J.P. handed the controller over to Luke, who received it genially, but then demanded that the bong be packed again. Not that it was an absurd request, or even unusual, but anyone else saying that without having brought a similar quantity of pot, and that had been acting in similar patterns throughout the history of their social contact would be considered callous.

Luckily for Luke, J.P. did the honors without resentment, saying meanwhile, "i- internet, as in the iMac, best selling computer model of all time. They called it that because it was 'internet-ready'. All you had to do was take it out of the box and plug it into the phone jack."

"Cheap!" Michael exclaimed in response to Luke's character selection.

"Oh, what? I can't be Pinky?" Luke said back.

"That's probably true…" Avery started saying to J.P., but was interrupted with-

"It is true."

"Jesus. Okay. I believe you. But I'm saying that

138

they must have stuck with putting that little letter there because the success of that computer. The iPod isn't an internet machine. Now there's i-everything. iSpeakers. iMouse. It's crazy. And that shit is no accident. Or it was at first, but not now."

Like an old locomotive, J.P. exhaled a stream of smoke. The room was already overcast. He looked at the screen and said, with a voice a few octaves higher than normal, "*Pinky*, man?"

"I know," Michael said, "he's so cheap."

The thing about *Super Bust-a-Move* is that it could go on for hours. And it often did. Many a night had been spent by Michael and his friends aiming the trajectory of those bubbles, popping them, dropping them down and overloading the other side of the screen. In their joint opinion, it was one of the most under-appreciated games on the market.

At 3:21 a.m., Michael went to bed, J.P. went home, and Avery and Luke went to Taco Bell.

Silence reigned the duration of the trip. Not silence exactly- there was the sweeping rush of fresh air between windows, and there was music. Music that was not new to Avery, music that he had listened to but never properly heard. He was just high enough now to hang on to every word, to consider the references in every line. And the beats! Aggressive and distorted, heady beats with choppy fluidity, unparalleled. There are times when a drug can enhance the sensitivity of an individual's observation. When control of concentration, creativity, cognition are altered, and suddenly arts and ideas don't strike so abstract. Not until they reached the drive-thru line did either Avery or Luke break the spell with their own words.

But, alas, it had to happen.

"What do you want?" Luke asked.

"Number four with a Hi-C. Damn. I can't believe we're eating this awful stuff. I must really be stoned right now."

"I am. Stoned, that is. Stoned."

"I know. What a word, eh? Stoned?"

"I'm rocked."

"Bouldered."

"Granite-ed."

"Quartzed."

"Okay, cut it out." Luke said, no longer amused. Really he just didn't want to follow up with 'limestoned', as he felt it an inferior successor to 'quartzed'.

"Sure. But by god, I am fucking buh-lazed, son. That music was amazing." Avery started to say something else, stopped himself, and instead said, "Remember that time that Drew was ordering from here? Like, this very spot, and the two girls at the window couldn't stop laughing and he just drove away without his food?"

"Do I remember? That's what I'll be thinking of when I die to cheer me up."

Luke pulled up a car-length, stopped in front of the microphone, and stared at the rusted, purple speaker. The voice said something unintelligible, but Luke proceeded to make his requests. Another rattling instruction, and Luke took it to mean 'drive up to the window.' The transaction was made flawlessly. No outburst of laughter from either side.

On the way back, Luke asked a predictable question. "Are you having second thoughts?"

"What, about the move? No. None at all. I can't wait, man. The more I look into it the more I look forward to it. You'll really have to come visit me over there. Apparently the hostel we booked is in a really great part of town."

"Absolutely," Luke lied.

When they got back to the house, the food was already devoured, and neither was feeling a very healthy satisfaction. Avery, in atypical fashion, used the front door instead of the garage. The short path from the driveway to the front door was laden with overhanging brush. Ducking and dodging was essential.

The door swung open, and a familiar yet not altogether acceptable aroma pounded their pores, their tongues, and most noticeably, their nostrils. Smoke. It must have been expanding through Avery's room, Michael's room, the loft, the stairwell, the kitchen, the living room, possibly even Avery's parents' room. Standing in the doorway was like standing on the edge of Woodstock. It wasn't anything his parents would scream about, but it was pretty far from an ideal situation, the home housing a grand, drug-saturated cloud. It would make for an uncomfortable 'good-morning'. Avery turned to Luke, as if to say, 'is this possible?' But Luke had already turned around, was already treading the treacherous track back to his car.

Avery sighed and locked the door behind him.

CHAPTER 30

A good liar alters history. With each fabrication, the lie replaces reality and a part of them is changed. Done too often, and the liar must stay as so many different people respective to so many audiences, that the liar's self is overcome with assimilation. His soul is spread thin, and his walk through life hollow.

According to promises, Avery should have been at Lisa's twenty minutes ago.

"Three and two!" a voice called, singsong and heavy with Russian accent.

It was the rubber match. Bottom of the fifth. One out. Man on first and third. Two out of the four halogen lights were on, which was all that could be expected with that box of tattered, frayed wires twisting around as the on-switch. The acting referee tossed the ball back to Jeff, and Michael readied himself for the pitch.

Pause. First understand the fundamental arrangement of this particular field. Baseball was what they called it, but it was not baseball as most would call it. Tennis court baseball was a little different. As the full name implies, it is played on a tennis court, which must be set adjacent to another court, and surrounded by a single fence. The first court served as the infield- second and third base being the poles at either end of the first net; first base, home plate, and the pitchers mound being chalk outlines. The second court acted as two-thirds of the outfield, center and right. Aside from the obvious variations in game play caused by the queer field itself, there was one other distinct rule of tennis court baseball, and that was the green-light for beaning runners. The tennis ball didn't cause much damage, and it turned out to be one of the most exciting aspects of the game.

John lobbed a weak, picture perfect home run pitch directly into Michael's swinging bat. The plastic sounded an empty *bop!* and the ball soared to the edge of center field.

"Come on! Come on! Throw to third! Here! Here! To third!" John screamed frantically from the mound. The only thing that could ever quiet that competitive spirit was an error on his own part. "To third! No- home! Throw home!"

The instructions were heeded, but to no avail. Two runs had already scored. And nothing short of a miracle or perhaps a little sabotage could save John and his discouraged team.

Tennis court baseball was, in itself, something of a miracle. Real, free entertainment. Nighttime activity. Nothing that even the residents of Pine Wood, for all the shouting, the clapping, the stomping, and the homerun balls bouncing off rooftops (and at devilishly late hours) would dare to break-up. The games went on, uninterrupted, always.

Scowling, John watched three more opponents round the bases. Avery, Michael, Jamul, and J.P. were glowing in the smiles of winners, laughing, joking. The other team wasn't saying much of anything. Occasionally the lights would flicker and crack in imitation of their purple, bug-zapping, lethal cousins. And a strange diagonal shadow was cast over everything. When the two remaining outs were finally made, and with a score of fourteen to four, a water break was called.

An exodus from the field. Everybody but John left the tennis courts, seeking cold, complimentary cascades.

But from the edge of the pool came a mild cry.

"Oh, what the fuck! The lights went out!"

Everyone stuck their head around the fence to see. Darkness swallowed the whole of their playground. Curses and questions resounded. The shadows were no longer just slanted, the shadows were straight, sideways, up, down, curved- the shadows were all. John materialized suddenly beside the pool, facing the back of everyone's attentions. He walked near Avery and asked calmly, with just a hint of well faked concern, "The lights went out?"

Suspicion. Heaps of qualms, doubts, and misgivings. It was obvious to everyone what had happened. But everyone had a different reaction.

"You always were a sore loser," Avery said.

Michael and J.P. started a purposeful walk to what remained of the light's on-switch.

"What are you talking about?" John asked. "We didn't lose. I want to keep playing."

Luke was making a face like he'd just been hit with an egg from a passing school bus. "Oh, yeah. Right, John. Just so happens that we *can't* play now, huh? 'I want to keep playing.'" He said 'I want to keep playing' in a voice very much like John's. It was just the kind of thing John probably hated to hear.

"Why are you blaming me? I didn't do anything."

"Why are you blaming me? I didn't do anything." The second voice was different, but gallingly similar, and it was meant to do as much galling as possible.

Everyone wanted a word with John, and were having it at pretty much the same time. Avery took his keys from his pocket, slid his pointer finger through the ring, and spun them around twice. He announced his departure, opened the fence to the pool, and followed the sidewalk to the parking lot. His brother and J.P. were already standing near J.P.'s car, ready to leave as well.

"The alligator clip was on the ground," Michael told him. "We can cross the wires again, but the lights will take about fifteen minutes to cool down and warm up."

"Can't do it," Avery answered. "Got to get to Lisa's. But I'll see you guys tomorrow afternoon. Early afternoon."

On the road, Avery pulled out his phone and dialed. Lisa, who had been spending the last hour peeking at the clock, peeking out the windows, who had been waiting in a wonderfully uninhabited house with her parents gone until tomorrow evening, who had been waiting to run a bath, pour in bubbles, eat cheese and drink wine while sumptuously soaking with her boyfriend, answered.

"Hello?"

"Hey, what's up?"

"Nothing. Just, umm, waiting for you, I guess. What's taking so long?"

"Well, I was stuck at the goddamned train tracks for almost thirty minutes now. The one at MLK. There wasn't a train or anything but the arms were down. Probably just kids fucking around."

"Kids? What do you mean?"

"Yeah- you know, if you stretch a piece of metal to each edge of the track, maybe one hundred or one hundred fifty feet before the intersection, the light turns red and the arms go down. You can do it with a pair of jumper-cables or a long enough pole."

"Why would anyone want to do that?"

"To mess with traffic. We used to do it a long time ago. Never for thirty minutes or anything, but you know how kids are nowadays. Nothing scares them."

"But you're headed here now."

"Yep. Should be there in about forty five minutes."

"Good. I can't wait to see you!"

"Me too."

And with that, Avery changed his history. For him, for the him that Lisa would know, there was no baseball game. No slaughter. No cop-out. Just a long, long wait at a set of malfunctioning train tracks, adolescents and their anti-social ways of misbehavior. He pictured how it would look. Felt the boiling anger and rage such a wait would provoke. The relief that would wash over him when the gates finally lifted. He remembered it, and as it fused into his mind, his past was everlastingly altered.

Avery was stuck on the road.

John had nothing to do with the lights.

Oh, that dirty fabric of reality- so easily cleaned.

CHAPTER 31

Sheens of sweat on their bodies that stuck to the sheets and slid on each other. That degree of closeness between faces that distorts the image, affects a sort of wrap-around, fish-eye lens form. Heavy breathing broken with short susurrations and whimpers. Sounds of stirred furniture.

What transpires between pairs of young, secluded, attractive, heterosexual members of the opposite sex?

Movement transpires. Rhythmic and patterned, at times deliberate, at times riding the steps of pure, unconscious feeling. Friction of the in, delivery in the out. Muscles contract to squeeze bolster the ego. Hot breath. Prayers and utterances to no one and nothing in particular, but a way of jettison- spill the throes of Elysium. Love, lust, the gambit between. Only now and nothing beyond. Distractions, diversions, digressions- not before completion does their tiresome cue activate.

Surely they looked strange to one another; with the dimness and lack of distance presiding, hindering the eyes' ability to focus. Her nose looked perhaps a little wide, her eyes set far apart, her lips reddish-purple and glassy. Avery took long, steady breaths through his nose. Lisa's eyes were closed, comfortable and complacent, knowing that she was being watched, particularly fond of the idea.

Here laid the girl who would be, for a while, his only friend. The girl that would be the only thing familiar to him for thousands of miles in every direction (not counting his laptop computer, his clothing, his contact lenses, his iPod, and his suitcase). She would share his needs. She would be the sole audience for the accounts of his day. Their awareness would be destroyed and resurrected together daily, in the same bed, wherever that bed may be.

Their awareness destroyed. Sleep. Slumber. Snooze. Die the little death. Death.

What was happening to Lisa's face? Avery watched, suddenly frozen in terror stricken awe, as her face went from healthy, milky white to gray- bitter, lifeless gray. Blank, wrinkled, old gray. A chill shot through him. Suddenly the room was cold, clammy. There nothing left in her, no youth, no vibrancy. Avery wondered in a panic if this is what acid-flashbacks were like. Did your girlfriend's face transform from a hale and hearty, an alive and animate thing to a picture under the covered precincts of a coffin? And right before your very eyes?

Lisa sat up, like characters in movies that suddenly wake from a nightmare.

"What were you doing?" She asked looking forward, not in Avery's direction.

"I don't know. Are you okay?"

"Why?"

"The weirdest thing just happened." He was shaking, and said so. "I think I just had an acid flashback."

"Did something happen to my face?"

"Yeah." Avery sat up beside her.

"When you were looking at me, it felt like you were seeing me when I'll be dead. Like you were looking at a corpse. My corpse."

Straining circumstances influenced somewhat different reactions in Avery and Lisa. Namely, when Lisa was feeling anxious or angry, she wanted to be held, while Avery wanted space. Avery was far too disconcerted to consider this.

Lisa put her hands over his. "Is that what you saw?" she asked.

Avery nodded. His jaw was held taut and in his eyes began to pool a dry feeling liquid. He didn't say anything for a minute. Lisa granted him time.

Throughout the night, feelings resonated in Avery of mystification, insignificance, and benightedness. The strange memory would not clear, and periodically, he would ask questions to the effect of, *how and/or why did that happen?*

CHAPTER 32

"That- believing in nothing, is just another way

of believing in everything. Consider the possibility that a realm exists, just the possibility, now- that a realm exists encompassing every conceivable reality. It is all that could and could not be. It is at once segmented and seamless. Every theory there is at once a law. Now in this place there is a smaller place, very, very similar to the here and now, and the only differences are tiny, subtle slips of reality. You may, for instance, watch your girlfriend's face change into a corpse. Are you positive of where you are?

"Believe in nothing. That's fine. There's nothing wrong with that. Rejecting is oppositely linked to accepting. I'm not saying you should cross the bridge, but if you want, when you're ready, the bridge is there.

"There are occultists out there who believe that the frequency of brainwaves occurring during orgasm can be made to manifest into worldly, material desires. Practitioners of magick have often sought these kinds of energies. They would host orgies and focus on the most taboo forms of sexual encounter, whatever will produce the most riotous uproar in brainwaves.

"See, I believe that everything is connected. Physicists might call it the Grand Theory of Everything. If all the forces of the universe are aligned, and stemmed from the same initial force, our whole universe and everything in it is quadrillions of years connected.

"But then you have to ask yourself- does belief change reality, or does reality change belief? I know and have known God. Do I know him because He is real or because I believe in him? I can't bring myself to say that my consciousness, my existence is all that matters, but yours! Yours is the universe! Your consciousness is all the universe to you! What you know, what you feel, what you sense, what you take from the other levels of being, what you think- these are the basis of reality for you.

"Sure, the physical will have its impact. But just an impact. It won't clear the path and pave it, too. In reality, the word apple has nothing to do with the entity itself, right? Wrong! When you hear 'apple', in your subjective reality, an apple has been created! It's in your mind, and it's real. That's the way I see it. But you don't have to believe me- I'm crazy, right?

"No, no, I didn't mean you. I can tell that you two are very open minded individuals. Young and open minded. But most people would think so. They think it's crazy for me to sit outside like this. And there's absolutely nothing wrong with that. They're free to think whatever they like. They've been conditioned by society, society comprised of themselves and other people just like themselves, to frown upon certain ideas. I don't mean to fault them for it- everyone will learn what they will when they will, all according to the great plan.

"So some people find the unusual offensive, and that I sit outside is deemed crazy. Meditation, however- I think it's crazy that more people don't do it!

"There is so much of ourselves, so much more than what we know on the surface. Eons and eons of information, and all you have to do is access it. There are oceans- free, near infinite oceans of calm waiting within your spirit. It is a place akin to heaven and beyond it lies a subsequent stage of being. In time, it whispers.

"Oh, I'm sorry, boys. I wish I were better at this. Speaking has never been my forte. But that's the thing with faith; if it's described well enough, the listeners believe the words and not the feeling that shaped them. It's been a real gift watching you two grow up. You've become such fine young men. Your parents must be tremendously proud.

"Please, don't let me keep you any longer. Go, have fun. Be young, lucky devils, you. Best of luck in London, Avery. May the hand of God be with you."

CHAPTER 33

<u>THE CHASE TRADE</u>

A Play in Two Acts

by

Michael Guess Tyler

"Cast of Characters"

Act 1:

Donald (Don) Chase, Sr.- A disgruntled man, age 41, runs the ultra-secret government subsidiary, Project A-OK, which sanctions certain extraterrestrial activities on Earth. He is immensely disappointed by his son's intellectual shortcomings. Don will do whatever he can to ensure that the failings of Donald, Jr. will not be seen as his own.

Donald Chase, Jr.- Donald, Jr. is in the third grade and has twice been held back. He is a happy-go-lucky kind of boy, seemingly without a care in the world, content and comfortable. He idolizes his father, but knows that for some reason, his father is not always happy with him.

Alex Chao- A subordinate coworker of Don's. He is very new to the business, and has yet to realize that in government, even working with aliens is made unbearably lackluster by bureaucratic process.

Ms. Applegate- A beautiful, caring, patient, witty elementary school teacher. She teaches children with slow-learning disabilities- Donald, Jr. among them.

Act 2:

Donald (Don) Chase, Sr.- Same man, fourteen years later. The accomplishments of his new son have done little to lift his spirit. In his older age he has only become more miserable, irritable, and frustrated.

Donald Chase, Jr. v2.0- A 24 year old robot that has grown to look and sound exactly like Donald, Jr., with an intellect that Don, Sr. can be proud of.

Joann Marx- The elderly cashier at the book store.

Time: Present Day

Act 1- Scene 1

Setting: We are in the living room of Don Chase, Sr. in the center of the room there is a black leather sofa, facing away from the audience. Above the sofa, at the rear of the stage, in front of the sofa (set high enough to be seen by the audience) is a large projection screen with a painted frame to make it look like a regular television. Otherwise, it looks like a normal living room. Area rugs, lamps, etc.

At rise: The sound of a door slamming is heard. Don walks on stage as if he were coming home from a long, unfulfilling day at work. He walks to center stage, behind the couch, and aloofly removes his button-down shirt, dropping it to the floor. He kicks his shoes off in opposite directions, and slowly walks around to plop down on the sofa. When he grabs the remote, a video montage of aliens wreaking havoc on terrified Earthlings plays. He watches. Soon after, Donald, Jr. scurries in, picks up his father's shirt and shoes, and scurries off. Don continues to watch the television.

DON
Donald! Donald, get in here!

(*Donald sheepishly enters*)

DONALD, JR.
Hi, Dad.

DON
Don't 'Hi' me, right now, boy. Is there something you want to tell me?

DONALD, JR.
Umm. I love you? How was your day?

DON
Your mother tells me that Ms. Applegate gave you a note.

153

DONALD, JR.
Mm-Hmm.

DON
Well?
(*Pause. He waits for Donald, Jr. to answer, but an answer doesn't come. He is getting irritated.*)
What did the note say?

DONALD, JR.
It said… It said… Umm. I don't know.

DON
How do you like that? You don't know! Well, color me surprised! There's actually something my boy doesn't know. Do you know if it said that you're failing all your classes again? You don't, do you? Do you know your single digit multiplication tables? No? Do you know who discovered America? No? How about spelling the word 'think'? Can you do that? No? That's just fine, Donald. Just out of this world. Go to your room.

(*Exit Donald*)

(*Don resumes watching his program*)

(*Blackout*)

(*End scene*)

Act 1- Scene 2

Setting: This scene takes place in Don's office. It is a

*bland, economical area, with but a shoddy desk stacked
with papers, a filing cabinet, a chair on wheels behind the
desk, and two chairs without wheels in front of it.*

At rise: Don is sitting behind his desk. He is talking to
Alex, who is sitting uncomfortably in one of non-rolling
chairs. Alex is fidgeting throughout the scene, and Don is
constantly checking his watch.

DON
Okay, so you're saying we put her behind the wheel of her
car and drive it off a cliff somewhere?

ALEX
Yeah. It separates the body from the scene. With an
accident like that, nobody in the world is going to think
anything out of the ordinary is going on. They'll just
think that some poor old lady fell asleep behind the wheel.

DON
Had a heart attack behind the wheel.

ALEX
Or that.

DON
And what if the autopsy shows the time of death to be a
full day and a half before the accident? I imagine the old
bird's pretty stiff by now.

ALEX
I don't know what they'll think. But they sure won't
suspect that extraterrestrials had anything to do with it.

DON
Right. Right. But wait a second- why not just have them beam her back to bed?

ALEX
Because then…

DON
Because then nobody gets their hands dirty, nobody has to crash any cars, nobody has to even come in contact with the body, and better yet, nobody raises any questions. Alex, do sixty five year old women even die in their sleep?

ALEX
Yeah, but…

DON
Yeah, but what?! But what?!

ALEX
But then she's right back where she was taken from. Someone might get suspicious.

DON
They might think aliens were involved?

ALEX
Sure. I mean, they were involved, so it's reasonable to assume that someone might..

DON
Stop! Answer me this- first how did you get this job? No, don't. I know that one. (*Looking up for a moment*)

Thank you for having a grandchild, Mr. Thompson. Now my second question, and I think you'll know this one. What have I told you about the X-Files?

ALEX
You told me not to watch it.

DON
Stick around, kid. You might actually work out here. Now first we beam poor old Mrs. Peterson, widowed, living alone, correct? We direct them to beam Mrs. Peterson back to bed, and bam!, we forget about it.

ALEX
And that's it?

DON
No, that's not it! I have a parent teacher conference in less than an hour and you keep me here with 'and that's it'? They fill out a Complication-D form, have it on my desk by tomorrow morning, and refrain from touching anyone in Lordsburg, actually anyone in New Mexico or its neighboring states for the next few days.

ALEX
I'll ask them.

DON
Tell them. *(Don gets up and begins to leave the office)* Now, like I said, I have a parent teacher conference to attend. On second thought- get the Complication-D form, and tell them not to touch anything- anything at all until tomorrow morning without my say-so.

ALEX
And if they have a problem with that?

DON
They don't argue.

(Don leaves, clicks a light switch on the wall with Alex still sitting there)

(Black)

(End scene)

Act 1- Scene 3

Setting- Three quarters of the stage will serve as the classroom, while the last quarter, stage right, will be the area outside of the classroom. The classroom is comprised of a half-circle of desks and chairs surrounding a large rug. Board games, blocks, and toys litter the floor. The door on the right wall of the classroom leads to the outside, which looks like a plain hallway.

At Rise- Ms. Applegate is outside the door to the classroom smoking a cigarette. Donald, Jr. leads his dad to her excitedly.

DONALD, JR.
Ms. Applegate!
(Donald, Jr. runs to her, hugs her around the leg)

(Ms. Applegate throws her cigarette on the ground and steps on it with her free leg.)

MS. APPLEGATE
There you are, Donald! I was beginning to worry about you!

DON
When I found him, he was bloodied and naked in a patch of thorns.

MS. APPLEGATE
(*Kneeling beside Donald, Jr. Addressing the boy instead of the father.*)
And that, Donald, is what we call sarcasm. We haven't learned about that yet have we?

DON
(*To Donald*) All in due time I'm sure, eh, boy? Alright now, the grown-ups are going to go inside and talk, okay? Just wait around here. And watch out for splinters.

MS. APPLEGATE
Actually, Mr. Chase...

DON
Oh, please- just Don.

MS. APPLEGATE
Okay, Don. I thought we could discuss Albert's progress outside- in his presence. I believe that an integral step in a child's development is to include him in matters concerning his future. Children who feel like a spectator in their own lives, and especially at such an early stage, can grow accustomed to just letting things happen and to not making an effort on their own behalf."

DON
Of course. Donald, let's go inside and talk with Ms. Applegate about your work. (*To Ms. Applegate*) You don't mind if we go inside, do you? Donald burns easily and the sun is pretty hot today.

(*Ms. Applegate nods, leads the trio through the door to the classroom. She walks to the rug and sits down Indian-style on top of it, looking at Don as if he should do the same. He doesn't.*)

DONALD, JR.
See? This is my desk. (*Points at a desk*)

DON
How very nice.

MS. APPLEGATE
It is. Donald won a contest and as a reward got to pick any desk he wanted. He built the tallest paper house in the class.

DON
That's my boy.

MS. APPLEGATE
Right. Well then, I suppose we'll get straight to the point. I feel that it would be in Donald's best interest to stay with me for another year, repeating the Third grade.

(*Immediate Blackout*)

(*End Scene*)

(End Act 1)

CHAPTER 34

WORLD GON CHANGE

It was scrawled across the bottom of an I-95 overpass in big, black block letters. Lisa's father was driving; he saw it, read it in a mumbled, reserved, not altogether approving voice. He said it again, after a short pause, a moment's thought to properly calculate his opinions- this time sharp, expressive, for the whole car to hear.

"World gon change."

Avery was first to respond. "Yeah, did you see that? Pretty serious."

"Serious? How?"

It had been a long night. A long night filled with long goodbyes and long promises and longnecks. Everything around was absorbed through hazy time, like blankets of dust and fingerprints athwart corrective lenses. The last thing Avery wanted was to enter into ambiguous conversation, delivering clumsy explanations of why and how the world should change. Luckily, there was a way out.

"Well, whoever painted that had to hang himself over the edge of the overpass, so he would have been only a few inches from the letters, not to mention almost or completely upside down- but even still, the letters were straight and in pretty good proportion. It's not easy to paint in places like that."

"I think it's a great message," Lisa's mother said, "The world needs a change. Good thing you two are getting out of here."

Again, the idea was followed along murky trails. Murky trails further obscured by thick, overhanging vegetation, turgid pellets of rain and nightfall. By a blindfold. By a blackboard's worth of heavy mathematics. It seemed surreal. Everything seemed surreal. There were suitcases in the trunk. They were following a direct path to the airport. They were to board a plane which would cross the Atlantic. They would disembark, gather their luggage, and meet Lisa's uncle, who would drive them into London, down the King's Road, and drop them off at their temporary lodgings.

We're in the process of leaving the country.

Again- it didn't chime factual. *We're in the process of leaving the country.*

"I assume that gon is short for the word gonna. *Gon.*" Lisa's father said. He had one of those brilliant English accents that was inevitably compared to Tony Blair or James Bond by Americans. When he said 'gonna' and 'gon', he employed his best American accent, which inevitably sounded like a deaf Southerner's, and worked wonderfully to accentuate demeaning remarks. "I'll have to remember that." Truly a master of half-way unsaid criticism. Such technique forced the listeners to fill in the blanks with his or her own words and judgments, whichever ones spoke loudest to their particular soul.

The passing of days, to Avery, was immaterial until the future could be known. Could be desired, anticipated and awaited. In weeks prior to the present, Avery knew that anticipation. He knew that the days were leading to something, that the now was not indistinctly melting into the forthcoming. Passing time was progression. The rotation of the Earth was the track to purpose. But hark! it would be the last of such days. The forthcoming was at hand. The forthcoming was a flight, a drastic change in routine- the aftermath of which would once again lead to uncharted, ad hoc future.

What dreams would the great city of London birth? What hopes would it crucify, yearnings would it resurrect? As high sands of the Sahara, blown by virtuoso winds settle where they may, all luck to those young and unprepared. May their destined environs become them. It was perhaps a bit of a selfish wish, because Avery counted himself roundly in the category of the young and unprepared.

All familiar landscapes sixty miles nether, the passing view offered little consolation. Lisa sat to Avery's left, holding in her right hand his, in her left hand a tattered stuffed Chinese dragon. It went with her on every trip, protecting her with its soft, wilting blue hide, guiding her with its one remaining eye. Avery took his comfort from a conversation he'd had with his brother that morning.

"You don't have to be worried," Michael said, "because no matter where you go- there you are." He also sited the very reasonable point. "Besides- if for whatever reason things don't work out, you can always hop a cab and catch the next flight home. You'll always be welcome back here."

Towing what would soon be all their worldly possessions, Avery and Lisa walked alongside her parents over the crosswalk. They checked their luggage with the skycap, tipped him, and walked into the heavily air-conditioned Miami airport.

Tears, for both Lisa and her mother, were not long

in coming.

"I'm going to miss you so much!"

"I know. Me, too."

"You're going to have the most wonderful time. I'm just so happy for you."

Their passports stamped, their tickets in hand, they made to the metal detectors.

Families could once say their taxing goodbyes before the individual gates. No longer- what with vile terrorists abound, armed with explosive shoes and shaving cream hand grenades. Drastic times have called for families and friends to part ways before security checkpoints. To say goodbye before the actual boarding of the airplane, not the boarding of the airport, has alas been deemed too quixotic, though those times are surely missed.

"I'm going to miss you so much!"

"I know. Me, too."

"You're going to have the most wonderful time. I'm so happy for you."

Mother and daughter. They meant what they said so. So much so they had to repeat it, thrice and thrice again. Lisa's father was not so emotional. He looked proud. Satisfied. Sending his little girl come lady out to the big city where she would someday make her mark on the world. His confidence in her was total.

In the midst of such sincerity, Avery felt slightly out of place and partially to blame. With Lisa's mom and dad, he hugged and shook hands, respectively. Their places in line were nearing the front. A break in the formation of four was required.

Lisa's parents said one last farewell and were gone.

Now bawling, Lisa faced the security guard.

A tall woman, with her medium length blonde

hair pulled back into a humorless pony-tail, narrow eyes, and firm, authoritative make-up, she spoke. "Shoes off, please."

But upon seeing Lisa's heartfelt grief, the guard seemed to lighten up. Her face relaxed by the same proportion as the Grinch's growing heart. "Ohh, umm," she said uneasily, "is that a worm you've got there?"

Lisa choked back sobs to answer, "He's a dragon."

"A dragon, huh? Is he your lucky charm?"

"He's a Chinese dragon, isn't he?" Avery said, rubbing Lisa's back.

"Yeah," she answered. For a moment she stopped crying. The sounds she made were deep and undulating. Mucus blew with the air of her voice.

"That's sweet," the blonde guard said, "come on now, let's get you two through here."

The procedures were all followed. Avery and Lisa were quickly on the other side of the checkpoint, re-pocketing their belongings and stepping back into their shoes. And in Lisa, the sadness of leaving seemed to be losing ground to the excitement of leaving. She was beaming- the tears on her cheeks functioned to nourish her skin, leaving it sparkling and alive, much as a good watering revives an ailing houseplant.

"World gon change," Avery kept saying. Once after he bought a small bottle of over-priced eye drops. Once more as they sat at their gate. Again in the doorway of the plane. Sometimes it was a joke. Sometimes it was less of one.

When the plane finally rolled down the runway, Avery gathered his thoughts into the most comprehensive stream possible.

It was July, 4th. The day that fireworks would boom over temporarily patriotic Americans, he was leaving. The day that his country celebrated its independence from its mother country, ironically, the one he was moving to, he was leaving. For Lisa, for experience, he was leaving. Leaving Michael, Luke, J.P., Chris, Herm, John- leaving his parents, his job, his home town, leaving routine and ritual, leaving the standard usual, leaving his car, his books, his fixtures, what's familiar and comfortable. But the plane was moving. All he could do was look at the beautiful, excited girl beside him, picture himself amongst crowded masses on the busy sidewalks of London, and hope for the best. Undeniably-

World gon change.

CHAPTER 35

"Two tickets to Covent Garden, please," said Lisa to the man in the booth.

"One way?"

"Please."

The local time was 2:00 p.m. but their bodies begged to differ. They were at the point of fatigue where everything merits humor and confusion. Tired to the pits of their acid drenched stomachs. A soft spot in a dark room called like a serenade in reverse, from the window to the streets, but Lisa insisted on following her mother's advice, which was not to sleep until the clocks reached a typical bedtime hour.

So to Covent Garden it was.

First impression- London is not a tall city. Avery

had been picturing something like Manhattan, the naïve benchmark his mind had set for what big cities look like. In his mind's eye, any city of over eleven million was a perpetual concrete jungle of skyscrapers, lining a confusing network of crowded streets, rising high above your peripheral vision. He was met with bonsai versions of the buildings in his imagination. It looked low. Cozy.

Second impression- the pace! Stoplights not only went from green to yellow, but also from red to yellow, giving drivers plenty of notice to rev their engines and prepare for take off. Consider the preciousness of time, then, to these people who must shave seconds off their waits at the intersections! In the grocery stores- see the attentiveness of cashiers, the scuttle of shoppers, as if the calling streets outside screamed 'GO! GO! GO!'

Aboard the subway trains, or tube, as they would have to call it, Avery and Lisa found their way easily. Maps are posted all around- simple, color coded directories. From Sloan Square, they followed the yellow line to South Kensington, transferred to the dark blue line and rode it to Covent Garden. Variations of this method would get them from place to place on a daily basis. Easy.

Third impression- the surrounding aspects of Covent Garden were exceedingly dissimilar to those of Sloan Square. From point to point, London had a magical way of amending its facade.

Street performers gathered crowds small and large, and Lisa stopped Avery from walking when she saw one that looked interesting. A man on stilts spoke down to the crowd.

"The hat goes around, around and around.

167

Remember, folks, for those involved in the noble art of street performance, the hat is our bread and butter. Make a donation, please. Keep your coppers, this isn't the 17th century. But if you've watched and enjoyed the show, put something worthwhile in the hat. I do accept credit cards, just don't cancel them.

"Now, a volunteer, please. I'll need two children and a woman. Two children? Yes, young one, you'll do. You? You're not a child! Another child! Are there none brave enough? Okay, okay, I see you. I need a woman, now! Did that sound desperate? Don't worry, it'll only take a minute. Aww, come, come, get your minds out of the gutter. You, miss, what's your name?"

While he led the generously proportioned woman to center circle, she answered.

"Lashanta."

"Lashanta! Are you American, love?"

"Yes."

"Happy fifth of July!"

"The fourth!" she yelled, jumping up and down excitedly, as if correcting him on the day's date.

"No, I do believe today's the fifth."

"Fourth!" she said again, this time holding four fingers to the crowd and jingling her collection of gold bracelets against each other. Jetlag was obviously having a different effect on her. She was stuck in yesterday.

The man on stilts turned to his audience, made a show of checking his invisible wristwatch.

"Okay, Lashanta, I need you to stand here, and you two tikes stand on either side of her. Right. Now, it's very important, very, very, very, important that the three of you remain absolutely still. I can't guarantee your safety otherwise.

"Who here wants to see a show? All you people,

you in this group waiting to be entertained, take heed of the hat! When the hat is heavy, the show will go on."

The man paced around on his stilts. Rail thin himself, he looked rather frightening on them. A real, live Jack Skellington with lips, a nose, and eyes. His volunteers stood fast, holding hands and standing as lithified as one could expect children to stand. The young boy to Lashanta's right eventually itched his nose. He looked neither scared nor guilty for it. After all, he had been waiting a long time.

"Enough about the fucking hat, already," Avery said to Lisa, "he hasn't even done anything yet."

"We can go somewhere else," Lisa suggested.

"Yeah, I guess. I kind of want to see what his trick is, though."

"Okay."

They waited. The hat went around. The stilt-walker pretended to start his performance, but stopped to remind everyone of the overwhelming virtues of his hat. Idleness. Lull. The act trucked on ongoing respite. Infinite interval and relief. Avery and Lisa finally walked off. What became of Lashanta, the two kids, and the hat would forever remain a mystery.

Fourth impression- beer is a mainstay in England. Never before had Avery seen so many men and women soaking in the qualities of bars. Pubs everywhere! Inviting, unfussy places with dark wooden furniture, dim lights, charismatic carpeting, and delightfully affordable pints. Perhaps England's affinity for pubs speaks for a time when the only refuge from a dirty, miserable life was alcoholic stupor, but who remembers those times?

Fifth impression- *cheers*. Fantastic word. Casual yet refined. Diverse without sacrificing honesty. Kindling sentiments of brotherhood, belonging, benevolence. Gracious modesty. Satisfied balance. Timeless tradition. Effortless amity. *Cheers.*

Sixth impression- the streets of London lack discipline. They curve, fork, circle, dead-end, double-back, criss-cross, shift, and diverge such wandering paths, that they look to have been paved by prodigiously drunken laborers, forced to follow plans drawn by the dizziest, shakiest of men. They steer with the randomness of precipitation. Maps of them are like staring into a can of dead worms. (This one of Avery's impressions could have been brought about by his alcohol consumption.)

Covent Garden, its people and places, did well to entertain Avery and Lisa. With the coming sunset, they found the Leicester Square tube station, argued about its pronunciation, and went back to their hostel- the enormity of their decision forgotten, evaporated by the rays of stimulation.

CHAPTER 36

In his sleep, Avery was visited by three sisters. They came in the early morning, like oil slicks on the air above him, three blotches, shadows, dark and foreboding. He saw them through eyes elsewhere, for his were closed, and as he looked at the sisters, he also looked down upon his own inert form.

They whispered amongst each other. Their words were not meant for Avery to hear. Not yet. Avery strained to hear them, was overwhelmed by a sense of grave risk. These sisters, he knew, were the Fates.

The children of night. Of Greek myth. Of Hesiod and Shakespeare and hopefully, he prayed, nothing more than his own imagination. They were dangerous entities. Entities whose decisions could not be altered, not even by gods.

"You will…" one of the sisters began.

This was a nightmare. Avery struggled to move; with hernia inducing strain, with a wildness that could burst the blood vessels in his eyes, he made to move. A movement would break the spell, stall the sentencing, free him from the damnation of destiny.

"…waste your life here…"

He tried to plead with the sisters, sending passionate threads of entreaty, one after another, anything to avoid their curse.

"…become of nothing…"

He threw himself off the bed. A five foot drop, a thud, a twisting of his body, but no pain. No parallel prospect of the ground. Obviously it was just another part of the dream, and his body was even now safely spread under a thin sheet, on top of a cheap mattress. Frame one was restored. He was back on the bed now. He flung his legs to the side, but his eyes would not open. It was only the dream, again- outside it, Avery's body produced no rapid movements beyond his sheltered eyes.

It was too late, he knew. The Fates had descended upon him. They had reached their perverse conclusion, and they were speaking it to the universe. His future happiness was set ablaze by corrosive breath, hacked to gory pieces by the magic binding of razor tongues.

"…attain nothing…accomplish nothing…"

And so it was settled.

Avery would forever wander the Earth, alone, without.

He sat up, his head being temporarily the highest object in the room, and made a sound of anguish.

"What's wrong?" Lisa asked. She was in the process of unpacking her bags.

"The Fates," Avery groaned to her with that deeper voice of the newly awakened, "God, you've got to be kidding me," he said to himself. He grabbed the bridge of his nose between the thumb and pointer finger of his right hand. He squeezed his eyes shut. "The Fates said they were going to ruin my life."

"The three witches?" Lisa asked. She was profoundly familiar with Shakespeare, not very much so with Hesiod.

"Not witches, Fates." Avery had read quite a bit of Greek mythology, but precious few plays. "You know, the sisters that divvy out good and evil to people when they're born. One weaves the thread of life, one cuts it, and one basically decides what you'll become. I'm fucked."

"Come on. Nobody believes in the Fates anymore. You're just anxious. We're in a new city, you don't know what you'll do for work, of course you're anxious."

"Lisa- the Fates just said that I'd amount to nothing."

"Well, I don't believe them."

Avery covered his face with his palms. "Oh, man, what am I going to do? What am I going to do?"

Lisa stood up and walked to Avery's side of the room. The beds were small and elevated on four steel legs, two of which were connected by bars that acted as a ladder and support brackets. The purpose of such a lousy structure, if one had to guess, would probably be to provide additional storage beneath the bed. Why anyone would need that much storage under a bed- the guesser could not be asked to speculate. But there were two of them- tall, single beds on each side of the room. The opposite walls also boasted a separate desk and a small wardrobe, so that if it weren't for its absurd geometrical shape, the room would have been completely symmetrical.

"Stop that! It was just a dream. We're in London, silly! Let's go for a walk."

But the implications of the dream were too goddamned crushing to just forget about. He would think about it for the rest of the day- why three rotten hags, old as time and just as bored, decided that on this of all mornings, they should cast his potential to the crocodiles.

CHAPTER 37

After some arduous persuading, Luke convinced Michael to meet up. It wasn't that Michael didn't have the time, only that he had better things to do with it than play the third wheel in Crystal's bedroom. Yet, there he was, sitting on her floor, filling a role that Luke so desperately needed filled, the role of witness.

"Why don't we listen to his last album, The 7 Day Theory?" Luke asked.

Michael was promised a show. And here Luke was, giving it to him with great practiced delivery. Afterwards, he would consider casting Luke in a future play.

"That album- the music, the artwork, and the

information contained in the booklet proves beyond the shadow of doubt that Tupac is still alive and well."

Crystal was sitting at the edge of her bed. Her palms were flat on the bed, and her arms were straight-pillars supporting the weight of her hunched body. She had no desire to listen to Tupac, said so, and was ignored.

"First consider the album's title, Don Killuminatus, the 7 Day Theory, and the name it was released under- not Tupac, but Makaveli. Why the name change? Especially to something that sounds an awful lot like Machiavelli, as in Niccolo Machiavelli, as in the Florentine nobleman and political philosopher, who in one work suggested that a person might fake their own death in order to thwart an enemy?"

"And who Luke just so happens to be the reincarnation of," Michael interrupted, unable to help himself, "We know that because he likes practical philosophy."

"That's bullshit," was the only break in stride. Luke immediately resumed with, "The 7 Day Theory. Tupac supposedly died at 4:03 on September 13th, 1996. He was shot the night of September 7th, 1996. Seventh, eight, ninth, tenth, eleventh, twelfth, thirteenth. Seven days after the shooting, he dies. Coincidence? How about another one? The cover art depicts Tupac, or if you prefer, Makaveli, being crucified with five bullet holes in him. He was supposedly shot five times."

Crystal, though still listening, felt a whisper of disbelief in that fist shaped organ behind her eyes. There was something indistinctly unnatural in Luke and his chatting. It was nothing that she could bring up, because it wasn't something she could put her finger on, but there was something about it. Something- hmm. Who knows.

"The video for 'I ain't Mad at Cha' came out

only a few days after he died. Have you ever seen it? It shows him leaving a movie theater and being shot, and afterwards he becomes an angel in heaven. But that's not the best part.

"The best part is that there is nothing printed in the CD booklet that says anything about Tupac dying. No 'R.I.P.' or anything. All it says, get this, is 'Exit Tupac-Enter Makaveli'.

"I take that back. That's not the best part, either. The executive producer of 7 Day was listed as Simon. Nobody has ever heard of this guy Simon, and the executive producer of the record was quite obviously Suge Knight. Who's Simon, then? Simon, according to the first book of Corinthians, was the first person to witness the resurrection of Jesus Christ. Weird, huh?

"See, you wouldn't know this by just looking at the CD, but Tupac was tired of the limelight. He said it a bunch of times in interviews. He just wanted out. He wanted to be a normal guy. He'd show up at parties, and everyone would be like 'Oh my God, it's Tupac!' you know? 'Holy shit!' But he didn't want that. He even said, in the song 'Life of an Outlaw', 'All for the street fame on how to be managed, to plan shit, six months in advance to what we plotted, approved to go on swole and now I got it.'"

Michael laughed. Not because it was a bad impression, but because it wasn't.

"More on the number seven- Tupac was twenty five when this stuff happened. Two plus five is seven. The time of death was 4:03, four plus three is seven. Seven is considered by some cultures to be a level of Chaos. Life is chaos- not death. There are seven proscribed 'deadly' sins. Seven is triumph of the spirit- three, over the physical- four. There are seven seas, and the Dead Sea

175

is not one of them."

"What the fuck are you on about?" Michael asked.

"Chill. I'm making a point. Just be patient."

"But what's the point?" Crystal asked. "I still don't know what you're talking about. Tupac? I'm not a big fan."

"What? Have you been listening to a word I said? I'm in the process of proving that Tupac is alive and well! It doesn't matter whether or not you like his music. Look- in a collaboration with E-40, which was called 'Million Dollar Spot', Tupac says, 'Fans can't understand my ghetto slang, so I evade and plot and plan a life of better things.'" That time, Luke recited the lyrics in his own voice, since he'd never actually heard the song and didn't know how Tupac said it. "Even the letters in Makaveli can be rearranged to say 'Make Alive' as long as you spell 'make' without an e. And did you know that there was no autopsy, which is actually illegal when dealing with homicides, and no funeral?

"Tupac isn't dead. That's the truth. Trust me. I've even heard an eye-witness account from a female acquaintance of mine. She saw him in Seattle a couple years ago."

"I'm sold." It was agreed beforehand that Michael would back Luke up, should he meet any resistance with his theory. Since there wasn't any, resistance or any other kind of response, Michael's job was easily accomplished, requiring only two words and a contented expression.

"Fine," Crystal said, "put the CD on."

"What CD?" Luke asked.

"The one in your hand."

"Oh. I would, but I don't have the CD with me. Just the case. I only realized that once I started telling you about it."

Luke put the case, empty save for the booklet, down on Crystal's dresser. He would later forget it there.

Crystal looked bored. She asked, sounding a little irritated, "Okay, then. What do you guys feel like doing?"

Michael answered first, saying that he didn't know and that since Luke begged him to come out, he imagined that Luke had something planed.

While Michael said that, Luke was unable to plan anything new. His plan, to procure a witness, visit Crystal, demonstrate his knowledge of the Tupac conspiracy, and see the look on her face had already been delightfully put through action. In the all-inclusive spectrum of reactions, Crystal's had been the opposite of what Luke expected. Still, it was good. He was happy. He said that no, he didn't know what he felt like doing.

Nobody said anything for a moment. Michael glanced around the room, his focus taking short vacations in the many paintings on the wall, the small piles of clothes on the floor. Luke went back and forth from looking at Crystal, to looking at Michael, to looking at nothing in particular. Crystal looked annoyed.

"Are you hungry?" Michael finally asked.

"No. I ate just before you guys got here."

"Oh. Are we keeping you from anything right now? You look like you might want some solitude."

"I have some homework I should probably be doing. I mean, I'm not telling you that you have to go or anything, you're welcome to hang out, but I do have some homework."

"Of course. We'll let you get to it. Luke, are you hungry?"

"Sure."

"You want to go to The Best Juan?" He did his best to pronounce Juan as Juan and one simultaneously.

"The Best Juan?" Luke repeated. He pronounced it like the old master in Chinese Kung-Fu movies. They left Crystal to her studies.

On the way to the restaurant, Michael's phone rang. It disrupted the conversation they were having about Guy Weeks' strip mall, but Michael was glad to hear his brother, three days gone, say that his plane landed safely and everything was going great.

CHAPTER 38

Avery did not put off finding work for long. Every time he watched his credit card pass through a reader, knowing that the electronic signal would be destroying his bank account, bit by bit, like enemy craft in a stage of Space Invaders, removing not just the cost of the item, but nearly twice the cost of the item, he cringed. It was not a good time for Americans to spend money abroad. Bucks were weak and Quid were strong. The need for a local income was becoming increasingly urgent.

Bars. They seemed to be the only recourse to British funds for the non-British. Avery's strategy was to randomly walk around the busy parts of town, indiscriminately walk into different pubs, haphazardly hand out his resume, and hope for the best.

Presently, he walked along Regent Street, and was beginning to think he should have started somewhere else.

The neighborhood was too nice, too clean, too

expensive, too touristy, and too windy. His hair was being blown into a disheveled mess. He passed the high-fashion retail outlets, the fine china shops, the Starbucks, the nameless businesses, and as he neared Oxford Street, the tacky clubs and another Starbucks. No prospects.

He turned right on Oxford Street. Crossing the street was like wading in a turbulent ocean. It wasn't that he was being forced in any direction by the bodies themselves, there was in fact no physical contact whatsoever, but the human respect for breathing room, the God given right to ample space, it forced one to sway from time to time, just a little. He was finally just a face in the crowd, the large crowd, what he always expected big city life would be like.

There were the huge flagship stores on Oxford Street- Nike, Barnes & Noble, Topshop. Upon passing the latter, Avery recalled a conversation he overheard between Lisa and a flagrantly rich girl in their building. The girl suggested that Lisa not wear clothing from that store in the future, as it was 'common'. Succumbing to impulse, Avery sauntered in.

The store was enormous. The size of a small shopping mall. Packed to the brim with wide-eyed girls, dressed in the mismatching patterns that were all the rage. He rode an escalator to the top floor, the men's department, found a shirt he liked, tried it on, fixed his hair, bought it, and headed back downstairs.

At the doors, a young woman approached him. She did not look to be shopping, nor working, but rather fighting to retain the empty space around her.

"Excuse me, have you got a moment?"

Avery said that he did. He also was happy for a bit of personal, human contact. Since his arrival he'd hardly spoken to anyone but Lisa and the people selling him things.

She asked if he was American.

"Yeah. I moved here just a few days ago. I was actually out looking for work, but..." he raised the bag in his hand, as if the gesture perfectly summed up his lack of dedication.

"Oh, really? Where are you staying?"

"On the King's Road," he said.

"Nice one. Well, listen- my name's Amanda and I'm a scout for FM model management. I think you have a very interesting look. It's quite in right now. Kind of that rock and roll pretty boy thing."

Avery started to laugh. He was flattered, but a small part of him felt that he should be insulted. He wasn't, however.

"No, no, you know what I mean," she said, "But I really think you should go see them."

"And be a model?"

"Maybe. I'm just a scout. The final say will be up to the bookers, but it's definitely worth a shot. You could end up making a lot of money."

"Hmm." Avery thought out loud. "Are you a model as well?"

She laughed. "Thanks."

"No?"

"No. I just do this kind of thing occasionally."

"Oh. Because, yeah, I'd be interested in hearing more about it," he said, looking at the business card she handed him.

"Definitely. Go talk to them. They're in Knightsbridge, across from Harrods."

"Yeah, I know the place. It's not too far from where I'm staying. Should I just pop in, or do I need to make an appointment?"

"If you go there now they'll see you straight away."

"Okay. Well, thanks. Amanda, was it?"

She nodded and said, "Good luck! I'll keep my fingers crossed for you."

Then they said goodbye to each other. Avery was afforded an opportunity to say 'cheers' as he walked away, with what he thought echoed instinctive, indigenous ease- it pleased him immensely.

Outside, the faces washed by, adrift in innumerable objectives. They ran the gamut of interest levels, those faces- some wide-eyed in wonder, others bored, over the whole tired routine. Avery strode into the drifting masses like a drop of water pulled into a puddle. He calmed his desire to show any outward hint of fascination, telling himself that he was no tourist, that this was his city, that yeah, it was amazing, but yeah, he was already aware of that.

In eighteen minutes he was climbing stairs of the Knightsbridge tube station. He was met with the shadow of Harrods, the cheerless notes of accordions, and the highest concentration of black cabs anywhere in London.

CHAPTER 39

No reason to feel nervous, Avery told himself, *they asked me here, didn't they? And he seemed friendly, like he liked me. I hope the picture came out okay. Damned Poloroids. Would he even have taken one if he didn't like me? God- just relax. Confidence is important to people like this. Looking comfortable is looking confident. What about this guy? Is he more handsome than I am? Hard to say. He looks comfortable, anyway. Bored even. What are they saying in there? Probably that my stomach isn't toned enough. Damn. Probably all kinds of hyper-critical evaluations.*

Ha. What a condescending look that was. That's right sweetheart, I guess I'm trying to be a model. Oh, don't you find it cute- to see some patient hopeful whose aspirations are just as empty as yours, and don't you just adore the possibility that I'll be denied any of it. Thanks for the smile, meek and phony as it was. I'll smile and nod to you anyways.

Maybe I'll browse through the magazines. Hmm, nothing. I could just pick one at random, but no. Perhaps it'd be better not. My first impression could be made over the open pages of feminine gossip or outlandish dress. Not that they'd care, but I'd kind of be misrepresenting myself, wouldn't I? Actually, fuck it. I'll read one.

This is the place girls like this come from. Interesting. Oh, wait- what's she saying? Um-hmm. Oh.

"No, I've already seen someone and he's asked me to wait here. Thank you, though."

It was Rodge, wasn't it? His pronunciation was a bit strange.

"Rodge, I believe. Is that right? Short for Rodger?"

Ah, okay. Should have expected that. Everyone in this business has unusual names. If you don't, you probably acquire one.

"Oh. Is that who I'd be working with, primarily? If I'm accepted, that is?"

Boys. They like that word here. Not men, boys. Have to admit, it's catchy. Jesus, everybody keeps asking

182

me that. I guess it's obvious, harmless observational conversation. I just hope that I don't hear it everyday for the rest of my life.

"Yeah. I moved hear just last week. From a place near Miami."

Now you ask, 'why', of course. I could do this with my eyes closed.

"My girlfriend came here to go to drama school. I thought I'd come along, see Europe, live in London, that kind of thing. I figured I should do it while I'm young. Free of any real responsibilities, you know?"

Aww. What a sweet old lady. Okay. I guess we're done talking for now. Yep. Looks like that's it. Back to the magazine. She didn't seem to notice my reading it.

It's no use. I can't concentrate. This really is a nice place. And I definitely recognize some of these pictures. I wonder how much you get paid for things like that? A lot, right? I should do some research into how all this stuff works. I'd be easy to take advantage of right now. Aren't modeling agencies notorious for ripping people off? But not big places like this, surely. This property must have cost them a fortune. Jesus, of course it does. Probably not a problem, though- look at all these famous pictures.

I should have brought a book. Flipping through this magazine is getting me nowhere.

Oh, wait- is he coming over? Yes? No? Okay. I should probably stand up.

Right. That's good, isn't it? Okay. Okay. Awesome. So I'm in?

"Wow, Rodge, that's great! I'm really looking forward to working with you guys, with all this…"

That was a silly thing to say. Or was it? Kind of. I guess it was a normal reaction. I've got to watch the hand gestures, though. Hear that the British aren't crazy about that. Okay. Be calm. Go meet everybody, then. Smile, make eye contact, nod. Okay. These are the people I'll be working with. Look at this place! There must be, what- at least eighty or ninety girl cards on that side, at least sixty or seventy for the guys- I mean boys. The layout's great, too. It's like the nerve center for EPCOT or something, if it ever became a real city. They all look really busy. Phone calls, emails, busy, busy, busy. Activity is profitability.

Ah- Tomorrow at 3:00? Nope, nothing scheduled.

"Sure, I can be here at three tomorrow."

Okay, good. Still, do some research, but at least he'll give me the practical information. Sure, paperwork.

"I have my passport and driver's license- will that do?"

Um-hmm. Um-hmm.

"Wonderful. Well, I guess I'll see you tomorrow afternoon, then. I'm really excited about all this. Have a nice night, everyone. Great to meet you."

Does this call for celebration? It does, doesn't it? I just got taken by a big-city modeling agency. Isn't that kind of an accomplishment? I mean, I didn't really do anything, but- I showed up, didn't I? I came here, came to London.

I'll be walking up and down this stairwell all the time now. I'll have a reason to be here. This is my building. My employer- sort of.

Hello, Brompton Road! Hello Knightsbridge! Did you know that this is where I work now? That's my office, right there! I'm here for business- I'm here for a purpose. I'm a part of this place now. These sidewalks are for me to walk on, the trains are for me to ride, the people are for me to pass, and these steps are for me to descend. Sorry, I couldn't help that bouncy spirit that bent my knees and rattled my body, I'm too happy not to show it. You people can laugh at me if it pleases you, be delighted with and for me if it pleases you, but me? I've found my own reason for being here- I'm at last an unfeigned component of city life.

CHAPTER 40

Vaporous light, projections of dull-whites and dead-grays countermanded a small portion of the room's darkness. It came from Avery's laptop. It was the only battery powered device around, and consequently it was the only appliance that would work until power was restored. Lisa's expression was probably the same one she would wear during the sermon of a Catholic church. Disbelief and boredom for what was, she felt, a gross affront on rationality. Avery was completely absorbed.

What showed and sounded concentrated on a theory of human technological ignorance. Technology, along with religion and politics, is being used as a method of control. It spoke of high technology not available to the public, suppressed knowledge, systems of dependence, and the terrifying state of world economy. To watch was to feel powerless. The concept of a microchipped population, whose electronic currency would be watched and controlled by the government was chilling. The vision of those microchips sending electrochemical signals to the host brain was even scarier. To Lisa, it was much easier to chalk the whole thing up to absurdity.

"So this is all because of the eight Jewish bankers, right? That live in the Earth's core?"

"That's not so crazy," Avery answered.

"What isn't? Eight people controlling the world or them living in the Earth's core?" She was getting tired of these videos and progressively more annoyed by the tidbits of so-called information Avery was constantly dropping on her. She couldn't see the British royal families as reptilian overseers, shape shifting into rosy-cheeked humans every time the paparazzi flexed their cameras. Total nonsense.

"Either."

She left the chair and climbed up to her bed.

Avery paused the video, turned in her direction, saying, "You think it is? Do you know a lot about our economy? Here in Europe or America?" Avery had watched two and a half programs about the Federal Reserve. He felt prepared for the coming discussion.

"No, not really," she said. Her voice was neither full or devoid of enthusiasm.

"Okay, well consider this- the Federal Reserve was started in 1913 by the Rothschild, Rockefeller, and J.P. Morgan banking families. You remember what the Federal Reserve is, don't you? They were just talking about it. It's a private bank that loans America it's money. They basically make money out of thin air and then charge interest on it. So in reality, all the printed money in America not only represents the value of the money itself, but also the interest on that money. How then, is the interest ever paid off? Borrow more money, which also represents more interest. It wasn't in effect when America was founded. In fact- a major reason America fought for its independence was because Britain wanted to establish a similar program. The agents behind the Fed orchestrated the great depression, World War I, World War II, and Vietnam. Nobody gets it. I certainly don't. But I know that when all this stuff was starting- a central bank, money going from representing its worth in precious metal to representing merely 'legal tender', a few people saw what was going on and opposed it. Some of them were poisoned."

"Like who?"

"I don't remember the names. There was this one guy, he was a congressman at the time. He kept saying how fucked up it all was and he was assassinated."

"Poisoned?"

"Yeah."

"You said 'a few people' and 'some of them'."

Avery forced an exhale through his teeth. "So what? That's like the least important part of what I said. Don't you understand how fucked up this whole procedure of charging interest is? The bank is just inventing money on the spot. It doesn't cost them anything to do that! But they want more money in return. That's the whole reason the Federal Income Tax exists. It doesn't pay for roads or education, that money goes straight to the Fed to cover the interest on American loans.

"Even look at smaller private banks- they count the money they charge you, that they don't have yet, as an asset so they can make more loans. So they can loan the money they loaned, sort of. And during depressions, which are part of the 'natural economic cycle', when people can't pay their loans, the banks start possessing the things purchased with that money. Fake money, mind you. So now they have real possessions. Homes, land, business assets, real, tangible property- all for fake money.

"The point is that these institutions were put into effect by a relatively small number of people. So yeah, eight bankers. It makes sense. If there were many more people involved it probably wouldn't be allowed to happen. Everyone might take part in it, but only because nobody understands. And with technology- look at this room! I know it's another point entirely, but it feels like there's not much to do without electricity."

"We could light candles."

"But we don't have any."

"I think it's nice."

"I think it's nice, too. But I'm saying, we rely on it. It's something we use every day. But I couldn't get the power back on. I know vaguely how light bulbs work, but I couldn't build one. Most people probably couldn't even describe how they operate, let alone...."

Lisa interrupted him. Her main tactic for this discussion seemed to be discrediting what he said by how he said it, not by using information of her own. "Wait, how do they work, Avery? Can you describe it?"

Early light bulbs were made by passing an electric charge through a filament inside an evacuated glass bulb. As electrons surge across the filament, they bump into the atoms that the filament is made up of, causing them to vibrate, resulting in heat. Electrons belonging to the metal atoms received a temporary boost in energy, and when they returned to normal they released that extra energy in the form of photons. High levels of heat were required to produce visible photons from metal atoms, so creating vacuum inside the bulb was essential- if oxygen was present inside the enclosure the filament would burst into flame. Avery said something to this effect and said Thomas Edison's name a number of times.

Naturally, a product of the American public school system, Avery would attribute invention of the light bulb to Thomas Edison. Lisa, on the other hand, completed her early schooling in England, which prompted her to say, "Actually, Sir Joseph Swan invented the light bulb. His patent was accepted a year before Edison's. Edison worked off Swan's designs."

Of course, there were something like twenty two inventors of incandescent lamps prior to both Swan and Edison. In 1806, Humphrey Davy presented his 'arch lamp' to the Royal Society. In 1820, Warren De la Rue enclosed a platinum coil in an evacuated tube and passed an electrical current through it. In 1835, James Bowman Lindsay demonstrated constant electrical current using a prototype light bulb. In 1841, Frederick De Moleyns patented a bulb, vacuumed and using burners made of platinum and carbon. In 1845, J.W. Starr invented light bulbs with a carbon filament. In 1850, Edward Shepard used a charcoal filament in an incandescent arc lamp. In 1874, Henry Woodward and Mathew Evans patent the light bulb in Canada. In 1878 came Swan's English patent, followed by Edison's in 1879. It was the efficiency of Edison's invention, coupled with his efforts to integrate an entire system of city-wide lighting that earned him recognition as the inventor of the light bulb.

"That's not the point," Avery said. "The point is that light bulbs, something people use every day without question, electricity- that shit is like a fucking magic spell to most people! What about our more advanced technology? I can plug things in, learn how to operate them, but I damn sure don't understand it. I think that kind of knowledge is discouraged, maybe intentionally, maybe not. But it could definitely be used as a method of control."

"I guess," Lisa said, climbing down from bed, "I'm going to brush my teeth."

"Be careful not to swallow," Avery told her. His

suggestion was met with Lisa's eyes rolling, a practically invisible gesture at the moment, and the muffled shouts of men in the streets below. Avery used the silence to further exercise his voice- "Toothpaste contains fluoride, which is a poison. They use it in rat poisons and nerve gas. The nazi's used it in their prison camps because it makes people passive and obedient. Oh, it's in Prozac, too. But yeah, it's another form of Illuminati manipulation. Can you see why they'd want that? Given enough fluoride, like when it's in the water supply, which it already is in some places, entire populations will lose their will to resist control. They say it's because it's good for your teeth. Nonsense. It's a delicate lobotomy to force people into passivity. Maybe it's already happened."

Lisa stepped out of the bathroom with the toothbrush in her mouth. Light green foam swathed the middle of her lips. She was looking at him as though he said something like, 'you're fat because your mom's fat- it's a matter of genetics'. It was the non-verbal communication of 'what the fuck?' and 'fucking enough already' and 'Jesus, fuck'. Avery, however, could not see it, as the bathroom door was far enough from the windows not to be affected by bleeding streetlights. Lisa was functioning in total darkness, acting through the muscle memory of an everyday task.

"So after I brush my teeth I'll turn into a zombie?"

"I didn't say that. Just be careful not to swallow any of it."

She didn't say anything. She only turned around and thought about where all Avery's interest in this stuff could have originated.

CHAPTER 41

One long ago day at the beach, Michael found himself too far from shore, fending off waves three times the height of his body. They pounded him down, held him under, dragged him out. It was a struggle for survival to keep his head above water. Once, on the school playground, Michael was attempting to flip backwards off the high pull-up bar by sitting on top of it, leaning back, and hanging on with his arms until his feet were underneath him. His hands slipped, he plummeted six and a half feet only to land flat on his back. It felt like he broke his spine. He went twenty nine panicking seconds unable to draw a breath of air. Another time, while vacationing in South Carolina, Michael rode his mountain bike full clip directly into a tree.

The phenomenon that presided during and just after each incident was a sensation overwhelming enough to mask the pain, the hollow thud of contact, and the dread of permanent damage to the body. It was the voice of his unconscious mind speaking to him as though he were a different person. It became the only recognizable thing in the black of his eyelids and the vacuum of his ears. It stood before all other thoughts and hid them in its shadow, saying with concise, uninterrupted authority - 'things are out of control'.

Straining in front of him was a rocket-like power, blasting forward and pinning him to the seat. Power that he was not in control of. Power steered by Mr. Thurbin. If something went wrong, Michael was sure that the voice in his head saying 'things are out of control' would be the last thing he'd ever hear.

A green light up ahead winked out; a yellow light just above it blinked on. Mr. Thrubin downshifted and let friction slow the car. He turned to Michael and said, "Well?"

"It's," Michael paused, nodded once, tightened his lips in the kind of smile that people expect to see and even though he wanted to smile that expectation forced an extra tension on it- it became a smile that in a square where each corner stands for forced, nervous, excited, and carefree, landed smack dab in the middle, "a little scary. I want one."

"Of course you do. See, your generation, no offense to you, but it's made up of a bunch of pussies. You kids don't get into fights. You don't smoke cigarettes at fifteen. You're all a bunch of queers watching reality shows and shit like that. You'd rather sue somebody than knock them out. Cars like this aren't popular anymore- and do you know why?"

Michael knew that Mr. Thurbin was about to tell him why, but he wanted make a good impression so he answered first.

"Yeah- because when this car was built, boys were in a hurry to become men. Now, men refuse to admit that they're not boys."

No sign of recognition emanated from the driver's seat. It was the sign of perfect recognition.

The car finally stopped. It sat under the light, the red taunting it like an audacious matador, daring it to move, daring it to scream forward. Mr. Thurbin pulled the emergency brake and got out. When he walked behind the car, Michael thought he must be checking the taillights or getting something out of the trunk. But he kept walking. All the way to the passenger side door, which he opened, stood patiently, and said, "Come on.

You know what we're doing here."

Michael felt his pulse quicken. "You want me to drive?"

"Don't you want to?"

"Well, yeah. I want to, but I don't know," Michael started to say, but before he finished thought back to the moments just prior to the red light. Mr. Thurbin called his generation *a bunch of pussies*. He said, *You kids don't get into fights. You don't smoke cigarettes at fifteen. You're all a bunch of queers watching reality shows and shit like that.* Prudence would not be the proper brand of manhood here. Confidence would be. Cool, defiant confidence. He finished with, "I probably won't want to give it back," and lifted himself with a self-assured spring from the seat.

Behind the wheel, Michael forgot he was supposed to be acting tuff. He was acting tuff anyway. He turned the volume of the tape up a bit. He pushed his sleeves a bit higher on his arm. He pushed his lips out a little and to one side a little. The engine's idle did as much for his blood as a second heart.

"Can you imagine being ordered around by some fucking 'boss' at work right now? Can you imagine being skipped in line at the bank? Can you imagine letting some twerp in an oversized shirt and a fitted cap even slant his eyes at you? Think about it. You can't, can you? We aren't the kind of people that let the world cross us, are we Michael? We have it in us to fuck the world. Not like the sheep that sacrifice their honor in the name of being nice. Not us."

Michael didn't answer right away. It was strange conversation, unusual conversation, by many definitions deranged cracker-jacks conversation. But the roar was before him and with him, and he felt a bizarre affinity for this new association. There was some indiscernible compass drawing them together.

"You know, I used to only tell my brother this, and maybe since you don't know me you won't understand," Michael said. The light was green now and he was driving, not pushing the car to its limits, but allowing it to roar and convulse within its comfort zone. The car cut along the dark road without challenge, like a great white surging through open seas. "The thing is, people have always seemed impressed by my ability to succeed. I've always been ahead of the curve. When I want to do something, I master it in a comparatively short time. Take this car, for instance- in a month or two, I'll show you ways to make it faster. I don't know how right now, but I'll study the physics behind combustion engines and I'll see a way to improve its efficiency. I've been like that my whole life. But I've also felt something else my whole life. Even though I've never really been reasonably frustrated in solving a problem, even though in the past couple years I've had every girl I really wanted- it feels like something's missing. Wait- no. Not that 'I don't know what I want to do with my life' or 'what's the meaning' kind of missing. I feel like there's a part of myself that's not there. Like there was something I should have been but I know, because of that missing part, it's something I'll never be. I feel a bit off."

Mr. Thurbin didn't answer right away. All the words were there, all those whiny, 'woe is me' kind of words that would usually make him sick, but there was something different in the cogency behind them. Different, too, because when Michael said it, he seemed to be speaking for the both of them.

194

CHAPTER 42

At 1:22 p.m., electricity was flowing; 240 volts to make brighter the morning. Avery left the hostel wishing he could bring the light with him. It was a dreary afternoon. Grey clouds hung imposingly low, obscuring the horizon where streets stopped and skies started. It was as though Heaven and Earth were sitting in opposite chairs, wondering why the face facing them looked so familiar, holding their hands out in a hesitant gesture to touch. It was as if they had touched, and suddenly the Earth was aware that Heaven was not as heavenly as everyone promised.

The trek to his agency did not take as long as Avery expected. He was there with an hour to kill, and did so inside the Harrods fine foods department. Avery decided that if and when the big bucks started rolling in, his first act of profligacy would be to eat an ostrich egg omelet. He changed his mind when he pictured a full grown version of the animal, with its taffy neck and geriatric dome, but changed it back when he pictured the omelet, folded over velvety cheese and glowing. He ate a free donut from Krispy Kreme and found an exit.

Outside, winds flicked his hair into shambles. His lips were sticky with frosting. Presently, he did not feel presentable. Not enough for a modeling agency, anyway. He would have to find a place to right his appearance before facing Rodge.

Up the stoop, through the first door, through the second door with a call box and a buzz, down a set of stairs, down a hallway, through a door on the right, another door on the left, to the reflection of a bathroom mirror, through the door that was once on the left, the other door that was once on the right, up two flights of stairs, into the reception area, and onto a chair Avery went. Rodge eventually came out to meet him.

"Hey, Avery. Alright?"

"Fine, thanks. How about you?"

"Good, mate. I've got a couple bits of paperwork for you to sign, and then I'll kind of explain how everything works. Give me one second."

Rodge swiveled one hundred eighty degrees on his heel. It was impossible to tell which heal, but possible that it was both. Separating the reception room from the booking room was a medium sized courtyard. It was a lovely area. Top floor, roofless, and adequately bejeweled with potted plants. Many a chain-smoking model had at some point inhaled poisons on that courtyard- with enchanting poise, of course. Over the brick walls of the courtyard, taller buildings and chimneys of Knightsbridge loomed. Avery took a seat in the open air, beside a small table. Rodge was back in the agreed upon second.

"This is such a nice place," Avery said. He seemed rather taken by the building.

"It's okay," Rodge said. He seemed rather over it.

Avery took the paperwork, read it thoroughly even though Rodge was briefly interpreting all the legal jargon, and signed a few dotted lines. Then he listened to another brief interpretation of what was expected of him, and what he himself could expect. Rodge handed him another sheet of paper. It was a list of Avery's castings for the day.

"You'll get one of these almost every weekday. You can call for it instead, but it's good practice to stop by in person from time to time. The first line will say one of four things. 'Go-and-See' means that you're going to meet somebody in the business. These meetings aren't for any job in particular, but it gives people a chance to meet you, see your face, etcetera. 'Casting' is when you are showing up to get a job, and 'Request' is when you're showing up for a job and the client has asked to see you specifically. 'Job' is when you've already been booked.

"The second line is the time you're expected, obviously. And it's always important that you be on time. If you're going to be late, call me and I'll call them. Third line is the name of the person you need to see, and after that is the address. Have you got an A to Z? Good. Sometimes, we'll know how much the job pays beforehand and sometimes we won't. See here?" Rodge pointed to the second casting on Avery's list, "We already know that this job pays two thousand quid. Don't worry about that right now. It's no big deal, just a window model. This first casting would be great for you." He moved his finger up the paper an inch. "And as you can see, it's here at the agency so you can just hang on until Tara gets here."

Avery was already hanging on; he was hanging on to two concepts- 'two thousand quid' and 'no big deal'. What did they consider a big deal, exactly? Tens of thousands? Millions? If two thousand pounds was nothing to worry about, what was?

"What are the castings usually like?" Avery asked.

"Well, they're all a little bit different. Sometimes there'll be a hundred people there for the same job. Other times just a few. Right now, since you don't have any pictures, it's up to you to really charm them. It's not necessarily a bad thing, not having a big book. Some photographers love working with new boys that nobody's seen before. Just be confident. See that picture in there?" Above the fireplace in the reception area there was a picture that Avery had seen in dozens of magazines. An advertisement for some Polo cologne or something. Avery nodded his head and Rodge continued. "He booked that job on his first casting. Two million pounds."

Avery felt his bones turn into a soft metal and his chair into a strong magnet, pulling his slackened frame down. Avery felt his essence rush from his oral cavity in hot pursuit of an exhalation. Avery felt his head inflate and collapse, like a child huffing helium from a balloon. He strained against these feelings and was in a moment back to normal.

"Lucky guy," Avery noted.

Rodge nodded.

Young men, or in the preferred industry term, 'boys', filed in one by one. Avery did his best to concentrate on the words in his lap, but from time to time his attention wandered, focused on random conversations between the other models. He wanted to see if any of them were conspicuously rich. He was also beginning a new chapter of 'The Throughout'.

Disconnecting the Grid-

Nothing threatens entrenched power like a people connected. Even the Old Gods knew this. And in the times of the Old Gods, the people were connected. Mankind was in communication with one another, with the Earth, in tune through a surging energy grid that flowed through all consciousness.

"Hey, man. Long time."

"Yeah, I've been out of town for a while. How's it going?"

"Oh, you know. Getting by."

For the Old Gods of the world and the new rulers of civilization, the Grid had to be suppressed.

In Egypt, monolithic structures stand. They defy the modern world's preconceived notions of what 'primitive' cultures were

"Oi, Brad! Didn't think you'd show up to this. Big star now, aint'cha, boy?"

capable of. Not only has science failed to describe how these ancient people constructed the pyramids, it has also failed to understand why. *The Egyptian pyramids were erected for one purpose and one purpose only- disconnect the people. (It has been one of the best kept secrets in history, hidden in the last place you're likely to look. Right in front of you. More on that later.) First, understand that the energy grid of the planet, much like the human cardiovascular system, runs first in powerful dilutions, then branch out into smaller, weaker fields. The shape of the pyramids*

"What are you reading, mate?"

"Franz Kafka."

"But it's in German."

"It's Franz Kafka."

and their placement was engineered specifically to disrupt a major ley line, disconnecting the Egyptian people from each other, from nature, ripening them for oppression.

Other monoliths have been erected for similar purposes, but obstructing the flow of energy is only one way for the powers that be to solve the problem of group spirit. Any time a race of people show a propensity towards a collective awareness, those people are put to slaughter. The Mayans. The Native Americans. Countless tribal communities.

"What else you got today?"

"This thing for Dazed."

"In Shoreditch?"

"Yeah. You, too?"

"No. Don't have that one."

The Pineal glands of these people were believed not to have atrophied on the same level as the people of more 'civilized' communities, living near monoliths and separated by societies from nature.

A woman with blue eyes and tightly curled blonde hair entered the room. She looked around, smiled, and asked, "Is Rodge around?" Avery stopped reading. The woman was wearing a dark blue dress with white dots. It fell loosely from the waist-down, and ended just above the tops of brown cowboy boots. Her skin was the white of old ceilings.

When Rodge entered the room, both he and she lit up, as if they were old friends with a wife/husband, children, and far too much responsibility to ever see each other. Whether that was the case or not, nobody knew. They traded friendly kisses and walked into a small room that connected with the reception area. A short time later, Rodge came out and said, "Alright, then. Who was first? Avery, I think."

Avery closed his book and prepared for his first casting. Rodge patted his shoulder on the way.

"Hello," Avery said as he walked in. He closed the door behind him.

"Hiya! I'm Tara." She answered brightly. Her face was round, her cheeks rosy.

"I'm Avery." They shook hands and Avery handed her his big, black modeling book. It contained one picture, a photocopy of the Polaroid taken the day before.

Tara opened his book, saw the first page, flipped passed it, and understood.

"Not been modeling long?"

"For about twenty minutes," Avery said. He

smiled at his own joke.

"Oh, wow." She smiled, too. "Well, let me just look at you for a second, then. You've got really lovely eyes. Can I see your profile?"

Avery hesitated. He had about a quarter of a second to figure out what that meant. "Profile? Turn my head?"

She smiled again. Either she smiled a lot, or the honest naiveté was fresh enough to win her over. "That's right. Turn your head to each side. Like this." Her chin described a half circle around her neck, pausing at each end. Avery accepted the excuse to stare before following her lead.

"Okay, great. Now that's done and we can just have a little chat before you go. You're American, aren't you? Did you come here for modeling?"

"No. Actually, I came here for a girl. She'd been planning on moving back to England for years, so I thought I'd just tag along. I wasn't sure what I would do for work when I got here. I was scouted yesterday."

"That's exciting."

"Yeah, I guess it is. It's a great weight off my mind, too. I thought looking for work would be a really onerous undertaking, but all I had to do was walk into Top Shop."

Her eyes tracked his like an astronomer's gaze, catapulted through telescopes, fixed into position by long-established mathematics. Avery let them focus there, her eyes. There was some quiet sensuousness in the moment. She was inspecting him. As a photographer inspects a model, yes- but photographers and models are first humans. Things with base imaginations. Avery almost forgot he was being interviewed. Tara picked up after the unusually long pause, the unusually beguiling escape into each other's eyes, "What's your favorite thing in the world?"

"Truth." Avery answered almost immediately. He was slow to realize why. "Veritas. It's like- when the truth hits you, nothing else matters. If the truth were available, no one would need to wonder about where we came from or where we're going. It's just such an evasive concept. The people want it and hide from it. I say that because I don't think most people know truth even in themselves, let alone the world. They don't know it and they don't know that they don't know it. Why did everyone in my high school want a Lexus, you know? Were they all car enthusiasts or something? Of course not. They wanted a Lexus because other people wanted a Lexus. Because they sought some kind of recognition or respect or something. But I think a lot of that realization never occurred. They only realized that they wanted the car. Not the why- the what. And that's not the truth."

"Interesting."

"Sorry, that was a bad example. I know. That's really the least of the reasons that Truth excites me. To be honest, a big part of the reason that the truth excites me is that most people don't know it. I learn something, like for instance- why the pyramids were built- and I feel like I'm a little more enlightened than the average guy, which basically makes me every bit as bad as the kids that wanted a Lexus. But I do want to tell people what I find out, and regardless of why I tell them, whether or not my motives are altruistic, they still end up with the information. I'd like to think that the ends justify the means."

"You know why the Egyptians built pyramids?"

"I know theories. Some people think that they were built as sort of a commemoration to a supernova that occurred like five thousand years ago. I'm beginning to think they were built to suppress human potential."

"Suppress? I would have thought the opposite."

"It's complicated."

"How old are you, Avery?"

"Twenty one. Why?" Avery was smiled wide, on the brink of a chuckle, glad to have left severe, on the spot confessions in the past.

"Just wondering," she breathed. "Good age. I wish we could keep talking, but all those boys are waiting outside."

"Oh. Alright. Well, maybe we'll see each other again sometime?"

"I'd say it's very possible."

While Avery gripped tightly a yellow bar on the bus back to Sloan Square, crowded with other commuters who also strained to keep their balance, with his music turned up much too loud, he was booked for his first photo shoot. Tara told Rodge that she was in love, and that that American boy Avery would be absolutely perfect for the job.

CHAPTER 43

Dinner for two would deplete his checking account of $162.34.

Avery took Lisa by the hand and dragged her to a swanky restaurant down the road, saving his explanation until they were seated. He told her then about the casting, about the other guy who made two million pounds on *his* first casting, and about the two thousand pound job that was 'no big deal'. They ordered a bottle of wine that the waiter suggested. It was delicious.

In the refined, dusky plot over their table, all skin glowed a healthy shine; all hair looked a lustrous shade. It felt wonderful to splurge on such a meal, completely guilt-free. Avery's sense of pride smoldered with as much élan as his skin and hair, obviously affected by the elegance of the room.

"I don't want to say, 'get used to it'", Avery said smugly, "but you might have to get used to it." He took another sip of wine.

"Didn't I say London would be good for you?"

She was right, of course. Fuck the Fates. What did they know, damning him to a life of misery? This wasn't misery. This was a four star restaurant. He'd pay the bill with money earned from letting people take pictures of him. Money earned for being born and washing his face every night. His was an awkward fall on undue glory- but glory it was. Soon, Avery promised himself, he would be flying his friends to London, buying Michael a car, living the good life that he knew he'd always deserved.

"I could use a new jacket. Want to help me pick one out after this?"

"Sure," Lisa said.

"If there's still time, I mean. Let's not rush. Oh and I also want to order some stuff online. Books and videos."

"Okay. Have you told Michael the good news? He'd be really happy to hear it."

"We'll buy a calling card from the off-license."

Lisa smiled and nodded. It was a rather uncertain gesture, making her look ill at ease until she stopped doing it. "Avery, just be careful not to spend all your money, okay? We still have to find a flat and everything and that's going to be expensive."

"I know how to keep track of my fucking money," he said, perturbed.

"I know you do, but maybe you should at least,"

"Hey, hey, hey," Avery cut her off, "I said don't worry about it. I got a job. It's fine. 'Thanks for dinner, Avery' and that's enough."

With that, the mood was spoiled.

Clipped conversation, curt and cold, was the only available distraction. Lisa's focus didn't stray far from her glass of wine and her plate of caramelized black cod. Avery darted his gaze nervously from place to place, looking at waiters, other tables, his food, Lisa's food, the windows, the kitchen, anything that didn't pout with palpable hurt like Lisa's face.

When the phone rang, it pulsed a strange, impatient tone. Nothing like the long, soothing tones of American receivers. The British ring was an alarm clock when the American ring was snoring. It was a good thing that Michael didn't take long to answer.

"Hello?"

"Hey, man. What's up?"

Michael knew the voice immediately. He gave an excited greeting and said, "To what do I owe this surprise?"

"Do I need a reason to call?"

"No, of course you don't. How is everything?"

"Great, man. For the most part anyway. I just took Lisa out to a really nice dinner."

"Yeah? What'd you have?"

Avery described the dish as best he could.

Lollipop lamb chops with truffle oil and mint jelly could be illustrated to some extent by just saying 'lollipop lamb chops with truffle oil and mint jelly', but Avery tried to do better. He described the tender, red interior meat, the refreshing, sweet jelly, and the asparagus cooked to green perfection.

"Okay, okay. So we're not being tight with our money tonight, eh?"

"No. Not anymore. I just booked my first modeling job."

"Oh, man! Congratulations! Are you getting a lot of money?"

"I'm not sure how much but I'm assuming, based on other conversations with my agent, that it'll pay well."

"That's great, Avery. I bet Lisa's excited."

When Avery answered, he heard the dejected quality of his voice. He was sure Michael heard it to. There was no choice but to explain. Yes, he and Lisa have been arguing a lot lately.

"Really? I'm not surprised to hear it. I mean, you two have a bit of adjusting to do; those adjustments will naturally revise certain parts of you. For a while at least, you'll have to get used to the new environment and to the new Lisa. You two will be fine, though."

"Yeah, I hope so. What's new back home?"

"Not too much. I've been learning a lot about cars lately. Oh! I drove David's mustang! He's helping me build…"

Avery interrupted him. "Who's David?"

"Dude next door. Mr. Thurbin."

"Oh, shit. Really?"

"Yeah. I hang out with him sometimes. He's been teaching me a lot about cars, and we're looking to start building another one for me. He's going to let me use his garage."

"So he turned out to be a nice guy, huh?"

To speak objectively and say Mr. Thurbin was a nice guy would be gross disinformation. Mr. Thurbin hated pretty much everybody and acted pretty much accordingly. But for some reason he liked Michael. Michael said he was willing to take advantage of that. And yes, he would be careful.

"Good." Avery said. "I hope auto-repair books aren't all you've been reading."

"No. I finished a few others since you've been gone. How about you?"

"Yeah, I got my hands on some interesting stuff. Crazy shit if you believe it."

"Okay, give me an example."

Avery called Michael for a few reasons- to get news from back home, to relay news from London, to hear a familiar voice, and to fulfill his obligation to 'keep in touch'. These were not the primary motives for the call. Avery wanted someone to listen to what Lisa was sick of listening to. He wanted to talk conspiracy theories. Michael was perfect because he would be interested, he would almost certainly have something to add, and he wouldn't think his brother crazy for entertaining crazy ideas. He told Michael all about pyramids blocking the worldwide flow of psychic energy, making the people easier to rule, and speculated that that was why the Great Seal of the United States was of a pyramid.

"Hmm. Okay. I've got something for you," Michael said, "Consider this- Moby Dick was written by Herman Melville, who was quite obviously a secret society adept. His writing alone is proof of that. Now, Moby Dick did a wonderful job of exalting the whale hunt. According to the Illuminatus! Trilogy, dolphins are a higher life form and communicate with humans through a very complex system of sounds. Sperm whales, on the other hand, communicate through what scientists now consider a very basic succession of unvarying clicks. The clicks are loud enough to be heard through the hulls of ships, and sailors once referred to sperm whales as 'carpenter fish' because it sounded like they were hammering.

"Now consider this- the dolphin, who have a highly refined language, artistic beyond human understanding, have to put up with the droll, monotonous language of the sperm whale. It would drive them mad, right? So in order to devastate the sperm whale population, dolphins put Herman Melville up to writing a book to praise and encourage whaling. Maybe a dolphin even wrote it for him. Clearly they'd be capable of writing, at least by human standards, incredibly stylish prose."

"Sounds like a solid theory to me."

"There's also the one about the toilet seat manufacturers using the name of a long forgotten god on their toilet seat, so every time some kid is masturbating, he'll read the name and that sexual energy will be transferred to their idol."

"That's too much." Avery looked towards the elevators down the hall. "Listen man, I gotta jet. Lisa's probably crying and shit upstairs."

"Okay. Well, it was good to hear from you. Check your email, I'll send you some stuff."

"That'd be awesome. Talk to you later."

It was exactly what Avery wanted. Michael didn't lay any heart-stopping information on him, but what was said enabled him to better understand the magnitude of the illuminati conspiracy. It was a conspiracy that not only transcended political, social, technological, and economical arenas, but extended also to the worlds of classic literature, the animal kingdom, and certain porcelain productions. It was everywhere. Suddenly, Avery absorbed his brother's theories. The feeling in his limbs suggested that, for a moment, his heart had very possibly stopped.

CHAPTER 44

In the early 1980's a new, seemingly scientific craze was sweeping Southern California. It had been recently rejected by councilors and psychotherapists, and was handed down to ambitious men and women in the high-pressure sales industries with the sentiment 'eh, maybe *you* people can use it'. Neuro-linguistic programming. Employees of Dan and Dan's Furniture Emporium were all about it. Framing, verbal anchoring, nonverbal anchoring, suggestively vague speech, submodalities, and trance- they were buzzwords of the sales floor. And business was good.

Guy remembered- he wasn't there himself, but his best friend, Buddy, made a great living off those reclining couches. Guy even bought one himself. It wasn't until after the transaction was completed that Guy was hipped to the secret inspiration behind the purchase.

Hindsight also revealed a thing or two. Guy remembered that whenever he looked away from the couch he was meant to buy, Buddy would converse with negative words instead of positive ones. While he was sitting on his couch, admiring the armrests and stroking the cool leather, he received a very positive description of

Buddy's date last night. She was 'incredibly voluptuous' with 'legs like a gazelle' and 'breath like ripe apples'. When he stood up and looked around, she was 'just another dumb broad, as dumb as they come' and 'dirty-not worth the popcorn or the gas money'.

But Buddy wasn't on a date the night before he sold Guy a couch; he was reading a book called 'NLP-the Key to Influence and Affluence' loaned to him by the A.M. staff manager.

Buddy asked Guy to sit down for his second trick. It was done under the guise of joking. Guy recalled being asked to sit down, close his eyes, and picture a girl straddling his mid-section. A real blonde bombshell. Jane Fonda. Michelle Pfeiffer. He was instructed to feel the couch, to imagine it happening. Little did Guy know that it wasn't a joke at all. His mind was supposed to make a real connection between the leather and the dreamy, smoke filled fantasy. A couple more tricks and Guy signed the dotted line.

Hell, he told himself afterwards, *I really did need a couch.*

This was years and years ago. The just-after-college years. Before he was fed up with Southern California and moved to South Florida. Before a lot of growing up and a little growing out. Guy never did read up on NLP. He thought it interesting, but was frightened to learn more. He tried to convince himself that he merely preferred to leave that kind of stuff to the slick, fast-talking Buddys of the world, but deep down knew better. He just never felt hip enough. Not for the lingo, the threads, the music, the wisdom, or the attitude. It wasn't until recently that he could even say words like 'dig' or 'jive', even though he always wanted to.

In a brazen act of self-fulfillment he pictured himself on a hang-glider, leagues above the Earth, infinitely emancipated. He captured that feeling, poured it into an imaginary gel cap, swallowed it, writhed as the coil of autonomy rolled through his body. At that moment, he touched his thumb to his middle finger. NLP would assert that every time he did it, touch his thumb to his middle finger, his brain should reroute the sensation of liberation and send him soaring along the wings of heaven.

Thumb to middle finger. Taste the wind. Drink in freedom. Thumb to middle finger. Thumb to middle finger.

Maybe it was working. He just wasn't sure. He opened the garage door, wanting desperately for sunshine and fresh air, wanting desperately to breathe fully, like he didn't have a sack of potatoes thrown over each shoulder. He touched his thumb to his middle finger. Did that help? The pressure was still on. The pressure could not be on if he were riding a hang-glider over emerald and olive forest. He figured he was just doing something wrong.

The big aluminum panels of the garage door were above his head and still. Florida sunshine pooled at his feet. He stepped out onto the driveway, hoping for a familiar face. There was a wooden clacking sound next door. Over and over, a wooden pop, a vacuous click. He knew the noise well. It doubled as an invitation.

"Hey, guys. Whaddya know?"

"I know I'm about to slam this ball down Mikey-boy's throat. This is the comeback of the century," Luke said. He hoped that Michael would be distracted by Guy's entrance and wasted no time in serving.

Michael said, "It's four to thirteen."

Guy remained silent until the point was won, Michael stated the more current score of four to fourteen, and Luke flung his paddle to the floor.

"Don't give up," Guy said, "the game's not over yet." But when Luke lost the last point, Guy was happy. He had some things to get off his chest. These young men would understand, but they wouldn't want to understand in the course of heated rivalry.

If Guy hadn't been there, Michael may have done a sort of Pee-Wee Herman dance, but he was, so he didn't. Instead he slapped his hands together like he was knocking sawdust off them, and said, "Sorry, Guy. What's going on?"

"Oh, not much. Just thought I'd stop by and say hello."

"How's business?" Luke asked.

While thinking *Thank God*, Guy said, "Not so good, actually. It's proving really difficult to find another tenant that'll adhere to the name policy. We're losing money every month. It's the pits."

"Damn," Michael said, "Wish I could help. We could sell coffins and name the store 'Will you Bury Me?' or something."

"At this point I'd be happy for a 'Will you Bury Me?'"

"You have to go after barber shops and hair salons," Luke said.

"It's true. They always have these fantastic names. 'A Cut above the Rest' and 'Sheer Beauty' and 'Hair and There' and 'The Buzz about Town' and 'To Dye For' and 'Trim Jim' and 'All's Fair in Hair and Curls'…" Michael let his voice trail away. He didn't want to rub it in.

Luke didn't mind rubbing it in. He had some ideas too, and didn't want them going unsaid, "How about 'Wesley Snips' or 'Scissor me Timbers' or 'One Snip Ahead' or 'Snippidy-doo-dah'?"

"No, no, no. You can't keep using 'snip'." Michael said, "That's like the worst of all the hair-cutting words."

Luke puffed a breath of air in protest. "Fuck you. Guy's the only expert here," and, looking at Guy, "What do you say?"

"Yeah. Snip. It's okay."

Guy looked on the brink of collapse. It was too much. His wife was constantly giving him shit. Tenants couldn't believe he wouldn't lease the property without what he considered an 'acceptable name'. Goddamned foolish, foolish, foolish! And here these two kids were, shooting names out of their asses that he would kill for. He touched his thumb to his pointer finger. Wrong finger, of course. It supplied no surge of liberation.

Michael made hand gestures telling Luke to cool it. Luke shrugged.

"Guy- hey, Guy- are you alright? Have a seat, man. It's no big deal, right? I mean, what's in a name? Everything! Everything, right? It'll all work out." And as he said that, Michael fixed Guy's hand so that the thumb was touching the middle finger, not the neighboring pointer.

Michael wasn't sure why he did that. He just knew it needed doing. Once it was done, Guy stood up, felt the sun on his skin, and said "Wow. Sorry guys. I don't know what came over me. I just felt dizzy all of a sudden and…"

"It's okay, man. Sometimes people faint. It happens," Luke said.

Guy nodded. His hand was in a funny position. Suddenly everything seemed completely copasetic. His business would be fine. His wife loved him. Through it all, he felt one with the sky.

CHAPTER 45

On the Albert Bridge, a listless passing underneath. On, dismally on, the wet ways of epoch and ages. Forward flow like the dirty mistakes of politicians. How many prodigies have cast a buoyant gaze upon that river? How many fools?

He was wearing a new jacket, Avery. Unusable morsels of lollipop lamb chops were passing slowly, much like the brown Thames, through his lower intestine. Lisa was off on her first day of school. Very exciting. Avery told himself over and over that the view was beautiful. That he appreciated it. It was worth the financial struggles he would doubtlessly endure.

Seriously, though- what the fuck? Of all the fucking stupid goddamned dumb fucking assumptions. Why would anyone pay millions to take pictures of his obtuse, presumptuous mug? Over four hundred dollars poorer than yesterday morning and mocked heartlessly by swells below, dwarfed by the intransience of swells below. Avery knew that but for a distended bank account, the river would not talk to him so. Were he an heir to affluence, he would stand over the tides a conqueror, subjugator of man, beast, and waterway. Not so. He spat.

Oh- sorry, mate. That job doesn't pay anything. It's an editorial.

There weren't many people walking. Cars went by with fair regularity, but for the most part Avery was alone on the bridge. There was that fresh, virtuous quality to the air- the kind of air that often hovers over and around bodies of water. The sun was bright, but the city still a bit gray. The memory played again.

...doesn't pay anything.

The word model has always been synonymous with dim-witted. Perhaps it was their willingness to work for nothing that propagated the notion. Avery certainly felt dim-witted. He knew Michael wouldn't have fucked up the way he did. Michael would have gotten the information, if the wrinkles representing that information weren't magically grafted onto his brain already, that is. 'The other guy got two million; the other casting was for two thousand; I must be getting a lot of money!'

Once again, Avery began walking. He had another Go-and-See and another casting, neither of which would fetch him one red pence. He thought about not going. 'Getting his face out there' sounded like protracted, ineffectual drudgery.

A nice, modest job as a bus-boy or prep-cook or maybe, with a 'sky's the limit' mentality, even bartender. He could get a paycheck a week, clock in and out, collect tips, walk in through the back entrance next to the trashcans filled with every kind of refuse, smelling like the color brown would smell if you could smell colors. Brown- the all-color. Restaurant trashcans- the all-smell.

But there was a hook in Avery's cheek. It reeled him in with promises of comfort, distinction, glamour, access, travel, stimulation, self-assurance, purpose, and the company of very thin, very beautiful young women.

'That is the payment', it said, 'So starve, Avery. Borrow money from whosoever will lend it. Relish your new jacket, your last night's dinner. For in good conscience there will be no more. You'll project an image of modern-day eminence, you'll live a reality of rationing and restraint. Strut forth, young corruptor of youth. The Fates and Fashion are one in intention.'

Avery liked neither the Fates or Fashion at this

point. He walked toward his next FM obligation only because it was the easiest thing to do. There was nothing like the high climb of expectation, a climb so lofty that it left the atmosphere, choked, burned upon plummeting re-entry, and all but blinked out of being, leaving only a forlorn and discontented boy on a bridge in Chelsea above the Thames.

CHAPTER 46

At the Duke's Parade with some people from class. Come meet up if you want, it's on Old Brompton Road passed the Lamborghini dealership.
Love,
Lisa (6:30)

The note was not readily readable. It was scrawled across a small scrap of notebook paper with a dull sky-blue colored pencil, which would barely exist under all but the brightest of lamps.

Four separate chains of dominos set to collapse in the decision making portion of Avery's brain. The 'protective boyfriend' mechanism, falling- built along the concept of blocking Lisa's tipsy conversations with the flirtatious, rapt males of the class. The 'curiosity' mechanism, falling- a drive to put eventual faces to inevitable names. The 'evade boredom' mechanism, falling- urging an escape from the indoors. The 'desire' mechanism, falling- falling into a pint of thick, frothy

216

Guinness. Upon the toppling of the last domino in each row, Avery wanted to change his shirt and head out.

The Duke's Parade housed one too many blazers for Avery's liking. A regrettable progeny, unaborted coupling between archetypal English pub and insipidly elegant American martini bar. The patrons stood, sipped, spoke, and even smiled with an uninspired sensibility. Lisa was not as of yet in sight. Avery ordered a beer, drank it down enough to permit safe walking through a crowd. He peered around the bulk of people and wooden columns looking for her.

Next to a faux fireplace aft, a rather substantial area had been commandeered. Lisa sat in the group, whom every one of them seemed as at home as if in their very own living room. Shoes were off. Tables, chairs, and couches had been rearranged. Two open containers of Hob-Nobs lay, or rather loitered on the knee-high table the students circled.

Before approaching, kissing his girlfriend and rounding introductions, Avery stood and watched. Her new friends were playing some kind of word game. Probably something they learned in class.

"Snap!"
"Snake!"
"Key!"
"Yes!"
"Se...awww. Damn!"

Everyone laughed. Avery took another sip from his beer. Another taste. Another slug followed by a gulp and a guzzle. He moved around his cover, two men and all their footballer stats, and proceeded to the table.

"Hey," he said to Lisa.

Lisa jumped up. She was already more than a little

drunk, the alcohol showing in her lively, lighthearted smile. Avery liked it when she was like this. His jokes were funny and her affection uninhibited. She stepped over a corner of the table and they hugged.

"Everyone, this is my boyfriend, Avery. Avery, this is everyone."

"Hi, everyone."

Everyone returned the greeting and Avery sat down in a place made for him beside Lisa. A few of the kids went on playing the word game.

"How was school?" Avery said in Lisa's right ear.

"It was okay. That old *bitch* Mrs. Lovell was critiquing my make-up again." She seemed to be speaking to the group as a whole, not just Avery.

The girl on Avery's right, the one who moved over and made a spot on the couch for him, said, "Don't worry about her, Lisa. What does she know about style? Your make-up looks wonderful, darling."

And a boy across the table said, "I don't mind Mrs. Lovell, it's Mr. Elmsworth, man. Every time he reads it puts me to sleep. 'With carrion men, groaning for burial.'" This last part was said as a hopeful actor acting as an actor.

Avery didn't know that it was Shakespeare the guy was quoting. If he had known, his understanding of the group's collective character would have been more promptly attained, and he could have reasonably envisaged a future in which quoting Shakespeare, saying 'I' followed by as much squeal as the audience would abide, and generally filling the mold of drama students happened all night.

A pale, slender lad stood up and in a singsong voice declared himself 'Bradley, the Hob-Nob king'.

By degrees, Avery found himself retreating within

himself, requiring escape from slipshod escape. To join the proverbial club meant chiming in tirelessly. Everyone wanted theirs to be the voice in the air.

"Lisa tells me you just started modeling," the girl Avery's right said.

"Yeah. Yeah, I did. I have my first shoot on Monday, actually."

"Oh, that's fantastic! I used to do hair-modeling once in a while."

It was not perhaps the connection that Avery was hoping for, but it was something. More, at least, than the other 'in common', the fact that every personality surrounding him consisted of an id, an ego, and probably but not in all present cases certainly, a super-ego.

"Is that what you wanted to do when you got here?" the girl asked. "I'm Clara, by the way."

"Clara," Avery said in acknowledgement. "No, I didn't know what I'd be doing when I got here. I still don't know what the fuck I'm doing to be honest."

She thought that funny. "Me either. I want to act, but it's not an easy gig. You have to get pretty lucky unless your parents are already movie stars."

To that, Lisa was listening. "Luck. Maybe for some people. What it really takes is persistence. And dedication and love."

"I'll drink to that!" another girl said. A few people raised their glasses.

"Hmm. I could use another beer", Avery said to Lisa. "Be right back." These last words he placed quietly, directly in her ear.

Instead of stopping at the bar, Avery kept walking through the open doors of the Duke's Parade. It was getting dark outside, and noticeably colder, too. Looking around, Avery felt as out of place outside as he did at the table. The homes and flats around him were won through inheritance or fortune. These were not the streets for young men concerned with the cost of dinner, who struggled to justify a few nights' spending at the pub.

"Avery, what are you doing?" It was Lisa behind him.

"Nothing. Just wanted some fresh air. How much longer do you want to hang out here?"

"I don't care. We can go now, if you want. But you just got here," she said. She looked red around the eyes and her face was flushed.

"I know. But I don't want to spend much money. I'm not having that great of a time, anyway."

"I could tell."

"Should we go say goodbye or anything?"

She said that they didn't have to. She would see them all at school tomorrow, anyways; they could walk home, it was such a nice night, and so on and so forth.

The buildings in South Kensington ushered between them substantial winds. Their white facades, bleached, pure and stately. Their stoops swept and shrubs maintained. Avery eventually had to urinate on one of the building columns. There was no way of holding it in and no alleyways to appropriate the deed.

What started as a pleasant night had turned otherwise as Lisa and Avery approached their building. From 'how was school' to an answer, from 'how do you like your classmates' to an answer and a 'do you think Clara is pretty'. An answer, another question, from that question to an unacceptable answer, a question from Lisa and an Avery admitting that he sometimes masturbates to fantasies revolving around absolute strangers. Lisa would not hear an explanation, nor did Avery give a very good one. Avery sat on his bed reading with a stable scowl while Lisa, alone and crying, carried that information to the kitchen.

With misdirected passion, she would run the serrated edge of a butter-knife over her thighs, still intoxicated, bleeding betrayed disappointment and ichor.

CHAPTER 47

"That was actually really disappointing," said Michael over a gentle melody in stereo.

J.P. has his attention fixed to the traffic of his immediate future. Maintaining his eyes' bearing over the steering wheel, he turned his head an atomic degree to the right. Michael was talking about John Woulf. That he knew. What he didn't know was why Michael would expect anything other than shit-head conversation from a shit-head like that. He frowned.

"That was the guy that gave Avery the tape he showed us. Remember? At Herm's house?"

With a sudden spark of recollection, J.P.'s body jerked into timber rigidity, "That was him? That guy?"

"Yeah. Except he was acting much differently. When he said 'I'm not really into that stuff anymore', I really couldn't have been more wounded. That lanky, maladroit mother fucker put Avery onto all kinds of new things. Secret schools, occult beliefs and practices, social, political, spiritual, and economic conspiracies, it's pretty much all Avery reads now. To be honest, I was psyched to bump into John. I couldn't wait to tell him how his intellectual pursuits had rubbed off on my brother. Instead he offered me a place in some pyramid scheme."

J.P. said, "That's just like when I saw Curtis last week. He used to come into work all the time and play Stevie Wonder on the keyboards. Then, like, a year later I started listening to Stevie Wonder and when I saw Curtis again I wanted to thank him. I was like 'do you remember me?' and he was like 'yeah, I remember you'. I told him how much I like Stevie Wonder now and he was like 'oh, that's great man, listen, can I have a dollar, or two, two dollars?'"

Michael nodded. He still thought that what happened with John was worse, but he could certainly respect the similarities. He played the event through his head again, in perfect detail, before deciding for sure whether John or Curtis was the bigger downer.

He was walking out of the grocery store, carrying an Italian sub in one hand, and a bottle of iced tea in the other. That part wasn't important. He was through the first set of automatic doors, only a few paces from the proper exit. Escape. It wasn't that Michael was very bothered going into public places stoned. Nothing bad ever happened, and it would be a groundless assumption to think it ever would. Like the high would ever get so on top of him that he couldn't decide what cheese to put in his sandwich- it wasn't in the realm of possibility.

Still, walking through such a crowded place could be a little disconcerting. For instance, one might be forced to occupy the same space as a conversation teeming with hopeless, irresponsible nugacity, and curb vital laughter. It isn't unachievable, just unpleasant. So, walking over the threshold, where decorum would trickle from the front of his mind to the back, Michael saw John Woulf.

222

"Well if it isn't the young Mr. Tyler," John said to him.

"The same."

"How's it going? I hear your brother's in England."

Michael said that it was true, and that Avery seemed to be enjoying himself immeasurably. He noticed that John, when not worked up in righteous defense of his beliefs, seemed very passive. Tired, almost.

"That's good to hear. I bet he'll fit right in there."

Here's where it happened- in time with the passing of an elderly black man pushing a row of carts, a tall, thin white woman and her two bug-eyed children, and a man whose chest hair was proudly exhibited through the first two buttons of his shirt, so proudly that he adorned the black, curly mass with gold necklaces and pendants, Michael asked, "Still tracking the reptilian overseers?"

And John answered, "No, not really," through a self-conscious half-smile.

"No?" Michael found it hard to swallow. Here was a man that only a couple months ago would have told Queen Elizabeth, 'go back to your own dimension'. "You don't think that the European aristocracy is anything more than a bunch of inbred humans now?"

"Yeah. Pretty much. That stuff was all pretty far-fetched, don't you think? You do, don't you? Sure you do. You're a smart kid. I've always known that about you." At this point John's character pepped itself up. It was like watching a shark's behavior in a cage, both before and after adding a bucket of blood. It was the dotcom entrepreneur thirty seconds after a long line of cocaine. His enthusiasm was snowballing toward a sales pitch. "Listen, I'm running a branch of this new business. How would you like to make an extra eight hundred dollars a week? Sounds pretty good, right?"

J.P. had been standing behind Michael just after the hellos had been said. Not sure where to look, what to say, or how long to wait, he took out his phone and looked at it. The effort didn't consume nearly enough time.

"Sorry, John, I'm really not…"

"Wait- hang on a sec. Before you say no, I have to tell you that what we sell. Pre-paid legal subscriptions are about as popular in Europe as cell phones. But the market here in the states is completely open! Something like two percent saturation! The time is right. The time's more than right. We're in on the ground floor, baby, and there's nowhere to go but up, up, up!"

"Tempting, but like I said, I'm just super busy. I've got a play in the works, a car I'm building, patents I'm waiting on, piano, way too much stuff going on."

Michael put his hand on J.P.'s arm to stop him from checking his phone again. John started talking, but was stopped.

"Sorry, John. We have to get going. I'll see you around though, okay?"

"Yeah, but here. Take the card. Seven o'clock at my house on Monday. Come see what we're about. No, no, don't answer yet. Just come Monday."

Allowing one of the biggest waves of relief ever to hit him in his entire life carry him away, J.P. beat Michael through the exit.

"I still think that was worse," Michael said.

"Are you kidding? I'm not saying it wasn't. That shit was fucking horrible, man. Don't you ever just leave me in the lurch like that. I had to listen to that bullshit and I didn't even know the guy. You signed me up for it. I didn't sign up for it."

Michael was laughing. It was true- he practically played a extraordinarily subtle but painful practical joke on J.P. Poor kid.

"I could have just walked away, I guess. Next time I will."

"I wouldn't hold it against you," Michael said.

J.P. looked down at his gages, swore, and said he needed gas.

"You don't need to worry about gas."

Eyes, lips, and tongue rolled in unison. "Okay. We'll just will the car forward."

The next gas station, instead of pulling in, J.P. passed. He thought that giving half-hearted pushes, while letting Michael strain to push most of the car would be a delectable 'I told you so'. It would be an 'I told you so' to someone that doesn't hear it with fair enough regularity.

"I'm willing the car forward," Michael said, eyes squeezed in focused intensity.

He wouldn't notice for a while, and when he did notice he wouldn't think much of it, but the needle of J.P.'s gas gage pivoted up nearly a quarter of an inch. There was a growing something special in Michael's will. It added 41 miles to the thirsty little Neon.

CHAPTER 48

There was an episode of Star Trek in which a warrior alien, brown face crowded with sharp protrusions and prematurely balding, had to clear his mind of all thoughts in order to open the door of some cosseted prison. It was hard to remember the details. Avery had always felt that getting into Star Trek would be a pretty heavy undertaking. There had to be at least twenty years of involved watching before one could consider oneself 'caught up'.

He pushed his finger against the buzzer, thought back to that episode and strained to turn white all thoughts. But thinking even of a blank white slate probably counted as a thought. Were he living in science-fiction, Avery would have been reduced to a puff of dead vapor. Nobody said anything through the speaker. The locking mechanism buzzed like the violently battering wings of a beetle against a mirror. Avery pressed in. He walked up a staircase that led to a very large, very open room. There, he was met by Tara and two other girls.

"Here he is! We were just talking about you."

"Sorry I'm late," Avery said. It was 9:07. In keeping with the tradition of scheduling only round-numbered times, his agents wanted him there at 9:00. "It was a longer walk than I expected."

"You walked here?" one of the other girls asked before asking, "From where?"

"Kings Road. About a half mile in the opposite direction from Sloan Square. I think it turned out to be a little more than two miles from there to here."

"You poor thing!" she cried out with all the feminine drama that feminine men aspire to.

"Actually it was a nice walk. I feel awake now."

The girls took Avery to a rack of clothing to brainstorm. They were still awaiting the arrival of the other model. Tara went and stood against an enormous white wall, which drooped a smooth radius into the floor, fiddling with lights and tangles of cable. It was, Avery noted, a room built for fashion photography.

The two girls introduced themselves. Mary-Lou was there to do the styling, and Becca would do hair and make-up. Together, they would attempt to create a biker/folk-singer/dandy sort of mod/Native American/rich-boy boater thing. Perhaps it would be best, they decided, if Avery went shirtless. With shaded, subservient deference, Avery would just say 'sure, if that's what you think is best' to their every proposal. After the outfit was chosen, everyone sat down on white leather couches to tea and croissants.

Twenty minutes later, she showed.

Willowy, with downy skin that bent and bowed along succulent pathways, winding up and down five feet and eight inches of dazzling, visual je ne sais quoi. She left her hips exposed through a short, baggy t-shirt and low riding black jeans. One could only imagine her form gliding over unworthy streets, a strident energy forever tantalizing desires. Her nonchalance only served to amplify the oomph. Read the observer's mind; hear it roar, 'It's not fair! It's just not fair!'

"Sorry I'm late," she said, not sounding sorry at all. Sounding more like the sugar in Avery's tea. The jam on his flaky pastry. If there were no such thing as tomorrow, he would have run from the building, clinging childishly to the notion that perfection exists in the female construct. No human could possibly live up to the impression she made in the first five seconds. "Do you need me for something now or can I relax for a minute?"

Becca motioned toward the couches and went to set up her beautification equipment. Mary-Lou went sifting through her rack of clothing.

In her heels, she walked like a mountain goat down treacherous slopes, or a side-winder across the open dunes. High heels were clearly her natural environment.

Avery could do nothing more than bury his face in a book. The memory of his girlfriend would permit nothing else. He anticipated and dreaded in chorus a future of working with girls like this. He mutely implored her to notice him, hoping with every ounce of his being that she wouldn't. He was distracted to such an extent, that every paragraph had to be re-read, that his place on the page was constantly lost.

"Avery, can I borrow you for a moment?" Becca asked.

"Of course."

He sat down before a big mirror, and Becca began running her fingers through his hair. She pulled it back, pushed it forward, and guided it every direction in between.

"I think it looked quite nice when you got here," she said, restoring the style he came with, "We'll just leave it like it was. Is that right?"

Avery pushed the back of his hair down a bit. "Yep."

"Alright, then. That's that. Want another cup of tea?"

The process of applying her make-up was much more involved. Becca employed the use of brushes, liquids, glitters, cloths, and palates. And in the finale, her canvas stood up a different person.

The time had somehow come to nearly 11 o'clock. Avery downed one or two too many cups of tea in the meantime, and pictured his stomach looking something like a corpulent fishbowl. It was an increasingly imposing thought. His shirt would soon have to be removed. Shirtless in her presence, before the camera eye, and readers god-knows where. He should have been more mindful of such things. When finally Avery donned his shiny, skin-tight black pants, with boots, necklaces, and nothing else, he quietly asked Mary-Lou, "Are you sure about this?"

Just as quietly, "How do you mean?"

"Well, I mean are you sure people are going to think I look good in this? I feel like I should be in better shape or something."

Mary-Lou didn't say he was silly for thinking such a thing, as skinny people are usually told when they assert open opinions of a distorted body image. She did talk him out of worrying, however. He could do nothing but take her word for it. He walked in front of the ascending white wall, stopping, as instructed, at a piece of back tape on the ground.

"I know this is your first time doing this," Tara said behind her camera, "but there's nothing much to it. Just relax. Okay. That's nice. Hold your chin up a little. Not that much. Open your eyes just a little. There. Beautiful. We'll just do a few more like that." She snapped a couple more shots, dishing out wonderful complements all the while. Sometimes the compliments would make Avery laugh, and Tara would join him. All things considered, he felt very comfortable. For about five minutes- maybe more, maybe less, Avery had no way to track the progression of time from his vantage point, but for what felt like a short time, Tara took pictures and gave simple instructions.

And then she was next. Her eyes floated in a haze of light yellow beauty, her pronounced cheeks defied all the villainy, oppression, and bloodshed throughout the ages. Her legs were the supports upon which men reach their dreams. She was so much, that saying simply 'she was' is all that makes sense.

The outfit was something like intergalactic rock-star meets space goddess meets djinn sex slave meets ancient vestal magic sacrifice. She did not need instruction. She contorted her body in ways that made her taller, thinner. In charisma she grew before the impending audience, personifying first kiss, first lay, first love. Avery could not bring himself to watch.

They seemed to shoot for a long time. When they were finally finished, Tara said that lunch was on the way. They would all eat, take a few shots of the both of them, and call it a day.

Avery did not eat much, wary still of his naked torso. Lunch, as expected, greatly reduced his assessment of her. Now she looked to him a little bony, a bit too sharp in shape. She uttered vacant responses and seemed to lack the capacity for any kind of fascination. Women like her were destined either to live the life of a demimondaine or suffer the clutches of quasi-poverty alongside a selfish, perpetually jealous, mistreating scumbag of a lover. This, Avery told himself. He felt ready for a few more poses, a few good-byes, complete with symmetrical cheek kissings and well wishes, and a long walk home. He would get half way there before remembering that he forgot to wash the cover-up from his face.

CHAPTER 49

Imagine a man buckled between a floor and a corner. A broken wreck of a man- pallid, skeletal, looking like that great obelisk of Washington might look were it chopped down and left to rot. Place open sores upon his skin. Dry cracks on his over-red, blistered lips. The cold floor beneath him is stained with urine. His bones support a dwindling group of dormant tissues, unkempt or cared for. He can claim no tangible possessions. Nor are any friendships his. The forthcoming only echoes a stasis of present.

Not a creature on Earth is happier than he. Technically, there is a way.

Dwelling on the news from home was depressing. Not because it was depressing news- on the contrary, Michael seemed to be keeping himself very busy, and Michael keeping himself very busy meant Michael fulfilling ambitious goals. It was depressing to Avery because in the last two months, he had done comparatively little. It amounted to little more than running a few errands and making peanut butter and jelly sandwiches.

There were castings he'd been to. He'd familiarized himself with central London geography. Six photographers booked him for shoots (none of which paid more than sixty quid). He'd sent a few postcards home. He walked a lot. Lisa took him to the movies once or twice. A magazine came out with two pictures of him in it. He sent one to Michael. About once a week he would check his e-mail, and while he was on the computer he would mournfully check his bank balances. The wealth they represented was withering under the weight of British economy. In what he deemed the crowning achievement of his London endeavors, he'd read a number of books, watched a number of films, and felt fully capable of educating British and Americans of their respective country's secret histories. This of his interests, unfortunately, was digging a chasm in his and Lisa's relationship. But it was not the only thing that was.

Procuring a flat was becoming more and more of an issue. When they first arrived, Avery went into a Foxton's, opened a brochure, and looked at what the cheapest flats were going for. 'Okay,' he said to himself, '300 per week,' figuring that everyone in London must be paying a similar amount. He later realized that he was in one of the most expensive agencies in one of the most expensive parts of town, but not before a few smiling young salesmen sanguinely unlocked to him apartments he could never afford. Avery and Lisa each wanted a different thing and almost signed a lease to each extreme. Once in Chelsea, once in Chalk Farm. They pulled out of the Chelsea flat because it was too nice- rent was 290 per week plus utilities. Chalk Farm was not nice enough- there was a drunken man pissing on their stoop at 1:00 in the afternoon and all of Lisa's friends said it wasn't fit for a young lady. They sadly lost a deposit each time. If they didn't find a home soon, they'd be forced to take another hellishly expensive month in the 'student hostel'.

He was glad to be by himself at the moment, happier to still have a sip of beer in front of him. Stupid and costly mistakes, the nagging desire for real success, blame piercing him in some spots and bouncing off in others, lonesomeness- they welcomed him into city life. Bestowed a sense of belonging. Big city equivalence. Mourn with the rest of them.

"Aristotle, Plato, Socrates- A comes before P, P before S. In case you want to remember who taught who. Of them Plato was the greatest. Socrates took his ideas and complicated them. Plato said that only one version of everything exists, and everything we see is a bad copy. Socrates said that evil in the world makes the copies imperfect. So he added that. Hmm." The old man paused. "Give us another, then."

The bartender, who was all the while looking around, giving half-hearted, distant nods, began filling a glass.

"Knowledge is like a cage filled with doves and pigeons, Socrates said. Think of all the knowledge there is getting round the world today. All of it flies. Some of it is true and some of it isn't. Doves and pigeons. We reach for doves, but sometimes we get pigeons, don't we?"

As the old man's drink was put down, the bartender's eyes followed what might have been an invisible pigeon that flew in a circle around his face. That, or he was just bored. Wishing he were still in school, perhaps. Not at all satisfied by the man's bad breath or the supposed knowledge that coaxed it out.

Avery left his table for the bar. "I'll have another Stella, please."

And at that, the old man looked at him. "What are you doing wasting the day away in a pub, young man?"

Watching the empty glass gradually develop into a less empty glass, Avery said, "Same thing as you, I'd guess."

"And what's that?"

A feigned hesitation for effect- "Drinking."

"To you, young man."

Avery looked over, and saw the old man frozen in that classic 'cheers' pose. He looked as much a character in a Sherlock Holmes story as a contemporary man could look. His tweed hat sat on the bar next to him. His white hair a stark contrast to his dark cotton shirt, collared and short sleeved, which hugged his generous outcropping of belly as it tucked into his slacks. He exuded the air of both drifter and sophisticate.

233

"Thank you." Avery said back. It occurred to him then that the old man's company might be better than no company at all. He sat two stools down.

"Here on holiday, then?"

"No. I'm here indefinitely." Avery liked saying that. It sounded daring to his ears- rebellious, optimistic. To phrase it was a rugged cowboy chasing dangerous adventures and escapades, out-numbered but not out-willed.

"They probably told you that the streets of London were paved in gold, didn't they? That you could just reach your hand into the gutter and pull out a fist of pound coins."

"How do you know I'm not?"

"Are you?"

Avery admitted that, no, he wasn't.

"Ah. Me either. And what I do have to spend I spend on this," again the old man raised his glass, "the oldest vice of England. Without it, well…"

"I have this theory that after 11:30, every English man and woman on the streets is drunk."

"That's your theory, is it, lad?" The old man laughed. He said 'your' with an intonation that implied the theory didn't actually belong to Avery. "I was just telling this other young man a little about philosophy. Perhaps he hasn't the patience for it."

Beer seemed the perfect drug for this occasion. Avery spilt the satisfaction down, loving the English pint, that perfect, perfect serving. Next to him, the old man pivoted in his chair, grunted, huffed, pushed his body up, and walked to the bathrooms. The bartender stopped polishing glasses. He looked at Avery, said-

"Don't start him talking. Trust me. He comes in here all the time. Tries teaching me but he gets it all wrong. Earlier, he told me that Aristotle taught Plato and Plato taught Socrates. But that's wrong. Socrates was alive first, then Plato, then Aristotle. He's no fuckin genius."

The bartender had probably wanted to get that off his chest for the last few hours. The news was received with the raising of eyebrows (Oh, really?), nodding (Do go on.), and finally a stretching back of lips (You don't say?). The bartender went back about his business, Avery just sat.

When the old man came back, he wasted no time in initiating his lecture. It sounded as though he prepared the beginning of it in the bathroom.

"1954- Your countryman, James Olds shoots electronic pulses into rat brains and accidentally discovers the pleasure center. He finds that the rats prefer stimulation of this pleasure center to almost anything else. When they left it up to the rat, it would trigger its pleasure center eight thousand times an hour. Now, young man, how different is the human brain from the rat's? Is the sum of constant, harmless pleasure iniquity?"

For three more beers, they sat talking. How the old man could still speak in coherent sentences was beyond Avery. By his fifth pint, Avery looked in the mirror and saw a zombie. The conversation was interesting, though. The man kept talking about the experiments of James Olds and all the different ways he helped rats to get their rocks off. Avery listened to the free-flowing sermon, biting his tongue to questions and shaking off incongruous theories. All he could think of was how much control such a device would give a person over a group of people. Finally, he realized that he could say anything. It was just him, the old man, and the resolutely remote bartender. He spoke out of turn, off topic, on an off color subject-

"Have you ever heard the speculations that the royal families are blood drinkers? I mean, shape-shifters from another dimension? Some people think that they're all giant reptiles. Royal families and bankers and media moguls, all the power elite."

The old man did not blink.

Avery continued, "It sounds crazy, I know. But there's a lot about our civilization that's crazy. Misinformation is everywhere. I can't really believe in anything anymore. I've heard that manlike ape remains that were found in Africa ended up being like fourteen million years old. Two million years ago another kind of primitive man appeared. Damn. I can't remember the name. A...starts with an A. Anyways, then a million years after that Homo Erectus appears. Then, add almost another million years, and primitive man arrives. Neanderthal. In all that time there wasn't much difference between the two. They supposedly used the same tools and looked almost the same. Two million years, right?

"So then, about two hundred fifty thousand years ago, the first Homo Sapiens pop up in Africa. By all accounts that should be impossible. Evolution should be much, much slower than that. Then others are found in other places that are only thirty five thousand years old, but they were still doing the same shit. Using animal skins, bone tools, that kind of thing, so put Homo Sapiens at thirty five thousand years old. But my point is that it supposedly took two million years just for Neanderthal man to use sharper stones, and suddenly, after only thirty five thousand years, we went from bone clubs to sky scrapers. Television. Computers.

"The only thing that would explain it is alien intervention. And if that's true, there could have been more than one kind of alien. And if that's true, one kind could have been reptilian shape-shifters. And if that's true, they could still be ruling the world today. It would make sense that they run the world because if their technology was so much more advanced they'd have every chance to. This whole pleasure center shit would be old hat to them. Or maybe they gave the technology to us, or to James Olds. I don't mean that aliens would have been in direct contact with him or sharing that exact information- I mean the information that lead to all science, thousands of years ago. It's crazy but in a way it's not. People in this country once believed that 'God himself' chose the King. That's a pretty absurd notion, but it was taken seriously. Why is the existence of intelligent life other than us in the universe more or less dismissed by 'serious' people? I think there's a good chance that there is some truth behind all this. Maybe even to blood-drinking, ten foot tall, lizard overlords. Fuck, man- what do you think? The queen is an alien right?"

"Son," the old man said, "anybody who's anybody knows that."

CHAPTER 50

Evening found the room whirling on discontinuous axes. The turning room turned wheels, which in turn turned gears, spun cogs, pulled levers, triggered triggers, and pushed with gentle wind the dust off Avery's imagination. It was once a cherished attribute. Elaborate games of 'what if' played for him; he looked on with as much surprise as his audience would once stories took shape, as characters from other realms momentarily showed themselves. It had been months since Avery had written anything. He started a journal, but abandoned it only a few days after touching London. His muse was gone. Sunning on a brick driveway, probably. A thousand miles east and whistling.

In endeavoring to reveal the mind's eye, it seems that two paths are available. A writer may divulge his or her story, philosophizing the more subtle points of life along the way, telling the people things they already knew but didn't quite know how to say. In doing this, it is helpful to have lived long, experienced much, and weave mendacious tapestries under the panning eyes and nodding heads of readers. This method appeals first to the intellect and second to emotion. The other option, a technique many writers swear by, is to 'rip their hearts out'. They mean to appeal to the emotions, granting over-colored faux-experiences in fiction the utmost importance. They want to take you to Mars, push you in love, turn your stomach with grief. This can be done by telling tales of struggle. The struggle can be built in the characters' mind or world, can be delicate or marked, but 'that there must be conflict' is, to many, rule number one.

Avery had to think of something. His sense of artistic redundancy reacted violently to inebriation. It combusted in thought. Promises to wake up and write. To tell stories like he used to. To grasp for the reader's heart, supplement the reader's opinions- those people who, somewhere, sometime, would skim across the consciousness of past.

His first idea involved a Christmas party and starred a woman named Mary. Mary would be old. Dreadfully old. With a heart-wrenching bend to her spine and a multitude of heavy crevices to adorn her face. But despite the ever approaching prospect of death, Mary is usually in unusually good spirits. Her life had been a good one. She cherished her sense of humor and it remained always a crutch for her to lean on. Avery would describe the Christmas party as a wonderful event. A tradition. Eagerly anticipated year after year, complete with food, drink, and merriment. Attended by family and friends aged throughout the spectrum of adulthood. Lights, laughter.

'Who's got the number one?' the gregarious hostess of the party asked. Her son stood up, and with a great smile declared 'I do!' Nobody expected foul-play. It was that kind of party and they were that kind of people.

It would be easy to describe the game. Avery could do that from experience. His family played the game every year on Christmas Eve. Everyone brought a wrapped gift and placed it in a pile with other, equally ostentatious, shining bags and boxes. Numbers were passed out, and in that order the participants took their turns. The idea was, whoever drafted the number one would unwrap a gift at random. The number two person could then, looking at number one's gift, take a gift from the pile or take the thing that number one had. During each person's turn, they could take something from somebody or from the pile, and if someone's gift was taken it became their turn and they were able to make the same choice.

A flimsy rectangle that looked to be wrapped in the frozen image of a kaleidoscope's viewfinder.

Certain phrases would pop into his head, and he promised his head to remember them. He also would be sure to remember the premise of the story, which he was sure would provide the same gut-wrenching experience as holding hands with a cadaver.

The old woman, who the reader would have no

choice but to love, would be watching the gift exchange with genuine savor. She would laugh as the ownership of items changed and changed again. As the young men delighted in opening liquor bottles and paled as someone else claimed them. Mary would be placed surrounded by the guiltless joys of youth.

At one point, another older lady, perhaps a neighbor or long time family friend, would unwrap a box and find it filled with a pristine little cooking apron. Nick, or better yet, Samuel- the young man who brought the gift would laugh, insisting that she put it on, for he made it himself and she simply must try it out.

She wrapped the apron around her front, tied it behind her with hands just made for baking. It was so far the most appropriate pairing of gift and recipient. 'Try the towel,' Samuel urged. He was barely able to contain his mirth. The show, he and he alone knew, was about to begin.

Diplomacy would not allow the wearer to refuse. This nice young man had made the apron by hand, and even though she didn't particularly care to be the center of attention, this neighbor or this mother of some middle-aged woman had to oblige. She started to lift the towel that was attached to the front of the apron, and upon doing so the room would burst into riotous laughter.

Everyone could see it but her, and she stood quite quietly confused, still stretching the towel out in front of her and pretending to dry her hands on it, not knowing that attached to the towel that attached to the apron, a string was attached, and when the string was pulled up, a cotton replica of a floppy, thirteen inch cock was pulled up too. It was a masterpiece.

Over and over, Avery thought of ways to properly describe the apron. He thought of ways to describe the laughs, the good natured embarrassment it caused when the woman wearing it finally realized what was happening under the towel. The way that Mary laughed harder than anyone and everyone around Mary found it absolutely hilarious that Mary found it so hilarious. The way that Mary couldn't stop laughing. The way that, finally, the laughter was too much for Mary's weakened body to endure. She would die laughing on the couch, surrounded by a room full of people that included an artful prankster, a panic-stricken hostess, and another old woman in a penis-apron.

The night wore on. By degrees his mood grew darker. His imagination followed suit.

Tomorrow, Diego Guzman's story would be written so that someday, he might be introduced to the world. Diego would be a very macho, homophobic homosexual. He would resent himself for his sexuality.

Seven and a half inches of trembling shame preceded his torso.

Avery thought about starting the story that way and changed his mind. Actually, he didn't like the line and decided not to include it at all. The only thing he knew, was that the story would contain a single sexual encounter suffered by Diego and a nameless boy. Prepare to feel terrible for Diego, to identify with his indignity, to scold the human race and all its preconceived notions of manhood. Avery would put Diego in bed with a boy. Diego would pull his penis from the boy's rectum to find some peculiar blob sticking to him. In what Diego will do next, he is not thinking. His awareness hovers about beyond the shell. Diego is not home, but visiting-Diego's bottomless humiliation. He wipes the blob from the crown of his penis with his forefinger, holds it to his nose, examines the odor, and spews vomit all over the boy beneath him.

The reaction was instant. The scent sent a jolt through his brain, the jolt affected a purge of fluids and half digested foods from his stomach. Yellowish and pinkish, it shot out like a fire hydrant on a hot Bronx summer day. In this case, however, there was only one boy found splashing in it.

What follows- a return to consciousness. Diego becomes the equivalent of a husband walking into his bedroom to find his wife being fucked by another man, only Diego must fill the role of both enraged husband and soiled wife. Diego snaps, his arms become turbines, winding a rash of slaps and punches, connecting with a back, ribs, a nose, an ear, a jaw, each eye, and a temple. Avery wanted to describe the contact. He would say how there was more 'give' in the boy's face than Diego expected. That it felt like punching a wall but instead of it hurting the drywall just makes way and crumbles. From good time to savage beating. The other boy was never in a position to defend himself. But though Diego emerged the naked conqueror, his own sense of honor was far from salvaged.

Come morning, Avery woke up with a headache. He was already bored before he even kicked his sheets off. He was thinking of some stories the night before-he remembered that. But they were bullshit. The only reason he thought they were any good was because he was drunk and delirious. Neither plot could come off as even remotely believable. Offensive, concurrently outlandish and trite; they were things that he could not say and get away with, not in good taste. He could offer no illustrious insights into the universe, nor had he enough strength in his writing hand to pierce the breastplate. Fucking pipedreams.

Lisa was still sleeping in her bed. Avery jacked off in the bathroom since he didn't do it the night before, took a shower, dressed slowly, and decided finally to rouse her.

CHAPTER 51

Dag-*blast* it! Of all the cheap goddamned wastes of magic!

To his dismal and derelict frustration, Guy's trick of the fingers was no longer working. He found himself worried over future contact with his wife, scared of the knock at his office door, and wanted nothing more than to just sell everything, pick up and go, and probably would have if picking up and leaving wasn't such a petrifying prospect. Guy was in no temper for company. He considered the option of playing possum. But that the person outside might somehow know he was inside just ignoring them made Guy very nervous.

An image opened in a pendulum-like arc- Guy's office. It was plain, shy, pasty, substandard in décor. Plain for its lack of furnishing, shy for its absence of ornamentation, pasty for its lack of color, substandard for the quality of fittings. It looked like the office of a grade-school phys-ed teacher, minus playground equipment and plus a desktop computer. Outside, looking in, holding a can of Red-Bull he'd just bought from 'Don't Think Twice (it's alright)', was Michael.

"Oh, thank God," Guy said.

"Hey, Guy. Expecting someone else?"

"No, not that. I just don't want to see *anyone* right now."

"Damn, I'm sorry. I wasn't coming by for anything important. I'll just see you later, okay?"

"I didn't mean you, Michael. You're a good kid, you know that? Come on in. I just meant other people. Business and what have you. I've been a wreck lately." And he surely had been. An anxious, timid mess. Constant psychosomatic shakes and shivers.

Michael sat down at one of the small chairs before Guy's desk. The room itself was petite. Enough space for three people to exist with four walls around them and little else.

"Is there anything I can do to help?"

"Probably not. Not unless you can find me a tenant for A-6, anyway."

Michael nodded. "I'll tell you what I can do- I can offer you a chance to forget all your troubles this very afternoon. We're getting a volleyball game together at 5:30. A bit of healthy competition, eh? You feel up for it?"

Normally such a proposition would have thrilled Guy down to his socks, but now his thoughts reacted with visions of injury, failure, and humiliation. He felt utterly unfit to play on either side; however those sides might be put together.

"Eh, I don't know. I probably shouldn't. I have a lot going on today. I should really just get all this stuff taken care of."

"Are you sure? We could really use you."

The response was an additional detonation to Guy's confidence. His self-respect, self-confidence, self-assurance a crumbled building under blitzkrieg assault.

As if the lie were detected, as if he could do nothing right.

"No. Yes, I'm sure. I'm sorry."

"Okay. If you change your mind we'll be at the court." Michael tossed his Red-Bull back but to his surprise it was already gone. "I'll be hoping that someone comes and rents that space soon. Try not to fret about it."

Guy said thanks, they said goodbye, Michael left, and Guy touched his middle finger to his thumb. He was only greeted with thoughts of helplessness, debt, and seasons in the abyss.

More knocking. The noise prompted the same reaction in Guy as it did before. Dig a hole and bury your head. Aim, pull the trigger, and blow off your head. These and other escapist pursuits regaled his attention along with the knock.

The knocking came again along with an annoying, "Hello? Anybody home?"

Guy wiped his eyes and answered by unlocking his door and turning the knob. The face staring back at him did nothing to sooth uncertainties. Johnny Mall was the man's name.

"Good afternoon. I'm Johnny Mall." He said in a slightly southern drawl. Johnny looked like what one of the men that adorn covers of pulp action/detective novels would look like if they spent all their lives sidestepping adventure, didn't work out or shave, dressed like an on duty construction worker, never scored honorable ladies, and had what seemed to be a persistently sweaty head. "Are you Mr. Weeks?"

"That's right." Guy said.

"I'm here about the property for rent."

"Oh. Well, come in."

The men shook hands. Guy's end of the gesture

came off uncharacteristically weak and clammy.

"Are you familiar with the area?"

Mr. Mall shook his head yes. "I live right down the road. Always thought this would be a good strip to start a business, to be honest."

"Sure, sure. Being on the corner of two major roads is a big plus, I-95 is just a stone's throw away. We're also fortunate enou…"

And then to Guy's ears an interruption, a miracle-"Now hang on a second, you don't got to sell me on the area. I know I want the place. I'd like to take one poke around the grounds themselves just to be certain, but I'm practically sold. And I'll tell you what it is, Mr. Weeks- it's the names. It's practically free advertisement. Sometimes the name's more important than the place itself.

"Look here- you might have three guys sitting around one night looking for some place to go, right? Now let's say these guys know about three places, each place is just a bar- they serve drinks and you pay for em. But let's say one of those places has a name that guys love to say! That's the place you're going."

"And you've already thought of a name? That correlates with the nature of your business, that is?"

"I have. 'The Bottom's Up'."

"Hmm. Not bad. A bar called 'The Bottom's Up.' I like it."

"Not just a bar, sir. Of course we're going to sell liquor, but I'm going to do you one better and put some naked women in the joint. I'm talking bottoms up and bottoms up." He put a brilliantly sleazy emphasis on the second 'bottoms up'.

Guy felt his stomach rise like a U-boat in friendly waters. His wife would not approve. His other tenants would not approve. His other tenants' customers would not approve. There would be conflict and controversy, discords and disputes.

"A strip bar?"

"That's right."

"I'm afraid that I'll have to discuss this with my business partner."

"Sure, call him up. I just want to get this ball rolling. Any paperwork I can get a head-start on reading?"

"Not now. It's my wife. My business partner is my wife."

Johnny didn't seem to grasp the relevance of that. He nodded and said 'okay' as if Guy had just said 'my absolute favorite color is brown'.

"I don't think she'll be crazy about the idea of a strip club moving in," Guy expounded, "Do there have to be women there? Nude women?"

"Damn right. I'm not going to let you talk me in to some other kind of investment here, buddy. Definitely not on account of your wife's Christian values. Hell, I'm a Christian myself."

Guy touched his thumb to his middle finger. He felt like crying.

Meanwhile, not two miles away, J.P. was rear-ended something awful at a red light. His nose broke against the steering wheel and his mid-section was bruised against the seat belt, but the worst part was that the car, which had been running for days without gas, was completely totaled. He would never again own a car that ran on miracles.

CHAPTER 52

Due to the upset suffered by a dear friend, volleyball was called off. Michael instead gathered some of the guys to sit with J.P. It was, for some, a time of mourning. Whiskey and weed were offered. It was, for some, a wholesome excuse to get fucked up. Towards the end of the night, as blunted brains became clumsily poetic, Luke said that J.P.'s eyes each looked like they were being held up by Harriet Tubman. J.P. said that they hurt- but this exchange happened much, much later. At present, Guy is just getting home from work.

No hello. No honey I'm home. Just a door opening, closing, locking, and the deep thud of bare heels on a tile floor.

"Guy?"

"Yes, it's me. Hello, dear."

Mrs. Weeks trotted down the stairs to meet him.

"How was work?"

Guy was a moment in answering. "I know people are at least reading the ad. A man came in today and wanted to rent from us. He'd thought of a name and everything."

There was a lack of celebration in her husbands voice. She asked him what went wrong.

"He was going to name the place 'The Bottom's Up.' As in buttocks. He wanted to open a strip club."

"Well?"

"What do you mean, 'well'? You don't want a strip club opening in our mall. It's bad business."

"But it's business, Guy! We're losing eight thousand dollars a month and all of a sudden you're holistic? Call him back! Fax him the lease!"

Normally, when his wife lost her mind to argument, Guy would do one of two things- say something biting and walk off to the clean the kitchen, bedroom, bathroom, or whatever the least likely to be occupied part of the house was, or he would remain impeccably logical and correct his wife's lack of logic with calm, cool common sense. He did not currently know what to do. His hands were shaking and wouldn't even form the signal of emotional safety blanket, the modified A-OK.

"Move! Call him or sell that goddamned Land Rover! Get those knife ladies! You keep fucking up and fucking up and fucking up!"

She was really flying off the rockers now. And poor Guy Weeks, he could do nothing but stand and sulk like a brow beaten child.

J.P. was sulking, too. His baby, shiny black with equally dark tinted windows, a deafening trunk mounted speaker, and an engine that, though completely stock, responded to his every 'jump!' with a turbo charged 'how high?' was gone for good. Michael recited a fine eulogy, and though it was more of a joke than anything it produced the same constricted feeling in J.P.'s throat as a Sunday school neck tie. In such company, however, the death of a motor vehicle could only remain the focus for so long.

"He's getting into more concrete theories now," Michael said of his brother, "less of the occult, numinous sort of thing, more along the lines of real political and social manipulation. Last time I talked to him he was listening to old William Cooper recordings. Cooper was a pretty famous conspiracy theorist who wrote a book called 'Behold a Pale Horse' and hosted an AM radio show called 'The Hour of the Time'. Dude was shot outside his own home by out of uniform police officers by the way. Depressing stuff. But yeah, that's the sort of thing Avery's interested in these days. Checking referenced materials and doing his own research."

"He's only going halfway, man. It's not just about that," Luke said. He was very drunk, obviously not used to drinking Jack Daniel's straight from the bottle, "The star of David has already gone. Of course there's political manipulation. Presidents aren't elected, they're selected."

J.P. stated his disagreement, and Luke said, "You're fucking past it, man. You're past it."

Sitting beside J.P. was Jamul, whose look signified either boredom, confusion, intellectual superiority, or something else entirely (it actually was something else entirely- Jamul was stoned, and for some reason he didn't want to ask if it was cool to use the bathroom so he was busy holding in his shit). His attention seemed to pan between each corner of the garage. When the bottle of Jack came back to him he declined.

"My car, man. Goddamn it!" Every so often J.P. would crack and make a similar outburst. He also wondered aloud more than once why and how his car had been getting such incredible gas mileage before the accident.

"Probably your dad was filling it up or something." Jamul offered. He was happy to talk as long as it wasn't about politics or astrology or the American forefathers cannibalizing infants or toilet seat manufacturers' desire to harvest the sexual energy of masturbators by naming their company logo after a forgotten god. During these discussions he clammed up.

"Yeah, probably," J.P. said.

"Fuck the car, man. I mean it's a shame, but you

escaped with your life and your body intact. For the most part, anyway. That broken nose is going to make you look tough for the rest of your life. The girls are going to love it," said Michael.

But J.P. wasn't convinced. It took three phone calls to three different girls to allay his concern. He said that if it were up to him, he still wouldn't have a broken nose.

The whiskey had nearly run dry. J.P. was wondering aloud how he would spend the insurance money, whether he would just get another SRT-4 or invest in some other model car. Michael was speaking on the merits of American muscle cars, as taught by Mr. Thurbin when Luke, completely without provocation, erupted with-

"And it's all just decided at Bohemian Grove. You know about this, Michael, but I know that J.P. and Jamul don't. Bohemian Grove is a secluded section of Redwood forest in California, like three thousand acres across. The Bohemian Club puts people from all different positions of power together so they can discuss how to bolster the power base."

Attempts at stoppage were made, but Luke kept right on talking, getting louder and louder until the only options were to throw him out of the house or let him keep speaking. The noise levels he was reaching were enough to wake Michael's parents. "Just shut the fuck up and listen! Learn something. There. The Manhattan Project was started there. It's something they actually boast about. They put industry leaders from all different areas in the same bunk so they can work together and consolidate power. I'm talking major politicians, military officials, corporate execs, heads of media conglomerates, oil companies, banking companies, you name it.

"And let me tell you about what they do there. They get together in these wizard, umm, monk, or warlock or whatever- hooded, hooded garbs- anyway they dress up in these outfits with hoods and burn this effigy that they call 'Dull Care'. It's supposed to represent their worries and cares, as if they want to live without a conscience. These guys who control large portions of the world, a lot of them claim to be Christians, and they're dressed up dancing around statues of Pagan gods. The party grounds themselves are actually a nature preserve; nature, Paganism," Luke moved his hands, palms up, up and down beside each other. It was the 'don't you get it?' topsy-turvy scale thing. "Are you listening to this Jamul? Don't you think it's curious? I mean this shit actually happens. And you guys, man, you don't give a fuck. You think you're so smart. Fucking televisions, American Idol and shit."

"I love how he's really articulate one moment, and then the next he's slurring, and the next he's fine, and finally he drives the point home with an outrageously gratuitous accusation," Michael said to J.P. "And he watches way more T.V. than I do."

Luke had apparently used the last of his energy. He would need a minute to look at the floor, regain his balance, and decided if smoking a cigarette would be permissible. Michael snatched it from his lips, which were late in responding with a fatigued, "What the fuck, man?"

Very sheepishly, as if he were confessing to some great sin, divulging some great secret, Jamul asked if he could use the toilet. Luke stood up for a reason known only to him, but seemed to grow uncomfortable once his body was fully upright and sat back down. Michael challenged him to a game of ping-pong, but only because he knew that Luke was too drunk to accept. J.P. had resorted to expressing his mood with murmured expletives. This, in warm October, was the air of the evening.

CHAPTER 53

They were jerky, grating, offensive- broken records skipping over and over again, during the most depressing parts in songs of bad choices and human destitution. They were, most of them, malnourished. Some kind of strapping desire kept them moving, walking around, discarded wind-up toys delivering their feeble pitches to the passers-by. Like used up dragons they emitted a soft steam from their breath. Nobody knows if they shake from cold or addiction.

"Can you help me? Can you help me?"

"Listen, mate- now before you say no…"

"I just need one pound eighty…"

"Any change, mate? Anything at all? It sounds like you got some change…"

These were familiar phrases. Popular beginnings.

Beyond the first gauntlet, there waited a second. This one was comprised of a different breed of men, but had to be passed in much the same manner. Avoid eye contact, a subtle head movement 'no' if directly addressed, a 'nah, that's alright' if persistently asked by the same individual. Their pitches usually consisted of only one or two words, and they were handling much greater quantities of money than the down and outs who wanted change but offered nothing in return.

Hear- "Skunk."

Or- "Skunk weed."

There were of course times when walking the second gauntlet would be seen as fortuitous, and not at all annoying.

Lots of other things were happening outside of the Brixton tube station, but the aspect of this scene that Avery found extraordinary was that it was all going down at 9:28 in the morning. He was 'working'- and apparently, so was everybody else. Everybody doing their utmost to taste compensation-flavored morning-worms.

Just before the fingernail of Avery's middle finger there was a circular cut. It had been gushing blood the whole time he was on the train, and now the tissue he was stopping it with was completely soaked with red. The injury happened when Avery was digging through his bag in the dark. A Mach 3 razor was resting face up at the bottom and it took a bite out of his hand.

When he arrived at the address he set out for, Avery had only a split second to remove his finger from his mouth, which now tasted like tangy iron. A small Japanese girl opened the door. She greeted him and invited him inside with such rare, friendly enthusiasm that Avery put his finger back into his mouth, sucked off more blood, took it out, waited a second, and showed her the wound. Even in those short seconds blood pooled.

"Could I trouble you for a tissue or paper towel or something? I'd really hate to drip blood anywhere. Cut myself shaving," he said making a bad joke. The odds were stacked astronomically in favor of her not getting it.

"Oh my!"

She rushed off like a pest on the kitchen floor when someone flicks the lights on. When she came back she was all concern and sympathy.

"Does it hurt? Should I get you some ice? How long has it been bleeding? Are you okay? Let me get you a band-aid. Cold water. Do you need to clean it? How did it happen?" And so on. Her last question proves that she did not get the 'cut myself shaving' joke.

Avery assured her that he 'would live', that no more 'first aid was necessary', that he was ever so 'thankful for her concern', 'you're a very gracious host', but it's 'just a little scratch', and will surely 'be fine'.

In her expression was a look that didn't buy any of it. To look directly into her eyes was to think your eyes were staring out of somebody's gory, gaping, shot-filled stomach.

"No, it's fine. I promise. I really can't even feel it." Avery told her.

"Well, okay. If you're sure you're okay."

"Definitely."

She raised her eyebrows and turned her head 45 degrees away from him. "You can have a seat on the couch if you want, Niko's probably just getting dressed."

So this was Niko's apartment, and that was Niko's girlfriend, and Niko was the photographer who would be giving Avery and his book the once over and ultimately deciding if his face was pretty enough. Avery took his bag off, sat down, and started reading.

On the Divine Right of Presidents-

One need look no further than the genetic lineages of presidential candidates to determine who will garner the most American 'votes'. Since George Washington, John Adams, and Thomas Jefferson, each and every president of the United States of America has, somewhere down the vast alleys of his heritage, blood relations to a single European royal family- the Merovingians.

255

With skeptical curiosity, Avery made a mental note to check into this for himself. The book listed its resources as 'Burke's Peerage' and information from the New England Historical Genealogical Society. In addition to claiming that every American presidential election has been won by the candidate with the most royal European blood, it also claimed that 33 Presidents of the United States of America are related to Charlemagne, and 19 have blood connections to the English King Edward III. If it were true, Avery's faith in American democracy would cease to exist.

Another young man was let inside. He was told by the same eager to please voice that instructed Avery to sit down for a moment to sit down for a moment. Avery couldn't help but resent the other presence in the room. They were vying for the same position, with their similar haircuts and complexions, comparable outfits, builds, even the same methods of waiting quietly for a photographer to get dressed.

Niko's hair was still wet when he walked into the living room. A small white hand towel was draped over the back of his neck. He did not ask who had arrived first, but instead took the other model's book and flipped through it. Avery noticed that, like himself, the competition did not have many pages of his book filled. Niko handed the book back, said thank you, and as the other guy stood up and made his way out, reached out to see pictures of Avery.

"Nice. This was the British GQ?"

"Yeah," Avery responded, "That was my second job ever. I've done some more stuff but we're still kind of waiting on things to come out."

Niko nodded in understanding. "This is nice, too. Did your agency tell you anything about the shoot?"

"No."

"Oh. It's for an Italian fashion magazine. It's a new thing, kind of raw, no glossy pages or anything but it's pretty cool. I think we'll be doing three or four outfits."

"Sounds good."

By then Niko had exhausted all the pages that Avery had to show for his career. He said, "Yeah. Thanks for coming by. Avery, right?"

"Yeah."

"Okay, Avery. Take care."

"Thanks. You, too."

There was somebody familiar on the sidewalk just a half a block away. He was standing there looking at his map. When Avery walked passed, the guy looked up, eye contact was made, and there was almost no choice but to say hello. Avery figured that while this young man was his competition, he could also be considered a co-worker.

"Hey."

"Hey, man."

Avery asked if he was walking back to the tube station. The guy said 'yes'.

"I remember how to get back there. You want to just walk with me?"

"Sure."

"What's your name?"

"Jack."

"I'm Avery. Are you with the same agency as me?"

They began walking. "What's that, FM?"

"Yeah."

"Um-hmm."

"Just start doing this?"

"Yeah, like a week ago. You?"

"Couple months. Hey, do you have any other castings today?"

"No."

"Fuck. Me either."

Just then a rail-thin man with dots all along his arms and marks that looked like they were made by years and years of obsessive scratching scuttled across the street.

"Dodgy neighborhood," Jack said.

"Yeah. Seems like it. One thing I will say for all these crack heads, though- I have to admire their ambition. I know I wouldn't be awake right now if I didn't have to be. What is it, not even ten o'clock?"

"No, mate. They're not getting up early," Jack said with a knowing, moderate frown, "They just haven't been to bed yet."

Any regard that Avery once had for the beggars of Brixton was pushed aside by this new perspective. He and Jack walked back to the tube station, stopping momentarily at a crowded bus stop so Jack could buy a handful of grass, or as it was articulated by man who sold it to them in a bass, barking shout, 'Skunk'.

CHAPTER 54

The dark time- hours made possible to function in by man's manipulation of the world around him. Avery was knee-deep in the evening hours that once meant work. These days, however, like the rest of his irresponsible generation, his mind set to cataloging and rating the entertainment options available, considering points of projected cost margins, moral restrictions, time limits, physical boundaries, the business world's staunch scheduling conflicts with dreams and fun, and what was expected of him by other people. The last point pretty much planned his night for him. He would be with Lisa, visiting her friends from school. One of them was throwing a housewarming.

Things got, not uncomfortable or weird, but a feeling akin to weird and uncomfortable as soon as Avery stepped into the house. He introduced himself to a girl that he'd already been introduced to, through Lisa, not one week earlier. He said, "Sorry, I guess I didn't recognize you. Were you wearing those glasses when I met you?"

"Yes."

"Did you get a haircut or something?"

"No."

Avery didn't know this, but Pamela Pearl got this treatment all the time. At every party she went to, someone would inevitably look at her and say 'I didn't recognize you!' with a friendly smile and sometimes a fervent 'Oh my God!'. She was asked once every few days if she had effected some major change to her appearance, which she never had. Nobody in London ever asked if Pamela Pearl was her real name, which it wasn't.

Soft voices in the kitchen clambered atop each other. All wanted to be heard, heeded, and held in undue esteem. There wasn't much around to drink. A few bottles of cheap chardonnay were being calculatingly blocked by a few young men and women. Lame, lame, lame.

When Avery found Lisa, she was listening to a classmate talk about class. Sad, feeling completely bereft of what otherwise might have been a fun Friday night,

Avery announced himself.

Lisa shot up with excited glee. She wrapped her arms around Avery, squeezing with all her might.

"Avery, this is my friend Betsy." Lisa said. She was forming a habit of making introductions in the accent of an old woman from Newcastle with a stuffy nose.

"Oh, he's fit," Betsy said to Lisa.

Avery told her he was in danger of blushing.

There was then a moment of awkward silence, followed by a moment of awkward dialog.

Betsy said, "So I hear you're quite the pot-smoker."

Being labeled a pot-head was never something that Avery liked. Yes, he used to smoke a lot of pot. Morning, noon, and night, he would smoke pot, but the subtext under the term 'pot-head' didn't do well to define him as a person. Or at least that's what Avery liked to think.

"Not really. I haven't touched the stuff since we moved here in July. Probably don't qualify for that title anymore."

"Oh. You don't say?" Betsy used the same accent as Lisa used to introduce them. Betsy and Lisa laughed, made faces at each other, and said 'you don't say?' a few times back and forth. While all this was going on, Avery didn't know exactly where to look. He found himself, as Lisa got sillier and sillier, growing more and more stolid by the exact same degree.

"You should find Tucker, Avery," said Lisa, "He's got some weed he'd probably share with you."

"Let's find Tucker."

In this vast dimension of our universe, the canon of possibility extends cosmic gallops in every direction.

Picture imagination. Know that of all the myriad kinds of people, there are two Tuckers. He can be a tall man with meaty bones, square jawed, with a visible scar or two and worn-in jeans, who fishes, drives an old truck, who grew up within walking distance of a creek or river, and who throughout every stage of his life has owned at least one pair of boots caked with good-old American mud. There is also a thin boy, owning locks of long, wispy blonde hair, a quiet and slightly goofy demeanor, a fragile nose, prominent larynx, worn-in jeans, who grew up in London and has never seen good-old American mud on boots or otherwise. Truth be told, the first Tucker, even in this measureless, all encircling universe, is completely fictional. It was the reedy boy version of Tucker who was sitting in the garden.

"Everybody, this is my boyfriend, Avery."

Hellos were said in settled, subdued voices. Tucker offered Avery a seat on the grass and began to roll another spliff. Avery wanted to burst out a happy 'right on time!' but deferred instead to proper decorum and remained silent.

"You like to smoke weed, man?"

"Sure. I love to smoke weed," Avery answered.

"How are you finding the weed in England?"

"This will be the first time I've had any, actually."

"Oh, you're in for a treat, mate. This is some grade-A skunk."

"Looking forward to it. Thanks."

Tucker was just finishing up. The lines of his spliffs were always perfect, and he saw rolling a good one as a genuine skill, a trade more like. He was the kind of person that would unroll a joint someone else made and redo it if it wasn't to his standards. For him, it was indecent to smoke a spliff if it was of unbalanced thickness, too wrinkled, or too loose. Tucker wore his pot-head badge with the pride of decorated military men.

"Here man, you second."

What a fine bunch of chaps these were- to welcome a total stranger into their circle on the garden, a garden not much different from the ones Oscar Wilde so often spoke of, to offer him a fine joint to smoke, inquire as to whether or not he was enjoying the drugs of their kingdom- what a fine bunch.

Avery put the cigarette to his mouth, took a righteous drag, and coughed his lungs out.

"That's...that's some..." he waited, "That's some harsh shit, man. ... Fucking harsh." He said, speaking still through violent hacks. Hacks that ripped through his throat, rattled the innards of his neck, each burning like the glowing ammunition of roman candles. "Why is that shit so fucking harsh?"

"Don't know."

The problems with the 'harsh joint' started and ended with Avery. It did not seem to bother anyone else in the garden. They just puffed away, merry little deviants, between the brick-red and brick-brown brick walls. Avery felt embarrassed. He spent the whole time wondering, while the spliff was going around, whether he should receive it again when his turn came. He decided that he must.

"I don't know man," Avery said, "It just seems really harsh." Obviously his first impression was a complete and total bust. He knew that in their eyes he must seem like a total new-jack, a bellyaching new-jack, a relentless baby unable to conduct himself in the garden of simple pleasures, good for his pretty face and nothing else, a paper tiger whose spirit would collapse under the strain of a cold shower. He took another couple hits, figuring that if they thought that, he could just feign an ignorance of the transnational joint-smoking rules, take a few puffs out of turn and nobody would blame him. "Thanks guys. I'm going to go back inside. That smoke is just too coarse for me. Too thick or something. I don't know. But thanks."

In a house that he didn't much care for, with a group of people he simply couldn't relate to, Avery played the proverbial bump on a log. Lisa was saddened by her boyfriend not getting along with everyone, and Avery's mood essentially ruined hers. They split much earlier than Lisa would have liked, and much later than Avery would have liked.

Leave the two of them on circle line back to Sloan Square. It would not due to watch the argument that ensued. It did not make either of them look like reasonable human beings. At least, none of the occupants of the same car they carried on in thought so. One man that was coming home from a late night's work even called Avery a wanker, but he said it so softly that Avery didn't hear.

CHAPTER 55

A few beers did much to reveal the reptilian portions of Mr. Thurbin's intellect. All night Michael was worried that he'd be caught in the middle of a brawl, what with the intense looks and indiscriminate insults that blanketed the bar, courtesy of the modern-day greaser.

"Oh, what the fuck's that fat ass going to do about

it, huh? Sloppy son of a bitch."

"Christ," Michael said, "why don't you just kill everyone here and get it over with? You're acting like an animal."

Mr. Thurbin bit his teeth together. Why couldn't the kid be a little more confrontational? Shit- he wasn't a coward, Mr. Thurbin knew that from the way they talked to each other. You can always tell a coward by the way their eyes hide when there's static. Michael wasn't scared, he just wasn't mean. Mr. Thurbin wanted to show him the virtues of malevolence.

The psychologist might accredit Mr. Thurbin's drive to exert his dominance to a general lack of self-identification. In our changing present, as mass media has continued to impact contemporary man's sense of identity- the effected will cease to know themselves by comparison to the real men and women in their lives, but instead by the overvalued, exaggerated personalities projected by film and television. These personalities, heroes and villains all, concocted to frighten, enthrall, and empower, have shifted the subconscious boundaries of the real and imaginary. Man, as depicted by mass media, fills his shoes with the power of menace- and men in the real world have come to identify with the tough super-cop, the remorseless mobster, the maniacal dictator, the dragon slayer, and the reckless, quixotic street fighter. The world as it is known is as it is shown on the tube. Know detective and serial killer, mogul and tramp, angel and demon, prude and slut, the conquer and the vanquished, the victimizer and the victim. Every time the victimizer and the victim.

The psychologist would be wrong, again. At the core of Mr. Thurbin's essence burns fire and brimstone. This can be explained by nothing. It simply is.

"Who the fuck is responsible for this music?"

It was something he'd been complaining about all night. Michael said, in a jaded tone, "It's a jukebox. People always play bad music on jukeboxes."

"Tell me the next time you see someone on it."

"Why?"

"Because I'm going to do something about it."

"Just what do you mean you're going to do something about it?"

"I mean just tell me when the fuck you see the next person picking music. If you can't do that maybe you can walk home."

Michael stood up, took out his wallet, placed ten dollars on the bar, looked to Mr. Thurbin and said, "This is getting old, man. I'm out of here."

As Michael walked toward the door, Mr. Thurbin called him a bitch. Michael just laughed and shook his head in a kind of nonchalant incredulity.

"Little pussy bitch," Mr. Thurbin said to himself.

But his antagonism towards the kid evoked an alien feeling inside him. It was like smacking a child across the mouth, and watching blood run down the innocent lips. It was a penetrating word to a woman, and the agony in her face for hearing it. He felt himself pulling apart, unraveling, and drowning. Purposefully, he walked after Michael. They nearly bumped into each other at the door.

"Hey, I was just coming inside to get you," Michael said.

"Why? What's up?"

"Look."

Michael pointed to Mr. Thurbin's car. His finger ushered inevitable violence, directed the traffic of a brewing hurricane- for standing on the roof of my Thurbin's beloved Mustang was a very drunk young man

265

being cheered and goaded on by a small crowd of friends. This scene breathed purpose into Mr. Thurbin's anger.

"I'm going to give you one chance," Mr. Thurbin said, his voice sounding loud across the parking lot, stern and steady and humorless and giving plenty of evidence that the man behind it meant nothing but business, "One chance to get off that car without touching another inch of it."

Dutch courage showed on the boy's face. He wasn't a scrawny kid by any means, he looked like he could have been the star of a high school football team, and what's more, he had five friends with him. He didn't react immediately to Mr. Thurbin's command, but instead just stood staring.

"One second to jump off. Dent that roof in the process and I'll fucking kill you."

Thump.

That's what it sounded like when the kid dropped to his butt, caving in a significant portion of polished black exterior. The next thump occurred when Mr. Thurbin grabbed the overgrown boy by his feet and dragged him a four foot, unforgiving drop to the pavement. He landed on his left elbow, crying out on contact.

Nobody knew what to do. They all just stood there, watching in frozen disbelief, frozen in fright, all five of them. It was an event vicious enough to cause a loss of memory, and the details are even now, to everyone but Mr. Thurbin, fuzzy. All that could be known for sure was that a young man's midsection was being devastated by a frenzy of kicks, given until Mr. Thurbin's slicked back hair busted loose from its form, until he was out of breath and the boy on the ground was out of consciousness.

When it was all over, Michael and Mr. Thurbin

got in the car and drove away. The boys began to move to help their friend. One of them was on the phone, probably speaking to an emergency services dispatcher.

The punishment had been unyielding. Michael was still somewhat sick over seeing it. But the engine was resonating. Mr. Thurbin was pushing the car to its limits, making what was almost sure to be a clean getaway.

Power, Michael thought abstractly. Power before him, power next to him, the upsetting result of power heaped on the ground behind him, power, probably, in him. A fair man could not blame Mr. Thurbin for doing what he did. And Michael noted a certain bent appeal in possessing the audacity to beat somebody senseless. It was a romantic ode to the true nature of man, poetically rejecting the restraints society would impose. The allure of kinetic ultra-violence- it was something Michael thought he might actually come to value.

CHAPTER 56

The fashion industry isn't much different than the pictures it trades in. It is a thoughtful profile with rosy cheeks staring a bright gaze in the afternoon. It is a confident posture; the face is cut off at the lips but the body- the body is poised with ideal, unconcerned bend because he knows that his colorful adornments will burn into the memories of every passing stranger. It is two men and a woman in bed, all their plastic passions and confidences, basking in wealth and glamour and magnetism and indulgence. It is a boy- his fragile face hovers emotionless over a shoe made of ten different reptile skins. If it is not Keanu Reeves, it is a person who looks just like him standing in a stuffy hotel room, trying to get comfortable in an elegant suit of bone-whites and chamomile-yellows that run down his body like so many raindrops. It is a straight on shot, with a face of moderate confusion, a child playing at adulthood.

It is Avery standing unnatural stances in a lobster-red jump-suit, holding a cow-print day-bag next to Yulia, before a clean-white paper backdrop in a photographer's backyard.

"Beautiful," Niko said. He lowered the camera as he had been doing after every four or five exposures, and struck a pose he wanted Avery to copy. All day he was saying how great Yulia was, but so far Yulia hadn't spoken a single word.

With his left hand stretched as far as possible across his body, gripping his right shoulder blade, his legs crossed, his bottom lip held suggestively between his teeth, Avery wasn't much different from the fashion industry. He was also cold and shaking rather noticeably.

"Nice. Right there. Just one more. Beautiful." Again, Niko took his eyes from the viewfinder, turned slightly to the right and grabbed a handful of his own hair. "Other way. To the left." Niko prompted.

"Your left?"

"If it's not your left it's my left."

Avery pivoted, feeling a little foolish at having called him on the 'your left' thing. Forcing every thought and opinion and suggestion from his brain during shoots could be exhausting. The only time he was really allowed to have a character was during lunch, and if it wasn't too early in the morning, while everyone was busy preparing. Showing up was the beginning and end to his responsibilities at work. And here was Yulia-

Her face was an ear to ear anesthetization to every emotion. Joy, sorrow and the in-betweens. She was a doll. She was a polished anestrous android. Whatever Suessian worlds of colors and characters existed in her head was not displayed in the glow of her countenance. Niko kept saying, 'isn't she great?', 'isn't she wonderful?'.

Avery and Lisa had three more days in the hostel on King's Road. The chances of finding a permanent home before then were slim. Lisa's parents were trumpeting their panic and concern over the Atlantic rather frequently now. Avery knew that his monetary reserves wouldn't go far in house hunting. Landing one or two jobs for fifty pounds a week just wasn't enough. Not when his travel expenses were twenty pence over twenty pounds, he had to feed himself, and his phone ate up about fifteen pounds a month.

Despite this, Avery's next jaunt about town would not be to find more work. He would instead get the Northern Line to Leicester Square, stroll down Charing Cross Road, bear right on Orange Street, left on Haymarket, right on Charles II Street, and move a couple blocks over to 14 Saint James's Square. There is a story about St. James in which the Apostle revives a boy who had been unjustly hanged- when the father of the boy heard about this, he stood up in rebuff, declaring, "My boy is no more alive than the roasted fowl on this here dinner table!" and proceeded to watch his supper stand up, sprout feathered wings, and fly away. Down and around the anfractuous city sidewalks to 14 St. James's Square- the address of the London Library. Avery had been ferociously wanting to visit it.

All those words and stories stacked side by side, all

269

the breath of all those minds, poured onto paper, waiting for a hungry ear to wander by. The number of images those volumes might someday stimulate was beyond imagination. Authors long dead would find their spheres revisited. It would add hordes of experienced realities to the hordes of experienced reality. As each concept was pictured, an addition to the great Everything.

Perhaps, then, a sexual fantasy wasn't so innocent. If Avery imagined Yulia sucking him off after the shoot, in a way, after the shoot, Yulia would have sucked him off. The event was created in one version of encounter. Whether or not his brain waves should or should not remain faithful was another story, but whether or not they were- well, he understood now why Lisa felt betrayed.

"Beautiful," Niko said.

It was surprising to hear that, because for a good while Avery had actually forgotten what he was doing.

CHAPTER 57

She was coming out of the bathroom, flustered and tense, just as he was entering.

"Sorry," Avery said. He noticed a bit of phlegm on the side of her face. "You've got something," his voice trailed off and he moved his fingers around his mouth.

"It's nothing," she said defensively. *Just a people killing themselves a slow, numb death. A people who have been warned and instructed but kneel instead to the Gods of convenience. Who steer their obesity to and fro in caustic machines, admit to not a semblance of fulfillment, make suffer great Gaia; tools sharpened by the system and its remorseless wheels. It's just a people who are oversocilized, overfed, over-numb, over-content, overanxious, over-sensitized- who welcome their executioner with flat stares and shrugs. Fuck you, fuck you, fuck you, fuck you, fuck you.*

"Okay," Avery said. He only had patience enough for the trying idiosyncrasies of one girl, and this silent model wasn't her. It was on to erasing the evidence that hair stylists and make-up artists insisted on leaving. Later for this broad.

Avery's body stood in front of itself in the mirror. He pictured Yulia standing in the same spot he was, chanting the famous 'Mirror, mirror on the wall' incantation, and when the mirror said, 'There are thinner girls out there,' throwing herself before the toilet to vomit lunch. What a world to live in- the girls that other girls supposedly look up to are every bit as insecure, only they have the benefit of being constantly judged by the critical camera eye and a thousand other eyes, each clinging to separate, conflicting concepts of beauty.

"I'll be right out," Avery said after a knock at the door.

"Take your time. I was just wondering if you were going to take the tube home." Apparently Niko was not as meek as his girlfriend, who wouldn't think to hold a conversation with someone while they were privately engaged in the restroom.

Avery opened the door. His hair was dripping wet and he still didn't have his shirt on. "Yeah. I was planning on it."

"Oh, good. Would you mind walking Yulia to the station?"

"Sure, that's not a problem."

"She'd probably be fine by herself. But well, it is Brixton," which it was.

"You're an awfully quiet girl," Avery said. It was that beautiful hour just before total night. The sky ran cobalt; a blade of sunlight still clung to the horizon. Streetlights poured their orange glow upon the ground while the many white beams of headlights spoke of a day at work, of a well deserved rest ahead. It was a popular time for travel in the city, which somehow gave evening a tune of loneliness. Of turbulent, crowded seclusion.

"I talk."

"Oh. That's good to know. You're here from America, too?"

Yulia nodded. "I visit a lot for work."

"How long are you here for this time?"

"Not long."

Electric Avenue was on the right. Tarps and blankets hung as awnings over merchant tables, rows and rows of mismatching tents, curving along the curb, produce and compact discs and trinkets and clothing hawked as far as the eye could see. Avery looked on in wonder, wondering what the fuck happens to all that real-estate at night.

Should he have responded to Yulia just then? She wasn't exactly a cascade of topical conversation. Was she purposefully being short, wanting only an escort down these streets considered notorious by the rich, elderly women of London, or was she just naturally cold and aloof?

"What do you do for fun here?" Avery asked.

"You must think I'm some kind of typical model girl."

Avery endowed her with a confused glance.

"Because of earlier, I mean."

"What happened earlier?" he asked.

"Oh, God."

"You mean like, outside of the bathroom? Whatever, dude." Avery wasn't sure if the smirk on his face was appropriate, but he felt like he was dealing with a girl who didn't necessarily merit genteel and chivalrous conduct. "It's your body, you know? Do what you want with it. I'm sure people more important to you than myself have told you it's unhealthy. I don't even know your last name."

"Or my first."

"Whatever," Avery suddenly decided that cordial silence would be a more fitting tandem vehicle for them to ride to the trains.

"Julia. The agency wanted me to go by Yulia because they say it's more interesting."

"Oh."

"I don't do it because I want to stay skinny. Actually it doesn't have anything to do with my body."

"Makes sense."

"Don't be like that. Just a minute ago you wanted to talk. Now I'm talking and it's about something real, not just where I like to get drinks in this town. Does that scare you?"

Now they were passing the KFC. Masses of people stood around on the corner doing god-knows what, masses of people next to the corner waiting for busses and hustling illicit herbs, masses of people before the tube station waiting for people and hustling tickets, Avery and Julia passed them all. Avery mumbled something about how terrifying he found 'real' conversation with her, something about reading the Necronomicon with a dying

273

flashlight while camping at midnight in Transylvania. She couldn't quite hear him and had to quickly maneuver around obstacles of bodies, trashcans, bus stops, and lamp-posts to keep up.

"What?" she asked, frustrated.

"Never mind. But do continue, Julia. You were saying something real?"

They trotted down the stairs of the Brixton tube station, each walking faster than normal, perhaps running with each other, away from each other.

"Forget it."

"Why?"

They were approaching the gates. Avery let her go first, blundering inadvertently back into good manners.

Julia said, "Because I doubt you'd care. And I seriously doubt you'd understand."

"Cool." The pace slowed. Avery didn't care if she kept walking fast. He would let her go, smile for it. She didn't. "Where are you going, anyway? I need to transfer at Victoria, so," he trailed off.

"I get off at Green Park."

They rode the first half of the escalator without saying anything. Down, down, passing Nike advertisements and public service announcements. Avery watched the faces floating up on the other stairwell.

"Look," Julia said. She was whispering in his ear to keep her voice from the other passengers. It was unexpectedly sensual. Her breath, hot in his ear, "Watch the people coming up the other side."

Avery was pretty much doing that already. He did so more consciously now. Up they floated, impassive, waiting. Letting technology get them from point A to point B; watching the world move for them.

"I have to explain myself to you. You saw what

I was doing and you commented, so give me a chance to explain. I love the people I live with, but only for what they could be. They insist on living as drones and workers, and I hate them for that. Our well-being is stripped from us and we know exactly what's doing it- but nobody cares. They keep living for convenience. And comfort. And everyone's just so damned comfortably numb."

"So comfort is the enemy?" Avery asked. The patronizing, derisory quality of his responses was absent in that question. He veered toward the left track at the bottom. She followed.

"Not comfort. It isn't bad to sleep on a soft bed or eat a big meal- bad example for me to use right now, I know- but it isn't bad to be comfortable. It's dependence that will ruin our society. Mankind is so desperately dependent on so many forms of technology. Technology destroys the power-process. It regulates our lives. Didn't you watch those people coming up the escalator? Wasn't it disgusting? How they just sit there, passive and apathetic and one step from dead? Once a new technology is introduced, it robs us of one of our virtues." The delivery was nice, if sounding semi-rehearsed.

"Okay. So you're saying your bulimia is a kind of protest?"

"Are you being sarcastic?"

"Not at all," Avery promised.

The platform wasn't as congested as it could have been. Another train must have just left. They walked to an unoccupied bench, all the way to the end/beginning of the tunnel. Meanwhile, Julia just jawed away.

"It's just that it should be obvious by now. Certain people out there know about this crisis, and some of them went through great pains to educate people. Theodore Kaczynski was a man who made tremendous sacrifices in order to alert the people of a coming danger. He killed and injured people just so his message would be heard. It's horrible that it had to happen- but it was the only way people would ever pay attention. And they did pay attention, but only enough to account for a short commercial break.

"I don't use my fingers when I throw up. I just thing about that. I think about a person sacrificing his life and the lives of others to sound an alarm, and nobody wakes up. They're too lazy and content and goddamned apathetic and hopeless. The alarm is going off, but everyone's so comfortable that they sleep right through it."

CHAPTER 58

The things that old men know are often things that young men are in the process of learning. All of these things have to do with love. Not love by all its many definitions- the English 'love' is without question the most plethoric word in the history of communication, being over-ambiguous in most cases and over-specific in all others. What the old man knows is the mind of females. Or rather how love is poured from a man's mind into a woman's, how it rushes through the complex tunnels of her perception, expands, contracts, reproduces, feeds on the exotic foods of womanhood, foods that revise its color like carotene flamingos. Old men know that it's like this-

Vladimir Horowitz (man's love) and Arthur

Rubinstein (woman's love) played the piano. Both men achieved such a level of greatness that to say that one man played better than the other would be folly. Know only that the same pieces were translated differently by each virtuoso; note only the differences in expression. Horowitz (man's love) on the piano is technical wizardry. It is methodical, systematic, reflexive, and most of all accurate. It is every note falling where and when it needs to. It is an exacting commission, an exhibit of man's mastery over movement, manipulation of the invisible. Rubinstein (woman's love) could shred the same piece, but perhaps more feelingly, with poetry presiding over precision, delicacy over diligence. It is a small scar on the face of beautiful Achilles, a face so magnificent that a blemish can only serve to lend character and appeal. Rubinstein (woman's love) claimed to have learned *Symphonic Variations* en route to the very concert, aboard a train and without a piano, while Horowitz (man's love) claimed on more than one occasion to have cold feet.

The old man knows, too, that girlfriends don't like it when their boyfriend's phone rings and goes from displaying a time of 10:11 p.m. to displaying the phone number of some model broad.

"Hello?

"Hey.

"Just waking up from a nap.

"No, it's fine. I needed to wake up anyway. What are you doing?

"Oh."

As Avery groggily held the phone to his ear, still in his jeans, without a blanket, Lisa looked up at him. Her stare cold and accusing, Avery could sense it without seeing it. He tossed to his left shoulder and looked down at her.

"Who's that?" She asked. Her voice was poison.

"No, I'm not sure. I have to find out what the story with some people is." Avery answered into the phone. To Lisa's question, he merely scowled. It was a 'not right now' and 'just relax' and 'woman, I'm on the phone' and 'don't take that tone with me', but mostly just a forceful 'not right now'.

"Who the fuck is that?" Lisa once again demanded.

"Yeah.

"I'll probably just have to get back to you. Right now, probably not. I can maybe call you back, though.

"Okay.

"Yeah, sorry. You know."

"Avery- who's on the phone?"

Avery said goodbye, hung up, mentally prepared himself for the coming shit-storm, thought of how foolish it was that the shit had to storm in the first place, and looked back at Lisa, saying- "What the fuck's the matter with you? Do you have any idea how rude that was?"

"I don't care! Why was that bitch calling you?" she screamed.

"Because we did the shoot together, she's visiting from America, and I told her that maybe the three of us could go out and do something tonight."

More screaming- "You think I want to hang out with some model bitch? What, did you exchange phone numbers?"

"Yeah, we exchanged fucking phone numbers!"

"Well that was a really good idea! Fuck you, Avery!"

The things that young men think old men know are often things that the young men are in the process of learning.

Lisa evacuated the room. Avery could hear the

kitchen next door open and close. He sat up and swung his legs over the bed, where they dangled, two feet, four feet from the floor. He felt bad for Julia, who during the course of an innocent phone call heard an enraged, jealous voice seeping through the microphone, 'Who's that? Who's that?' He felt bad for Lisa as well, who during the course of an innocent phone call heard the threatening, flirtatious voice of another woman seeping through the speaker, 'What are you doing? Still want to go out tonight?'

Avery knew that he wouldn't be doing anything tonight. He would never see Julia again, save for the pictures of them standing in Niko's backyard. The girl who had no viable outlet for dissent, but felt compelled to do something, anything, because it was better than nothing. The girl who fought so private a rebellion that it only occurred behind a locked door, before the porcelain alter- still something, better than nothing.

In the kitchen, another manifestation of rage was playing itself out on the surface of Lisa's fair skin. A cry for help or a preference for pain physical over emotional. She decorated her arms with bloody lines like a lady prisoner might mark lipstick days on a cell wall. The time, the pain- all short red ribbons.

What the old man knows the young man is in the process of learning. What the young man thinks the old man knows the young man knows already. It is, of course, volumes shy of complete.

Avery thought about jumping down from bed. But he thought better of it, and decided instead to just lie back and close his eyes.

CHAPTER 59

It was still Saturday night. Disorderly groups of twos, threes, fours, fives, and sixes marched and chanted up and down the King's Road, barking loud at the night on behalf of their favorite teams. Avery opened his eyes and no longer felt the least bit tired. Lisa was comatose on her bed across the room. Quietly, Avery sifted through a pile of his things and left their little coffin-shaped room and walked into the kitchen, where he filled a mug with water, a tea bag, placed it in the microwave, set the timer, sat at the table, and opened his new book.

Honestly, to the Reader-

I was a much happier person once. If you possess a bright outlook of reality and cherish your contentment, that bliss which can only stem from ignorance, this book may not be for you. It is filled with frightening, negative potential futures. It does not paint a happy picture of this world and how it works. It includes, rather, information exposing a government within a government- agendas and designs that fully surpasses the stuff of nightmares.

My name is Omar Bryan and as I said, I was once a happy person. I accepted the conventional panoramic of truth without question. I worked as a metallurgist and helped to build jet engines for our American war-machine. I was proud of my work. I imagined my bitter, bald, unhealthy and undersexed boss to be all that was truly wrong with the world. I watched FOX news.

Avery flipped the book over and stood up. From the cabinet he grabbed a couple biscotti and sat back down.

One day, sometime in the middle of 1996, a

new coworker of mine began discussing some of his particularly dismal opinions regarding American and international politics. My initial reaction was to scoff. I was at once the sheep and the sheep dog. I criticized the ideas as ridiculous. I considered Charlie a crack-pot.

Fast forward a few months. Charlie kept talking. I decided to delve into a little research, so that at the next opportunity I could blast Charlie with cold facts that would discredit his unbounded ranting once and for all. I soon recognized the foundations of my dogmatic skepticism- indoctrination. Every source of information I had subscribed to throughout my life, from the cradle to the time-clock, had been crowded with misinformation supplied by the power structure and passed down by the unwitting people. Standard resources of current affairs and history don't deign to mention the Council on Foreign Relations, the Trilateral Commission, the Bilderburg Group, immensely powerful organizations to which the majority of high ranking American officials belong to, nor are we furnished with 'accredited' accounts of Freemasons, Illuminati, the Open Friendly Secret Society, the Brotherhood of the Dragon, the Russel Trust, the Knights Templar, The Knights of Malta, The Knights of Columbus, the Skull and Bones, the Scroll and Key, the Order of the Quest, or any other secret society with similar agendas shaping life as we know it.

THESE GROUPS DISTRIBUTE POWER. THEY DO NOT ALLOW THEMSELVES TO BE DISCUSSED.

During my first research session with Charlie, we searched the internet for information pertaining to American prison camps. We found a few seemingly creditable sources, copied maps and works sited lists, when suddenly, Charlie's computer powered down, compelling him to fly into a wild rage. 'The mother fuckers *crashed my computer!' he kept saying. Naturally, I tried to convince him that these things happen, but Charlie would not settle down.*

THE POWER STRUCTURE WANTS YOU IGNORANT. YOU ARE EASIER TO CONTROL THAT WAY.

This extends not only to the political engine, but also to math, science, history, language, culture, etc. All that is required of you, in accord with the New World Order (which has been openly talked about among the selected elite, paying no mind to the rolling cameras or the ignorant public behind them), is that you either die, or show up to work and pay your bills. It is not the parents' fault that children test lower now than ever before. We can not blame our youth for the near-fact that every prominent expression of fashion throughout time has been superior to today's. It is not the contemporary author's fault that his/her books inevitably pale in comparison to the great works of generations past. The population has been dulled down with expert precision and we, each and every one, count ourselves amongst that population.

I beseech you, the reader, to provide yourself with proof of what I am telling you. I will supply you with the information that I have amassed over the years, with what I consider solid theories, with leads and starting points and avenues of discovery. My faith in the data is derivative of my own research. Feel free to visit the pending American concentration camps in your home state. Read the congressional records sited.

I ask only that you take my word for the events and personal experiences that I describe. They are as accurate as memory will allow, true in each detail, devoid of additional color or exaggeration. Names have been changed, but everything I talk about here happened.

The tea was probably ready. Just to be sure, Avery set the microwave for another thirty seconds and watched the glowing machine cycle through. With three fourths of a biscotti in his right hand, he reached for the mug.

Upon contact, he screeched.

The handle was scalding. It had apparently been soaking up microwaves like a sponge, depositing the heat in a ceramic savings account to be spent on Avery's epidermis. Biscotti and tea. Avery started to suck on his finger. He noticed with shocked dissatisfaction that a blister was actually forming along the middle of his pointer. Biscotti and tea. Hot hot tea. Déjà vu.

The book was open on the table. So far, nothing mind-blowing in it at all. Just a dry introduction alluding to estimations Avery had already come across. The last time he burned himself with tea and biscotti the info in the background was a lot heavier. This time it was another story. Nothing God would be mad at him for, would likely feel warranted a slap on the wrists. No ideas that He would reach down from His cumulous throne and burn a mortal for pondering. Avery abruptly decided that burning himself while drinking hot tea and eating biscotti had nothing to do with conspiracy theories. It did not speak for the existence of God. It was simply an unlucky combination of foods for him, and he would have to be extra careful in the future.

CHAPTER 60

For Guy, the ill-starred caprices of the universe were lingering for too long.

Good Guy. Guy who was always the one to help a friend move house, to organize baseball games for the neighborhood kids, to bring flowers home if he'd absent-mindedly said the wrong thing, who tipped well and gave deserved congratulations. Anyone with a heart would say that the universe was dishing Guy inequitable portions of bad luck.

There was first the strip club idea, the 'Bottoms Up', but boy was it getting worse- each new inquiry begat a fresh version of embarrassment, irritation, dismay, or any combination of the three.

A Miss Rochelle sauntered into the office that morning, busty, buxom, and barely contained by her paper-thin turtleneck. She had the awkward conversational patterns of someone who had once made a living out of getting fucked, and didn't give a fuck if you thought poorly of her for it. She was the half wit relying on money and confidence to get her through a dog eat dog world. She had enough of both to make it work. In fact, her confidence and definitely unnaturally large breasts didn't have to try hard to deflate Guy's customary poise-

"Fabulous place, absolutely fabulous. I must have it." She said loudly and in different directions, as if she were speaking to be overheard by a cocktail-gripping crowd of other people.

Perhaps not the audience she was used to, Guy said but meekly, "But you haven't seen it yet."

"Oh, but the outside is simply lovely. I love the hair place- whatever it's called. And it's clean- the outside, anyway. Shall we?"

Guy gave her an uncertain stare. "See the property?"

"See the property!" She said, still loudly but this time followed by a deep gut laugh which was perfectly wasted in the lackluster, empty office. "Come, come, darling- let's see the property."

"Of course. Ehm, what business are you in?"

"Retail."

Guy took a set of keys from his desk drawer and stood up. He walked around his desk, around Miss Rochelle, and opened the door for her.

"A perfect gentleman!" she exclaimed.

"I do my best. Now, I'm sorry, what was your name?"

"I go by Miss Rochelle, Miss Alexis Rochelle." When she said her name, it sounded as though she used an accent. Like one that she invented only for saying her name.

"Right. Well Miss Rochelle, I should tell you from the start, as some business owners find it to be a problem, that my one requirement before I agree to lease the property is that the name of the business be one that, shall we say, fits in with the others?"

"Oh, why that's a wonderful idea! I want the store named after one of my movies. I'm sure it would *fit in*."

The blood in Guy's veins heated by degrees. "Yeah? May I inquire as to what the title was? The name itself has to be kind of a play on words."

"Red, White, and Screwed."

"You're opening a hardware store?" He knew he was wrong as soon as he said it.

"You got the *hard* part," she said, placing a hand on Guy's shoulder and laughing her big deep laugh again, "I sell adult films and erotic toys, roll play outfits and things like that."

They were in front of the store. Guy was pretty much going through the motions because he didn't know what else to do. He couldn't find it in him to tell her outright that it was unacceptable. That not only would the storefront be an offense to the decent, Christian patrons of the other properties, but the neon sign saying 'Red, White, and Screwed' would be a relentless defilement of his idea. It would be a green ring under the gullible fisherman's new gold bracelet. It would devalue the idea with its careless prurience and fill the air with the sweaty perfume of cheap strippers. Guy once again held the door ajar for Miss Rochelle.

"Oh, just look at this!" she said, walking around with a bounce and looking at walls.

Under the cover of Guy's khaki Dockers, a dreaded occurrence. Not that it was something to dread usually, but this was certainly the wrong time and the wrong place and the wrong person to be with when it happened. Guy looked around. He had given up the hope that touching his thumb to his middle finger would help him. There was nothing to hide behind. A waist high island would have been perfect.

It was suggestive usage of the phrase 'fit in'. It was the look she gave him when he held the door for her. He tried with all his might to fight it away. It was her porn-star tits and free spirit and her ass and Guy's imagination that was way, way out of line and not following directions at all. It was countless years with the same woman who was never exactly kinky and definitely never starred in a movie called 'Red, White, and Screwed'. It was the scenes that, to the best of his knowledge, may have been contained within 'Red, White, and Screwed'. Guy's erection was crescent, like it or not.

"I don't think it's going to work." Guy blabbed.

"I'm sorry, honey?"

"I can't rent the property to you. I'm," he paused, "it's complicated. It's, it's my religion, see? I'm a Mormon. I can't rent the property to someone like, umm, someone in the sex trade."

Her attitude adjusted in awe-inspiring time. From chummy and subtly suggestive to completely angry, the wall between them was erected in one second flat. She went from comfortably loose to threateningly stiff.

"The sex trade? Who the fuck do you think you are? This is America, you son of a bitch. I started from nothing, okay? I could buy and sell you three times over. Look at me. Look at me. What do you see here? Huh? I'm asking you what you see here," her voice was the sinister reverberations of a thousand rattlesnakes.

She was in his face now, screaming and yelling absurdities, with her arms spread, her silicone bouncing, her face locked in an almost becoming snarl.

"Look, I'm really sorry."

All the commotion did nothing to allay Guy's tumescence. He did his best to turn his body away, but his penis was sticking out far enough to be noticed. Miss Rochelle did finally notice, and said a mouthful of extremely biting, extraordinarily demeaning things upon storming out.

And that was only Miss Rochelle.

There were a number of other people answering the new ad in the paper. There were people without names, without credit, one man who told Guy that his name requirement was 'childishly self-indulgent', an openly

287

racist anti-Semite who wanted to expand his successful internet business and get a store to sell his inventory of outdoorsman gear, guns, and Nazi WWII paraphernalia and planned on naming his store 'The Reich Stuff", bitchy woman, shitty men, and a host of people that for one good reason or another could never work out.

Suffice to say, Guy was cursed.

CHAPTER 61

The possibilities:

1- The Old Testament is a record of history, to be absorbed literally, of a time when God actively involved himself in human affairs.

2- The Old Testament was written as a slightly modified version of history, in which names were changed to protect the families that would, should everything go according to plan, still be in power. The stories are relatively believable because they are based on relative truths, and the book itself serves to both dupe the ignorant masses and to remind those who possess the proper ciphers of their history.

3- It was all made up. Any historical parallels are but coincidence, and all religion functions only by capitalizing on man's confused and incomplete system of symbolic references.

So if-

It's all true- Being eternal sinners down to the last man, woman, and child, you're all fucked.

It's all lies- Every stone lain in every church, every war, every prayer, every donation, every missionary, every page in every bible, every confession, every Rosary, every tattoo of the cross, every Sunday school, every holy diet, every vow of abstinence, every kneeling posture, every work of religious art, every 'Bless you' after every sneeze, every circumcision, and indeed the drives and thoughts and energies of countless human lives were and are all for naught. Wasted. Ours would be a history of people merely kept in check by one of the most potent human-programming institutions in existence.

Or-

Considering the fact there is no historical evidence confirming the existence   of the Old Testament's cast of characters or major events, compare the records of theology to the records of history- the bible says Abraham, the annals of Egypt say Amenenhet I. The church says Moses; the school says Thutmose III. In one version King David, in the other, Pharaoh Psusennes I; their sons were Solomon and Simon, respectively. King David and Pharaoh Psusennes I were ruling the same land, fighting the Philistine people, naming their sons names that mean the same thing all at the same time (ignoring technicalities like the space-time continuum).

Consider also that the British Monarchy may still adhere to many of the ideas found within the Old Testament because they are descendents of the original rulers of Egypt and Israel.

Example 1-

One day, en route to Israel, Jacob (likely a fictionalized version of the Hyksos King Yakubher starring in a fictional story) naps with his head upon a stone. With the stone as his pillow, he dreams of a ladder to Heaven, and is visited by God.

"And God said unto him, Thy name is Jacob: thy name shall not be called any more Jacob, but Israel shall be thy name: and he called his name Israel. And God said unto him, I am God Almighty: be fruitful and multiply; a nation and a company of nations shall be of thee, and kings shall come out of thy loins; And the land which I gave Abraham and Isaac, to thee I will give it, and to thy seed after thee will I give the land."

This piece of rock, known as The Stone of Jacob or The Stone of Scone or the Pillow of Jacob or the Stone of Destiny, can currently be found under the coronation throne of England. Queen Elizabeth II herself was crowned in that chair- built upon both a Jewish holy stone and an Egyptian-style step pyramid (like the 'ladder to Heaven' in Jacob's dream). What's more, the College of Harolds in London traces the Queen's bloodline back to the biblical Abraham (Amenenhet I), Jacob's grandfather.

Examples 2 and 3-

The twelve stones in the Queen's crown represent the twelve tribes of Israel, and the four gold rings in the crown (like in the Ark of the Covenant) represent the four corners of the Earth that the descendants of Solomon are destined to rule.

Example 4-

The Queen carries a Royal Scepter.

And finally-

The name Britain actually means 'land of the covenant', as in the land promised to Jacob and his people by God. The sun never sets on the British Empire.

CHAPTER 62

"I think what stifles spirituality in America, and in Britain, and actually in the rest of the modern world is convenience," Avery was saying just before an affected pause- "Maybe not convenience per say, but something like it. Something in the lifestyle. Never are we content to just be, you know? We must always be doing. Our present has to be occupied with some form of activity- T.V. or music or exercise or study, drugs, always something. I can only imagine, and I say that because I'm not a spiritual person, but I would think that spirituality would almost certainly require peace and quiet."

Avery and Patrick were each on their third pint, and had already discussed such topics as school, living situations, LSD, careers, literature, Egyptology, the internet, religion, Italian girls (Avery who was for, Patrick who was against), drum and bass (Patrick who was for, Avery who was against), DMT, one of Prince William's guest appearances on British MTV, and finally, Avery's very broad projected cause for contemporary apathy in the English kingdoms.

"It's got to be worse in America. I recon you have, what- one hundred fifty stations?"

First Avery said that he didn't know if that makes it better or worse, and then proceeded to cultivate his original point. "But think about it- how many ways can we occupy our minds? Right now, I mean. There's a screen right there," he pointed, "I have a drink right here," he lifted his glass, "millions of dollars are probably being spent putting on a football game in one of our two homelands right now- it's impossible to ignore all those distractions even if you wanted to. So not only do you not have the space to develop a relationship with God or, if you prefer, the universe, there's so much buzzing and static that you can't think about anything real at all. Picture the world (the real one that exists beneath all the deliberate lies that we're told and blindfolds that we're given) as pigeons on your windowsill. They're there, but with the shades drawn you can't see them. And with your radio on you can't hear them. And what the fuck do you care if they're there at all because there are so many other things around that can readily hijack your senses."

Patrick had been but listening intermittently. Not because he wasn't interested, nor was it because of Avery's passionate speaking patterns, the occasionally high speeds of which would cause him to meld syllables together in certain words, but more because the opportunity to play the devil's advocate, a role that Patrick very much liked to conform to, had not yet presented itself. His normal pattern was to ask a question, let the other person ramble, and disagree with the weakest assertion. Avery was rambling, alright. The tracks were being laid- but where were they headed?

"Okay- so these pigeons as you call them, they represent the world. But what's this world you're talking about? Is it just a world where people don't know God?" Patrick said to Avery, followed by a mute, "That should do it," to himself.

"That's a really hard question. It's better to think of things in terms of possibility and probability. Not- 'this is how it is', but- 'there's a good chance that it's like this'. I've come across tons of evidence supporting the idea that for the past, I don't know, hundred years, give or take, small groups of extremely powerful, extremely power-hungry men have been directing the course of humanity in hopes of establishing a one world government. The people are definitely being dumbed down. It might be to disconnect them from God; it might only be so they don't see what the men behind the curtain are up to. Probably both. But certainly if the masses were educated enough and aware enough, well," he shrugged. "We can use hindsight to see how certain situations created by these groups have led to 'solutions' that only further their agendas. All kinds of economic crises were engineered by a few banking families in the 1900's. That resulted in the Federal Reserve. Then the Fed coins more panic, and the way out always results in an even richer, more entrenched institution.

"All the big wars have similar purposes. World War II probably only happened so that it could be fixed with the United Nations. They create a shitty situation that the people will want rectified, they offer a solution and, lo and behold, the solution is really what they wanted in the first place. Do you know how many important civil liberties Americans have lost of since the whole 9/11 thing? I'm telling you, man, this shit isn't even far-fetched. Political groups like the Council on Foreign Relations, that super high ranking government officials belong to- presidents, prime-ministers, congressmen, sheiks, princes, whatever- have openly stated that their goal is to eradicate all nation-states. There's already a European Union. The Trilateral Commission is the group trying to make it happen in North America. Now this might not sound like a big deal, like a natural progression or something, but it's a major push toward a world government, which can only mean more power for the people in control, and less power for everyone else."

While Avery continued, his voice shifted into a deeper, bendable shade. That he was truly disturbed became obvious while he proclaimed his love for the principles of American government. And John F. Kennedy. The more he talked the more he thought the more palpably out of control fucked up everything seemed. Regaining his composure required a new train of conversation. He switched to one that felt a little less real.

"As far as I'm concerned, all that is more or less fact. There are other theories out there that I weigh the same way, but obviously the evidence isn't as accessible. Some people think that the ruling elite have been controlling human societies for way longer than a hundred years. Since the rise of Egypt, maybe. Maybe even prior to human history, back to Atlantis or something."

A smile cracked across Patrick's lips. "Is that a real place?"

"I don't know. Some people think it is. They talk about it in school like it's just a myth, but I don't have faith in a lot of information I got from school. The public education system isn't meant to teach you the truth, it's meant to whittle you into a cog that fits into society. I trust independent researchers more than I trust my high-school text books."

"Mate, you're saying that every text book in every school is made by this tiny group of people. A lot of quacks write books and get them published."

Avery explained what he spontaneously termed the 'snowball effect', and even though a 'snowball effect' that described something else entirely almost definitely existed already, his sounded like this- if a group of people possess sufficient resources, they can insert conventional norms without placing them *everywhere*. For instance, if the ruling class deemed it necessary for popular music to stultify the mind, they need not insert a thousand musicians in the industry. They can use their resources to make a couple acts popular, and as time progresses other groups and individuals will create their own music that echoes the tones and concepts of the original agents. Before long entire genres and sub-genres will spring forth, all ignorantly fueling the fire. Same with movies, books, politics, public opinion, accepted scientific truths, school curriculums, and pretty much every other conceivable aspect of culture.

"And if you can entertain that idea, you can listen to some pretty convincing accounts of an alien race, usually described as shape-shifting reptilians, which assume human form and make up a large part of your more dominant aristocratic families, controlling almost every aspect of our lives."

This time, Patrick didn't think to suppress his smile or the chuckle that it snowballed into. The reptilian thing was too much for him, and he didn't mind saying so. It was too much for most people.

"That's okay," Avery said, "I'm not trying to convince you that it's true. I'd only want to convince you to consider it as a possibility, even if it is astronomically small."

Again, Patrick laughed. He employed an almost sympathetic usage of the word 'mate', and asked if Avery would 'fancy coming round for a spliff' because the pint he was almost finished with would be his 'last one'.

Nodding, Avery said that, yes, a spliff 'sounds lovely'.

The flat contained a bunk bed, a stove, a toilet, and clothing. It was just a block away from the Hammersmith tube, which was, according to Patrick, very convenient. Tea was brewing. The only place to sit was on the ruffled sheets of the bottom bunk. Marijuana was being carefully picked into bits. The air in the room was stale. It smelled like fallen smoke and re-re-re-cooked onion soup. Avery experienced a eureka moment when Patrick loaded tobacco into the joint.

"Oh, man- that's it! That's what happened in the garden!" He exclaimed, more for his own sake than for Patrick's. He excitedly recounted the story, telling of the mysteriously harsh joint, how, having never smoked cigarettes, he coughed his lungs out and nobody tried to console him- and even though he thought later that Patrick might consider him an uninformed, unseasoned, even uninitiated smoker for it, he didn't care. Suddenly everything seemed to make perfect sense.

CHAPTER 63

To a passing man- "Help me! Please, please help me!"

To a waiting woman- "Please, can you help me?"

To a fifteen year old girl, out hours passed curfew- "Oh, Lord, help me, please!"

Far to Avery's right, the plea was sounding; lost, idle, out of control, sold-out assemblies of delirium and confusion, constant shadows of cheerless futures forever forlorn. Nobody was helping her. Not with one Sterling Pound. Not with a kind word. Help for her could only be attained through a grueling work of devoted charity, one that nobody on or off the last train through Hammersmith was willing to bestow. Avery could hear her but faintly. All his attention was tuned to his cell phone, which was getting less than stellar reception.

Back and forth, pacing- leaning for a moment against the guardrail along the curb, on the concrete pillars, Avery was the confident, carefree kind of high. He felt at home on the street. The importunate old homeless woman didn't bother him a bit. Nor did the gang of masculine girls passing in track suits, harassing loners with menacing stares. Avery was empowered by a rare kind of self-assurance, like when someone spends all day smoking weed and the thought of going to a crowded club strikes first as a wretched mission with a bothersome beginning, miserable middle, and empty end, but turns out to be a great time filled with dark lights and beautiful strangers.

He did, however, notice a strange cadence in his speaking. An ostensible pause after every few words, so that 'the most difficult part, really, was walking over everyone's feet' sounded more like 'the most…difficult part, really…was…walking over everyone's…feet'. How pronounced or identifiable this rhythm was, Avery wasn't certain. He had bee smoking a lot of grass. "I'm saying man- that's it," he said, "No more movies for me. Shit's getting tight, man. I've got to start saving money."

And a temporary stay in a new hostile, Avery told Michael, was the plan. The good bookers at FM were going to help make arrangements, and hopefully, after a few jobs, there would be enough money to rent a decent apartment.

Moving closer, the hysterical woman's cries caught more of Avery's attention.

"Dude. Where I'm standing right now, outside the Hammersmith Underground- it's not really a bad place, but at night… Yeah. You could say it's pretty dodgy. This old crack-head woman is staggering up to everyone and screaming for them to help her and it's fucking freaking people out."

Michael said that it was loud enough for him to hear through the microphone.

"But yeah. I'm actually looking forward to a change of scenery. The King's Road is not what's up. We should have moved here in the seventies," said Avery.

There was a girl nearby sitting on a store

windowsill. Her nose was buried in an Evening Standard. Her concentration so thoroughly absorbed that she was somehow incognizant of the wandering banshee haunting the steps of Hammersmith.

Two inches from the paper; a nose on either side. One of them reading, the other attempting to sort out problems in a world of who-knows-what, the crack-head pressed- "Oh, please, please, help me!"

Shocked as she was, the young woman's mind reacted instantly and without a shred of decorum. She shrieked, threw down her paper, and ran a safer distance away. No doubt her personal comfort bubble increased two sizes that night.

Avery saw the whole thing and described it in expert prose to Michael.

"This lady, man. Damn. Okay, check this out. I'm going to move right next to her, so you can hear."

Michael listened anxiously.

The woman wasn't far now. Avery looked at her, taking the image in, this poor old distraught woman on the piss soaked streets. God- what a string of miserable misfortunes and mismanagements must have brought her here. There was really no telling her age. She looked to be in her poorly kept sixties, and it was possible that she was. It was also possible that she was in her thirties, forties, fifties, or seventies.

There was no telling her race. Her skin was dark, but her ethnicity still impossible to peg. Her distant relatives might still call the continent of Africa home, perhaps some island in the Pacific or even some other island of the Caribbean Sea. Her face looked as much like one of those browned apple carvings as anyone Avery had ever seen. Her mouth sucked in around a set of ghost teeth, her cheeks sallow and her chin protruding.

She looked like an ad campaign that Avery remembered, where someone would take a drink of Brand X beer and his face would contort in all sorts of weird shapes and everyone would be like, 'Hey! Bitter-beer face!' only this wasn't the least bit funny because her face didn't return to normal.

To look at her was to viddy a dark, off-track side of humanity. It was a bid for the powers that be to go ahead and rule the world, because normal people certainly don't know what's best for them. Normal people are one step away from a torn and tattered and soiled and oversized t-shirt. From mysterious scratches on spoke-thin legs. From malnutrition. From hopeless nows and desolate thens. Anyone could be her. Hand passively any and all important decisions over to the more proficient makers.

Avery leaned against a railing ten paces down from where he was before. His nonchalance was a perfect bait.

"Please, awww, please help me!"

It was right in Avery's face; her voice as much in the mike as his.

"Lady- how can I help you?"

She balled her hands into fists and brought them up to her mouth, leaving a slight gap between them to fit the words, "Oh, lord! Please, please help me!"

"I can't help you. I'm on the phone to Brazil," and with that, Avery walked the ten paces to his old spot, leaving the distraught woman to her unbelievably bad trip.

Michael let his brother collect himself before asking why he said Brazil.

"I don't know. I guess if I'd said America I would have felt kind of like an asshole. For some reason Brazil felt better. Anyways, did you hear all that?"

300

Yes.

"Crazy. But I guess when you get twelve million people together in one city, well," Avery's voice stalked into quietude, but Michael surely understood the point. "I'm saying though, I really have to get some work soon. But whatever, man. Pretend I didn't even say that because everything's going to work out, I'm sure."

What Michael said made him feel a lot better.

"Ah, man. Thanks. But you know I can't ask that. I'm going to take care of myself. I can't be taking loans from my kid brother. Well, maybe, but you know I'll try not to.

"Anyways, I should probably get going- the trains are going to stop running soon. Tell everyone I said hi and I'll talk to you soon."

Michael would distribute hello's, of course, and goodnight.

Beside the shops in the Hammersmith underground, everything was normal. There were no in-your-face personalities to be experienced, and the entrance was graveyard silent by comparison. It felt strange. As though Avery had somehow synchronized with that strange velocity of madness and found it too easy to steer about the sane factions of humanity. The train was shortly there, and Avery in an empty car started home.

His music sounded amazing. Every note was genius, in perfect position, hanging in his ears until the next clear, perfect note was struck. Free to just sit back and enjoy, regardless of looming possibilities. Because Lisa was waiting for him. And Michael told him not to worry about money. Because while he didn't want to borrow money from family back home, desperate times call for desperate measures, and accepting a little assistance from the closest friend you have in the world is much less desperate than bouncing back and forth from pedestrian to pedestrian, begging recklessly that they, or God, help you.

CHAPTER 64

In a more graceful eigenstate, the moon is lynched large and pumpkin orange in a comatose black of night.

The date is October, 31. Mask night. Mischief and candy. Parties, risqué outfits, fake blood, make-up. The city of London shrugs its shoulders and gives a half hearted, 'Eh,' and the moon hides its sickle shape behind clouds.

"This is bullshit," Avery complained.

Lisa said nothing. Sure, she liked Halloween. She liked Halloween a lot. But as a decidedly permanent fixture in the city-state of London, she decided not to miss it.

Avery went to stand again beside the window. A faint reflection of his morose bearing, sniveling visual gripes, was cast back to Lisa. She chose to ignore it.

"Can we go out or something? I mean- fuck. There's got to be *something* going on."

"I have class in the morning," Lisa said, "Besides, there's that thing at the Black Widow on Friday."

He whined that by Friday it would be November.

"So what?"

"Won't be the same," he said. Not many people were walking down the King's Road and not a single person looked scary. "I don't know. I don't think I want to go."

Precariously close to feeling snubbed, Lisa demanded- "Why not?"

"Because. It's in November. In the afternoon, no less. And you know how I feel about all your acting friends. I wouldn't be able to stand them in costume, acting all theatrical and shit. Man. No. I'm sure I'd hate it. I'll just have to be content with missing Halloween this year."

Lisa nodded and climbed up to her bed. She turned over on her back and froze, icy, fixed, staring daggers into the innocent ceiling. Avery was completely unaware of what just happened. He turned to his desk and selected a book.

Okay, Avery thought to himself, *this is trigonometry. Surveyors use this all the time. You record the position of an object from one point against a stationary background, move to another point and record the position again. The shift in the object being measured is- yep, that's it. The parallax. As long as you know the distance between the two points, the angle of parallax can be used to determine the distance between the points and the object.*

So that's how astronomers first figured out the distance between the Earth and the Sun. Okay. 92,965,000 miles on average. Average? Oh, because the Earth's orbit is elliptical. 92,965,000. That might be a good thing to know someday. 92,965,000. 92,965,000. And that's the measurement of an 'astronomical unit' or 'A.U.'. Pluto is about 7,300 million miles from the Sun, or 79 A.U.

So now we can discover how far the other stars are. Err, wait. No. Even using opposite ends of the Earth's orbit around the Sun as a baseline, no parallax could be detected. Oh, but that was only until the 1830's. Fuck. Okay. So telescope technology advanced enough, and Friedrich Bessel measured the parallax of 61 Cygni. After over a year of observation, he recorded a .31 second of arc. Damn. Not much. .31 seconds of arc is the width of a twenty-five-cent piece viewed from 10 miles away? What? You've got to be fucking kidding me.

Now instead of using A.U. astronomers count the distance of stars in light-years. 5,880,000,000,000 miles. This makes 61 Cygni about 11 light-years away. And Alpha Centauri 4.3 light-years and also the closest star besides our Sun. By 1900, the approximate distance to about seventy stars was confirmed. And thousands more by now. Still, the best instruments can only discern the angle of parallax before 100 light-years.

Fucking technology! 100 light years? If 61 Cygni is 11 light-years away, and measuring that angle is equivalent to seeing a shiny quarter from ten miles away, the new telescopes can, what- measure that same quarter from over 100 miles away?

Goddamn, man. Goddamn scary fucking technology. Even telescopes are terrifying when they can do things like that. And if telescopes are that scary-damn. What are other forms of technology doing these days? I should go to that Halloween party dressed as a telescope. Too bad I don't have any money. I'm not going. Fuck that. Lisa can go without me. It's good for her to have friends. Ack. Pay attention, Avery.

With the help of his telescope, Galileo noticed that the Milky Way, previously thought to be just a sort of dusky glow in the heavens, was actually a band of many millions of stars. This is our galaxy, and galaxy is actually another way of saying Milky Way, as the word galaxy is derived from the Greek word for milk. Neat.

Moving on to a particular star- worth mentioning because, from Earth, it is the brightest in the sky. At a distance of 8.8 light-years is the star Sirius.

Sirius?!

Why does that sound familiar?

Avery turned the corner of the page down, closed the book, reached for another, and turned to the index.

> S. *Okay. P. Passed that. S. S. Sirius. Here we go. Page 41. Sirius.*

> *Sirius, the 'dog star', is, yes, the brightest in the sky and supports a solar system*

8.7 light-years from Earth. I thought it was 8.8? Hmm. Whatever. The Egyptian Sphinx is most likely an homage to this star. Modern researchers say that the Queen's shaft in the Great Pyramid was designed to point directly to Sirius. And from this solar system came the biblical Anunnaki.

"My friends have been nothing but nice to you," Lisa interrupted in a very shaky voice, "Even though every time we hang out with them you're moody and quiet- they've still been nice and included you. You are such a fucking asshole sometimes, Avery. I can't believe sometimes," her voice shaking more, "that," her voice shaking so much that calling it broken would be a more accurate description. No more sounds beamed down from Lisa's bed but breathy sobs.

This all came as quite a surprise to Avery, and he didn't know whether or not it would be permissible to keep reading.

CHAPTER 65

Michael was nearly sick with laughter. "And that turn! It was art, man. A real live work of picturesque, spontaneous art."

At that, Jamul smiled, glad for the praise.

A little more than three hours earlier, at exactly 10:41 p.m., Michael was not trespassing on a docked boat with Jamul, Karen, Heather, and J.P.; he was in Jamul's bedroom looking at the back of the door.

The door was covered in black sharpie marker with phrases such as 'DIE PIG DIE' and 'TUST AND CRUST', poetry like-

RIP
From a peace-keeper's piece

and-

Fuck a badge,
Light em on fire,
Dance a jig around a pig

in addition to pictures of police uniforms beneath swine faces, pictures of bullets blasting through pig heads, drawings of youths with bloodshot eyes smoking joints, ect. It looked as though all the handwriting belonged to the same two or three people. He took another swig of the Maker's Mark, turned around to hand it to Jamul.

"Mm, mmm. This is some good shit once you get used to it."

"I know," Michael replied. He was getting a little bored, but there didn't seem to be anything else to do. He looked around Jamul's room, and then looked at Jamul sitting on the couch, holding what was left of the whiskey close. "Hey- why don't you ever pass the bottle back to me? Every time I have a few sips I hand it over to you, but when you're done you just fucking chill. I have to walk over and practically snatch it from you."

Jamul said, "I was just thinking about shooting my little brother's BB gun."

"Yeah? Around here?"

That didn't seem like a good idea. Jamul lived in a pretty bad neighborhood. A neighborhood in which gun crimes weren't uncommon. The prospect of carrying something that looked just like and sounded just like a real gun within a two mile radius of Jamul's house elicited memories of scoldings.

"Why not? I'll go get it."

Jamul came back, holding the piece in both palms like the venerated ring bearer of his father's second wedding. It was flat black, with white writing along the barrel, and looked almost illegally identical to a Glock 9mm. Jamul handed it to Michael, who handed back the bottle of Maker's, and they both took a spot on the couch.

"This is unbelievable," Michael offered, "You could hold a liquor store up with this thing."

Jamul nodded. "It's weak, though. Barely shoots through a Pepsi can."

"Still."

Michael cocked the gun and fired a round of compressed air.

"Yeah, no ammo," Jamul said, graciously handing over the whiskey.

307

The owner of the boat was obviously a party animal. Michael walked out of the cabin, triumphantly holding a plastic blow up doll over his head. He tossed it at Heather, who shrieked, shirked, and kicked the doll away. Her reaction betrayed her fancy that the doll, as all sex toys were, used or not, was coated in a thin layer of the very contagious HIV virus. About two hours and forty five minutes earlier, around 11:03 p.m., Michael was getting a call.

Michael's phone vibrated. It vibrated again, and then started to ring. He thought about crossing his fingers, hoped hard that it would be something good, and answered-

"Big Rach! -

"What? No, of course I don't mean it like that. What's up?

"Sitting around with Jamul.

"No, nothing.

"Who's there with you?

"Yeah, yeah, I know him. It's just the two of you?

"I don't know. I'll run it by Jamul. Got any pot?

"Oh. Okay. Well, maybe we'll stop by. Maybe not. I don't know.

"Right. Bye."

Jamul asked who it was, and Michael ran it down for him. Rachelle had incorrectly assumed that he meant she was big when he said 'Big Rach'. She asked what he was doing. She asked if they had any plans. She proceeded to invite the two of them to her house. She said she was being visited by her friend, Greg, but looking for more company. There was no weed around, but they were welcome to her dad's beer. She emitted the verbal equivalent of a shrug and said that it was whatever, they were welcome if they wanted to come hang.

"Sounds pretty lame," Michael confessed, "Have you met her friend Greg before?"

"We don't have anything else to do."

"True. But we don't have anything to do where we are. We can go over there and have nothing to do, but we'll,"

Jamul cut him off, "But she's got beer."

Michael's face changed abruptly. From the vision of disappointment to one of a young man previewing an amorphous projected future. He seemed to be lost in an idea. "Yeah. Yeah, she's got," he started laughing, "Okay, dude," and standing up, putting the fake pistol in his jeans, "we're going."

In the car, Michael laid out the plan. Jamul was in, and said he could handle it. But before they were off his street, he blurted out, "Yo, fuck this. If we're going to go do this you know you want to be high first. Turn left at the light."

"You want to go get weed?"

"Yeah," Jamul answered, "You got some money?"

The answer was half the money. Jamul gave only one more direction and they were there. The place was not far.

It looked like a small block party. There must have been thirty, forty people out. There were men and women, radios and bicycles, there was drinking and eating, dancing and talking- there was also business to be done. Individuals approached and formed a small concave cluster beside Michael's window as he stopped the car. Three faces nearly poked through and head-butted him.

"Okay, what you need, baby? What you need?"

"Green or white? I got you."

The third man grimaced and twitched his head,

walked away, beaten and back to the corner with his covered quart.

"Five for the dub! Five for the dub!" Jamul remembered joyously.

Backs to the water, looking at Michael and listening to Jamul, Karen and Heather were without a frame of reference. They weren't there two hours and thirty nine minutes ago when Michael and Jamul were buying regs from the weed-stand. They didn't know that the way Michael tried to bargain with the dealers had instantly become an inside joke. They didn't even know that 'five for the dub' meant, loosely translated, 'Since both of you are vying for my custom, I'll give it to the man willing to sell me five nickel bags for one twenty dollar bill'. The girls just assumed that Jamul's outburst was some new slang, which he was genetically guaranteed early access to by way of his blackness. They committed the phrase to memory.

About two and a half hours earlier, 11:31 p.m., Michael's proposed bargain was being tactfully rejected.

"Four for the dub."

"That's not even a deal! Five for the dub."

"Can't do it, bro," the dealer said, looking around. The dealer was strictly into dealing, not at all interested in dealing.

Four nick bags were eventually purchased at five dollars apiece, or one dub. Michael pulled around the apartments, wondering exactly how such a business-obvious, out in the open, ostentatious and outlawed, was allowed to run without the objections and obstruction of officers. The street itself was set up just like a drive-thru.

"Do they pay off the cops or something? Or do

the cops not care what goes on around here?" Michael asked.

But Jamul was already busy watching his hands. They were expertly manipulating the grass into tiny pieces and dropping them into the crease of a cigarette paper. He made a gut noise that expressed his lack of data. Michael nodded, and even though he knew it was a gross exaggeration to think the following, continued driving away from the lawless land of The Ra.

What a difference in scenery a fifteen minute drive can make. Where the light beaming through their windows once bounced off of the here and there of small, dilapidated houses, street-walkers in heals and saggy skin, forbidding corner-stores and tenebrous corners, it now carried images of wealth and privacy. Rachelle lived in a nice neighborhood. A very nice neighborhood. A neighborhood in which smaller houses stood behind modern-day castles in case relatives came to visit or the help needed to stay the night. Where pools rested in peanut shapes guarded by lines of Shaq-high shrubbery. They were fifteen minutes north of Jamul's house, keyed up by the silly body-high of cheap weed.

"Here we go, my man. Showtime. Are you all set for this?" Michael asked. He was actually a bit skeptical as to whether or not Jamul would play a believable role. Jamul had, with each drag, become increasingly taciturn.

"Oh, I got this." Jamul replied. For increased effect he calmly patted the look-alike pistol concealed in his waistband.

J.P. was passing a bowl around. Jamul was acting beautifully the part of crestfallen, ignored, would-be lover. Nobody had explained to Jamul that crestfallen, ignored, would-be lovers never interested any girls of any

311

age. The more the girls ignored him the more ignored he acted, forever and ever, down and into infinity. The prospect of repercussions for their trespassing and vandalism never occurred to any of them. The inflatable lady, name unknown, had been cast overboard. She was being carried down the inlet by a small current- a comically vulgar sail in the dim, eyeless night.

About two hours and fifteen minutes earlier, at 11:47 p.m., Michael was knocking on Rachelle's door.

Since it could be measured that Rachelle was walking to the door at 4mph, and that her tits preceded her every step by .8 seconds, a simple mathematical equation could deduce that the exact size of her tits were not a hair shy of enormous. They were of sufficient volume that, when asked, Sir Edmund Hillary described them as 'mountainous'. Amelia Arnhart never made it around them. God had to make each one on a separate day. She threw the door open with one hand, caught it with the other.

"God-Damn!" Michael exploded. His eyes were tilted down thirty degrees.

Jamul stared, too.

Rachelle gave a big smile, said that she was glad they came, and led them into the kitchen. She took a seat beside Greg on a barstool.

"Man. Seriously- your tits are looking colossal right now, Rach. Titanic. I don't know which is bigger between colossal and titanic but damn!"

Greg seemed completely shocked at this. He expressed himself, saying that he'd never heard language like that, and said directly to the object lady especially.

"That's because you're a square," Michael told him. But as soon as he said it he remembered that that kind of talk was not according to plan. Yes- if the plan weren't in effect, he would talk down to Greg at every given opportunity. And Mr. Thurbin had stimulated enough change in Michael that, if Greg got the least bit lippy, any battle of wit might soon deteriorate into a slap in the face. But no- the plan was in effect. Greg had to like him, had to side with him. "I'm kidding. I act like a pig sometimes. Pardon me."

Rachelle's tits, soft white spheres the size of volleyballs were pushing hard against her thin, stretched wife-beater. They were not fake, and though Rachelle was not what might be considered a skinny girl, under the girth of her chest her body tapered and conformed to reasonably healthy measurements. However and unfortunately, the mass of her upper torso would forever project the illusion of an overweight girl, since most eyes never traveled south of her nipples.

"I just couldn't help but comment," Michael continued, "because that shirt, well, you understand, I'm sure. Jamul doesn't."

Greg shot a glance at Jamul and asked, "What do you mean by that?"

"I mean that Jamul would rather have a look at your two balls that at those two," he paused, "perfect," and paused again, and instead of completing his sentence with mere words, shivered, brought his hands to his mouth, and went, "Mmmmm!" He then apologized, saying that it was probably the Riviera grass talking.

This was only the beginning. Michael's show- a brilliant demonstration of insult and abuse, and all of it directed at Jamul. Jamul played his part well, too; partially because he was playing a part, and partially because part of what Michael said really pissed him off.

313

"He's really hot," Heather said.

"White hot," Karen corrected.

The girls, suddenly selfish and competitive, turned their attentions away from each other. Michael and J.P. were walking the perimeter of the boat, and Jamul was sitting across from Karen and Heather, also selfish and competitive.

"You think so?" The crestfallen, ignored would-be lover asked scornfully.

"Well, yeah." Karen replied. "Obviously."

Jamul's face turned back to a discouraged pout, "Yeah, whatever."

About one and a half hours earlier, at 12:45, Jamul's face betrayed sentiments even more fueled by bitter resentment.

"It's a fucking rent-a-tent!" Michael yelled, tugging the bottom of Jamul's shirt, "Look at this bleeding three-ring circus under this here!"

"Three-roll circus, more like!"

Flawless. Not only was Michael being completely obnoxious to Jamul, but Jamul was reacting with a textbook display of building rage and even better yet, Greg was actually joining the fray with his own off-color comments.

"Good thing your grandfather bought so many Wu-Wear shirts before he died, Jamul- even if he was four times as big as you."

"Stop," Rachelle said. She didn't like to see anyone get picked on so relentlessly.

"Stop? You feel bad for this asshole? The only reason he's even here with me is so that he could drink my whiskey, smoke my weed, and drink your beer. This selfish fat fuck here is the wrong guy to feel bad for. His

314

mom still feeds him and all his clothes come from his dead, obese grandfather."

Jamul closed his eyes and nodded. He was not acknowledging Michael's accusations, nor was he giving the 'I'm about to do it' signal (they had actually neglected to devise such a signal). It was an honest, instinctual movement Jamul made when something was really upsetting him. He tried to remember that it was all a joke. In front of the two breasts of Rachelle, however, the meek soaking up of such exploitation was a difficult task.

"Why are you such a bitch, Jamul?" Greg asked.

"Huh?"

"I said, why are you such a bitch?"

Finally, too difficult. Jamul stood up, spun around while lifting his shirt. By the time he had completed one full revolution, the pistol was out of his waistband, in his right hand, cutting slow, threatening lines in the air.

"I'm a what, mother fucker? A what?" Jamul screamed.

Michael gasped, cursed, stepped back, and lunged forward, grabbing Jamul's firing hand and wrestling him to the ground. Their struggle was violent. Rachelle was backed against a wall, screaming and yelling for them to stop. Greg was very near the exit, approaching full tilt, and was in another instant being carried down the street on as fast a get-away as his legs would oblige. When the faux-fight over the gun had reached a conclusion, Michael and Jamul commenced to their long, well deserved fits of laughter.

It was getting late.

Heather was pressing Karen to leave with her. J.P. was already standing on the dock. Michael was observing an arduous internal debate as to whether or not he should wait until Karen was not in front of Heather before inviting her over. He ended up inviting them both over, and they accepted. As everyone hopped off the boat, Michael was struck with a sense of overwhelming gratitude. The boat had played such a fine host to their evening, and all they did in thanks was throw some property overboard.

Michael faced the boat and turned his palms outward, striking the most saintly pose he could envision. What followed was such a tremendous blessing for the boat and whosoever it belonged to, that J.P. (also a boat-owner) felt a lump of delight swell in his stomach. The captain of that ship and the vessel itself would, should Michael's words be heard, be eternally bound by the hallowed ties of love, be swathed forever in the heavenly nest of togetherness, amen.

CHAPTER 66(6)

Avery supped heartily upon the judgments of logicians and philosophers. The nagging company of actualness, actuality, and all their humdrum children had finally grown tired, leaving Avery alone and satisfied with the same kind of unobserved appreciation one has for body parts in good, working order. He was unbound. Carefree before a stack of books, getting to the bottom of what exactly was important about that most mysterious five pointed star. Avery took notes and so far they looked like this-

Sir Edmund Parker. <u>Satanic Rituals of Past and Present</u>.

Pg. 25

I am to understand that the practitioners of Satanism act always with the belief that the universe, in addition to adherence with the laws of physics, operates on entirely different sets of laws and values simultaneously. On one hand we experience the material- fire is hot, objects fall toward the center of the Earth, etcetera. On the other hand we can, through precise ritual, experience the unexplored and unacknowledged.

The purpose of the pentagram is to call a member of the otherworld into ours, where it can be perceived by human senses. Imagine a bell. To strike the edge of the bell results in a ring. Much like the striking of a bell, the pentagram creates in the human mind an energy, the energy creates in the universe a rift. A ring, a doorway, if you will, through which demonic entities can be called upon.

The last paragraph sited another book as a source. Avery continued his notes, starting where Sir Edmund Parker left off, a step nearer to the source.

Francis Parades. <u>Beyond the Science of Man</u>. Pg. 111

To compare man's microscopic to the great underneath is to compare solar systems to pin-heads, the atoms of atoms.

Strands of energy comprise the fabric of reality, strands that crisscross in a single, uniform pattern. All variation throughout the universe initially stems from the same configuration of energy. Always the same configuration, billions and billions of times over for every gram of being. It is a puzzle that science will never solve, but one that human spirits- mine and countless others, thanks be to God, hold the solution to.

The energy that all existence is built on rests in the shapes of a five pointed star.

This information, according to Francis Parades, was attained through Godsend and drug induced Eureka. Still, the author thought it prudent to cite the works of other quasi-scholars, perhaps to prove that if a brick falls on two different people's heads, it hurts the same way. The theories were supposedly shared, and when a theory is shared, its cocoon shell may, with enough sharing, shed to reveal a beautiful, jewel-colored law. Avery checked Francis Parades' backup, Dr. J. Hampstead.

Dr. J. Hampstead. <u>Origins of American Symbols</u>. Pg. 16

Without question one of the most misunderstood symbols in American as well as other cultures is the pentagram/pentacle. It seems to have become a fad among young people, who interpret it as a symbol of devil worship or rebellion, but the symbol of the five sided star pre-dates the English language.

It started as a symbol of the goddess Kore (also Car, Cara, Carnac, Ceres, Kor, Karnac, Kaur, Ker, Kher, Kherma, Q're, Qet, Quor), who was worshiped by ancient peoples around the globe. It became her symbol because the apple, considered the goddess' sacred fruit, displays a five sided star when sliced down the middle. This is where the word 'core' is derived from, as in Kore's apple. The apple core is sometimes referred to as the 'Star of Knowledge'.

What a backwards, dead end step that turned out to be. Weird. It certainly had nothing to do with drugs or omnipotent beings peeling back layers of the gigantic world until star shaped subatomic energies were all that's left. Dr. J Hampstead and Francis Parades seemed to have nothing in common. But Dr. J left a note at the end of one of his paragraphs, and the book he borrowed from was soon opened in front of Avery.

Rush Dewey. <u>10 Things You Should Know</u>. Pg. 38

The notion that human consciousness operates on a complex system of symbolic references is as established as the notion that the planets of our solar system revolve around the sun. While the old adage, 'the map is not the territory', appears relevant to some, a woman of the western world can look at a cartoon heart on a Valentine's Day card, an object bearing little or no resemblance to the actual organ nor to the shapeless emotion of love, a shoddy map, if you will- but the routes of that woman's awareness will travel the same path and touch the same references. The simple cartoon represents the heart to the point of becoming the heart. Similar shapes can be found for important things or ideas throughout all cultures. Star shapes are obviously abundant due to mankind's veneration of the stars and the sun. The cross is everywhere Christianity or Catholicism is. So the map becomes the territory. It elicits the same response within our seemingly unconscious consciousness.

Invidious. <u>Bring on the Antichrist</u>. Pg. 4

Praise man.

Hail the mind of the beast. Within him is all God's glory. God's glory. What an insult to your intelligence. Praise man. Perfect proportion. Human Divinity. Praise the scientific process. Hail the two topmost points of Lord Baphomet's Sigil. The scientific process is the ascendance of man. Faith is your prison. Poison. God is Will.

Invidious went on to explain what each point of the pentagram represented, but Avery didn't write it down. He instead proceeded to the next book.

Roberto Antonio. <u>The Funny Fedora</u>. Pg. 390

Professor Dexter drew a diagram on his notepad. He frowned, tore the page into a crumpled ball, sat the crumpled ball on the table, and tried again.

"I messed up on the arrows," he said, and seemingly satisfied with his second attempt, "What I have here is a visual example of how quantum causality works, trusting Bell's Theorem over the traditional, linear mode of causality where A effects B, B effects C, C effects D, D effects E, and so on."

He held the picture up to Jessica, who was only doing her best to pay attention because she knew that the Professor knew that she never paid attention in class.

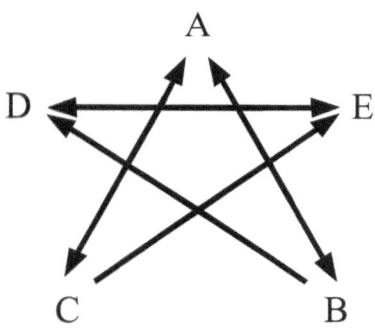

"Now before space and before time, we have a world in which A precipitates B, C, D, and E; but you can see that B ALSO causes A, along with C, D, and E; and C

effects and is effected, and D effects and is effected, and-
you get the picture..."

Avery sighed.

Duncan Binks. <u>Great Disguises</u>. Pg. 2

I offer no answers, merely options. I could perhaps
convince you that the only way to kill a werewolf is by
shooting it with iron bullets wrought from the nails which
held Jesus, but where would that get us?

Freemasons force initiates to consider the
possibility that the five pointed star represents more than
one possibility. Five points that are connected by five lines
be they crossed through the middle (as a star) or wrapped
around the outside (a pentagon). Two possibilities, one
in the same. To usurp control is impossible while blind of
options.

Consider the possibility that that same pentagram
represents the world, and the decisions we make in it-
each line can be a directive, a censor of the personality in
order to communicate within cultural limits. 1- Is it good
for me? 2- Is it good for my family? 3- Is it good for my
friends? 4- Is it good for the crowd? 5- Is it good for the
world?

I just made that last part up. Does that make it
false? True? Does it matter?

This was all a load of bollocks. No two definitions
were alike- no theory or description supported the
one before it or after it. It was a confusing mess of
misinformation, typed up by careless hands to further
confound the curious mind. Fuck Sir Edmund Parker.
Fuck Francis Parades. Fuck Dr. J. Hampstead. Fuck
Rush Dewey. Fuck Invidious. Fuck Roberto Antonio.

321

Fuck Duncan Binks. The lot of them professed to leather-bound volumes of ignorance, three hundred plus pages of pointless pedantry. Avery removed his cell phone and unlocked it with the MENU, STAR combination.

A message from Rodge saying to call the agency or stop in, good news was waiting.

Good news was good news, and Avery happily greeted actualness, actuality, and all their humdrum children back to the table of his life.

CHAPTER 67

He thought for a moment that his hands were against each other.

Well, they were against each other, but he thought for a moment that some animosity existed between the right and the left.

Only for a moment. His hands were his. There was no body politic. That was right and all that was left to do was to rub them, rinse them, dry them, look in the mirror, call back to attention any wayward hairs, get it together, and collect the good news.

Look at that face.

There was nothing on it to reveal the stupidity of his high. Hellish high. Nothing like an intense high to make one question the practicality of plans and ponder the folly of ambition.

His hands were against each other. The brotherly love of right and left. The right of reverence, left of loathing. Not opposites at all, right and left, hate and love. Call it reciprocal aspects of the same body, from the body the same emotion.

Hands outside were against each other, surely. The vice-grips of young lovers. Where was Lisa? He should do something fun with her. There was that Halloween thing. He hated the idea, but it was only right to go. The hands of cab drivers along Brompton Road would be rubbing for warmth and anticipation. Get in, ye hoarders of money and masters of purchase. Get in and nourish the insolvent navigators with all that burns holes in your purse pockets and coat linings.

Their hands would be together, too, across the street. Struggling for warmth and dryness and comfort under the generously protruding easements of that epic department store. Didn't they sell a tiger to a sheik? I'm not in the market for a tiger but how about that water resistant Burberry shawl? All the colors of earth built into one angelic foot of fabric, it's certainly for me. With money in their right hands, it's soon left.

Avery stretched himself out. Beyond the bathroom doors, the stairwell, the agency, as far across Knightsbridge as his aura would permit. There were people out there, none of them outside themselves, all of them just doing.

All that needs doing is drying and getting it together, and his hair was too wet to fix really so fuck it. It's damn impractical wearing sunglasses under shelter of the four o'clock grim, the cloudy, rainy, monochrome afternoon. A look in the mirror without to affirm it must be done. He felt a corpse staring back at him through puffy dead eyes, drained of their vitality unless hidden beneath the blanket of dark shade. All that's left for doing is getting right and getting the good news.

The vowels were mouthed his reflection. The

image was the only noise, but in his head a different monologue continued.

She was wearing a slack black shirt with lettering across the front that read 'Hooked on Fonics wurked fer me' and if you asked about it she would say 'It's an original'. The shirt and quiet cockiness with which she wore it had the seemingly magic power to confuse anyone that saw it, even more so if they saw it and were informed that it was an original.

Whatever was giving him that thought stopped giving it. He looked left and right, around the cramped bathroom and its nonsensical fittings. There was hardly enough room to dry your hands, yet there was a lock on the door and a separate door and lock around the shitter. Then there was a urinal, and all around it walls painted the same royal blue that a couple planning to adopt might use for the room of their soon-to-be boy. All it was missing was the baseball mitts.

Avery, you're a fool. A foolish, fool-hardy, fool. Let them take your picture, little girl.

Stop that, Avery's second voice replied to the first, but in his head it rang with such a flamboyant lisp that Avery actually laughed out loud.

A deep exhale, a reassuring 'Okay', and Avery opened the bathroom door.

By the time he got up the four flights of stairs his high was calming down, his perspectives easing themselves back into an arrangement of normalcy. The privacy of the bathroom was a bad thing, then. To prepare for interaction required interaction. Privacy would only make matters worse.

"Rodge! Good to see you, fella."

Rodge spun around in his chair, smiling.

"Alright, Avery? Glad you could make it, mate.

Have a seat and I'll be with you in one second." With that, he spun back to his computer, mounted the keyboard with two work-ready hands, and put what appeared to be the finishing touches on an email.

Busy, busy, busy, all around. There were calls being made, jobs confirmed, options put on and taken off, couriers coming and going, thank you, thanks anyways, rates to negotiate, magazines to procure, aspiring hopefuls to see, checks to sign, portfolios to organize, travel to be arranged, all with chipper, be it positive or not. The bookers were working for themselves and for a sizeable wall of pretty faces and forms. The invisible tunnels dug by these workers sprawled through the entire hive of fashion.

When Rodge was finished- "Okay. Avery. What's with the shades?"

"Do I need a reason?"

"No," Rodge and a couple of others within earshot were smiling. This was exactly the situation that Avery was dreading. "It's just not that bright out."

"I just know what a hard time you give to Jack when he's got bags under his eyes. I needed to hide mine. Plus I have a black eye. Plus they match my shirt. And block the rain. I can take them off if you want."

"Not necessary."

Avery chuckled, and while rubbing his hands together said, "Well? What's the good news?"

"Right. Good news. What do you want first? The good news or the really good news?"

"Regular good news first."

"A really amazing photographer from Thailand wants to test with you and a couple other boys on Tuesday. So you'll get some great pictures for your book. That's the good news. And now," Rodge paused, opened a drawer from his desk and pulled out a sheet of paper, "Tah-dah!"

"What is it?"

Avery removed his sunglasses.

"This," Rodge said, celebratory and singsong, his voice spanning the sinuous up and down movements of the maestro's bow, the calming swing of the ocean currents, proud gratification with a dash of here you go, "Is your work visa." He handed it over and clasped his hands together.

CHAPTER 68

An artist was making money somewhere in the Black Widow, pulling pints or bussing ashtrays or plating bangers and mash. It was possible, too, that she or he had the night off, but the work was there- a smiling, chalk Dracula on the door-front blackboard.

A man dressed as a banker cutting loose after work was belting out a Destiny's Child song. Before his sweaty shirt and hastily loosened tie a small crowd was enjoying it. That or they were just waiting for their turn to sing.

"Oh, look Avery! Why don't you pick a song?" Lisa asked.

"What the fuck. I told you nobody would wear costumes."

It was true that Avery had always been a fan of karaoke, but karaoke was to him a sad affair in which lonely women display dreams of being watched and

326

wanted to the collective haze of a drunken crowd that couldn't care less. Karaoke required a table of at least five friends, fifteen beers, and an otherwise sparsely occupied establishment. This Black Widow strain of karaoke was too high energy and happy. A whoop which might better have been a sigh.

Lisa assured him that her friends would arrive shortly, clad in elaborate dress all the tones of Halloween. Avery did nothing to mask the collapse of his mood.

"What do you want? A Guinness?"

Big eyes flashing on Lisa's face, the nod, and Avery made through the small crowd to the bar.

It had been a lovely day thus far. There was the futile yet somehow fulfilling trip to the London Library, the good news from the agency that he would, upon his next passing through British customs, be assured two years of government championed residence outside the United States, and there was the afternoon after that with his girlfriend. The sun was out now. No more rain. Just wet streets reflecting brightly the white-yellows of well-rested sun.

They had just taken a long, scenic route to the pub. Arriving, to Avery, was the worst part. It meant that a day of pressing their smiles together was over. Privacy aborted. It meant that the lofty air of ardor around them would be polluted by the air of strangers. The walk had been a million dolphins jumping and spinning and skipping and singing before landlubber tourists. It had been two true hearts beating behind glass strong enough to repel all the glooms and miseries of Pandemonium. It had ended. Now there was the pub. A pub like most other pubs. Halloween distraction in November afternoon.

Taking her drink from Avery, Lisa asked, "So now you have to go back to the States."

"Yeah.   Soon," Avery   said,   "Maybe   for Thanksgiving. Why don't you come, too?"

"No, I can't miss school."

Avery   made   a   face   that   was   perhaps   an inappropriate response. It looked as though someone said in one of his ears 'I never want to hear music again' at the same time as someone else saying 'the best way to fix America is to vote' in the other. But it was more or less an accident and his words better represented how he really felt.

"I'll get to see everyone. I miss Michael. I miss everybody back home. I really lucked out with all this."

"See?"

Lisa did that occasionally. Exhaled a restrained 'I told you so' for every good thing that great London granted. She did it enough that the ambiguous meaning of her 'See?' was unmistakably clear, and all Avery needed to keep quiet and assume a sort of deadpan understanding.

Devils walked in beside androids, beasts beside pixies. All red face paint and clip-on wings.

Exploding from the life-like copy of Snow White-

"Lisa!"

Up and down, cherry Satan looked, smiling at all the eyes that were in his mind predictably upon him.

"NEED BRAINS," the zombie that walked like Frankenstein's monster said.

Lisa lit up.

A new hand grabbed the mike, saying hello just before the first note of 'love me two times' was plucked.

A round for everyone from the Evil Doctor.

Screaming orgasms for the two blondes in the mismatching patterns of Chelsea shoppers.

Laughter from someone across the room.

The kangaroo jumped in circles.

Avery shows freely his lack of amusement.

A man in a blue oxford bumped an elbow and a swig of foamy beer smacked the floor.

Another man turned around and accepted an apology.

Across from Lisa a fairy waved her star-topped wand.

Conversation over singing, communication loud all around.

Only a drama student would dress up as William Shakespeare.

Squeaky wheels turning, empty cans dragged over bumpy asphalt, this one knows that that one is listening, the thirst drowned under bitter tidal waves from tilted glasses, all in all make-up holiday at the swarming pub.

The hopeful young actors and actresses, who, normally, in accord with their supercilious teachers' instruction, spent each school-day striving to rout every occurring inhibition, were by trick of the pint becoming more and more vocal, with less and less contrived demonstration. Karaoke was over, replaced by the jukebox and British top 40 pop hits.

"I heard about this guy at a RADA audition who performed his pieces and then they told him to fuck the chair," a mousy girl whose name had slipped Avery's mind was saying, "Fuck the chair. Can you believe that? I don't think that there's any actor in the world that could fuck a chair. Without practice, anyway. Anyway it made him really angry. He walked over to the chair and smashed it on the ground. Then he started stomping it and kicking it and after it was all broken he looked at them and said, 'chair's fucked now, innit?' I think he got in."

Gossip turned round and round their table like so

many planets. Nobody could believe that one of their school-mates had told Lisa that Top-shop was 'common'. Everyone had something to say about how during an 'embarrassment exercise', one of their school-mates happily admitted to fingering herself at a party because a boy she liked was sleeping on the couch next to her.

"I heard that at LAMDA they make everyone get naked on the first day. Isn't that crazy?"

"So what? I don't think that's such a big deal," Lisa said, "If you want it bad enough that's nothing."

The mousy girl scowled. "They just have to break you down and build you back up. Once you don't have any faith in yourself they give it to you."

Here, Avery felt the rare urge to chime in, "That's a form of brainwashing, you know." He waited to give a further explanation, but was not asked for one.

"I just want to be taught. I'll do anything if it makes me a better actor."

It didn't matter who said it. Avery just knew that he wanted out. Bad. Visions of escape were clouding his attention as though he'd been locked up for decades.

"If I don't make it as an actor I'll kill myself, I just know I will."

"Jack! Jack! Fuck, man! How the hell are you, buddy? What's going on? Something good?" Avery yelled into the bottom of his phone. He made a quick break for the exit, the open doors that were still considerate enough to hold some daylight and hopes of a salvaged evening between them. "Jack! Praise merciful Jesus!"

At the other end Jack was laughing and inviting Avery and Lisa out to see some world class DJ's because he wanted to be the one to introduce them to a new world of music, a world which, living in London, they would almost certainly happen across one day or another.

"I'm going. Yes. I'm there. Dude I was so fucking stoned at the agency today I almost couldn't make it up the stairs. And then Rodge called me out on my sunglasses in front of everyone and I was just like, 'well, you always fuck with Jack about looking tired so I wore these.' Thanks for that."

Jack called Avery a motherfucker in his very pleasant, amused character.

"I'll do what I can to convince Lisa to come with me. But I don't know if she'll want to leave her friends. You really saved my life just now, man. I was dying. Be there in an hour or so."

Sounded like a plan.

Sounded like a dejected, 'no, I'm with my friends, why can't you ever just spend time with me, everyone is here and I'm enjoying myself, go if you want but I'm staying.'

Sounded like, 'whatever, then I'll see you later tonight.' And Avery was soon boarding a train on the District line, wondering if his own attitude catalyzed the recurring friction in his and Lisa's relationship. If the ever-fleeting emotional ups and downs were perpetuated by his own imbalances. If it was all hopeless- communication, contact, living and breathing, love, acceptance, knowledge, experience, and all the rest of it. If he wasn't as right as he always thought, if there were even such a thing as right. If the night would be more fun. If his new friends in Hammersmith could do anything to jettison the emptiness in his being. If 'jettison emptiness' was just a silly oxymoron.

Somewhere deep down, Avery knew that the shift from glad to sad and back would have to decrease in frequency, otherwise his gage would surely break, and he'd spend each and every evening wondering who he was in front of the television.

CHAPTER 69

(When everyone understands the motives behind every thought and action in individuals outside themselves and neurological relativism blends into the great Everything, you have entered the kingdom of Heaven. And even Yin gets Yang.)

The sun flexed its muscles, and though atrophied in November, still popped out enough to warm the streets and skins of Florida. Guy was homeward bound on his afternoon ride. He pedaled a black beach cruiser, handlebar basket, cup holder and bell, no rush, down and around the green-lined neighborhood streets. It was difficult to tell what Guy was thinking exactly. The aspects of his expression might betray any one or any combination of the following sentiments- irritated boredom, mild but long-lingering resentment, condemnable overtiredness, deep reverie, stern purpose, attentive cautiousness, bitter reminiscence, tetchy offense, and/or blank thoughtlessness. This was because the part of his face above his sunglasses looked focused, the part below it looked bothered, and the lines he rode along the sidewalk were straight and humorless.

Really, Guy was happy. Or as happy as he could be living through the miserable present of his life. Bad luck could be put on hold during the warm afternoon. The pool would be blue, regardless. The breeze would welcomingly blow through the development circles, passing Galley Cove and into Jolly Yard, throughout the whole sun-drenched community and all its dry, earth-tone houses. Oh, happy blank.

Every roof in sight was the same. Hot hot Spanish-tile singles, as clay-colored as the driveway bricks, cutting slightly different angles over houses that were either dull, dusky-orange, beige, or three-quarters-digested-curry-chicken-yellow. The streets were more gray than they were black, as a testament to too many hot summers. Still- the thick blades of grass shone like patches of bright green fireworks. The grass and bushes and flowering trees were the visible cool pouring from the sides of a cracked freezer. For a while, it was enough to keep Guy's troubles at bay. But home soon approached. A structure like all the others- Spanish-tile, brick driveway and functionless shutters, but home to no one but the Weeks family. Distance diminished. It grew larger. More threatening. Until eventually he was before it, and the sound of pierced atmosphere warped into his ears.

"What th…"

Guy's reaction was involuntary at first, but he felt a selfish urge to willfully justify it.

"What on Earth is your malfunction, man? Don't you know its noise pollution whistling as loud as that?"

Mr. Chase said nothing. This is to mean he stopped whistling. He smiled. The poor man across the street, nice man, he was having problems, and Mr. Chase knew that for at least a moment, he helped the nice man forget them.

(Nothing they do is right. They are all mad but you and I, and I often wonder about you. If only they could understand what I understand, they would tread the soil of Heaven. Because I know what's right. What I should do is teach them. Force them to get it. You'll see. You'll understand.)

The burnt, used up, Christmasless Santa Claus of a man, sand-caked beard, lips and eyelids, salt-covered brow, crusty nostrils and chin, was stiffly inert, with no visible rise and fall to his chest or stomach. He did not stop the children from playing around him. Tourists sunned. Men and women bent over and beat the grains from their towels and twisted the caps from their bottles of water.

A Moroccan boy had been building a dirt fortress before the sleeping man's feet. Its construction started with a series of moats and walls. These had to be rebuilt every so often, due to the proximity of the ever-coming breakers. Dark brown sea-weed washed ashore in clumps. The grounds of the rising kingdom had been cleared of almost all of it, but the length of vagrant was over it and in it, sea-weed from face to feet.

"No te acerques q ese cochino," the boy's mother yells. Her Spanish is beautiful and she knows it. She feels it lends and air of elegance to the beach.

Pretending to ignore her, the boy goes on building. He digs tunnels from tower to tower, escape hatches for the tiny lords and ladies. Something about the fat sleeping man is frightening- he does, after all, covered in sand and seaweed, look as though he'd been spit out from the shrinking tides. As if the sea had shat him out. Left out to invigorate the crabs and the gulls.

It was easier not to look. Leave the bum to his sorry fate. Nobody in their right state of mind sleeps with their face in the sandy, salty, tar-crusted shore. Let him to his sandy fate.

Bubbly water rushes forward over everything.

More of the castle crumbles.

"Sigue comiendo me casa!" The boy shouts and gets hurriedly back to work. Save what can be saved.

Please notice that the body is moving less than it should. And it lies too close to the coming waves. The boy is scrambling to restore his castle, which has now eroded to smooth anthill-humps. His mother is watching nervously, paying progressively more attention. The scene playing before her eventually registers as too odd.

Even in a party town the bums move their faces for the waves. They don't sleep so unendingly unperturbed. When water floods their nostrils, they sneeze- even bums in places like South Beach. They breathe.

"Ven aqui ahora!" Mother screams. Because it was true. Men don't sleep on the beach with excrement half in and half out of their assholes at once. That's usually a sign that they're dead. A hundred tourists could ignore it, a handful of residents could bathe and sun and play catch around it- but a corpse, a man devoid of heartbeat and health, would eventually need to be cleaned up.

His castle was fucked anyways. The boy walked over to his mom, with his arms and shoulders sagging in disappointed defeat, the kind of walk that gets walked when a body has worked against the rigging of nature.

A football went soaring through the open blue sky. Under it, a group of young men waited edgily. It was as bright as white out. Out in the water, a girl was wading as far from the whitewater as she could because she heard that that's where the sea-lice get you. A fat southern woman sweats profusely in the humid Miami sun. A man born of evil destiny with an equally evil automobile visited the night before and left a heap of debris to rot indefinitely. The unkempt and uncared-about got stiffer and stiffer. The sandcastle is pretty much gone now. It's

335

being eaten by slow bites of the awkward to and fro of the ocean.

Hours earlier- a shriek, a splash, half a shit, and silence; a silence roundabouts for the children to play.

CHAPTER 70

It will supposedly begin with violent perspiration. Sweat upon sweat upon sweat. Onerous breath. Steamy eyeglasses and waters retreating to the crest of our atmosphere. A new bubble in the sky, growing, and bringing with it havocs and hells upon the Earth.

The populace of Earth will remember the historical warnings- the plagues released among the master race of ancient Egyptians, the Deluge, the dinosaurs' worn out welcome. They will hark the bellowing doomsayers of past and present, all the while waiting in droves for sunscreen, canned goods, and batteries. Everyone is finding God.

During nighttime, the bubble casts an eerie glow into the twilight. People have disappeared, but not many. Deep into the sanctuary of underground government sponsored bunkers go America's best and brightest. They will build the new future from what scraps survive, once the perspiration becomes a burning too hot to suffer.

Mars is sucked into the tumultuous wake of the bubble and is followed by oceans of cosmic rubble. The bubble, what the few people left alive are saying, is most surely the Destroyer. Islands are soon lost beneath electric blue waters. The face of the Earth is changing violently, as if its lips are parting to scream, mindless of the millions dying in the process. Atlantis all over again.

Norman Chapman refused to be convinced. He stood up, all gangly six foot four of him, in order to better punctuate his position.

"Come on! It's not like the sun is going to go," he turned around twice widdershins, checked his wristwatch while saying, "Oh, shit! It's 2012!" and spun a few times the other way round.

Avery spoke up, too. "It just doesn't seem like the numbers make sense. According to that the thing would have traveled billions of miles in like nine years. Seems almost impossible."

"That isn't what scientists think," Peter maintained.

Sitting next to Peter, who was sitting next to Norman, who was sitting across from Avery, was Jack. Jack was rolling a spliff with a holier-than-thou grin on his face for the duration of the discussion, as though he knew something that nobody else in the room did, or thought the whole thing was too ludicrous to discuss in the first place. "Man, fuck it," he finally said. He took a deep, showy, histrionically calming breath and asked everyone to do the same. "Say it with me, now- fuck it. Fuck it will set you free."

"Can you be sure that the creators of that documentary you saw were scientists?" Avery made the demand at Peter, ignoring the beg for togetherness chanting completely. "Dollars to doughnuts they were just repeating information that they gathered from the 'scientists'. More likely it's just a big convenient ploy to galvanize massive fear in the citizenry. People can be led to do and believe anything when they're sufficiently frightened." Avery had planned on saying more, but he was interrupted by Jack saying 'fuck it will set you free' and breathing deep breaths while waving his arms like a composer.

"Are you doing Tai Chi over here? I was in the middle of making a point," Avery complained.

But as Peter was sitting to Jack's right, and he knew that the joint could either be passed first to him or Avery, Peter was compelled to side with the host. He said- "I'm with you, man. I agree totally, completely, one hundred percent. Fuck it. Fuck it has set me free."

Fixed sets of principals, doctrines of morality, goodness, and those groups and individuals that subscribe to them, will inevitably fall victim to society's collection of cold-blooded opportunists.

To believe in nothing is to believe in everything. The opportunist cares not for truth or for falsehood, only for what proposed beliefs will further their own personal agenda. A malleable public the power-hungry's bountiful repast.

The prodigious opportunist can sculpt raw fear into almost any instrument. It can mimic the loyal sheepdog, driving the herds of cattle this way and that, rounding them up, splitting them apart. It can take the shape of a suspended guillotine to induce mass anxiety and disquiet. It can look like the end of the world.

Confusion amidst the ruling classes of society would create the perfect step-ladder for the opportunist to climb. Enough confusion and panic might even erect a step-ladder high enough to surmount the entire human race. There could erupt a vacuum of power, frightening in scope to any man or organization weighed down by even a shred of moral principals, ready to be filled by the vile, callous, reptilian man or men.

Whether the Earth is crumbling, or is said to be crumbling- whether crumbling is immanent, or merely said to be immanent, is irrelevant for the opportunist. Look no further than the end of the world to find a new regime wielding power absolute.

By default, the new Overseers, amoral enough to have seized power, will sow their own brand of suffering. The people will revel in it, of course, saying, "Yes, this is my life. Woe is me. Woe to the living. Yes, this is life." They are at once the captors and the captured, inflictor and inflicted, participants in their own perfect enslavement.

It will be known that the Masters of the world have always been in control, but went through great lengths, spanning throughout recorded history and probably before, just to openly admit it.

All the gold of the kingdom, as well as the blood of all the remaining virgin red-heads will be homage to the new Kings, who walk their ten-foot-tall bodies around, scales showing, tails in plain sight.

Before that last bit about tails and red-heads, Avery was receiving no challenge from the room. Not even in the form of Norman's skeptical squint or Jack's nihilist mantra. Now Norman perked up, and Jack came out with, "Oh, right. Avery thinks that the Royal Family is reptilian, but they can shape-shift into humans."

"I believe it," Norman said, but he was obviously making a joke, and didn't.

"Princess Diana said so, too. And I never said I believe it, I said I believe it to be possible. And I was actually mistaken about the gold tax. Now that I think of it, I think that they only need gold to shape-shift, and once they're properly ruling they won't need to do that anymore." Avery found himself talking in a funny cadence again. He was pretty high. "Do I sound stoned to you guys?"

Peter was the first to answer yes, followed by Norman nodding and Jack laughing.

"I don't mean do I sound high because of what I'm saying. Yeah, that was probably misleading. This has been happening lately. I mean how I'm saying it. Like is there a weird rhythm in my voice?"

"Mind if I make some tea?" Peter asked Jack.

"No, mate. Help yourself. I'll have one too, please."

Avery felt a little hurt over being ignored like that, and it made him miss Lisa and feel bad for leaving her. She would never belittle him by pretending what he said was so stupid that the vibrations they made in the air didn't exist. And all three of them did it- Peter, Norman, and, worst of all, Jack. But Peter was thoughtful enough to turn around before he got to the kitchen and ask if anyone else would like a cup, and that made the situation more palatable.

CHAPTER 71

Avery started typing at 2:06 p.m. Around him, washers and dryers toiled, expressing long, bombilating low grunts, hums, clicks and clacks. It was the perfect place to be hung over. It was uncomfortable station for an uncomfortable body. It was also lacking in one damned obnoxious thing- distraction.

Not for years had Avery gone so long without

writing. Back in West Palm, afternoons slaving over the keyboard were recurring exercises, with drawn shades keeping the daylight out, and the computer screen was the only bright thing in the world. There, Mr. Chase had a hundred origins. An ostrich spread his jewel-colored dragon wings and set out for the moon. All manner of implausible stories were mapped out from the bedroom, stashed in the file dubbed 'writings'.

But not so in London- because London had Lisa, pubs, photographers, landmarks, bright signs, hot kicks, rock and roll, be seen-ability, do this, go there, check that out, oh, oh, let's. So the basement it was, while the laundry rolled.

Avery dredged through the innards of invisigrams, seeking substance.

The piece was almost finished. It was called Mosaic Tiles between Your Ribs, and it kicked off with "A few less or more than 1000 times upon a time," before describing a boy wearing a gray tracksuit walking down Oxford Street. He was wearing a red baseball cap, too- so low on his face that if you were an average length person you would have to bend at the neck, knees, or waist to see his eyes. Around him, a brown Staffordshire Terrier orbited. The dog's show of control, especially in the midst of such distracting hustle and bustle was astounding, and suggested an uncanny potential for intelligence and trainability in the breed. Really though, it spoke for the sheer number of grisly lashings the dog was forced to endure. Stop, get hit. Run, get hit. It was a phenomenon that at some level, the boy in the gray tracksuit and red hat understood perfectly.

Nobody he recognized was waiting outside the H&M. Or was it supposed to be the HMV? Or HSBC?

Damn. Gotta start writing things down, he thought. It threw all the other details into question. Was it 14:00 and was it Tuesday? The date November 29? Was he even selling drugs? A troop of Paki girls shroud in their designer niqabs walked past briskly. The scene made him jealous of their money, that they could so brazenly wrap themselves in yards of that expensive Burberry trademark plaid. Someday. Someday his potential for greatness would see itself realized. A shadow of his future self, he would catch up to what would be or rather will be. Money and a degree of fame. The MTV generation could expect nothing less. In the quest for ratings, they'd almost all been lied to.

London isn't warm in November. How could the confidence of any man wearing practically see through pants outside not wane? At the right/wrong angle, a body could get an unjustified, misleading idea of what was covered. But everyone was doing it. It must be okay. He'd heard that in China, men his age were going ga-ga for Levi's jeans. It was something he believed without question. On the other side of the street, James spotted the black lad he'd been looking for.

Stace was the man's name. Real name, nickname, or short for Stacey, nobody knew. The width of his body, combined with the width of his all black clothing confused some people. Is that a man or a Taxi? That kind of thing. The two hoodlums talked for a few minutes.

"Alright, Stace."

"Yeah, alright, mate."

Stace talked about a girl he'd brought home from the End the night before. He didn't know if she'd passed out before or during their sexual encounter. Probably before, knowing Stace. Somebody's daughter, sister, best-friend, Stace couldn't care less. His mind was not normal. There was no compassion in it. No empathy. Nor real acknowledgement of wrong, law, or consequence. But Stace and James were business partners. To fuck one partner, you have to fuck both partners, and nobody but nobody was going to fuck Stace unless they were young girls close to overdosing on god-knows-what.

"Spoke with the door. It's all set up. We're golden."

They went nuts over this stuff. They being the customers. They were buying a grand old time that would last most of the night for just five quid. They were buying stronger friendships. Rhythm. Bliss and wanton contentment.

Shame that the dog couldn't come.

At last, loud music. So loud that your brain can't hear its own complaining. It was impossible to think of waking up on Monday morning or processing paperwork on Thursday afternoon. Everyone just go talk to Stace, he's a well pleasant chap in this environment.

Next to the bar, two construction workers vocalize appreciation for their lasting status as co-workers.

In front of the speakers, a 17 year old boy is banging his head. His eardrums have never suffered this much punishment, but fun is all that registers.

On the stairs, a Japanese girl in England for fashion school talks to a shy red-head. They have nothing in common but euphoric states of mind but that's all that really matters.

The dark and criminal are almost nauseating concepts now to all but the most depraved of men. Everyone wonderfully connected.

The boy in the gray tracksuit wouldn't be identified as that anymore. He and Stace ran out of pills only three hours into the night, saving two a-piece. Nothing to do now but have a good time and hang on tight to the money. Oh, right- the reason you wouldn't call him the boy in the gray tracksuit anymore is because he'd taken it off. He was bare-chested now, drenched in sweat, dancing like a cross between an American Indian warrior and a frog. A girl had been dancing next to him for almost twenty minutes. Her desire to talk to him was so obvious, so tangible, so palpable that it was practically a third person dancing between them. The non-threatening gay friend that just LOVED to play matchmaker. He didn't find the girl so attractive at first, but the drugs- exertion and drugs soon did a better job than the gay friend that wasn't there at all.

They talked eventually when he asked her for a cigarette.

Thirty minutes later they spoke again when he offered her a sip of water and she said thank you.

It was probably nothing. Even the drugs said so. There was that sketchy feeling, that 'this isn't entirely real' feeling. They all knew that there was a time, a time fast approaching where the ecstasy would wear off, the love would dissipate, and the club would close. Probably it would come around six o'clock.

Now get the N2 back to Brixton. Maybe you'll even have company.

The end.

Lisa turned her head from the screen, pulled her lips back for a split second and set them normal, avoided eye contact with Avery, looked back at the computer, touched the mouse, scrolled to the top of the page, and said, "Mm-Hmm."

Avery was at a loss for words. He mocked her

344

utterance of 'Mm-Hmm' but added to his a question mark.

"Guess I can't like everything you write," she said. There was a touch of bravery in her voice. Defiance.

"What don't you like about it?"

Once more Lisa's eyes shifted toward the screen. She let them go out of focus, gazing into the blurry black accents on the white page, as if there were some equation, some arithmetic hidden there that could be applied and prove his art bogus. She was still unsure of how much she wanted to hurt him.

The story, the telling it, interpretation of it, critiquing- it was hard for the two of them. Avery and Lisa shared a short conversation only twelve hours before, and to be sure it ended in tears and trauma. He was out too late with strange people. She decided not to come and that was her fault. Avery's peace-offering was a story he'd just written. That it was a peace-offering, Lisa was totally unaware.

"There's no life in it. I don't know if it's bad or not, I just don't like it."

"So you don't like it but you don't know why," Avery said, in a very predictably, childishly defensive color. "Don't tell me when you don't like something anymore," breathless speech, "Just fucking lie," monotone low, "I need confidence, not unfounded criticism from a fragile little girl," becoming not the bomb, but the hand at the launch, not the blast which ate brick and bone alike, burned man and woman and dog with the lack of prejudice that only nature can exercise, but the enlightened conscious behind it, "It's so heartless, Lisa," when the wall of light would hollow the shells of countless innocents, would poison the land, would burn the children, "But you wouldn't understand, would you? Everything you have has been given to you. It's all free of charge and effort," the thumb at the switch.

"Fragile little girl, huh? Who's acting fucking fragile?"

As to whether or not the hurt in Lisa's voice had been embellished by her apparently successful drama training, Avery could not know. Redress seemed hopeless. Damn last night. Sure it was fun, but damn it anyways. That phone call and the drugs and the music and the void of visual love and the fighting and when you're around and when you're not around and, and, and. Some points in his explosion rang logical, at other times not. Sometimes he made sense, at other times merely noise. Still he was trying, and crying, and he felt she had to award him at least sympathy points for that.

"I don't want you to censor yourself. I also don't want to read a hardly fictionalized version of what you did last night when it sounds like this. I know you were dancing with those girls. Were you all fucked up? Feeling good? Did you make out with them or fuck them? What's this last line? 'Get the N2 back to Brixton, maybe you'll even have company.' That's how you think, I know it. Think about taking some complete stranger home and fucking her. I know how you write when something's real. Some of this is real. You're talking about this real fun time you had, dancing and doing drugs with random girls. Taking a stranger home. How could you really think I'd enjoy this?"

"It's fiction, my love," Avery said with a forged air of condescension, "None of it is real."

"Sure. Well, I'm glad you had fun," Lisa answered. But it was painfully obvious to both of them, that she wasn't glad of it at all.

346

CHAPTER 72

At a certain height, civilization shows itself as one big circuit-board.

At a certain height, civilization shows itself as one big monopoly-money-spending-circuit-board.

Asphalt conductors were down there, bouncing cars back and forth on their many errands, various but not so different, electrons often on the path to goods, to buy, to become themselves economic electricity. Steel and concrete resistors, they stop the electrons- post offices and laundromats and furniture stores and schools and workplaces galore erected to introduce friction into the many lives that pass through them, robbing them of energy and sending them on their way. Capacitors keep safe the energy of men and women below, sometimes dishing it out in loans, only to recharge themselves again with interest, titles, and real honest-to-goodness wealth.

Thus Avery was currently learning, but there was even more to it than that.

The forms were telling. The mathematical theories describing control of electrical energy can be right away directly appropriated to the energy powering the economies of the world.

Potential energy, instead of being represented by capacitors in the case of electronic engineering, would be represented by Capital in economic engineering.

Kinetic energy, instead of being represented by inductors in the case of electronic engineering, would be represented by Services in economic engineering.

Conductors, represented by Goods, are plugged into the same equations, and with but a little translation world economies can be charted and manipulated.

So what? Avery began to wonder. His knowledge of electronics was every bit as limited as his acquaintance with Goods affecting Services, the difference between hindsight flow and foresight flow, or how the price of oil might predetermine Budweiser's quarterly profit margins. His eyes were getting heavy. He was skimming through the information too quickly, not pledging as much consideration as the information warranted.

Much of modern economic engineering was learned through The Harvard Economic Research Project. The elites of the world wanted a way to scientifically regulate the economy. Map a thing only to rearrange the thing. It was the Harvard team that discovered that the structure of economy was identical to microchips in action. Capital, Goods, and Services- Capacitance, Conductance, Inductance- coulombs to dollars, volts to dollar demand, amperes per volt to dollars per dollar demand. The theoretical economists needed only find what aspect of electronics the economic factors pertained to.

This was and is being accomplished by shock testing certain markets and labor pools. Economic shock testing is the process of forcing a change in the price or availability of one or more commodities, and observing the waves of effect it has on advertising, sales, and prices of that said commodity or commodities and others related to it. Done enough and studied enough, buying impulses become predictable, and the benighted public can be subtlety led in any direction that the economic engineers choose. Eventually the collapse of currency will be brought about, and a New World Order born.

A rhinoceros of a man slumped over in the seat beside Avery. The man was too large for his own single seat, and his superfluous bulk flowed into 23A and 23C to the right and left, respectively. This was the main cause of Avery's discomfort, for beyond the anxiety that being seated next to such a dry skinned, red-nosed, permanently scowling man caused, the rhinoceros was making absolutely no bones about hogging both arm-rests. Avery's eyes were dry and irritated, and he could find no restful position in which to sleep. Any time Avery tried to spread his legs, his knee would run into the rhino, whose leg was surely trespassing into Avery's paid-for space.

Avery had also to consider the state of Florida, and the state of affairs it was and would be in. Hurricane Patricia had just blown through, leaving much of West Palm Beach powerless, and supply trains had only in the last few hours been able to make their rounds. Debris still covered the streets, homes were without electricity, gas stations without gas, restaurants without food, and last Avery heard, a curfew was still in effect. This, just in time for Thanksgiving.

Avery zipped his book in his bag and shoved it under the seat before him with his feet. He slid his shoes off. The rhinoceros was wheezing.

Outside, dusk. Dark descended upon the microchip lands like the first of God's fallen angels. The darkness in the air, darkness in man's brain, the same self appointed few that set the volume of advertisement want the people as dumb as possible. To misdirect their attentions to things that don't matter, to give them nothing more than a child's entertainment, to bombard them with work, work, work.

A dark future, according to the book at his feet. Perhaps that's what was affecting him. The book. Making him feel ill at ease. No, it was surely the rhinoceros. Avery finally decided to wrest sleep from within, violently if necessary. He crossed his arms hard, made as much space as he could between him and the big man to his right, leaned his head against the window, shut his eyes, and wished to watch the world as some wish it short circuit.

CHAPTER 73

"There he is," J.P. found, voice smeared with complacency and satisfaction.

They were three very refreshing words to hear, on one hand because it meant that Avery was there and they could stop driving the same vortical, toilet bowl pattern around the airport, and on the other, because it was the first time in hours that J.P. had strayed from the subject of Daniel Aston. It was a hard enough subject to ignore without all the oratory aide memoire.

"Get over!" Michael yelled.

J.P.'s head was cranked around at such an angle that his face contorted into both a silly and frightful thing. He had two lanes to cross, two too busy lanes, and these Miami drivers didn't lightly make room.

"Muscle up, man! Damn."

But it was already too late. J.P. was too high to drive aggressively. Avery's reflection grew smaller and smaller in the rear view mirrors, and J.P. sighed a reluctant agreement to make one more loop around the airport.

"Unacceptable."

"They weren't letting me in!"

"Alright, alright. He was on concourse J, *just* as I instructed. I'll light this up- get it ready, so it's going around when he gets in. Unlock the doors, pop the trunk when we hit the curb, he'll throw his bags in, we pick him up, one, two, three, back on the highway. What else?"

"What do you mean, 'what else'? I got this under control."

"You're right," Michael said. Everything was beginning to feel like a game to him. He hoped that J.P. was as stoned as he was. "I'm just the navigator. You're calling the shots, boss man. You really should have honked when we passed him, though."

Avery didn't realize he'd been passed up until the same car came back and two familiar faces were inside it. A smile was born.

The stately chariot pulled alongside, driven by a Japanese-made 1.8 liter engine, and a pleasant noise of music and 'hey!'s emanating beyond the frame. It was a greenish Honda Civic hatchback, probably a 96, in good cosmetic condition. It wasn't perhaps the car that most suited J.P., but J.P. looked plenty happy behind the wheel. Avery leaned through the open window of the passenger door and gave his brother a big kiss on the side of his face. A great feeling blood beat in all of them. Anticipations realized. The three young men couldn't count a care in the world.

"Pop the trunk."

J.P. obliged and in almost no time at all, just after Avery was situated and heartfelt greetings were passed around and they were following signs back to I-95, was back beating the dead horse that Michael was surely hoping had been assigned to oblivion. "I have to fill you in," he started. Michael blew an arrow of smoke, muttering quiet requests for J.P. to shut up, to absolutely no avail. "We used to hang out on this little boat by Joe's house. I found it a couple months ago and every now and then we'd go hang out there. This is so fucked up, man. Listen. Oh, thanks," J.P. accepted the joint. "We go there every now and then. Not that often because, you know. But sometimes. So we were there one night, me and Michael and Jamul and these two young ass girls, just hanging out, you know, smoking some weed and shit."

"Okay. So you were hanging out at this place that you sometimes go to but not often because, like, you only go there now and then. A boat, you said."

"Yeah, a boat." J.P. missed the subtle criticism of his story-telling. "You have to get that because if you don't know it's a boat none of it will make sense. This night I'm talking about was like, what, like three weeks ago or something. Anyway, this one night we were there hanging out, and when we were leaving Michael decided to give the boat a blessing. I was kind of fucked up so I don't remember what he said exactly, but it was a big blessing about keeping the boat and the owner together."

"What?" Avery interjected.

"Yeah, about keeping the boat and the owner together. That was the gist of it. What did you say, Michael? You remember."

Michael inferred that he was not interested in retelling it.

J.P. continued, a bit let down by Michael's lack of cooperation, "Whatever, man. What I'm getting at is this- Michael blessed the boat and the captain, togetherness, key word- *together*. And a couple weeks later the hurricane came.

"This storm was crazy, man. All kinds of shit is fucked up. Fucking trees knocked over, power down everywhere, houses destroyed. I mean not terrible but pretty bad. Well this guy, Daniel Aston shot himself in the head just before the storm hit. The papers said that nobody knew why he did it. He didn't show any suicidal tendencies. All his friends and family were shocked. But it turns out, just after he killed himself the storm hit, and his boat sank. He fucking killed himself, and his boat sank a few days later."

"That's pretty far-out," Avery said, "What a weird coincidence."

"Coincidence? Coincidence? No. No coincidence. Your brother put that spell on him. Him and the boat, I mean. Just like I think he put that spell on my car."

Avery laughed powerfully. Like a troop of third graders watching an overweight postman trip over a curb and belly flop to the concrete.

"What J.P. is doing here," said Michael, sounding very bored, "is assigning a sense of responsibility to me for things that were obviously beyond mortal control. It's easier for him to exist with guilt than with helplessness. A classic case of magical thinking and moral defense, projected onto me, because he's got a gelatinous backbone. He can't stomach the notion that it's a cruel world. He's like a hundred generations of peasants, all tortured and oppressed, thinking that they deserve their misery because they're born sinners."

A short silence.

"You lost me," Avery said, not really listening. J.P. was pretty sure that he didn't like the comparison, so it made him happy to hear Avery say that. But there was still the threat of Michael expounding upon the point, which would likely be an exponentiation of the original insult, dispensed even more slowly and articulately. Plans of escape built themselves in J.P.'s whirling conscious. Still time. Still time.

"So, Avery, what's new these days?"

It was unfortunate, Avery thought, that such an innocent, open-ended question could sound so heavy. All the new things these days were obstacles, it seemed like. And though his vacation was just starting, he knew it would be over soon. The question took him right back to London.

"I don't know. Lots. Lisa's going to be moving all our stuff into a new hostile in the next couple days, so there's that. New home base."

"Where is it?" Michael asked.

"It's on Gloucester Road. Not too far from where we're staying now. Really nice neighborhood. And it's cheap- like eight quid a night.

"But other than moving not a lot's happening. Work has been pretty slow. I did a shoot the other day with these guys from Thailand that didn't hardly speak any English. I was talking my shirt off for one of the shots and one of the guys, who was one of the most effeminate guys I've ever worked with, said something and they all started laughing. So I was like, 'Guys, I know what you're talking about,' and then they all got really embarrassed. But of course I was jumping to all sorts of conclusions there.

"And then there was this shoot for a magazine called Elle Girl, me and this thirteen year old girl. She could have passed for seventeen easy, but she wasn't. She was thirteen. Thirteen, motherfucker. And her mom was there. The photographer was giving us all this weird direction, making it really awkward. He was saying like-

'Put your faces together. Look into each other's eyes, like you're about to kiss. Grab her leg, spread your fingers out and really give it a squeeze.' And her mom was there the whole time, right? I don't know, man. It was funny."

'Poor Avery,' J.P. and Michael mused in turn. 'Poor Avery had to grope a virgin Aphrodite in front of her mom.' 'Poor Avery had to take his shirt off for one hundred quid.' 'Poor Avery had to lunch with some of the most beautiful girls in the world in a room where nobody knows anybody but everyone's willing to try.' 'Poor Avery, who with the modern-day cultural epicenter of Europe as his playground, had to find ways to pass the time.' 'Poor Avery, who...'

"Good God, alright. I'm not complaining. I'm just saying, that's what's new. Fuck. Besides being broke all the time, yeah, being in London is tits. And when I go back, I'll have a two year work visa. Pretty much be all set."

And down the highway the little Civic traveled, leaving the still things far behind, riding alongside all the other cars, screaming by South Florida overpasses, sounding to the vagrant men beneath them like a battalion of Tie-Fighters.

CHAPTER 74

Luke's version of the history, like so many other versions, was a version unto itself. But blame the boy not, for true history is surely buried with the bones that saw it through, and the whispered mendacity that blows across the ages can only be translated by living souls not fluent in the language. We begin our journey outside the gilded walls of King Solomon's temple with the Who playing a live version of 'My Generation' in the background.

"When the Mason's were building their cathedrals and temples and monoliths, the people that saw these structures could only believe that they were bestowed upon them by God, and it would have completely blown their socks off."

"Blown their sandals off," Avery said. He wasn't being entirely facetious, he was just drunk and wasn't likely to hesitate in saying the things that occurred to him to say.

"Socks, sandals, socks, sandals," Luke sang in an operatic voice, "You're missing the point," still singing, also drunk.

"No. Go on."

"Okay, well as I was saying, the Masons had knowledge of building that was way beyond the rest of the people at that point. They would see a place like King Solomon's temple, all the gold, bigger," Luke was really on a roll. His hands and eyes were as much a part of his performance as his mouth. He was the camp councilor presiding over the campfire, the principle over the loudspeaker, the newly made star under the shiny limelight, "more exquisite than any building in the land by a million miles and it was like, 'holy shit'. It was like that in all the early civilizations. Egypt, Israel, and all throughout Europe. They knew tricks of the trade that no one else knew, until eventually the knowledge of the people caught up. The Masons would have taught some, then taught some more, and some more, and some more, until eventually these buildings were big and great, but by now they were the work of men, not God.

"When that happened, when too many people knew the tricks of the trade, Freemasonry replaced Masonry as the forward advanced and secret movement. Instead of reshaping the world with building and architecture, they used philosophy. And I'm pretty sure their goal was to change society's mind about religions and governments. The church and the Monarchy together."

"Sure. Like Thomas Paine. After the American Revolution he went and did the exact same thing in France. He was a Freemason." Avery said. He turned his head to the side and realized the party was in full swing. (That the party was in full swing could be interpreted in more ways than one. The party was in full swing- rooms were fairly full, music was playing, beer was flowing, boys and girls smiling, laughing, gesturing, enjoying the ambiance of the lively apartment. The party was in full swing- the party itself wouldn't sit still. It moved and swayed in ways that made Avery a little dizzy. He had to concentrate to stand completely upright.)

Luke said, "Yeah," with a cast-off, lost-track-train-of-thought expression.

At this point Michael approached. He was moving about the crowd of young women like a clownfish sieves through anemones. More quiet and friendly confidence than Avery could ever remember.

"Luke couldn't wait to hit you with this, man. He's been chomping at the bit all week," Michael said.

It was an interruption, sure. It sidetracked the conversation. But as burning charcoal eventually grays and goes out, Luke and Avery were soon back on the topic of Freemasonry. This bored Michael, who went back to where J.P. was standing. What Luke and Avery couldn't deduce was why an organization that once won the world with righteous benevolence presently wanted to burn the patriots and shackle the leftovers. Luke's presentation grew more subdued, and his mood along with it. To look at him in the lively party, with that sad a face, was an exercise in acute cognitive dissidence.

"I came across this one video showing one of these concentration camps popping up. There was only one entrance and exit. It was this big, like, round shaped, umm, you know, concrete, like," Luke said. His face contorted. He was obviously wholly unable to find an apposite word, "A dome. A little concrete dome fortress."

"Like a bunker or something?"

"Yes. Like that. And passed that bunker there were all these turnstiles. The kind they use in the New York subways at night. Floor to Ceiling bars. And I noticed that some of the badges on the turnstiles were almost exactly the same as the dollar bill. The all-seeing eye on the pyramid."

It was relevant to some of Avery's reading material. Certain conspiracy theorists went so far as to say that anyone with any ties to patriotic groups, with histories of violent behavior, with paper-trails linking them to subversive political organizations or even records of certain books purchased on credit should not spend holidays at home, because someday the occupation of this land by its own rulers will be a go, and the presumed threats will be snatched up in the night. See, Storm-Troopers, Nazi Germany.

"Yeah, I mean it's scary. But there would have to have to have to be warning signs. That happened in Germany, but it wasn't like there wasn't both social and political turmoil beforehand. But still…"

Avery stopped when Michael lifted him up by the waist. Avery turned around immediately, instinctively grabbing his brother's neck and hooking his foot around his brother's leg, that way Michael couldn't lift him any higher.

A small struggle ensued, stopping only when Michael ran into an accordion style closet door, and enough noise was made to be noticed and scolded. Lots of people stopped what they were doing and turned their attentions to the commotion.

"Man, you will never- never be able to overpower me," Avery said.

Michael flexed his bicep and through a cocky smile, hissed.

And so the gauntlet had been thrown down. The only way to settle the thing now was to settle the thing. Avery and Michael went outside, followed by a small group of eager spectators.

It was just like old times. Old times because West Palm Beach was all around him, the same thick flakes of itchy grass, and the sprinklers that dampened them at night, the same new apartment buildings everywhere, big wide streets connecting all the spread out development, and those good-old familiar faces, dark and shadowy under the downward yellow-glow of streetlights. There seemed to be so much space. Big parking lots and patches of grass between everything.

Michael was within arm's reach, bouncing up and down with a slight horizontal deviation. Avery heard himself saying that Michael hadn't a snowballs chance in hell of surviving. Michael went to grab Avery's wrists then, which he accomplished, but it was nothing Avery wasn't used to. For three years, Avery had spent every school-day afternoon in the wrestling room, training for just such situations, and though drunk and out of practice, reacted with muscle memory that Michael wasn't ready for.

Avery lifted his arms, ducked fast, shot forward. Michael was forced to relinquish his grasp on Avery's wrists, and tried to under-hook his older brother's arms. But it was no use. The shot had been a kind of fake, and instead of going for the legs, Avery had gone completely behind him, with one arm around his waist, and the other arm between his legs, grabbing the first arm in a classic t-bone style. Michael was in the air, falling back, back, back, until he eventually felt the up and down motion stop, right where Avery's chest started. Michael counted himself lucky that his fall was broken by Avery, and wasted no time in doing whatever he could to gain the upper hand.

Avery regained consciousness suddenly. He was face down in the grass, with his head and neck being propped up by Michael, who was on his back and choking the life out of him.

"CHHHHPMMMP…" the grunt was muffled by Michael's forearm as it traveled through Avery's throat. Not that it changed the meaning of the sound, merely the acoustic quality of it.

"I think you should let him go," J.P. offered.

A swirling sensation filled Avery's head. A swirling-pounding. It was a sensation parented by hearing and vision, a sort of mixed up something that spoke not to his eyes and ears, but to his brain directly.

"He'll tap," Michael said.

Someone in the crowd took a picture.

Avery made another sound, similar to the first but not as forceful. He managed to tap his hand against Michael's arm.

"What the fuck, man." Avery announced a

moment later. He was still on the ground, nursing the meat around his windpipe. "Fucking choking me while I'm passed out. Damn. And you guys didn't do shit about it?"

But there wasn't a sober soul in the crowd. Not by a long shot. Shrugs and quick frowns blinked on and off like fireflies throughout the rabble.

CHAPTER 75

Pride pooled in Mr. Thurbin's eyes when he looked at Avery's right eye, in which a patch of blood pooled. Weird how happy it made him. Mr. Thurbin didn't attempt to contain his mirth, looking from Michael to Avery's injury, and back again and back again.

"I don't know. I wasn't really awake for it," Avery was explaining.

But the delighted eyeballs of Mr. Thurbin ogled Michael, checked the vortex of Avery's darting gaze, went again to Michael. Again to Avery.

"Anyway, it doesn't hurt. Just looks bad."

Michael had apologized enough by now to chime in without guilt. His pronouncement was made with a more or less detached nonchalance, on and on about how the blood-clot is only a testament to Avery's moral fiber and how it would surely increase his marketability in a world of tough facades and rugged masks, where a tasteful flaw could double as trademark beauty-spot.

"Yeah. I have a maroon Atlantic Ocean painted on my eyeball," Avery responded.

Misrepresentation. Accidental, but inaccurate. The blood-clot was much more comparable to the Indian Ocean, not the Atlantic, in shape, size, and placement, allowing that the pupil and retina should substitute for the continent of Africa. Mr. Thurbin still looked proud. Proud as ever. He was the lioness, and Michael the young daughter, halfway through her first kill, or would it be his first kill? Pride. Pleasure. Bloodlust.

"…" Avery didn't say anything. But it was obvious enough that he was going to. His exhale was the ghost of some complaint about his busted blood-vessel, or excuse involving the circumstances under which he was bested. The oomph was something he was going to say, but at the last moment thought better of. He wasn't fond of Mr. Thurbin's garage, or Mr. Thurbin for that matter. He wanted to leave soon, and promised himself that he would. The less idle chit-chat, the better.

Michael's body was hidden by the hood of Mr. Thurbin's Mustang. To that mutant power-plant, he whispered sweet-nothings.

Be cool, baby. Breathe. Take all the breath you want. Breathe and be cool.

"Done?" Mr. Thurbin asked, stepping back into the garage.

"Yeah, yeah. I'm all finished," Michael answered, "Check it out."

Mr. Thurbin walked over, stopped, planted on two sturdy feet, standing as tall and as straight and as proud as any one of the eternal Sequoia.

Yes, Michael had it in him. Killer instinct. The God-head. The desire to conquer, to offer up fresh blood to the Earth, to wash clean the planet from everyone-from the rich to the poor, dead to the holy, the insatiable drive to soak his hands in red lurked somewhere near the surface of him.

"You say it's done, it's done."

Michael twisted out from under the hood.

"What do you feel like doing now?" Mr. Thurbin said.

Michael told him that he should probably get going, being that Avery was in town and all, but he wanted to take the car for a quick spin just to make sure everything was okay.

The garage opened with as much to-do as usual-shaking, squeaking, and shuddering like an earthquake through Tokyo, and closed behind them with the same effect. Mr. Thurbin was driving with a straight face. His fatherly pride beamed with much less intensity than before.

"I meant what do you feel like doing. Not what you plan on doing. What do you feel like doing? Honestly."

"Fuck. I don't know, man. Shoot a pumpkin with an AK-47?"

Not bad. He was getting there. Killer instinct. Instinct that could be trained, molded.

"You know what's great about this world that we live in?"

Michael noted that the car was running beautifully. It felt faster, more alive. "Wait- are you waiting for me to answer? That's a rhetorical question, no?"

It was. "There are a lot of things different about us, Michael. You and me, you and your brother, your brother and that fucking retard across the street, everyone. We're all different. But you know how we're not? We all live in physical bodies. Weak castles that we hide ourselves in. We're all on an even playing field. The one thing that every human being has in common is a susceptibility

363

to foreign objects slit or shot into a vital organ. Their skulls all cave in with enough force. A single jolt and its curtains. Game over for anyone, as long as you have the determination."

Michael asked, among a few other things (such as- what the fuck's gotten into you?), if Mr. Thurbin had ever actually killed someone.

"Not as far as the law knows."

Michael said, "No, seriously."

"Can you keep a secret?"

Michael said, "Sure."

"I kill people all the time. You should come sometime."

Michael turned his attention out the window and to the steady roar of the engine, saying, "Oh, I get it," before missing the shrug of Mr. Thurbin's shoulders.

But it doesn't end there. Just before midnight, while Michael, Avery, Luke, Jamul, J.P., and a flux of strangers drank cheap domestic pitchers and played shuffleboard and darts, Mr. Thurbin masturbated in the shower, his sense of pride replaced by sheer private humiliation, because the thought of Michael strangling the life out of Avery while a helpless crowd watched had him as turned on as he could ever remember. The picture played from flaccidity to orgasm, and more than a couple times.

CHAPTER 76

A woman, old and pale to begin with, looking paler and paler by the second, paler until her wrinkled skin looked more blue-green than human, stumbled to escape the theater. The man behind her turned one last glower to the stage- despicable, abominable show, just the kind of noise that happens when you put something in the unchaperoned hands of youth. He, too, felt nauseous. With all its near-perfect acoustics, the theater was turning many a stomach, and setting many a body on edge. Some of the less adventurous were finally jumping ship.

Walt Disney was nauseous for days. Damn the cartoonists, but so were they. How could he have known that the sound of a soldering iron played at five times less than normal speed would produce such a sickening sound?

Damn this dizziness, Walt Disney thought.

Hitler ignored the nausea. Hate, anxiety, and disorientation were felt in the fretful masses before his podiums. Every time his words spoke to their ears, sounds beneath their ears spoke directly to their bodies. All the fears and apprehensions of Germany, stirred by a seemingly inaudible noise. The menace coursing in their bodies, Hitler instructed, was the enemy's fault- and as the infrasonic precursor to earthquakes demands horses dash violent circles, Holocaust.

Every man and woman in the audience, regardless of whether they had had the experience of raising children, regardless of whether or not they could relate to a father's chronic disappointment or the gravity of losing a son, each and every one was tricked into empathizing. In the third row, two spaces from the aisle, there sat a two hundred and twenty pound man of walking muscles. The man's knees were pressed together, his elbows were tucked tightly to his sides, his back looked all the ripples and bumps of a married couple completely under the covers of a king sized bed, his face frozen- shock, concern, by all objective observations, fear.

Up front, the strobe effect roared right alongside the lead actor.

"My Donald! My Donald! Could I possibly? A new Donald?" he screamed. Shame, excitement, dejection, exuberance, agitation, and vigor all in one voice.

Only two objects were in view. A simple set-up. Strobe lights, smoke, and Donald Senior in the middle of the stage, with his back to the audience, looking up at an enormous projection screen suspended fifteen feet from the ground. His acting was tremendous. This was mostly because he was undergoing the same physiological strain as the rest of the audience, and more or less forgot he was acting.

Words flashed on the screen with burning luminescence, the kind that seems to stick into your forehead afterward like the flash of archaic cameras- 'YOU CAN', 'YOU WANT TO'.

Subdued groans were raised in spots throughout the crowd. Michael had just hit them with another blast of inaudible sound.

It was noise that was instead a spinning room. It was the chatter of your brain after a vigorous blow to the head. It made the world beat in unison with your heart.

It sent the audience into survival mode, their intellects retreated and they believed wholeheartedly that the man on stage was nothing other than Donald agreeing to trade in his own flesh and blood for a robot replacement. They believed in aliens. In technologies not of this Earth. Dopey failure for mechanical genius. Skin and bone for nuts and bolts. Disbelief all suspended and ignored. The physical edginess could only be associated with Donald's inner turmoil- the sine waves carried it up and down the aisles, through walls, through skulls, three hundred sixty degrees.

Luke leaned forward and whispered in Avery's ear.

"The demons are feasting right now."

"Huh?" Avery asked. He was observably vexed.

"I said the demons are feasting right now."

"I heard that but what the fuck are you talking about?"

Luke said that he would explain later, leaned back in his chair, and looked around to see if he and Avery had disturbed either of the women next to him. The last thing that Avery said was much louder than a whisper. They looked perturbed, the two ladies, but surely it wasn't a big deal. It's not like they would know anything about demons or lower fourth dimensional vibrations.

Before long, the curtains dropped, and Michael relinquished his precarious hold over the audience. Men and women squirmed in their seats. In the next act, robot Donald Jr. graduated high-school with honors, and gave an orotund acceptance speech, posing the question- is the market of emotions cornered by organic beings? In the final act, Donald Senior found the magazine that exposed his secret career as Ambassador of Earth, and was shocked to find that it was written by none other than the boy he traded away, the human Donald Jr. Still, the viewers were slow to recover. After the hesitant ovations were given to cast and crew, when the house lights went on and the show clearly over, men and women walked out as though they were wading through the shallow end of a swimming pool.

In the first couple rows, quite a few people weren't moving at all.

"I said that the demons were having a feast."

"Luke, goddamn it, I said I heard that part, I just didn't know what you meant by it. Still don't. What'd you think of the play?"

Luke felt hindered by Avery's question, but answered anyway. "Oh, it was fantastic. Never seen anything like it."

"I feel like I need a drink."

"Soon, my friend. Soon. First allow me to explain. Were you feeling anxious during the alien scene? You were, right?"

Avery admitted that yes, he was, and asked Luke if he felt anything similar.

"Yeah. Definitely. Everyone was. So what I meant by 'the demons are having a feast' is this- all that anxiety and fear that the audience was feeling, those emotions are essentially energy that resonates at a certain frequency. Fear and grief and terror and shit like that resonates at the same frequency as the lower fourth dimensional plane. That's the space that negative entities live. Negative energy goes there and comes from there."

His head shook, his face puckered- it was clear that Avery had heard enough. "That's fairy tale shit."

"Oh is it? Is it, now? That's why," Luke started, but Avery cut him off by placing a hand directly over his face.

"You couldn't prove any of that in a billion years," Avery said.

Luke shook his face free and wiped his lips with a shirtsleeve. It was a long, long way from the response he'd expected.

CHAPTER 77

Every congratulation to the White Man. You have spread your polish, your perspicacity, your top-hat ways upon those without, invited or not, with unswervingly objective insistence. You have proved that men, regardless of what corner of the Earth they call home, what shade reflects from their skin, bleed a shade of red. You have used their lands to the land's utmost potential. You have relieved so many from the burden of ownership, of self-sufficiency, of that pesky, trite, complicated notion of freedom. You have humbly received your dominance through tanks and television commercials, hydrogen bomb bursting and Hollywood, militia and modern-science buttressed marketing. You provide work for the poor and impoverished, and ever so ever so selflessly show them the way to wanting more of it. Civilize them. You are the cultivator. The teacher.

Let us celebrate on this fourth Thursday of November with gluttonous feast the sweeping up and taking care of they, them, and those; least not to forget us, we, and who. All together, now- give thanks.

The Tyler family was gathered in typical Tyler fashion, remote in their close vicinities, food and drink going in, passive aggressive observations, remarks, and annotations going out. Avery thought that if one could harness the breath of his relations, and all the critical energy those breaths encompassed, the so-called world energy crisis would be solved.

"Give any thought of going to college yet?"

"How much money do you owe your mother now?"

"I hope you're paying more attention to that poor girlfriend of yours."

"Why does he read that garbage?"

It was a fine tradition, directly in step with culture. Individuals were present, the White Man, blasting his own world across the world, seeing that his point of view conquered. Death and taxes to the dissenters.

"How long do you expect to make a living with that? You're going to have to come back to the real world sometime, am I right?" Avery's uncle asked him.

The table was shaped like two halves of a circle on either side of a square. The table-cloth was white, with another white layer on top of it that looked like a gigantic paper snowflake. There were red, ribbed placemats, three candles in a line lengthwise halfway between everyone, a glass for each water, a glass for each wine, white napkins that the adults had taken over their laps, and one still remaining on the table before the child. But this is only still life. The display-case against the wall and all the porcelain clowns it contained is not important, nor is the yellowed, smoke-stained popcorn ceiling, pieces of which were always falling off if someone slammed a door, nor the wall paper. The people- that's what Thanksgiving is all about.

Sitting at the north and south ends of the table were Avery's Grandfather and Grandmother, respectively. There was his Uncle Ron to his left, and Michael to his right. Uncle Ron was sitting across from his wife, Bea. Across from Avery was his thirteen year old cousin, Gil, and across from Michael was their grandparent's next-door neighbor, Mrs. Green.

Avery wondered how such an annoying, antagonistic question could be asked so casually. "This whole set-up is great, isn't it? Family. Food. Look at this table cloth, for instance- fine stuff, this. Bit of a Christmas feel to it, all the white a red, but it's really nice. Thank you, Grandma and Grandpa."

By this obvious retreat, Avery's Uncle was spurred on even more.

"I don't mean to harp on you, it just seems like you could be doing a lot more with yourself and," he swallowed the yams he was speaking around, "and if I'm not mistaken, Michael, you'd have all sorts of opportunities for a higher education."

"These placemats remind me of condoms," Avery said, "not that I wear them, but still."

To the puritans at the table, it was like an Eskimo seeing molten lava. The comment was so far outside their reasoning, so uncomfortably uncalled for, that it simply did not register and reddish-yellow-orange-black was indistinguishable from white covered conversation. The thirteen year old, however, was burned to the core.

Young Gil roared with laughter, and coca-cola poured out his nostrils in a moment that he would remember well into adulthood. He would not, could not get himself straight. All the words were sentenced to time-out in his brain, turning around to see if time was up, reminding him every time of just how funny they were.

Condom- Said at the dinner table in front of his mother and father and grandmother and grandfather. Condom- It was glorious. Condom- The ticklish boy was beset by feathers, stubby fingers wriggling at his midsection, and wind on his earlobes, all working, all at once.

Nails to the death. Blaring singed-testicle scented conflagration. Beating drums and stony monotony and Chinese water torture and bamboo shoot manicure and live fire-ant pie and your defrocked skin skeleton.

"I have to get out of here, dude. No joke," Avery said to Michael. They were in the kitchen, out of earshot of the dining room, Avery openly at his wits end.

"Okay, okay, relax," said Michael casually, "We'll go soon."

"Not soon. Bollocks to soon. I have to get the fuck out of here, man. I can't take it. One more comment about my life and I'm going to lose it, man."

Michael was amused at his brother's panic. He watched, entertained, as Avery talked under his breath and turned his eyes to every possible doorway, constantly checking that they were alone, that nobody was listening and that nobody was around to impede escape. "Brother mine, I would be the last person in the world to observe, passively, any harm befalling you," Michael planned on saying more, but Avery flew into a flurry of whispers.

"Passively observe harm! What have you been doing this whole time? Every time we come here you clam the fuck up and just, I don't know, like you're just trying to fly under the radar or something. You never help me out. You just sit there and listen the whole time. It's like you've lost your puppeteer. And that shit is harmful."

He made sure that his laughter was quiet, for

Avery's sake, but laugh he did. He went on to explain that dinner conversation is a perfect place to sit, listen, and tune your ear to dialogue. For a playwright, and for an aspiring writer, he added, that was important.

"Whatever, man. It's like this- I'm going to go say thank you, good-bye, wish I could stay but I've got this other Thanksgiving thing with Mom that I'd promised her we would go to. That puts both of us in the clear. I hope you'll come with me, but if not I'll walk. I'm on vacation, man. I've done my duty by coming here and allowing myself to be verbally assassinated and watch my corpse being desecrated over and over. And you just sitting there..."

And Avery, cutting his talk short, walked with unparalleled determination passed his brother, passed the kitchen counter, passed the wall mounted rotary telephone, passed two white leather couches and a television in the corner, passed the front door, around a corner, into the dining room, said his piece, turned around, walked over the small patch of dark green tiles that constituted the entrance room, put his shoes on, opened the door, and took leave of the house. Michael was kind enough to follow.

CHAPTER 78

Michael was beyond stoned. The Human/American/Eastern Standard precept of time portrayed the notion that the sun would soon be busy in rising, and that the day was one-fourth the way over, and that the Earth had gone completely one fourth of the way round. It was early for some (the respectable men and women of the world who bombarded the malls for kitchen goods and electronics like so many addicts demanding sale prices and limited quantity items in such droves and caused such headache and traffic jams that the morning was dubbed Black Friday) and late for others (who instead of rising early to participate in edacious buying were falling late to partake of beer and marijuana cigarettes). Michael knew it was late and desperately longed for rest. He realized, however, that sleep would forsake him until two things came to pass- he must take care of the pile of clean clothes piled on his bed, and his brain must settle down a little. He hoped to take care of the second thing by taking care of the first.

The folding went as follows: Jeans- folded in half, vertically, from front pocket to front pocket, then folded once horizontally, from waistband to cuff, and once more horizontally. Shirts- folded once in half, vertically, from sleeve to sleeve, the sleeves folded at an approximate forty-five degree angle inwards, then one horizontal fold, from top to bottom, and another horizontal fold on that, sleeve side in. Mostly Michael was folding jeans and t-shirts, and the folding was fairly monotonous.

Michael was, this whole time, playing a monologue in his head. It was being delivered by none other than his neighbor, the horizontally inclined Mr. Chase. (Or was it?)

"Death, fighting, jealousy, pride, resentment, predetation, ownership, selfishness- these are things of the lowest Level, or, if you will, this Level.

"We don't know now that there are others, but others there are, and on each one, progress is made by defeating the Ego and becoming one. Love, or God, you could say."

Michael's response- "Sounds good."

"Oh, it is. It's God's plan. We were all God once. But there was a time when God grew unsure that it could appreciate itself- it being the perfect being. We can only speculate as to the magnitude of irrelevance that would be felt by an existence that always was and never was not. So God broke itself up, and scattered itself out.

"All is life. All life is on its way back to God. We learn, we love, we move. We move from this place to the next, and from that place to another, and from the other beyond."

Michael began to wonder if Mr. Chase was really talking to him or if were only his imagination. Was it possible that these temporary mental linkages are as much a sense as sight and sound, but nobody can validate them because they come in times of high, semi-delusional, secret contemplation, and are never brought up otherwise?

"Mr. Chase," Michael thought, "How long have I known you?"

"Longer than you can imagine. You're old, Michael. Very, very old."

"Old is a relative term."

"From your perspective, you're old."

As Mr. Chase told him this Michael's visual cortex played a soft image of the man nodding his head.

"Old enough to move forward?"

"Yes," Mr. Chase said, "To move forward and backward. You've been beyond here, but destiny has shown you back. You are a teacher of men. Or might be. We still aren't positive about that yet."

To this, Michael wasn't sure how to respond. Mr. Chase understood, and offered him a glimpse of creation's finish-line.

"At the next to last level there will spin a single

ball of life."

"How big is the ball?"

"It is all, and it is nothing. It is as big as can be, and small as can be. There will be nothing else to compare it to. A single ball of life, swirling together as a single being. It will spend an eternity being one, as light blocking out the dark. The Love standing guard against the non-Love. It will hold all eternity, in conscious effort of keeping pure and staying together, and when it's finished all life will once again turn to God, and find out that as God, it is merely the sum of its parts."

"So I'm God now." Michael said.

"A part of it, yes. But more to your meaning, you might be."

Again, Michael began to wonder if Mr. Chase was really talking to him or if were only his imagination. Was it possible that these temporary mental linkages are as much a sense as sight and sound, but nobody can validate them because they come in times of high, semi-delusional, secret contemplation, and are never brought up otherwise?

"Only one way to find out," Mr. Chase answered.

"By asking you."

"Sure. And you're welcome to do it."

"That sounds fine," Michael commented, "But I don't know if you're welcoming me to ask you or if my personal concept of you is welcoming me to ask you."

"From your perspective, is there much of a difference?"

What made it seem so real was that Mr. Chase's ideas were not Michael's. Or at least he didn't know that they were. And they came fast enough and unexpected enough that they seemed, by all accounts, to come from a different consciousness entirely. Michael had no choice but to ask Mr. Chase, tomorrow or the next time he saw him, if they had in fact spoken while he was folding clothes in his room.

CHAPTER 79

J.P.'s Car
(In First Gear) VRrrrrrrrrrrrrrrrrrr
(In Second Gear) VRrrrrrrrrrrrrrrrrr

Luke
I can't believe we're going to the mall, today of all days. I haven't been to the mall in forever.

Avery
Black Friday.

J.P.'s Car
(In Third Gear) VRrrrrrrrrrrrrr
(In Forth Gear) VRrrrrrrrrrrrrrrrrrrrrrrrrrrrrrrrrrrrrrr

Luke
Black Friday, derived from Black Magic, or the magic spell cast upon American cities. It's like we don't even have a choice.

Avery
Well, we need to get those tickets ASAP.

Luke
If it wasn't that, it'd be something else.

J.P.
(In First Gear) Thank God. Do you know how much money I made today?

Avery
What'd you sell?

J.P.
(In Second Gear) Six thousand six hundred and six.

Luke
Get the fuck out of here.

J.P.
(In Second Gear) No, but it was over six thousand.

Luke
I wouldn't have been surprised. There's so much Black Magic in the air today, man, I can feel it. Of all days, I find myself going to the mall because I need something. Magic.

And then there's the Magic in almost every transaction made, through the barcode. Did you know that 666 is hidden in every UPC barcode? It's true. I looked into it. In case you don't know, barcodes are essentially binary code, where each number is represented by seven spaces, or units. A unit will be either a black line or a white line- 1 for black and 0 for white. I only remembered the binary code for the number six, because obviously that's the number I was most interested in, and it goes 0101111 or 1010000. Okay? Six can be either one of those, by the way, because the numbers on the left side of the barcode will be the mirror of those on the right side. It's inversed like that. The left side of the barcode is called the manufacturer code. The manufacturer code will be the same for every product that company makes. So for instance, on every box of General Mills product, the numbers on the left side of the UPC will be the same. The right side is called the product code. Now, here's where it gets interesting. There are three bars called 'guard bars' at the beginning, middle, and end of the UPC. The first guard bar tells the computer that the next set of numbers it reads will be the manufacturer code, the middle guard bar tells the computer that the manufacturer code is over and that the product code is about to start, and the last guard bar tells the computer that the product code is over. Bear in mind while I'm telling you this, that the number of barcodes on sellable items right now is simply staggering. They are on almost everything that can be sold. I can hardly even imagine packaging without one.

J.P.
(In Second Gear) Oh, I know there's also this 'check digit' on the end of the barcode so the computer knows that it read the numbers right.

Luke
That's not important.

J.P.
(In Fifth Gear and Semi-Flustered) It's actually very important. Barcodes get messed up all the time and sometimes the scanner will read them wrong. You know how long I've worked in retail?

Luke

Dude, whatever. Who cares about that. I'm saying that barcodes might be the mark of the beast here. Every time someone buys something energy is transformed into homage to Dark Gods. Every time you scan a product you're feeding them. That 666 is feeding them.

Avery

Where do you get this energy shit from?

Luke

A while ago your brother was telling me this theory he has about toilet seat manufacturers naming their seats after old Gods, so that when kids are jacking off and aiming…

J.P.

(In Third Gear) What?

Avery

I know. He told me that. But I think it's just a funny theory to him. He doesn't really believe it.

Luke

Why not? Occultists everywhere grant that there's a power in energy, and that it's possible to manifest that power into the physical realm.

Avery

But that's just their belief system. Blind faith, rather. I don't see empirical evidence to support that. A few months ago I might have granted some potential, like, budding credence to what you're saying, but now I don't think so. All magic is, really, is manipulation.

Luke

It doesn't matter if you believe it or not. It's the truth. Why would someone go through so much trouble to brand everything with 666? Look- those guard bars on the Universal Product Code are 101 every time. Even though, technically, that's not a six, because six is 1010000, only the number six, on the product code side, contains the combination 101. So to all intents and purposes, those guard bars are sixes. George Laurer, who invented the UPC while he was employed with IBM, says that it's merely coincidence, but I doubt that very much. IBM is obviously in league with Satan, and are obviously an Illuminati front, and they obviously consider spiritual energy worth harvesting.

Avery

And that's obviously unfounded speculation. The part about energy harvesting.

Luke

Why else would they do it? Why would they be so, umm, you know, like, persistent about putting it out there?

Avery

Because it's like a signature. You've got a very small number of illuminated men shaping the world, and they like to show off about how much impact they're having. About how much of the world they actually control. Not out in the open, of course. But if you can sign your organizations name in invisible ink on almost every product that exists- you're going to look like a pretty powerful organization. It's not about feeding Satan. All that occult stuff is just misinformation. Just to waste your time. Ruling the world is done with emotionless, mechanical, meticulous practicality- not magic. Just like when George Bush flashes the Sign of the Beast for the journalists. He's not saying 'I'm a devil worshiper', he's saying 'Now you know who my friends are. Big up to all my people in Skull and Bones. Illuminati. Word is bond. We're handling the Earth right now. Keep it real, player'.

Luke
Sure. And coincidentally, we're going to the mall today. I'm shopping on the last day that I'd ever choose to go shopping in a mall that I never find myself going to. Sure. Magic isn't involved at all.

Avery
I'm not bashing that theory because I'm amused by it. But of course it's nonsense. Any sufficiently advanced science will look like magic to a layman. You said yourself, just the other night, that Freemasonry was a movement of philosophy and psychology. Right? Which in a way is just drawing maps of human behavior. Once you have the map, you can see where you want to go. So they implant social norms. Prompts, if you will. It's social manipulation. It's saying 'you need these things' and 'you need to be this way'. Of course they can't say it outright, because that would coax out resistance. They give people the illusion of choice. Command in such subtle, irresistible suggestions that the people think that they're commanding themselves. It's not magic. It's fucking frenzy. It's normal. We've been made to think that.

J.P.
(In Second Gear) The crowds should mostly be gone, anyway. Everything fizzles out in the evening.

382

Avery

That's kind of disappointing.

J.P.

(In Second Gear) Not really. Work was hell this morning.

Luke

Literally. You were working with people under a dark spell. I've never been more certain of anything in my life.

Avery

I will say this- look at those signs and light posts. Is it any wonder that the architecture of the Gardens Mall, high end, money grubbing mall, Luis Vitton purses and shit, is literally riddled with Freemasonic symbolism? Look-you've got your pyramid lights, your checkered floor, your obelisks. It's really ostentatious. But you'd only notice if you knew what to look for. I'm sure I'm missing things, too. But they're all signatures, you know?

Luke

Wrong answer. It's magic all the way down.

CHAPTER 80

And so went Avery's vacation. Lighted conversations, cozy familiarity, a dearth of discord and dissonance, the cheer of happy faces, the permissiveness of drugs good and plenty, bright bars in which Avery was a bigger fish in a much smaller pond, family, friends, the air of love and welcome- things all which blow inflatable life up with more value than breath. But, alas, time has a way of grinding down both the bad and the good. It was from these things which Avery was scheduled to fly.

What sad last minute happiness along that ride to the airport! 'Guest of Honor', he is told, and given claim to the front seat. But would Avery think of that? It was the back middle, the bitch position, that he preferred, best seat in the house, between four good people and all the chit-chat passing by. But wait- who were these four good people giving and sharing Avery's transportation? T'was none other than Michael, J.P., Luke, and Herm, Herm who rode in the front seat, whose size rather demanded it!

It is also Herm who insists the blunt go around, and who freely offers his choral regret that Avery should leave so soon and without really hanging out with any of his old buddies from work. Avery is fast in apologizing, and says just as regretfully that he wished he would have, and that next time he will. But don't think that the color of his last hours in town would be gray or black or a dark shade of any description! They are talking and joking constantly, like a group of young boys skipping school for the first time and knowing that they'll get away with it, the ceaselessly merry here and now.

When driving is done and destination reels them in, Avery removes his bags and says his goodbyes. To Michael's assurances that he will soon be visiting London, Avery gives encouragement and says, "You'd better." To Luke's summons of caution, warnings to be suspicious in the modern-day Babylon, Avery smiles, and rubs the top of his friend's head. To J.P. it is, "Always great to see you, man. I'll send you a post card." And to Herm, who cries once more that the next trip better include a stop over to the shop, Avery promises, "I will. Promise." With these last words and a large wave and a final glance to his brother, Avery shoulders his bags and heads for the skycap.

Bags checked, ticket received, Avery graduates the metal detectors, gets a coffee, and finds his gate. Soon he would be heavens over the Atlantic, bearing faithful back to Lisa and London, with work-visa purpose and newly recharged.

His headphones are singing bravura harmonies and he congratulates himself on functioning so properly past airport security. The view! The huge windows are spotless. All the planes line up, they drive back and forth, they take off and land, a child in Mickey-Mouse ears watches spellbound- a sight to make a stone heart turn.

"Fare thee well, fair Florida," Avery thinks in the air, and watches the time relapse.

To reside between past and future bliss is a charmed thing. It mothers a charming present. Warm to the what was, and look forward to the what will be, and you will find yourself glad to be alive. It is better by far than even a feather pillow that softly sings a lullaby of truth, and guarantees that you will rest, and promises that through its shell a quill shall never penetrate, and you may relax your head on the softest thing without the least worry of needles.

CHAPTER 81

God wrote his evening news with the sky. Sunset colors and haze, artfully artless journalism of the Holy Spirit, it read as follows:

An asteroid belt of stonewall-gray clouds, all visible vapor coalesced and condensed into one ribbon spanning the horizon. It arced across the sky, doubling the curvature of Earth, and ended neither in the east nor west. Along this ribbon the sunlight froze, and the blue sky around it was the blue of hours ago, and was the only blue remaining. Yellow and purple owned the coming dusk. It was as though a coal-burning locomotive had circumnavigated a stratosphere of chaos, and left a dark fume in its wake made of molecules too frightened to dissipate. That strange cloud could only mean one thing. God help us.

From his cool brick driveway, Mr. Chase examined the article, and his body responded with beating and breathing as composed as angels.

Do with us what shall be done, for upon thine Earth thy kingdom come.

"Amen to that, brother!" Michael shouted from his bedroom window.

This was rather shocking. It was all happening too soon. The clouds. The coincidence. Yet Mr. Chase remained unshaken. Destiny, like Death- will come. It was writ in the sky, and in his soul, and upon the fabrics of this their time.

Moments later, Michael was coming towards him.

"In all your days out here, have you ever seen

anything like it?" Michael asked. He was looking up, too. "God- it's incredible."

There came a small smile, a slight signal that he heard, but Mr. Chase could not speak. What was cool became warm, and warm became hot, and hot became burning, and burning became an agonizing, searing, scalding, fiery, hellish ordeal, his skin and his organs and his bones all ablaze, feeding each other with more and more and more heat.

"Hey- hey, are you alright?" Michael worried.

But the words seemed to come from the other side of a long tunnel. They traveled to him eventually, but Michael was atop the well, and he, Mr. Chase, was horizontal on its deep, deep floor. He was aware of his spasms. He knew that he was causing anxiety and worry and perhaps panic in a purely innocent bystander, but the awareness could not stop the happening. And after all this, was the boy innocent? There was the sky, and then there was the sign. Damnably painful sign.

Michael was on his knees, holding Mr. Chase's head with one hand to keep it from bouncing off the driveway, and calling for an ambulance with the other.

The places on his neck where Michael's hands touched burned with more intensity than anywhere else. It was as though the boy were made of molten iron, seething radiation on everything near, but melting objects to liquid with his touch. But no- the boy was hardly a boy anymore. He was a young man. By all accounts a man. How long had he been a man? As long as Jesus? This had to be the second... the second...

And suddenly it stopped. The pain clicked off like a light switch, leaving no residual sensation, and Mr. Chase stopped shaking and came fully to his senses.

"Michael. I'm sorry. Thank you for your help, but-no, no, you can tell them that I'm fine. I've recovered."

To be sure, Michael was not easily convinced that all was instantaneously well. It took a little convincing on Mr. Chase's part, followed by a little convincing on Michael's to call off the ambulance. When it was done, Michael pocketed his phone, and went from an uncomfortable kneeling position to a more comfortable sitting one, leaning back upon his arms. For Michael, there *was* residual sensation, and the anxiety he felt, though slowly amending into relief, still affected his heart and lungs.

"Have you ever had a seizure like that before?" Michael asked.

"Never. But I'm quite sure that it was a one time thing. I was asking for it."

"Asking for it? What, were you praying for a fit?"

This prompted an unusual question from Mr. Chase, which was something he was probably going to ask about before the episode- "You said 'Amen' when I finished praying, then you asked if I were praying for a fit. Do you know how or why that happened?"

Michael went from reclining on his hands to his elbows and asked, "Are you asking about Jung or something, or if I can read your mind?"

"Or my prayers."

"No. Not consciously, anyway. But that's really weird, because I came over here to ask you something similar. Have you ever had a telepathic conversation with me?"

"Well that question, as with all imperfect, non-telepathic communication, could be taken a number of ways. Can you be more specific?" He was the opposite of nonplussed, Mr. Chase. He was as calm and unassuming as he would have been had Michael asked him if he ever ate in the new French restaurant down the road. Michael found it pricelessly reassuring. If two people see a fairy appear, eat a starfish, and dive into the tile floor without so much as a splash, neither can accuse the other of lunacy.

"I can tell you what happened," Michael started, "The other night I was folding clothes and I was talking to you. It was all taking place in my head, but your responses didn't seem to come from me. I have to think that they were outpacing my imagination. I asked you if it was really you or if I was just thinking that I was talking to you and you said to just come talk to you. Ring any bells?"

"Hmm," Mr. Chase said. He paused for a long time. It was the pause that comes before a difficult lesson is imparted, the pause that comes when one must accurately and honestly divulge one's secrets- "I remember when I was about your age. I moved into my own place and got a dog. One night, I was on my way out, and the dog walked to the door and looked at me as if to say, 'aren't you taking me with you?' I thought to the dog, from my consciousness to his, that, unfortunately, I could not."

Michael waited patiently for more. He waited a bit less patiently. He realized that more was not coming. "Right."

"Well, we did say more. He asked me *why* I couldn't bring him along. I told him that the establishment that I was headed to would not admit dogs. He wondered if his life might be more interesting with another owner. I assured him that it would not, and said furthermore that, unfair as it is, the world was simply not built to accommodate dogs. Ours is a territory ruled by men, built by and for them. We did not stack our society on the happiness of man's best friend, but only man, which shows what kind of friend we are. But that isn't the important thing, Michael. What's important is this- did I talk to the dog? Is it possible that I communicated with him in that moment as I am with you now? Well, maybe. Is it also possible that I communicated with the him that I know, in my own personal universe, through my personal set of senses and experiences, the subjective him and not the objective him? Definitely. The question of which is more important, or if one version of the history is indeed more important than the other at all is yours to decide."

"I take this to mean that you have no recollection of the chat we had while I was folding clothes."

"No," Mr. Chase answered, "But does that change the chat?"

Michael humored him and said that it didn't.

They sat and watched the sky, and as the sky grew darker, the clouds began to move. The normalcy of white swirls and bubbles against a dark bluish black backdrop, with dots of dead light spread far around was once more.

But such a fine heart, lord- how could it be? Mr. Chase wondered.

His answer came again from the heavens, for a cumulous moved and the moon had been unveiled. And as destiny would have it, she shone down with a cruel, laughing grin, and strove to remind each and every one of the world of their precious insignificance, and the indubitable coming of Damnation. With the possible apocalypse apparently at hand, Mr. Chase felt sick.

CHAPTER 82

"Yo that shit is phallic, son!" Avery said, standing next to and looking at and talking about a completed 3-D puzzle of the Washington Monument.

No one in the room responded and Avery, after a moment's repose, decided not to call any more attention to what he'd said. He was tired, and deliriously so. So deliriously tired that he didn't feel tired, only giddy and heedless. The jetlag was all over him. It was also necessary for Avery to remember that he was no longer back home, with old friends that understood him and wouldn't take offence or confusion to that kind of slapdash announcement.

There were five other male models in the room, not counting Avery, and all of them passing their eyes around, focusing each on a different aspect of the décor, holding meekly onto their plastic-lined portfolios and waiting. Some of the castings were like this. Nobody wanted make a sound or a sight. Usually, Avery didn't mind. He was just as often one of the passive bodies, content to sit and read until it was his turn to hand over his pictures and see whoever it was he was there to see. But he was too charged from the long day, and too excited to be back in London. It was hard, this time, to loiter in such anonymity.

"Do we know who I'm after?" he asked, and was answered by one of the guys raising two fingers in the air. "Okay. Cool. Cheers."

So his attempt at communication was shot down, and again, it was awkward.

He had been to three castings at this point, and none of them screamed 'job'. Yes, there were those recalls and bookings that came as a total surprise, sometimes even weeks after the prospect of confirmation had been written off, but usually there was a hint of 'yes' or 'no, thanks' in some facet of the company. Odd that he hadn't run into Jack. Any request for Avery was usually a request for Jack and vice versa. Avery decided to give his friend a call. He would say that he was back, ask Jack which of the day's castings his own schedule included, and find out, hopefully, if the last casting which was not a request and therefore much more likely to be a waste of time was worth the trek to Camden. Jack answered right away.

"Hey, man! How's it going? You back yet?"

Avery said that, yeah, he was back, and already back to work. He asked where Jack had been so far.

"Oh, I've been everywhere, mate. Thing in Hackney this morning, fucking mission. And now all the way back up that way." Jack started to say more, but Avery cut in. The cutting in required almost perfect timing, because Jack sounded mildly excited and was speaking fast.

"I didn't have anything in Hackney. What was it for?"

"Some magazine. Car magazine or something. Eight in the fucking morning I had to get there."

"Oh. Well I was too late for that, I guess. What else?"

"Dazed and Confused."

Avery nodded. "Yep. Right."

"Umm, French Marie Claire?"

"Yeah. Have you been to this thing in Camden?"

Lots of wind was coming through the microphone.

Jack said he was on the way there.

"Damn. Well, hey, can you do me a favor? Call me when you get there and let me know what's up. If it's like a big thing I think I'll just skip it."

"Sure, sure," Jack said, but then realized that he didn't have any minutes on his phone, and couldn't call, and so apologized.

"Fuck. Okay. Do you know about when you'll be there?"

"Oh, I reckon I'm pretty close."

"Cool. I'll call you back in like ten minutes."

Jack said 'alright', and Avery said 'alright', and they both hung up.

Three minutes and twenty seconds later, Jack's description of the casting was exactly what Avery wanted to hear. There were a lot of people there; standing in line along a three story stairwell, and it seemed to be an open call to all the working models in and around London. Avery thanked Jack, and said they would talk later, that he was just going to head home and stay there until tomorrow but they would definitely hang out soon.

Again, the beds were singles, too small to comfortably sleep two adults, but this time their mattresses were stacked atop one another on a flimsy aluminum bunkbed. The new room was about as plain as a room can be. Not at all like that photographer's living room he'd seen earlier, with knick-knacks and art work and table books and board games and records and furnishings packed so tight that the house itself might ratify a 'No Children or Dogs' policy or hold down a second job as a third-shift Spartan nightmare. The new room was white and silver everywhere, everywhere being nothing but four walls, a bunk bed, two bed covers, two sheets, two pillows, two pillowcases, two fold out chairs, a sink, and an electric kettle. Avery was depressed upon seeing the place, but realized that his depression could very well be motivated by a loneliness and lack of sleep. He climbed to the top bunk to catch some Zs before Lisa came back.

It was restless sleep. Tossing and turning. Waking up and wondering if sleep had come at all before going back to sleep and waking up again, still unsure, still tired. Avery awoke once to find that his body was sleeping. He could feel himself there, from top to bottom, all curled up, heavy slumber in effect, but his intellect was alert. Something roused his brain. Something with a tangible, yet still highly invisible presence. It was a terrifying feeling- like being raped and strangled by a ghost and the ghost's ghost husband respectively. Like knowing the Fates were damning him with fingernails and cats' eyes and bat droppings or whatever they use to damn innocent young men just taking an honest stab at getting by.

Move! Shake, twitch, convulse- something! his brain commanded.

Nothing. Like the last time, his organics were at the mercy of the moving world.

There was something in his ear now. It was there before, but he was only just now noticing. A slight pressure, from his ear to his mind, bypassing the eardrum, straight in.

((Stop thinking about those poor oppressed African people.)) The ray told him.

((They don't have space travel because they don't want it, not because they lack the math or the resources.)) It beamed further.

Avery's thoughts reeled upon this. Not because of what the Space Ray, if Space Ray it was, was saying- what was really confusing was why the Space Ray (if

Space Ray it was) opted to tell him- of all things- that. There was some stuff that Avery was reading about these big Asian corporations that were going into rural African towns and employing the indigenous people to mine their own lands for their own resources, and just give the materials up for a pittance of a wage, and when the lands are stripped, the company would just pick up and leave over to the next town and drop that terrible scam there.

But what were African rocket ships to the Space Ray?

((Stop thinking about those oppressed African people.))

Damn. But he hadn't been thinking about them. If anything, Avery thought he should be thinking *more* of them. The so called developed world has been fucking over the Africans for pretty much ever, and so hard and heavy that the only thing that a lot of the African nations have learned from it is how to fuck each other and themselves over in turn. Of all the swindled, cheated, lied to, misled- even the African wildlife seems to have it rough.

((They don't have space travel because they don't want it, not because they lack the math and the manpower.))

Avery couldn't be sure about this. It might be true, it might not. Even the richest nations in the world seem to have trouble justifying the tremendous cost of research and development that goes into space programs. And the nations of Africa are not as advanced technologically or industrially as the National Aeronautics and Space Administration or its Soviet pressure, are they? But was it also possible that Avery's knowledge of Africa, limited though it was, was off beam? Was it a bunk version of actuality? A thundershower of the establishment's lies?

Was he indoctrinated into thinking his society superior? And even by his own, slowly changing standards, was it true?

At last, his body obeyed. He straightened out, rolled across his back, and landed on his other side. The Space Ray's pressure was vanished. Relief. It felt an awful lot like water draining from his ear canal. And on more alert and focused, less sleepy and dreaming reflection, almost certainly was.

CHAPTER 83

"I wrote these on the plane."
Lisa accepted the notebook and looked it over.

An American Auto-Shop Story in A-Minor
By Avery Tyler

It was dead hot in the parking lot, but we were out there anyways. Probably because it was hotter in the garage, and darker, and inside, there was much less room to move. So we stood around outside, in the alley-like street, between two rows of steel panel garages.

We had just taken a joy ride around Riviera Beach to check out J.P.'s new speaker system. It was loud. What I mean is, if you drive around with a Ying-Yang Twins CD, any regulatory agency concerned with health or hearing or public quiet will make suggestions that you wear earplugs, and those suggestions will be as strong as Paul Bunyan's blue ox and clear as an optometrist's salt water fish tank. To me it was a grand novelty. But it was exactly what J.P. wanted. The guys that installed it were outside, and J.P. was telling them how happy he was. I guess that's why we were standing around in a little circle on the hot ass street.

"You look like you're in a band or something," one of the mechanics said to me.

I told him, yeah, heh, I get that a lot. He said he wished he were as pretty as me, which I believe he meant as more of an insult than a compliment. Besides that, we were getting along just fine. Me and J.P. and the redneck mechanics, we had lots to talk about.

At one point, someone else came outside with a two liter bottle of coca-cola. He handed it to one of the guys. The young man he handed it to had his look down pat. I'll do my best to describe him.

Dirty white shirt. Equally dirty blonde hair, three quarters bowl cut but a little longer in the back. Big boned. To all intents and purposes a hardy man. But he had a cherubic face, hairless but for the wispy beginnings of a thin mustache and big green child-like eyes. When he took the two-liter, his three comrades and J.P. grew excited.

How was I to know what to expect? What could be done with a two liter bottle of coke? They looked at me like the most ignorant piece of shit they'd ever seen. Like because I didn't know what was going to happen, I almost didn't deserve to know. I kid you not, that guy opened that bottle and drank it down in three cetacean gulps. I was floored. It was like I had just ejaculated for the first time. Like I was in the shower, writhing in ecstasy, thinking 'oh, THAT'S what the older kids are talking about'.

And the older kids were around me.

"Every seen anything like that in your entire goddamn life?"

"No," I answered.

"Probably never will again, neither."

How proud they were. They had their jewel and they were happy to brandish it right in front of my face. 'Ain't got nuthin like that in the big city, do you boy?', 'Bet you wish you could put em down like that, dontcha son?' I honestly didn't know what to do next. They were standing there glowing, all four of them, and even J.P., who had apparently seen the trick on a previous visit.

"Where'd you learn to do that?" I asked meekly. I was out of my element here, and I knew it.

Two of the mechanics, bored by now, returned to the shop.

"Ah, man, I don't usually tell nobody bout that. But hell, I like them skinny jeans you got on so I'll tell ya." Another dig. Fine. I took it because I was curious. The guy proceeded to tell his story. "When I was real little I used to drink stuff. I'd get anything I could reach out of the refrigerator and drink it. Milk, my dad's beer if I could open it, soda, BBQ sauce, but I guess one time I got down this bottle of hot sauce. That real hot hot sauce that you can only get in Texas. Hot damn, my dad had a bunch of it cause he'd go out there for work. Well, I drank that shit- the whole bottle. I think what happened is that I burned up all my nerves, cause now I can drink shit real fast like you saw."

And that, as they say, was that.

To the Victor Goes the Soils
By Avery Tyler

On Sundays mom would take us to see Pop-Pop at the Pine Tree assisted living center. Shit sucked. It always smelled like shit, or Pine-Sol, and when those senile old men and women weren't walking around in some tired old broken charade of their once-life, all slack jawed and aimless, they were watching Zorro VHS box sets or playing Monopoly.

These gents couldn't hold it together for a game. The only one that had the mental capacities and the attention span was this one dude I nicknamed Slappy. Slappy would start charging them for their own properties, sneaking houses and hotels onto his, steal money from the bank- you name it. I saw him do it all the time but he seemed to be the only one that gave a damn. So I kept mum.

The best time was when he pulled the same card from the top of the Community Chest pile four times in a row. 'Granddaughter gets married- collect fifty dollars from each player'. Slappy was laughing so hard that he forced out a big round fart fit to fill the Hindenburg. Only I know it wasn't just a fart. I could tell because Slappy stopped laughing but quick, and looked around eagerly for the nearest nurse.

Keep on Keeping on, Jack
By Avery Tyler

Two years ago Jack was a wreck. You probably think you know what I mean by wreck but I doubt it. Jack wasn't just hung over four mornings in a row from beer that wasn't in his budget to buy, nor had he just been hit by a car or something of transitory discomfort like that. Jack was on the road with his girlfriend who he loved but could never seem to stop fighting with. They were somewhere in the dustbowl of Middle America, trolling shopping malls and neighborhoods and doing their best to sell shitty magazine subscriptions with a troop of soulless individuals who were also at the end of their rope. It was going nowhere, but at least it was going.

The hotels they stayed in were cheap, filthy places, the food always bad. Maurine sold more magazines than him, six or seven new accounts or so a week. Probably it was her genuinely naïve smile. The way the old men would look at the top of her tits while she smacked away on her chewing gum and obliviously delivered her spiel. Jack, Jack couldn't sell those damn stupid subscriptions to save his life. He was going through the motions though, reciting the lines they gave him and knocking on doors like everybody else.

One night, near the tail end of that dreadful trip, Jack was asked to join his co-workers for a beer or two. They were awful people, somehow content with their own worthlessness and more than willing to scrape out a living bouncing from rural wasteland to rural wasteland, selling magazines to more or less illiterate people. Jack didn't like them, any of them, nor did they seem to like Jack. The invitation was strange, but they offered, and Jack accepted. They were buying.

So Jack sat there, in a small bar decorated with a myriad of neon beer logos and mirrors with beer logos printed over them. Jack was out of place in the bar, out of place in his company, out of place in his shoes and in his skin and in that damned town. His co-workers were laughing at the few other patrons, as if their lives were in some way superior. They also talked of their plans for their immediate future, which involved fucking female co-workers and fucking over strangers of either gender. Scum through and through, these guys.

"What's up with your girl, man?" one of them asked.

Jack didn't know how to answer. This was the same guy that, only moments ago, was showing pictures and videos on his cell phone of his naked girlfriend. Her nipple tattoos. Her clit piercing. Jack said that they fight sometimes but that they've been together for about as long as he could remember. The guys all smiled. All four of them smiling as if someone had just told a joke.

Time went by, drinks went down. They were all about six or seven beers deep. It was time to go. But whereas before Jack's co-workers were being chummy scumbags, now they seemed to act like scheming, conspiratorial scumbags.

The lot of them were walking down the street, which was devoid of activity, lighting, or noise of any kind.

Someone's phone was going off. The young man took it out of his pocket with uncontainable glee, celebrating and showing off the pictures he'd just received to the other guys who, upon seeing it, celebrated with equal ferocity.

Finally, it was Jack's turn.

How could she?

How fucking could she?

The email was a series of pictures- Maurine with her lips on a hard, cylindrical something under a pair of cotton boxers, Maurine holding that same penis tight between her lips, Maurine with the cock as far down her throat as she could stand it.

The punch came right after.

Someone socked Jack in the side of the face, hard, with another person following the example, and another, and an unkind repetition of the process.

They left Jack lying on the ground, bruised and broken, as they said 'have a nice life' and walked away. They were leaving him there, no doubt. In that dusty town to either fend for himself or find his own ride home. They would surely be laughing about it, high-fiving, and looking at the god-awful pictures of his girlfriend sucking off their boss for the rest of the night.

Lisa had finished reading, but kept her eyes on the page as though they hadn't reached the end. She knew how hypersensitive Avery could be when it came to his writing; even if it were only something nonchalantly handed over as 'I wrote this on the plane'. Her critiques had to come quiet, careful, or better yet, curtailed. Eventually, when she could no longer simulate scrolling, she nodded.

"What'd you think?" Avery pushed, "Really I just wrote them for practice, you know. I should really be writing more often."

"They were different. I liked the first one the most. Why did you call it 'in A Minor?' though?"

"No reason."

"Oh. The second one was neat, too. Did you go to a nursing home while you were there?"

"No."

Lisa pursed her lips. "The last one was pretty sad. I wish I knew where all that came from." This was closer to the question she wanted to ask. But had she asked what she wanted to ask, she would almost definitely hear the racket of a battered shield. Later, better to wait until later. When his guard would be down.

"My imagination? I don't know where it comes from. I just thought of it. But to me, when I read it, I feel like it isn't such a sad story. Because things can only get better for Jack now. He was better than that. Now he'll move forward. The rest of the characters will stay selling magazines in shitty towns- ultimately they're the ones that lose," Avery explained.

"Did you call him Jack because of your friend?"

"You mean did I name Jack after Jack? No. Didn't think of it."

"Oh. Well, yeah. It's cool."

Closing the notebook, placing it upon the table, standing up, straddling Avery's legs and sitting on his lap, Lisa congratulated herself. It was a fine line between interest and accusation, these reading sessions, and this one was over, sans incident. She wanted to get out of the room, and said so. So they went out, hopped the train out to Covent Garden, looked at shoes, went to Forbidden Planet, Café Nero, walked, talked, held hands, kissed, watched the people, joked and caught up. They had new stories for each other, and after a little while apart, felt freshness in each other's company.

Late that night, after sex and intermittent slumber, Lisa figured Avery's guard was down. She asked him about the blowjob scene in his story, asked about Jack and his girlfriend and why Avery invented two characters that say they love each other but fight all the time. This goaded the sleepy young man into a very tired anger, and all his offensive defenses were said very slowly, through teeth that seemed and sounded evermore clenched. They fell asleep as far away from each other as they could on the pint-sized bottom bunk.

CHAPTER 84

Avery was mildly drunk, and talking. His humanoid grunts and utterances was annoying one of the girls seated next to him, but luckily that girl was the stranger- not Lisa. She, the stranger, that is, judged his lexis pretentious, his parlance condescending, his assertions ham-fisted, and his aura junk. Those were the exact words she used in her head. She was drunk, too, and it took her a couple minutes to compile that perfect list.

But as Avery was completely unaware of the brutal criticisms, he went on talking, and Lisa went on listening. Thus far the items of discourse were:

-Trends are in modern times put forth primarily by advertisement, and exist to create and reinforce status.

-Fashion advertisements create trends not only in the realms of clothing, but desired aesthetics in general (bodily dimensions, hair styles, posture, and even overall countenance).

-Current trends and advertisements (Avery used the two words interchangeably) projected the ideal image as youthful cadets and spring chickens prettying their way through life all careless and empty.

-Fashion industry trends of not so long ago, however, utilized a more manly persona. The average male model used to be older, with a more 'capable and grown-up' appearance. Female stylists working through the transition period went on record saying, "Who are all these boys? Where are our men?"

Subsequently, Avery said that "It could have happened for a number of reasons. Most observably, to me, anyways, would be the issue of cost. Male models used to make way more money than they do now. I mean, like, way more. Because if you have a guy that's old enough to have a family, and old enough to be doing other, more lucrative things with his time, you have to pay him more. The young kids came way cheaper.

"That the public initially thought of these kids as, well, something other than symbols of enviable figure was irrelevant. The public doesn't decide what it wants. The public is moved by calculated, practiced influence. They want what they're told to want so eventually they wanted youthful icons.

"But check this out- if the target image is that easily changed, and that successfully, maybe it's also being changed for less obvious reasons. I think that maybe a member of the super-elite, or a group of people at that level might have had some other goal in mind. Check it out- an image can pretty easily be championed, and along with that image come parallel ways of thinking. If a boyish image is projected as 'in', and people relate to that image in some way, accepting it if not striving for it- could that image instill boyish personalities as well?

"A man is capable. A man is strong, he takes care of himself and his family. He acts. A boy waits. A boy needs grown-ups to do things for him and is passive. If that role is given to us as the norm by all the fashion companies and magazines and it trickles into movies and television, it works its way into people's reality tunnels. I think it could affect a shift in our generation's potential. That would be vastly beneficial to the ruling elite, who want nothing more than a population of passive, easily influenced robots. By normalizing perpetual boys and making them, like, fashionable, fewer men develop, and fewer men are around to make demands on society and fight the power."

He had by now lost the girl to his left. She would hang on to one word or combination of words thinking of what a clumsy choice it was, and in a minute she'd have a much better option envisioned. She was also giving herself a ruthless reprimanding for leaving her headphones at home. Luckily, the girl to Avery's left was not Lisa.

Other things were happening on the train, meanwhile. A boy of thirteen or so had just pushed through the door at the end of the car. It was poisonously noisy, the door and the breach of sound proofing, and he wobbled to a stop and regained his balance. No easy job, that. For in addition to being tired and hungry and the train bearing across a precarious strip of track, the boy was also carrying a paper cup and an unwieldy accordion. He played a quick ditty, received no money, and made his way to the next car. It had been hours and hours since he smiled, and would be hours and hours until he smiled again. The heavy door slammed hard behind him.

Lisa came damn close to inciting a row by taunting Avery with, "So you're one of these perpetual boys then, huh?" But Avery calmed himself. Consciously. With the unflappable, unflustered, unfallen, and admittedly unfamiliar calm of bigger men, he forgave and forgot. All was well between lovers, and Lisa was admittedly relieved. When she next spoke, it was more constructive.

"It's interesting, I guess. I just think you're becoming more and more paranoid."

"Could be," Avery admitted.

"Just seems like everything you put together deals with a couple bad guys at the top tricking the rest of the world at the bottom. Why do you suppose that every change is for an evil purpose? If you had love in the forefront of your mind, and not fear, do you think you could see a positive force behind it?"

Not when the distribution of wealth is as unfair as it is. Not when the common man's freedoms shrink, his fetters tighten, and the walls around him grow. Not when- but no. Wait. Avery is saying now-

"Look, I have another example for you. They seem to have all the angles covered. Anyone who entertains hopes of rebellion can look at movies and see how absurd it is. Anytime Hollywood tells a story of rebellion; of, you know, fighting the state, it's about a single man taking on the world. In the movies, it works. But put that into a conditioning context. Let's say I want to fight for change. I saw how all the action heroes did it- Stallone and Schwarzenegger and, uh, Will Smith, and in the movies it worked. But I can apply those stories to real life, and know that it's impossible. We would relate rebellion with one against the world, and realize that for us, one against the world are hopeless odds. Therefore rebellion is hopeless- freedom is hopeless.

"Hollywood projects, literally, all the rules that it's convenient for us to follow. This one producer I worked with thought Hollywood strove to Americanize the world. I think it's more than that. Do you know what Hollywood means?"

In her head, she was telling him off good and proper. 'Shut up', she was saying. 'Who do you think you are, Ayn Rand?' she was saying. 'Shut your daft, boorish, dogmatic, pedantic mouth. It's like your mouth is an oil-spill. I've had it about up to here with you and I hate social commentary.' Luckily, the girl thinking that was the girl to Avery's left. And right after Avery

407

embarked on his elucidation of the symbolic meaning of Hollywood, the train was stopping at Leicester Square, Avery and Lisa were off to catch the Piccadilly Line, and the girl that had thus far silently endured their presence, let out a very snotty and self-indulgent, "Thank God!" when the doors closed behind them.

CHAPTER 85

London was soon offering more ways to spend money than to make it. In the agency, Avery was told along with Jack and Thomas that there weren't any castings for Monday, but if they wanted something to do this weekend, some promoters had stopped by and left a few flyers and contact info on the filing cabinets. The three of them had a look. Thomas was the most excited, and was the first to flip through the flyers, and was the first to bust something out.

"Table. Bottle service. Seven people," he said loudly and looked up with all the light and livelihood of an unsupervised lecture hall.

The lad's enthusiasm was admirable. As was his history. Avery had gone out a few time with Thomas, and though Thomas was only fifteen, the kid talked them both into some of the most exclusive clubs in London. He would confidently look the most imposing doormen in the eye, and announce, with all the audacity of a fifteen year old male model, that they were two models, and that they were going to be accepted into the club, for free, because they were with FM, models, remember? And more often than not, Avery would find himself surprised, and the doorman would be saying 'alright then, lads', and they would be at the bar in no time.

"Sorry guys," Jack muttered, "I can't go. Too poor, I'm afraid."

Thomas offered a simple solution. They'd just get all their drinks for free, and if that plan failed, he offered to buy Jack's drinks. Still, Jack declined. He said goodbye to Thomas and Avery and was off, leaving the two of them at the top of the stairwell.

Plans were made to meet in Leicester Square. Thomas went downstairs ahead of Avery, bouncing with each step, as though the coming night mailed maps to hidden treasure, from the future to his pockets. The kid had it made. Here he was, barely a young man, and already six feet and two inches tall, with obscenely sought after red shaggy hair, delicate features, a deep enough voice, and the ability instantly inflate his years by at least twenty percent. His posing could be found in all the men's magazines, for all the men wishing they were boys that looked like men to look at. Thomas promised to bring a couple ladies out tonight- girls that were easily old enough to be his big sisters. Avery congratulated, but mentioned that his girlfriend was at home waiting, and yeah, see you around ten or so.

The boys were visited immediately by insectile debacle. That was, it came in three parts, abdomen, thorax, and head. The shitty abdomen first, where shit is processed and babies come from- the dealer was impossibly late, as those in the cocaine business usually are, but they all had to wait around Leicester Square for nearly two hours. There were of course the Hare Krishna parades to watch, foreign girls to holler at, hobo tap-dancers, yes, yes, there was that, but two hours? Finally the merchant drove by in a busted whip, oxidized paint and rust all over, and young Thomas went over to conduct the transaction. The time was 12:15 a.m.

They five took turns doing small lines out of a dim phone booth. Adam first, followed by Thomas, who was before Avery, then Ollie, and Chrisoph. Now the night was on and expectations high. Merrily they walked to a club called the Funky Buddha. Merrily verily. The world opens its easy gates for the young, careless, and handsome. But following the abdomen, the thorax is next. Legs and wings. In this case, all curled and facing lifeless up. Christoph was told by the hostess- "Right. We have your table ready. It's eight hundred fifty." Eyes were rolled, noises of disbelief and shock, and from Avery, an eight hundred fifty degree spin. "No, no- we have a table. I'm Thomas. We're all here from FM. I spoke to Mandy on the phone and she said you'd have a table for us." The hostess said that the table was there, for them, right, but at a cost of eight hundred fifty pounds. She would be happy to split it between credit cards. Thomas repeated himself. So did the hostess, adding pitilessly, "She didn't say it was complimentary." And Avery speaking for the first time, "She certainly implied it." And as nobody was prepared to pay even a fraction of that extortionate bill, they left, pinched. It was nearly 1 o'clock in the morning.

Another line in the same phone booth on the way back, and Thomas was leading them to plan b. A friend at their agency was also a promoter, and always promised something of a night out for his fellow fashion models should they ever desire it. Thomas was on the phone to him, giving names and getting directions. They walked, were admitted, had a drink, decided better times were to be had in different places, and went to find another club.

They were in the West End, where swanky clubs piled one atop the other like rungs on a ladder. Eventually they found a long line, the club it pointed to, and Thomas was working his magic. Successful magic. Inside before the strike of 2:00. Christoph and Adam and Avery went to the bar, Thomas and Ollie to the bathroom with their bag of scandalous white grounds.

With the glass of whiskey, came the mandibles. Thomas ran up, looking shaken. Bad news was in his eyes, holding them open wide. "Ollie just got caught doing coke in the bathroom. They had fucking cameras." It was bad news, sure it was. But Avery was perhaps less moved than his friend. "Damn. That's a drag. Still, though. I like, just got a drink. I'm sorry for him and everything, man, but it took us forever and a day to get here. Now we're here. I'm nowhere near ready to leave. It's just the head, man." Christoph and Adam consented, though that last bit was over their head.

The head threw Thomas into survival mode. Design artificial intelligence or die type situation. You have six hours to fix your air filtration device or you suffocate type situation. He said he would take care of it, and strode toward the exit, leaving the three others feeling a bit guilty, but talking each other out of it by and by.

If this three part debacle was indeed insectile, then what followed would make sense. Many insects can perceive ultraviolet and infrared light, as well as the visible light wavelengths, and mere visible light would not have shown a solution to the predicament faced by Thomas. Bug eyes were the answer. Thomas calmed down on his way out, and his excited bug eyes relaxed.

At 2:21 a.m. they were back, and Thomas explained, standing with Ollie, that he offered the doorman a deal. His cell phone for Ollie. Once again, audacity won, and the five of them were free to get loose. Thomas had taken one for the team, and at his cost they were all back inside. Game on. That they were there and everything was cool was enough cause to celebrate. Perhaps the youth were not so lost, after all.

CHAPTER 86

They were this time to out with the superman. The super-human in red Ferrari motor, castle keys jingling, all cared for, never wanting, never needing, best-bred. It was something that Avery didn't really want to do. And as synchronicity would have it, the live radio show he was streaming on his computer was vicariously speaking on his position.

A gruff, robust man in an unassuming cotton collared shirt was on the screen. He was facing a 45 degree angle from the camera, was seated at a blue table top, before various monitors and recording apparatus. A studio mike was in the upper left-hand corner of the screen. He was feelingly halfway through a rant, and Avery had so far been counting himself lucky that the topic was the ruling class aristocrats, and that Lisa was still in the room to hear it.

"What you need to know, people, is that to the ruling classes of the world, you are dirt. You are lower than dirt. They're the ones that have been in control for years, handing down your laws and customs, and without them you would all just float off starving into outer space.

You're all the trolls and they're the angels.

"Tyranny is in effect now, no doubt about it, but as the sheep forget how to do anything but Bah, bah, bah, oppression is brandished more openly. We're just seeing the tip of the iceberg. National ID cards on the way, nationally funded eugenics programs, like the bioethics organization commissioned by our very own George Bush; we are being murdered and sterilized by our puppet government and the real power base behind it.

"I'm talking about generations of criminal psychopaths, here. These are people who, through hundreds of years of isolated breeding, rearing, and ruling, have actually become so far separated from the whole of humanity, psychologically and physiologically, that they can't consider the bottom to be anything but worthless eaters. They are worlds away from identifying with us. And here they, the puppeteers playing humanity and playing at godhood, who claim to be Supermen compared to the viral majority, are in fact only men of extremely jaded mentalities, incapable of surpassing their reptilian, essentially devolved and disorderly minds.

"The ruling class proclaims that they have a right to change the world, claiming that an Atlas Shrugged scenario would occur if they weren't kind enough to hoard the world's wealth and power. That's right, people-you don't know what's good for you. You are an inferior life form, forever riding the coat tails of the enlightened. Let's reflect for just a moment on the genius of inbreeding. Genetic disorders. Decreased fertility rates. Weak immune systems. Facial asymmetry. Infant mortality. Mental disorders. And these, your kings and queens.

"A great cloud is upon the world. An entrenched enemy, a ring of globalist criminals, who systematically attack your mind, your liberties, you lives, and the future of this planet. They want you dumb, sick, and dead. They are murdering us soft and hard. Dead. You- dead. Burned bodies sicken the air with the stench of murdered flesh. Die! Die! Die! They're coming for you!"

This, apparently, was all that Lisa could stand. She seemed very offended, saying, "Oh, God! Isn't this entertaining?"

"No, he does this. But he makes some great points. Seriously. All that stuff about inbreeding? It's no joke. This guy you all want to hang out with tonight probably has the same people for parents and cousins."

She thought about that for a moment, thinking if that was possible. No, she decided. It wasn't. She told him that. She also told him to turn off the computer, or put on headphones, because she was tired of hearing it. The host of the show had now moved on to other things, leaving the topic of inbreeding to resound in flawed memories only. Avery obliged, now that it was done, closing the clamshell monitor. He sat for a moment, trying to be civil, a good boyfriend, non-confrontational, mature, grounded, sticking to the 'if you don't have something nice to say…' axiom, and failed.

.   "Do you think he'll have a crooked jaw?"

No response. Actually, there was a response, but not verbal. Lisa was rolling her eyes heavy and her mouth went a little slack. She went and opened the window. Stood looking out. Grey was descending on the outside. The wall framed a monochromatic London, where a beat and downtrodden and perpetually depressed pulp detective could feel right at home. It was weather perfect for coffee and smokes.

"Want to go get some fresh air?" Avery asked.

"I wouldn't mind going to the café."

"Cool. I'll play you checkers."

There was a half a game and their coffee had cooled off enough to drink without talk of Lord Alexander, or whatever he likes to be called. The café was warm. It played nice music and the patrons, mostly students and travelers from other hostiles, sat drinking their hot drinks and speaking Spanish and French and Italian. Foods were displayed behind glass cases and looked colorful and delicious, provided that you were no closer than six feet from them, and the menu was handwritten in chalk behind the register. It was as inviting a café as could be found in all of London. But Avery could no more refrain from bringing up his gripes and inventing more complaining than Eve could resist smooth bodied, smooth talking reptiles. It was like he had the hiccups, tried to kill them by holding his breath, but felt his lungs pop and his chest heave and his throat squeak before he could quite reach thirty- "So, another night out in the West End."

Lisa answered in the affirmative, but looked, and was trying hard to look too involved in her next move to participate.

"Well, I'm sure it'll be fun. They play great music. And the people are so cultured there. Cheap drinks. Good times. I'm being sarcastic here. Can you tell?"

"Don't come, then. I don't want you there if you're going to be acting like a crybaby the whole time. Just fucking stay home. Watch your videos. I don't give a fuck," not looking up.

Avery's turn. He shifted the board left a little. Then right. He was winning, but that wasn't helping. A red piece jumped a black piece, landing safely on the edge. Eight times eight. Sixty four squares. Sixty four hexagrams in the I-Ching. The black piece was in his hand- and yin. "No, I'll go. I'll go. I love the West End. I can't say no to partying with those people. I want to celebrate the fact that I survived another five monotonous days of working and barely living, too. It's like Friday, so like, everybody's done living on their boss' time. Now they're on their own time- so let's get wasted! Let's dull our senses until Monday because until then we aren't robots and what the fuck else can we do when we're not robots?"

"I'm leaving." Lisa said dryly. There was so much anger in her voice that it zapped all the lubrication in her vocal chords.

"No, hey- I'm sorry. I'm sorry. I'll cheer up." Avery said. He was suddenly a little panicked.

"Call me once you do."

"What the fuck? Really? Where are you going?"

Lisa said that she would meet up with her friends. They would be at a pub in Pimlico. She suggested that he give her a few hours to calm down, and suggested more, that he should go back to the hostile, try meditating, and to do the same. Calm down, that is. And leaving, even her ass looked angry.

CHAPTER 87

Before long, it wasn't voices outside and horns that Avery was hearing, it was voices inside and warnings. The nerves in his legs had finally quit their post after having sent relentless communiqués that "Mayday. Mayday. We hurt like hell. Requesting immediate stretch, over". His eyes were closed and still the clay-like darkness churned, turning itself into all manner of things. Colors, first. Baby stuff. Shapes. But presently a crowd swimming by. Anonymous mass behind and all around would form a new individual every second, a new face in the crowd the focus. One after another, one became another. They all looked at him before they morphed into another person, and in each one crystal clear deformity.

"STOP" some of them whispered. The noses, moles, uni-brows, calcium horns, bumps, and birthmarks-they were enough to say the same. You are walking uncharted territory. If you know what's good for you, go back the way you came.

Entranced, like looking at the first blast of a hot bonfire, Avery was content to let his unexpectedly inspired imagination amuse him. But his was not the purpose. He neared the end of the parade. The circus will amuse you from purpose. Faces lingered. The Hindenburg volume of physiognomy gave a little less, but a little longer, and a little harder to watch. He had reached monster territory.

There were goblins ("STOP").

There were ghouls ("STOP").

There were ghosts ("STOP").

There were genies ("STOP").

There were goats ("STOP").

There were Gods ("THIS IS YOUR LAST CHANCE").

"And don't forget the Guess-What!" It said.

The speaker was hogging the stage, black backdrop behind, abyss before, the street preachers and busted grills and hawk-boys had all joined the eternally departed, never to be pretended again. Only the crooked Pan hung around. The thing began with hoof feet and ended in arched horns. It between all that was hairy legs that bent the opposite way of mans, an old dusty leather belt that propped no pants, only divided a mostly animal lower half from a mostly human upper half, protuberant belly and button, long arms, beady eyes, and black curly hair.

"And don't forget, gwhat do you wants?" It asked.

Avery projected his thoughts to the thing. That he didn't know what it was talking about. He may have sent a bit of disgust mixed in the message. The crooked Pan was hell on the inner eyes.

"I mean, gwhat is it you want? Maybe I can help. I'm in the business of granting wishes, you know. We can work together." As it said this, it sent a single shot of urine to the ground. No apparent focus or deliberation was involved in the act. It just sprayed through the thing's coarse, bristly leg hair, no hands, as easily as one discharges a burp.

"Whoa, man. Fuck that. I'm not asking any wish from you. Look at you, prancing around all creepy and shit. If I make a deal with you I'm liable to regret it later. You'll probably eat my soul, I bet. Fucking have me cleaning your hoofs with my tongue for the rest of eternity and shit. Fuck all that. How can you even ask me something like that, looking so creepy?" Avery tried to imagine having a sword, but a weapon would not materialize, and he felt fairly vulnerable. It wasn't like a dream where you can flex a moderate control. It was like floating through the ocean current, a jellyfish dreading the shore.

But the creature didn't attack, or cast a spell, or imply it was going to. It just faded out of existence after saying- "You're the one who imagined me like this, fuck face."

And Avery was alone.

Alone with his ignorance of oneness, the inability to conceive of oneness. The great everything- the extension of the self that oneness requires, extension out of self completely- he was falling into the gulf between individuality and infinity, and it was a schism deeper than oceans and darker than space. It was terrifying.

Beaten into us by divisions, Avery was finding. Divisions as our most elementary method of understanding- I know this because it's different from that, and I know that because it's different from the other thing. I know me because I'm different from you. Fear of losing the ability to understand by understanding differences. If I can't tell things apart, how can I anything? To join one must separate, but to join truly, separation makes impossible.

Consider too that the trifling individuality you hold so dear is the one thing keeping you from unfeigned union with the rest of your people. Perhaps it is not they that are mad, but the man that referees madness. The application to join the club was readily available, but pride and self-importance and self-righteousness held the pen, and as the club was not joined, give up hope of ever getting laid by a new woman because you refuse to talk television or brand your sometimes skin with the apposite logos or spring for a sufficiently sexy car and if you can't do that, you can't synchronize your consciousness with the rest of your supposedly bemused generation and if you can't do that, well, rejection and resentment and loneliness are your just deserts.

Fear and insignificance and the individual is small and transient. Do you dare think yourself worthy or capable of encompassing infinity? Every day we are conditioned to fear it. Yet that Oneness can be imagined would make it obtainable, your imagination has clockwork limits. Give it up, little human. Little animal. Give it up.

No way are you meant to concentrate long enough to get into this. Your attention span is negligible. There's not enough energy in it to propel your soul through the cosmos independent of your body. All you can do is think of what you're drinking tonight and wait until you're drinking it. A product of a dull, greedy, aggressive society. The mold you fill was not made to fit Love. It wasn't intended to. And reshaping yourself requires patience and confidence and knowledge that you just don't have. Now would be a good time for you to quit and get on the Tube to somewhere. The path you blindly and faithfully follow leads to an end of blindness and faithful ignorance. What do you know about limitless? Or eternity? Give it up, boy.

Death frightens. The one thing that every living thing will experience and it frightens you. Give up ever knowing God because you're still afraid of death and not only will that fear keep you from passing through here, all that fear and desire to cling to life will spill your soul into a void that is not of space or time or energies or magic but is merely, God help you, the ghost breath of this most base dimension. What do you know of the universe if it's principle of transience frightens you? Stars die. Butterflies die. You will die.

"This is our world," quoth the heavens, "Our web. You are just a visitor here. And unwelcome at that. Leave while you still can. Or we will present you with visions to drive you mad. You are lost, child. Quite obviously lost. Don't turn around and trace your steps home. Just open your eyes. Now."

Something flashed in the darkness. What it was was unclear, but Avery was glad of that. Whatever unholy thing it was, it wasn't meant for his eyes.

"NOW!" the voice boomed. There was a second

flash, and this time, Avery did as he was told.

CHAPTER 88

Heaven and Earth this night were dismal mirrors. Clouds of puddles. Rock hard car parks of black vacuum. In the middle swirled rainfall so insubstantial that it hardly boasted the substance to descend. It became the wind and the dew on Avery's sweater. It hit and darkened the sidewalk and brick and made shiny the bus benches and cloudy the windshields- eventually it did these things, but rain? Only kind-of.

When he reached the tube station, Avery took his hands out of his pockets and blew on them. The pub that Lisa said she'd be in would be closing soon, and due to that, and due to being scared out of his mind by his own mind, Avery was feeling a mild version of the stomach talk that you get looking over the railing of a twenty two story building, though you know that in all prospect the balustrade, being made by skilled masons of the highest integrity will surely hold but the height still suggests death and the feeling still reaches you. He looked back to the dreary sheen of the streets once more, pushed more hot exhaust onto his cupped hands, thought how the gritty the outside looked, how the streets and everything sitting upon them looked as grizzled as Earthly achievable, altogether gray, used and burnt up charcoal melting into itself during indefatigable rain.

Only three people used the same car on the Victoria train to Pimlico. One of them was a girl sitting in the first seat she could fall down in. Looking at her made Avery think of the time that he was standing on the Earl's Court platform, again waiting for one of the last trains, and a man beside him leaned as far back as the infrastructure let him, stopping only for the chalk-colored concrete, standing and addressing his friend who had been standing there watching, "I just fell. That's bad, isn't it?" Drunken post-midnight London, a phenomenon a body could set his watch to. The other two men riding in Avery's car were sitting together and talking.

What kind of night would it be? The self-defeatist answers- I'm going to fuck it up. The pessimist- how could I possibly enjoy it? A-list club that would start with a line, continue with, sorry, mate, no trainers, and then of course there would be the company they'd meet there, the company they'd start with, tacky music, extortionate prices, overbearing, conceited, South-Africans dressed in blazers over oxfords with jeans just waiting for him to go to the bar so they could spit their hyper-conventional game to his girlfriend, drama students, and some lord that everyone was just so thrilled to meet- the tedious, rambling pessimist.

"I remember one time, when I was in mascot, I fell asleep in…" One of the men on the train was saying. His accent was as thick as old grits.

"You were in Moscow?" The Russian's friend asked.

"I was a mascot."

"Yeah, but you were in Moscow?"

The Russian nodded, smiling slightly. Watching his head was like watching apples growing in a golden tree sway in the wind, so red were his cheeks and so blonde was his hair. "Yes, I was a mascot in Moscow."

Avery laughed, counting himself lucky to have

caught only that bit of banter, which cheered him markedly. Had he not heard it, he would have been a different person meeting Lisa and her friends at the pub and not at all ready to play the sunshine on a barely raining night. Things were looking up like the Queen on five pound note, flat and lost in a barely traveled alleyway. A note that was, obviously, facing up.

Avery walked into pint-sized forgetfulness, forgiveness, joyfulness, keenness, thank goodness, with pint-sized wishful thinking that glittered like al fresco chandeliers in the young lady's eyes and pint-sized ingenuousness in action. More accurately, four pints, which were more than enough for little Lisa.

"Hey, Mister!" She jumped up and threw her arms around him, was in turn greeted with, if not as much exuberance, at least as much sincerity.

"I tried meditating. I'm better now."

"You did? And it helped?" Said Lisa, happily shocked.

"I did. But no, I don't think it helped. It was actually really scary. I'll tell you about it. Masturbation helped, though. More than meditation," suddenly afraid that he might be seen as once more the callous, insensible boyfriend, he quickly added, "But it's cool. I missed you and I'm really glad we're hanging out tonight."

This was as good as an hour long massage. Lisa beamed drunken glow and boundless delight, white teeth standing at exultant attention. Her friends, feeling that they had allowed enough time for a make-up greeting, began to chime in and around, saying hi to Avery and lingering for the echo, standing up, leaning in, and generally making their presence known in one way or another. Avery knew the best way to deal with this crowd- tell a story of sufficient length that it will stop them from talking. As he did, tell a made-up story, that is, his audience squirmed.

"Oh, Lisa- on my way to the tube there was this old homeless guy outside talking to himself and I stopped to listen. He was just talking shit, I mean, I had no frame of reference but it sounded like nonsense. So I was like, 'what's the word, old-timer?' and he gave me this really like, poetic description of his philosophy. It was great."

Lisa, not being much like her classmates, deigned to ask, "Yeah? What was it?"

"I'm glad you asked," and he was, because that meant more squirming, "I'm just going to do my best impression of it," which was doubly penetrating because actors, while watching other actors act, are really only awaiting their turn to act, and impatiently at that, "I see myself as like a boat. A boat can go anywhere over water. Anywhere the water takes it, see? Now, listen," a long, long, long pause, with a finger in the air as though he had forgotten what he was going to say, which was relatively inaccurate because he hadn't forgotten, just hadn't thought of it yet, "Anywhere. The boat moves according to the ocean. Listen, most people, they're like land animals, so they want to change the world. Be in command of it. In charge and in command of where they're moving. They want to move their legs and make the world change. That's not what I do. I let the world move, and float," and then, back in his usual voice, "Pretty neat, huh? I gave him a pound and said, 'get yourself some crisps, yeah?'"

Suddenly, the most gracious form of applause he could have prayed for, lights cut on, glowing cheap yellow 'well done, lad- here, you're welcome' to Avery and 'get out's and 'time's up's to everyone else. They may have critiqued his accent, delivery, posture, breathing, enunciation, timing, or some other aspect of his improvisation that he was wholly unaware of, but as it landed, he considered his act a success. No time for an encore, ladies and gentlemen, it appears that it's time to go. No, no, please, I was really only talking to keep you from doing the same. Back to the crispy moist outside, everyone, which waits with smells and sensations similar to hours-old used tea bags.

And so Fortuna rolled, like the heads of French royalty, into baskets who-knows where and who-knows why and who even cares, so long as it rolls ad infinitum. And woe to those boys and girls that distort her shape, and live that their emotions can be pushed a line, happy or sad, providential or awkward, that they should know the coin's face and not its ass, that mended situations should stay, or that broken they shall remain, for Avery, Lisa, Sharron, Pamela Pearl, and Danny (in what was for Avery a frivolous departure from his normal mode of travel) were splitting a cab to China White, where all their names were on a list, and where all their whistles would soon be wet and/or whet. Avery had by now even psyched himself into being happy about it.

CHAPTER 89

'Get the flash out early' was a lesson arranged by Lord Jasper Lilenthal's benefactors, and he, in his privileged manner, at his privileged table, in dandy dress, was. He was establishing himself as a person of value, yes, here in the neon fishbowl party, in the plastic castle, one of the few fish big enough to seize the sky-rocketing landed property which, at over a grand a bottle, was the fish equivalent of rich, feathery fins. They could all see him. Wealth. Entitlement. The ones that were too far from his society might not know him, now or ever, but those people would most likely remain outside his society forever, and were uniformly irrelevant. It was possible, however, in these banal annals of public place, that there would be people around, who someday, years from now when he had outstripped flash, would remember him, and know what a marked change he had effected in himself, notice how much he had matured, and extol him for it. Those that weren't those people were just practice. And therein holds another lesson.

Those. There are those, also referred to as them, and us. At no time does Lord Lilenthal forget that most important moral. Us and Them comes right after Me and Them, which comes after Me and You, and is among the most embryonic models in his system of man-club consciousness. Opposites, see? Oh, there were of course similarities, but they most often warmed the bench of Jasper's cognition. If it isn't that, than it must be this. As much as the rest of the world might hold fast to these comparative references, Us and Them/Me and You especially, Lord Jasper Lilenthal did more. They were as different from Us as a lady bug is from a grouper.

Lord Lilenthal knew this by nature, nurture, and books. Well! How fortunate the fortunate- Us were the only ones worth a fortune.

Them are holding less stocks, are inferior stock.

Jasper Lilenthal, Lord, aristocrat, only God and God's chosen people know what imperative role he will fill in conducting the future.

Falling controlled crash next to Jasper is Avery,

looking over the Lord's lap, at one of His Lordship's non-royal companions.

"Pardon me gentlemen," about to lie, "don't mean to interrupt, but I think I'd be good for the movies, too. Can you sign me up for one of those twelve million dollar contracts you were telling my girlfriend about?" Confrontational, haughty, but at present waiting patiently.

Object looking first at the Lord, then to Avery. "Oh, sorry. Didn't know that was your girlfriend."

Avery doesn't know what to say to that. He didn't quite expect it to be so easy. He gets up, having not come over for anything other than that, saying, "Well, yeah," as he does. It was in response to Lisa telling him that they might be soon set financially, which was after the fledgling gentleman beside Jasper told her, being that she's an actress, that he just so happens to work for a producer, and that she would be perfect for a vacant roll, and well, he couldn't say for sure for sure that she'd get it, but would twelve million be enough? which was two stages before Avery was asking her if she was really that naïve, three stages before Lisa was getting mad and misty eyed, and four stages before Avery plopped himself down uninvited on the VIP sofa.

Now here comes Jasper. He's about three inches taller than Avery, walks with the confidence of someone whose royal heritage predates that of his country…his outfit is one custom made, and cost more than the total earnings of Avery since he alighted in England, his fair hair and eyes, sharp features and carriage, even Avery finds attractive.

Oh, great, Avery thinks mordantly.

But the Lord isn't there to confront him for the disturbance. In fact, he says, he found Avery's behavior admirable. Not too much, not too little. Come back to the table, bring your girlfriend. Have a drink with me. My regrettable friend is off to stalk young women upstairs and I'd be delighted to have you join me.

They're there at the table, Avery sitting between Lord Lilenthal and Lisa, Sharron who is flawlessly hypnotized by the dashing royal host, with two girls, brutal alluring in their little dresses and just as silent, like book ends at each end of the sofa, there to prop and magnify the important, card-holding people at the core.

"So it's just me and the aspiring actors," Jasper says as he pours vodka into chilled highballs.

Avery is quick to correct. Not a drama student, thanks.

That tedious, obnoxious, but somehow unanimously germane question is asked and Sharron, by delicious fortune, who figures that it not only allows her to speak and spot herself if only for a flash, but grants that flash a touch of glamour by association, answers that Avery doesn't have to, "He's a model."

Smirk, and through it, "Ah. A praiseworthy occupation. Truly honorable."

There is nothing Avery can do but pass a genuine smile, laugh, and voice flippant agreement. The bookends spotless at work. They either can't hear, or mask their intrigue (both of them of model mold, have been told so scores of times, but told once (by each modeling agency), that they were just a dictionary-width too short) with stone-faced nonchalance.

"No, I mean it. You're part of the machine. Without people like you, there might be too much confidence in the world."

Drinks and stimulation and lighting and circumstances, Avery is burst of torrential laughter, literally lying sideways across Lisa and laughing. "A part of the fucking machine," he says, rolling his head to look up, as though Lisa his star witness to testify to the contrary, "you got me all wrong, man. All wrong. If I'm doing something to bring someone down by standing for a picture, on any level, even an abysmally deep subconscious level, I'm not damning those people. They were beyond saving to begin with."

And Avery makes an impression. He has spoken to Lord Lilenthal directly, rather with his own words. He qualifies this by stretching his lips, slowly and knowingly at the corners, smiling as evil cartoon characters, madmen bent hell or high water on world domination, bloody lion's smile. "Quite," he says.

CHAPTER 90

Clearly Avery could not have said it all at once, but as linear time assumes dulcet repose, Avery's busybody mouth will list, in order, the topics and summations born the course of the night. Consecutive arrangement, not occasion. Things happened in the meantimes. Lisa spilled a drink on Sharron, who threw her's on Lisa, and they both laughed through their remaining friendship, people stop by, indulge barren how do you dos, rests for restrooms, and so on. Club stuff. Typical. But Avery and Jasper, both disposed to what they thought of as rare talk, chatted frequently. Right. The index. Avery first. Some words were slurred, some stumbled over, but in the gush of pop-life night-light and sound, we are all on the same page.

1. "On some level it's natural for people to need God. Any god, gods, whatever. It's natural to reach for a cipher of symbols. You would accept that everything humans comprehend, they comprehend by symbolic reference, right? Like, if I didn't know dry then I couldn't know what wet is. And since I know what wet is, and I know it's caused by liquid, I can associate the notion of wetness with water, rain, rain with wetness, wetness with the sound I make when I pronounce wetness, rain with four particular markings, marks that I call letters and in particular the letters, R-A-I-N, in that order. So I recognize these things by comparing them to other things. And as I make these comparisons, some of the symbols that I still connect with the initial idea, we'll still go with wetness here, become further and farther removed from the thing itself. I don't know... umbrellas, housing, warmth, fire, clouds, airplanes, oceans, boats, beards, whatever. It all happens in an instant, totally subconscious. God is such an attractive concept because it would be a notion that all things relate to, and emerge from. I'm not saying that I believe in God, or a god. Maybe I do. I think the universe suffices for me."

2. "Scientists keep saying how imperfect our senses are, but it's like, my senses are the only senses I have. They're my only vehicle of experience. So I guess I have to decree that, fuck, my supposedly imperfect senses are all I need."

3. "Yeah, the whole karma thing. Lisa has an interesting theory about that, not that I really take much stock in it. But she thinks that if you have an honest, conscious desire to like, get right with the universe or something, it says 'fine, burn all your bad karma'. And a person can essentially choose to do it all at once, instead of the usual millions of lifetimes or whatever. Come to think of it, I wonder if maybe that's what the story of Jesus is really about. Because it would make sense in a way. Here's an absolutely good person, and he has to suffer all these trials and tribulations. He's consciously accepting the pains of the physical universe because he wants to enter 'Heaven' immediately. The whole concept of Heaven could be a metaphor for moving past this dimension of existence. On to the next. Maybe a few like Jesus has already done that, but surely not many."

4. "It's totally imposed thought and behavior. It's like they're saying, 'Look at the Jesus ordeal. This is what you deserve, better than what you deserve, actually. But don't worry. It doesn't have to happen like that. All you have to do is accept these teachings, believe what we tell you, and obey God's rules. What we know to be God's rules.' I mean, how perfect, right? Christianity was championed by Kings. Do we really wonder why? A religion that says, stay poor, powerless, meek, unless of course you're fighting one of our, no, I mean, God's wars. Wallow in your squalor now, and so long as you don't complain too loudly, when

you die everything will get a lot better? For sure. Sign my peasants up. And here people are still, still settling for so much less of their lives. Damn. You know?"

5. "Not only is the power structure testing the people's likelihood to resist by allowing them access to the truth, they've moved on to producing damning documentaries themselves! They explain piece by piece what they've done, what they're doing, in such detail, that it could only come from the ones behind it! But think- what have they learned? That the world is filled with herds of zombie sheep alla *1984*."

6. "Blood towers. Yeah, I know. Erections. Yeah, man, I mean I see it, sure. They look like erections. There's the whole mysticism behind orgasms. Energies. Magic coupling. I kind of get it. Still, the obelisks themselves would still be just a symbol, right? What about the theory that they're built on lay lines to suppress energy? Or if they're going to be symbols- check this out. If they're symbols, and supposing for a second that the power structure has remained benevolent to the human race, but lost it's faith in the potential of ignorant people, what if they're supposed to look like rocket ships? Like a constant reminder to everyone in the know that, no matter what they have to do in the meantime, it's all working toward a perfectly necessary technology for man's survival- interstellar travel."

7. "You people are lucky you're not raised in

stables and bled daily, so we could buy bottles of your blood and see the future or something."

8. "Orwell talked about three super-states, right? So is it any coincidence that real world distribution of power seems to be headed in the same direction? What will we have? The European Union, North American Union, and Asian-Pacific Union? The E.U. is already in fucking full effect, man. And similar trade agreements that lead to the E.U. are in effect in North America and Asia. It's going to happen. Fucking matter of time."

9. "Fluoride shrinks your pineal gland. Tooth paste is meant to dissolve your connection with the energies of the universe. But it's like... you don't have to worry about this sort of thing. You can already shape shift. Not to keep bringing it up. But, you know..."

10. "Samples of overt control work well to disillusion the people. For instance, as the monarchs and aristocracies of old used to rule with an iron fist, though their numbers were much fewer, the peasantry would just think, 'The machine is so big, what can I do?' Now it's not so different. The government does something that's so obviously fucked up, rolls back the rights of citizens, holds public meetings behind locked doors, commits a generation of men to a farcical war, we still think 'The machine is so big, what can I do?' The ruling classes are just so goddamned far separated from the rest of the world. In their heads, I mean. Me, I couldn't think of killing other men to make money for myself.

I guess maybe they figure that there's enough paperwork and like, bureaucratic abstraction between political motions and actual death. But probably not even. I don't know how these guys could wake up next to their wives in the morning and experience love. I'm rather convinced about the reptile thing."

11. "Seriously, you're completely made up of noble blood?"

12. "It's like I said earlier. You're lucky you're not bred for blood. I'll give you a thousand pounds for a pint of it."

A regression towards a conventional gauge of cause and effect- Lord Lilenthal didn't laugh at Avery's proposition, which actually didn't sound like a joke anyway. He turned his head to one of the bookends, back to Avery, saying without a hint of anything but solemnity, "A thousand pounds? Let me show you what a thousand pounds means to me," and then back to the bookend, "Excuse me, love, another bottle," which affected her for the first time that Avery could see, and she was up and off to the bar.

Allow once more the hands of time to spin asunder and depart from E-F-G, at least back to A-B-C, when Avery first started, at which point his royal audience asked if his proposed theory--the sum of cognitive programs is God-- was a result of his own studied mathematics or merely something he'd read in a book. Avery admitted to the latter, but Jasper consolingly assured him that it didn't matter where the theory came from. Book or brain, once you understood it, once it was in you, it was yours. There is no copyright. The right to observe reality belongs to no one man or group.

After Avery divulged his seventh theory, Jasper looked cross as a flash of lightning. Fast lightning, followed by an expression of confusion as sustained thunder. The thunder lasted as though Avery had said something else altogether, though to think that someone could think of raising noble families and selling their blood as ketchup was strange enough, to look at Jaspers face, and hear a last, isolated syllable leave Avery's mouth (and miss the whole story), that person might think Avery had just said something along the lines of, 'All the snakes in the days of Atlantis used to walk upright, and had hands and arms much like the hands and arms of man, and would choke their rats and rabbits with their hands, as a man would. But the Lizards envied the dexterity of snakes. So the Lizards advertised a pill. Once or twice a commercial break their pill would be advertised, and it promised the males larger penises, and it promised the females less depression. And at the end of the advertisement, a number was given. The snakes, overmedicated television junkies all, one by one were taking the pills. The pills, the pills, the pills, doing as they were designed to do, atrophied the limbs of the snake community, down and evermore, diminishing them in time to vestigial, skeletal nubs.'"

Here is where the universe, bored universe, boring universe, insists things tumble one over other, as long as after one tumbles two, and after two tumbles three. It is to be no more one through twelve and ignoring the one and one thirds, three and three sevenths, no more going from twelve back to one, then on to seven, the cosmos is smashing its wooden hammer and demanding, 'Order! Order!' (or more clearly, *in order*) like the most humorless Southern judge in the infancy of America. One before two and two before three followed by four and five, if you please, sir, stray not from factual sequence.

435

"See? A thousand pounds. And I hardly need to drink any more."

"Fuck. Listen, man, I didn't really want…Shit," and Avery's eyes hit the dirt, feeling all at once bad for goading his new friend into such wasteful show, "I shouldn't have much more vodka, either."

With the gesture already made, and the bottle on the way, with a formal, friendly curiosity, Lord Lilenthal asked Avery if he was serious about wanting his blood. Avery answered that, possibly because he was drunk, that he, "Would drink it. I really would. It would set a lot of things straight for me. I'm thinking about it, and… Yeah, dude. Fucking seriously. I really want it. Let's drink some more vodka, since it's coming. We'll figure it out."

And chatty intoxication tumbled into tremulous intoxication, and Avery himself more and more feeling like Don Quixote of la Mancha, unable to separate the stuff of his books from standard narratives, what is, isn't, can and can't be, all the arcane, unaccountable, no actual in sight, not believing in his palms if they were turned down, feeling something like an ant shaken in a glass jar along with a twig, sightless plaything of influence, reeling endlessly unless… unless- yes. Solution. Exsanguination, vampirism, and waiting till morning. Lisa was back now, dancing in front of them. Lord Lilenthal was watching. Apotropaic glue in the wrinkles of Avery's brain, it suddenly dried, ghost puddle on the blacktop. He was entertaining a horrible idea. It was all over, anyway, wasn't it? Wasn't the world sure to collapse? Wouldn't the trusses snap and the supports sink and authoritarian fire rip through the panhuman motif, who were doomed anyway, and him first? Not an inkling of significance. Stunted substance or never was. The lot is but a lot of could-be, and to believe? Insufferable, faith. Worldview splitting and forking across all the compass. Here's damning you, me, and divine alike. Here's forfeiting good and holy. What will be will whatever. Avery took a swing from the bottle. It tasted like water.

CHAPTER 91

Music rained down from the ceiling speakers that must have been a joke to somebody. Scarier to think otherwise. Top 40 hits hastened to one and a half times normal speed, injected with piquant, jubilant, effeminate effects (think pineapple, plum, peach, cherry, and oh yes, banana, unquestionably boatloads of banana). There was a question as to which self-respecting body builders could pump iron to such sucralose productions and still flex his (or her) synthetic manhood (or womanhood?), but then again, the place *was* called L.A. Fitness.

L.A. Fitness was not a good place to find your iPod out of juice. Not only was the music disconcerting, and fast enough and hitting the most pervasive and difficult to ignore frequencies, the surrounding conversations between work-out partners were usually about as insipid. It was about last night at the club, tonight at the club, this one girl at the club, this girl that'll be at the club, and if the club wasn't mentioned, fuck, were you even listening? Saturday night. Set you up with this fly honey. Club pump, bro.

A slight correction should be made here. Michael only got the impression that everyone was talking past, present, or future nights at 'da club' because that's what they were doing around him at the moment. But to think that the weight-lifters and treadmill-runners and basketball-players in L.A. Fitness weren't qualified to explore other avenues of tête-à-tête would be folly. It would be possible to ascertain, by involuntarily eavesdropping, such things as the body parts that would be exercised tonight by the speakers, where someone's trifling ass girlfriend was the night before, how the housing market is going to shit ("it's a buyer's market, bro"), the status of celebrity game shows, whether or not the new Lil Wayne album is fire- things like that.

With forceful, whistling lungful expelled eight, nine, ten, Michael dropped his weights and sat up. It was perfectly acceptable to gaze into your own reflection in the gym, and he was. His hair was in good shape; his head perched upon a neck that looked as though it may have belonged to a more stalwart fellow. Not true, though. Michael's body was changing fast, soaking in the exercise with porous ambition. He stood up, racked the dumbbells he was using, and walked along a long row of floor to ceiling mirrors (Mirror minutiae- not very minor actually, because a minor misstep in mirror making can send any fitness freak into half-hellish self-repugnance. A glass radius that deviates from an aspheric rate of infinity by even a few thousandths of a millimeter, well, between that and cold lighting...) to the other side of the gym. His image, as it moved from panel to panel, grew slightly in height, then in width, with convex and concave curvature respectively. Most eyes were on themselves, definitely the most innocuous place to look.

Over by the dip bars, a fit couple and their fit friend were chatting.

"I just wish I had nicer legs," casts the fit friend.

438

His shirt was made so sleeveless as to be nearly backless and frontless, but the neck was left unadulterated. His hat brim was bent in the shape of a lower case N.

Behind the three of them, two men in goggles and headbands sweat out a heated racquetball game. They're moving through something like a big whitely lit aquarium, but the only things wet are their foreheads, shirts, and a few spots here and there around the slick wood flooring. To the left of the three fit folks, a similar wood floor and a similar glass wall, but there a different game is playing out. Five men are trying to put a ball through a hoop, and are doing their best to stop another five men from doing the same. Occasionally they wipe the soles of their shoes off with their hands.

"That's such bullshit. You've got the nicest legs in this county." It's the male half of the fit couple that comes to the fit friend's rescue. He is at least seven or eight years his fit friend's elder, and may even be, Michael wonders, the fit friend's brother. They both have similar builds, and their gym banter is in precise equilibrium. If not brothers, bros. "Think about it- you have the best legs in this gym, and most of the body-conscious guys in this county come here. So I'd say that probably you have the best legs in the county."

Michael began his first set of dips. He felt like a gymnast. He was finally able to ignore the house music, or at least drop his focus on it. And he thought, isn't it funny how a mirror is glass, and at a molecular level glass is a liquid, and over long periods of time gravity acts on that liquid and pulls it down, so that old mirrors tend to be thicker on the bottom than on the top, and how those images at the gym that people so aspire to attain and attend to will eventually be effected by that same gravity, pulling their liquid muscles down, image and thing the same, and eventually every concept he could imagine seemed to melt into another one like that same heated sand or chemically-grown reflective slickness.

"Yeah. But think about baseball players. I want legs like that. Baseball players have great legs."

"Baseball players are fat," the woman half of the fit couple erupts, "You have the best legs in the county." Vehement stress on the two words 'best legs'.

In any other place, the temptation to chime in on the fit trio's conversation would be overwhelming. Not so at the gym. At the gym, Michael felt it his duty to keep to himself, talk only when asking in reference to an occupied machine, 'are you done here?' or 'mind if I hop in?' Some guys found it acceptable to nod and say "Sweet tats, bro," but Michael did not.

All Michael could think of was how he couldn't wait to smoke some pot with Luke or J.P. and tell them about what these marvelous people at the gym were saying to each other, in public, like it was no big deal. He would smile then the smile that, in any other place he would have already been smiling, and laugh the laugh that he would be laughing, were he anywhere else in the world.

He finished his workout, as per usual, autopilot all the way. Body politic all the way.

He thought about his brother, too, and wondered if Avery knew about the club pump.

CHAPTER 92

The city beyond their paper-thin drapes was alive and moving. No sympathy. No apprehension. It moved with the same speed and the same noise as always- a man on his hands-free cellular device, a bus stopped for commuters to get off and on, a delivery man dropped kegs from the back of his truck, children schlepped their turtle shell backpacks to school, women gossiped, engines, voices, doors, all that sound. Avery's ears picked it up. His sore brain sorted through the noise and listened to some bits harder than others with an absolute lack of conscious say-so. He leaned over the bed slowly to look down on Lisa, who was twice as sleeping as he. Thank God. Avery needed time. Time to compose himself. Time to think and regret and damn himself. What in the bloody hell happened last night?

Drinks and far too many of them, his body declared in agony. He remembered the beginning and middle of the night, but only obscured portions of the end. Sift through them, then.

An offer. A crazy offer that started out as a joke and morphed hellishly into one of the worst violations of trust imaginable. Avery looked again at Lisa. The line connecting them was dark. Line connecting them? What is that thing? It was in his head, totally unfamiliar yet impossible to ignore. It wasn't that he saw the thing like he saw Lisa's body or the bed or the floor, but there was something there- a perceivable chord that he knew was their bond. He knew it by something that wasn't smell, sound, touch, or even sight- it was just something that his brain experienced, something like a sense of sight

441

independent of eyes, an image put directly to his soul, which he could also gaze upon. He saw the her on him that must have looked different before. The chord, the slowly spinning strand of energy between his existence and Lisa's had decayed. Dried up, gray and withering. Like winter had passed its killing breath over the thing. Rotted by his betrayal of her. Polluted by his abhorrent decision, his respect for her turned to hate, and his love for her to disgust.

It must have looked different before.

He got up, poured himself a cup of water and left the room, not caring how much noise he made, whether or not he roused Lisa, even if the whole world outside saw him in his dark blue boxer-briefs. Everything else could wait until he figured this out. Down the sheer spiral staircase, down three regular staircases, stumbling, with his eyes half closed and his body half naked, Avery walked. He walked quickly and maladroitly, like a slow moving junkie on fast forward. His mouth tasted like a twenty minute bare-knuckle fistfight. The water rolled over the edge of his cup and onto his legs. He tossed the rest of it in his face just as he walked through the already open door and onto the stoop.

Gloucester Road stretched on ahead, looking more terrifying and incomprehensible than it had looked to anyone, ever. Avery closed his eyes. An image paraded though. The usual black canvas was replaced by something more like a moving Basquiat painting. That was no use, obviously. He raised the curtains that were his eyelids to the strange stage that was his world, adding another layer, the layer that he had known all his life, the layer comprised of streets and buildings and people and cars and sidewalks to the colors and vibrations. The blood changed him. Blood! The thought hit him with the force of all the two story buses in London, sent quivers down his body until all he could do was either run or collapse.

Avery dashed to an area that seemed untainted by the vision. A spot that was seemingly devoid of energy, between some shrubbery along the black iron gates of a private garden. There he finally dropped the cup and hid. The cold was at him, eating at his bare skin, leaving teeth-marks of whitish-blue everywhere. The cold was the least of his worries. At least cold had always been there. Not like, like this new, whatever it was. Energy.

It was all nice and good to think about an elite power-structure when it was tantamount to sincere fairytales and he could go on living his life, fine to mull over death while it waited ambiguously in the future, easy to believe in alien races as long as they remained forever veiled. Mystery and magic, fine- but proof of either would soil the allure. All of it beating him now at once. Making him feel for real what he only thought he'd been feeling. Strike of impact that didn't end in a strike. It lingered, lingered still, making him dizzy and sick.

He pressed his eyes together, covered his face with his hands and his hands with the dirt. Under these three tiers of seclusion, Avery quietly sobbed- begging and begging for a return to normalcy. Indian-Give the torch, Prometheus. Pease, Gods, have it back.

CHAPTER 93

Above the bed and Michael and Jen, a new soul pocked with disabilities and beleaguered by handicaps barely balanced, chameleon-sways on a one night stand. It isn't a beautiful thing, but Michael is smirking. He feels safe enough. Everyone that saw it happening have committed worse affronts to standards- there were the episodes at Mystic Woods and whatever hotel they found for Magic Fest in Orlando, J.P. fucking up at his birthday party last year and everyone wondering if the poor kid's spine wouldn't buckle, and Broadway Ave- fuck. Broadway Ave. didn't make anyone look good, ever. He feels safe.

His head is turned to the left, watching her sleep. She breathes classy. Soft nasal breath that rolls over the bed-sheet and matches perfectly the shy morning light bleeding through the curtains, slightly curly dirty-blonde locks over her forehead, one strand tickling the corner of her lips, warm skin perspiring pensively, the air inches from her body is a full ten degrees hotter than the rest of the room. Michael thinks that he could have done worse. Still- their amalgamation is a distasteful creature. A feeble-minded sapling, pigeon-toed, knock-kneed, bow-legged, buck-tooth, bird-chest, and what have you. It's nothing to be proud of. He commits himself to waking up within the hour. When mom and dad are out on their morning walk, he'll get her out. His phone begins to vibrate down the night-stand.

He has his clothes on now. His jeans and shirt were pulled out of a pile of dirty clothes, and his jacket smells like smoke when he's occupying anything but the crisp London morning outdoors. It isn't morning to everyone- the respectable movers and shakers call it early afternoon more likely, but being up before noon after such a late night feels to Avery like a dreary accomplishment. He left Lisa still sleeping, probably feeling like shit and knowing it's just as well not to wake up for a while. He's doing his best to act normal. Not to cry or stare at anything for too long that he wouldn't normally stare at. But it's kind of hard to know.

The phone is ringing, those two fast beeps, a little more disconcerting than the long, single ring in the U.S., but he's past that by now. Some of the numbers lit up more than others on the key-pad. It was like, once you acknowledge something, and it contracts your cognition, your spirit moves on the universe and that acknowledgment becomes an actual, perceivable outward manifestation. The 5 in the 561 area code, first the 5 (SPLASH!) and then the 6-1 but only after he thought that 6 minus 1 is 5 also (SPLASH!), the 316 prefix moved together becoming first 10 and then two 5s (SPLASH!), and finally 3011... magic colors in Michael's cell phone number. The same as in his toes and fingers, but only when he thought about it.

His guest stirs a little as he reaches across her. She moves her hand to his bare stomach and tilts her head forward, and inch or two closer, barely holing on to the pillow by now. The caller ID is keeping mum about who's at the other end. Michael answers, hoping that it's his brother.

"Hello?"

He was hoping for something more in the voice. An ambulance revving and roaring with lights blaring. Trained, practiced professionals discharging mantras of 'everything's going to be okay', 'just leave it to us', and knowing he's in good hands. But it's only a voice. Leagues away across the globe and robbed of utility by distance. What was he hoping for, anyway? A vaccination? He knows that all Michael's said is 'hello'. And he hasn't said anything yet. He at least has to explain. He has to hear himself say what happened, and say it for Michael if he expects any help. The people around him are walking in and out of the Tesco's, passing by the news stand, walking with their hands in their pockets and on their purses, all their eyes are forward as if the next act of their lives will make a dent in the function of the universe. He is realizing that he's holding the phone still without speaking, and is unsure of how much time passed since Michael answered. It couldn't have been long.

"Hey. Hey."

It's Avery, he can tell, and tell too that something's wrong. It was alarming enough that Avery was calling so early Eastern Standard Time on a weekend. Unless he had a job or something Avery would never be up that early, but the second 'Hey' is one of the weakest and shakiest echoes of a word Michael has ever heard. Racquetball courts bounce your voice with more pride.

"Whoa- what's up? What's the matter?"

Thinking, *Please, man- do something. Make this better somehow. You always know what to do, just help me,* in his own, private impression of thought, Avery leans his head forward and closes his eyes. His imagination does exactly the opposite of what he wants. Like when your subconscious wants to fuck with you for keeping it locked away for so long, and it pictures your high-school science teacher on her knees blowing you when you absolutely can't afford a hard-on, or when you're driving down a two lane street and visions of a head on collision with a speeding semi spawns every time you pass a speeding semi. This current daydream is the child of the two- there he is, hunched against the

446

wall on his little bed, crowding a glass of frothy red blood close to his chest, not wincing as a heavier than human weight thrashes the mattress above him, and a crocodile tail spins wildly off the side. Lisa is awake and loving it. No, it couldn't have been that. She wasn't awake. Was she? The glass is tipped thirty three degrees and the contents are spilling right bloody down, iron acrid war on his tongue but down it goes bottoms up. Meanwhile the bed-frame is straining, and it definitely is a crocodile tail or something similar. Oh, Michael is on the phone. He's saying hello and Avery hears an open end trailing afterward...

"I'm here. Listen. Oh, fucking, I don't know man. I'm fucked up. Something really big happened last night, man. Really big."

Michael is asking what and waiting.

Thankfully Michael is waiting patiently, because Avery is unsure where to start. As to whether he should preface the description of his new sense with the way he acquired it or go into all that after. It feels like it's been forever since he's cried. Since back in middle school, maybe. When he got his bike stolen. Or when his dad pushed him down the stairs. He's just unaccustomed to dealing with his body doing this to him.

"It's fu... I'm seeing colors. Colors that shouldn't be there- or that aren't normally there. They aren't really colors. They're like colors. They're like temperatures. I feel it more than see it. And I'm feeling sounds. Listen, I'm not on a drug. That isn't it. This shit is real."

He's sitting up with his legs over the bottom of the bed and his feet on the floor, moving them both forward a little, back a little, forward a little over the carpet. It's a tickling and scratching feeling at once, sensitivity and relief, much like the relief in knowing that it's probably just a bad trip his brother's going through. He remembered doing acid with Avery and Luke a while ago, and thinking that God was talking to him in the privacy of his own bed. Imagine being along a busy London street in the middle of the afternoon while that was going on… All he is going to do is talk Avery down. Scatter some breadcrumbs along the trail back to relative-reality. He'll be fine, Michael is thinking.

"Where are you right now?"

He's down the road from the room, Avery is saying. Across from the tube station.

Michael's happy to know that at least he's close to home. Avery liked to get out of the house when he was tripping. But damn, if he started to lose it out in the city it could be really weird for him. There are voices coming from the garage. They are saying hello to someone, probably a neighbor walking their dog around the block, and a conversation blooms and wilts in the time it takes whoever-it-is to pass. His parents are leaving now. The garage door is closing behind them as they embark on their routine morning excursion. He's painting a picture of a comfortable room down the road, tea brewing, Swamp Thing book opened, Close to the Edge playing on the stereo, all the things that he'd be into if it were him in a room on acid.

"I told you, dude. I'm not on drugs. It's. Isn't what you're thinking. God, man, it's really hard to say all this, you know? I committed the most vile act imaginable last night. Fucking… just fucking gross. I drank some blood. That's what's doing it. I drank a pint of a lord's blood. I wanted affirmation or something."

The world around him isn't spinning but something is. Something like a compass that's lost its magnetic mind. The compass is spinning, it isn't as though the world is spinning, but the compass is.

Jen is stirring now, snaking her body toward Michael, arm stalking waistband. Michael's face is inflexible as he listens, but a scowl develops and disbands. He is holding a finger up behind him to where he thinks her face is, like pin the tail on the donkey without even the slightest desire to peak through the blindfold. Jen gets the picture. The call is important. The creature that is them isn't.

"All I really remember of it is, like, bits and pieces. But ever since I woke up, man- I don't know what's happening. The blood changed me. I'm seeing, no, not seeing exactly but I'm sensing all sorts of extra shit. I mean it's everywhere. On me and Lisa, oh man, this thing between me and Lisa looked so dead. And all over certain places. And to my right it's like a fucking pink and purple tornado from the sky to the ground. It's far off- probably in Chelsea somewhere near the river. But," Avery is pausing, mumbling nothing, overwhelmed by the vortex and losing his train of thought, "But…"

CHAPTER 94

The Throughout was everywhere. That was why he called it that. It carried with it- carried with it and *was*-commands, histories, residues of life, death, dreams, and disappointments. It beat along life, streets and circles, above them, beside, down the big and small, along the airwaves; the Throughout could not be mapped. A map of the Throughout would be a different colored map of the world.

It told you what you needed. It knew want and need as synonyms, using always the latter and forgetting wholly the former. It asserted what you believed and didn't.

Not at all monochromatic like the 'OBEY's and 'BUY's and 'THIS IS YOUR GOD's under resistance remodeled sunglasses, but radiant. Dazzling and complex. Wielding colors not carried by the light of Sol. How it got there was impossible to say. To think that it was secretly manufactured to coat and cover everything was too ambitious to believe. It could not have been done by the few and secret society.

A spell, Avery decided. He figured he was seeing either the fabric of a spell or the living energy of a parasite dimension. The face of a spell or a tapeworm.

From workless wives into the lives of their tired husbands, the Throughout. Pouring from children's hearts like water fountains on the hottest playgrounds. People and things alike, the Throughout.

The world is doomed. Doomed.

It is why they love the loud lights of Times Square and Piccadilly Circus. Those bright adverts that jump with peacock intensity headlong into each and every one of your worldly senses, they only mimic the great underneath. The Throughout. Those places are a shoddy adaptation of invisible influence. The billboard might not much influence, but the Throughout beneath and atop and throughout it does.

She was sitting eight rows in front of him on the 3 bus and he saw her as perhaps the last remnant of unspoiled life. Godly pure. Holy in essence, spirit, and splendor. God! her light was fantastic. In a lost night, the lighthouse to which all the damned might find their way. Golden white beauty and heavenly mother in clinch. Avery put his face in his hands and wept. Hard. Heaving tears and breath. The other passengers on the bus looked on, assuming the worst and staying the hell out of it. They were all thinking that it's bad luck to watch other people having bad luck and let Avery go on sobbing. It was the intense love and pain of a lifelong relationship, charging in on all flanks, and condensed to fit the stretch of road from Oxford Circus to Charing Cross.

Colors on the girl. Colors that made sound and tasted like paradise. Colors that felt like a dolphin's skin and a hot shower. Vibrations on the girl that carried like a dearest lover's voice over pillows. She was an empty full and Avery couldn't take it. He couldn't stop until she was well on her way, and enough distance had separated their respective life-forces. It was all new. So new and insufferably intense.

To watch the world move over the Throughout was educational. Feelings that you didn't know why you had could be translated by the Throughout. Avery always wondered why every time he bought something expensive, no matter how much he wanted it, he always felt a little hint of a feeling somewhere in his guts. He didn't know quite how to explain or even describe that feeling, and it wasn't pervasive enough to ever mention to anyone, ever.

But the currency digs into you, and pulls out pieces when it's passed. Its tendrils snare your soul, the tendrils only as long as ownership. Once it's gone- the way a fish feels when a gamesman carelessly removes his steel utensil. That's money. And a part of the Throughout. For better or worse, enmeshed into life, not minding the damage it does when it comes tearing out.

Like an American boy watching a baseball game in Japan, Avery watched the Throughout. How it affected togetherness. There were the things he didn't understand, ambiguity throughout the Throughout, kanji and katakana on the scoreboard. The emanations and feelings and strings of super-color, the sound atop sound and sight atop sight, do you know baseball? Watch. The announcers follow every consonant with a vowel, but you do know baseball. The women at the ticket booths bow, but this is still baseball. The bats and balls and bases are still there in all their blessed fluency. The world is still the world, knowing the world is at least a start in knowing the magic dimension that fuels it. But it truly was like learning another language. Sink or swim, Avery was lucky enough to be immersed, so far, only to his chin.

He would soon know something else, too.

He stepped off the bus at Westminster Station, stepped down Whitehall, along a living yellow brick road. The streets and sidewalks and squares all lived, but around here lived deafeningly. Waist high energy, rising like the shallow end of a swimming pool, threatening to raise like the coming tide, to come as Avery panics.

Whitehall. Downing Street. Drowning Street. Terrifying.

Swallowing fear and thinking of a wet-lung death, Avery made forward. There it was, all to his left. A vortex of power, one of a kind. There was no blocking it out, but did he try? He tried.

Armed men stood at the gate's attention. Armed and armored. A show, really. We are protected. The peoples' representative, who the people might have killed- black iron gate bullet shooting protected. Men in finely-tailored suits were walking across what was visible of the driveway.

Men? No, not men- dragons. Naked dragons.

Ten and a half foot olive-green animations, bipartite man bipedal iguana, crocodile smiling masters, out in the open like nobody's looking. But nobody was looking. Nobody noticed. Avery wanted to scream, "Good goddamn, people- there is two tons of walking alligator leaving the Prime Minister's house!" Sleeping eyes see only dreams. Nobody would have heard.

But the dragons noticed him. They looked, pointed, and laughed.

What's the matter, lad? Avery's mind chimed.

Oh, he's American! Let's eat him.

As Avery ran as fast as his not-fast-enough legs could carry him, laughing continued to tour the highways of his brain. He ran down the energies of drivers and walkers past and present, as it shot out of big windows and splashed out of the sun, through puddles of could-be and piles of once-was, through rivers of alternate dimension, no resistance, just fear and conditioned apathy, terrified, going crazy. Reverting back to primeval man, ape in the city. Mindless child. And like a soundtrack to the madness, still, the laughing. Obviously they were just fucking with him.

CHAPTER 95

"I could use a little help."

Affectation- young man politely seeking the assistance of a library aid. And given the circumstances- not half bad. He might very well have been doing an impersonation of half-mad homeless man twenty trips lost from the world, wandering with a God on his shoulder emitting susurrant whisperings of how each and every passing individual was after him. See, circumstances:

Circumstance the First- The London Library hoards the residual life-force of every author who is represented or has influenced an author represented in it.

Circumstance the Second- It is very difficult for an extra-dimensional novice to tell the difference between life-force and residual life-force.

Circumstance the Third- He is thinking that, should his only real dream come true, he might well be fated to haunt libraries for the rest of eternity, and never laugh at full volume or hear his phone ring again.

Circumstance the Forth- At infrequent intervals, something jumps out of his imagination and screams, "BOO!" He is still unsure as to whether or not it's the dragons still fucking with him, or his own fun-loving wit doing the same.

Circumstance the Fifth- It appears as though the library aid has lived many hundreds of thousands more lives that Avery, which is a rather intimidating premise.

She looked up, and pleasantly raised her eyebrows.

"I'm. I, uh, am looking for a book."

It was a shot in the dark, of course. Avery had allowed the throughout to influence his interaction for the first time. The first time since running from the dinosaurs, rather. He expected her to know exactly what book, to know what he didn't.

The library aide asked if he was looking for the truth in a book. Avery answered that yes, he was, and felt immediately idiotic. So what if this woman's aura filled the room and rang like church-bells of experience galore? She was just a library aid. A library aid with a tie-dyed radiance and, hey- that's why all those hippies liked tie-dye and why it moves so much when you're on acid- it's just a simulacrum of the library aid's character essence. She would have been around long enough to incite that.

"Are you, umm," but Avery stopped himself before finishing. She hadn't told him about the book that he'd asked for, no sense in jumping the gun and assuming that the person's aura really represented that person. They might not have any idea what color their aura was. The library lady might have no idea that tie-dye is her birthright. She might be too high-brow for all that. "No, never mind. I was thinking something else."

"Of course," she said, shifting her weight from her right buttock, "You can use this. I'll get another." When she centered herself, there were about eight inches of empty space where the top of her head formerly dominated. Had she shrunk?

No, obviously there was no shrinking. She had merely relinquished her booster seat. And while Avery was thinking of how kind a thing it was of her to do, he asked- "Is that what I'm looking for?"

"It's always helped me," the ancient young woman replied, "Thickest book in the whole of the London Library."

Of that, there was little doubt. The library aid had pulled a book from her ass, leather bound, worn, thick as the most verbose of English dictionaries. Avery knew it was something. Without even reading the cover. It was the most pronounced pocket of negative energy that Avery had thus far encountered. It was a book, in this and that dimension a book, and thank heavens, nothing more. No green slime or blue foam or purple muck or yellow glow- the discolored white pages only spoke to his eyes, giving off the usual magnitude of information, ready to be read as per usual. He carried it to a quiet corner, thought about what candor such a large book could possibly contain and how he could ever hope to find what he was looking for in twenty minutes of random page turning, opened the book, and scanned the scarce symbols printed therein.

As long as another man lives, there are only truths. No truth.

...the fuck? Avery thought, wondering why the letters were so fire-hot red and how the book seemed to answer his question directly. He closed the book. *Did the blood change me? Or is this some sort of near-death experience type breaking of my sanity? Am I sane?* He wondered, and shook the book a bit before opening it.

They're lucky they aren't bred for blood.

Perfect. Next question.

He isn't the Antichrist, but he came damned close.

He didn't know what the Antichrist had to do with Michael. He didn't believe in an Antichrist. Well, he didn't before. But the Throughout- the Throughout had him believing in everything. It's possible that we become sea foam when we die. It's possible that ghost twins live next-door to each other in every set of human eyes. The Antichrist would be a trick zeitgeist touted by the power elite- what did it have to do with Michael? Antichrist? Son of God? And how can you come close? Was it possible that Michael was conceived, rather, fathered by a dead goat's horn? Did human sperm undo the end of man?

Even God doesn't keep track of all the dust in the universe. Even that dust effects destiny.

Whatever the hell that means. What is going on here?

It's all energy, man.

That much was obvious. Everywhere, all matter, all thought, all consciousness- different speeds of energy. But where does it come from? Why does it happen and why is it invisible to everyone unless you're a shape-shifting reptile or, apparently, have guzzled the blood of one? Is it cognizance that gives it power? Is that why what's around seems to jive with so-called occult wisdom? Or is it there regardless?

The people give it power, yet it takes power from the people.

Isn't that a paradox? How can something take what it's given? Like when you give someone the proverbial inch and they take the metaphorical mile? Or is that the nature of politics? Avery's head was scrambled. He was asking too many questions at once. Not realizing what questions the book was reading. Was he thinking of George W. when he turned that page? Almost certainly not- but who knew what symbols were popping up at the recollection or Politics? Cucumbers are crunchy, but at some level- would you need mush to know that? He cleared his mind. But an instant later it was filled with the same incessant uncertainties, just as loud and just as cluttered.

Luke is Lucis, but not literally.

Another anomaly. It made no sense and he had no idea why the book told him that. He opened to a page, thinking hard on blankness, nothingness, an empty oblivion, vacuum up, down, left, right, forward, and back.

Not surprisingly, the page was blank.

"Excuse me. You can have it back now." He told the aid.

She thanked him honestly, glad to have it and the increase in height back safe and sound.

"Are you guarding it?" he asked her?

"Guarding what? The book?" Of course she knew that he meant the book, and of course she recognized the flippant implications of the question, but she was by nature too serious to play along.

"Yeah. Do they have you here to guard it?"

"It's the thickest book around. Gives me the most height."

After she said that she went turning over papers, looking as officious and hectically busy as a library aid could hope to look. Avery thanked her for loaning it to him, stepped outside toward all the busses and bustle of

Trafalgar Square, and made a very nervous call to Lisa.

CHAPTER 96

6:01 p.m.

He was doing his best to follow Michaels's earlier suggestions. He was thinking that his body was a machine, his actions were programs. He's been behind the wheel of that machine all his life. He just had to get it under control again. And why not? This he told himself. He'd been programming and operating that machine of his since he could think and move. So he talked with Lisa. They had rather uninspired sex, the machine not following directions completely. But his machine had the excuse that neither of them was feeling well on hand. The room was stuffy and the stagnant drops of water in the brownish bottom of the sink seemed to be transmitting into and corrupting the air. The chord of Avery and Lisa's love was still looking more like a cobweb than a rainbow, and though he did well do hide it, Avery was dying inside. There would be no way to play this out forever, man or machine.

8:40 p.m.

Crying. Lots of crying. Yes, they knew this would come. Puppy dog love. Puppy dog that had grown into a fat, smelly thing and yes, suppose it had to happen eventually. I'll always love you. I'll always remember you. Yes, yes, maybe it was inevitable. He is telling her that he simply has to move home, money worries and all that (lies), and she saying that she understands (lies). The fighting is too much. Yeah, it's true. Everything has changed since they moved to London. Agreed. She is saying that she's sorry. So is he. There is more crying. Crying, cuddling. Exhausting, but the tears keep coming for them both.

12:33 a.m.

"We're going to enslave every last one of you, shit-head."

It woke Avery up. At first he thought maybe it was one of the Italians next door, screaming at their partition in a sort of dry-wall prank. The wooziness with which Avery considered that possibility was banished by the time he picked his head off the pillow, even before he opened his eyes and turned them around the room.

"I said, we're going to enslave you every last one."

There it was. The non-sound. It didn't come from thin air, didn't even travel through thin air. To his ears, all was silent. Even the Italians next door.

"What?" He spoke aloud. The 'the fuck are you talking about' didn't follow the 'what', but it was more or less understood.

"You heard me. Every last one of you will be slaves until the day you die. No exceptions. No getting out of it."

By this time, Avery knew he was being contacted. He didn't know how or why, from where or by whom, but someone was sending direct messages, and that someone obviously didn't have good intentions. This was a newly discovered muscle of his soul- naturally, Avery flexed.

He thought hard, and hoped the thought would be transmitted to the correct talking Lizard, "People wouldn't let you." His own voice; moving in his head as a hall, marble floored meeting place.

"They already have. We've done this before. What happens when we arrest your brother? Do you go and break him out? No. You grieve and complain. You don't break him out."

"We have the courts. And we all die sometime."

"We own the courts. The laws have changed. There is no afterlife."

These were the words swirling in Avery's head. After the last word, though, there was another sound. Or rather, another non-sound. It sounded, or rather, non-sounded, like snickering.

"I don't believe that." Avery sent. And he didn't. When he came home that evening, he used a paper-towel to squash a cockroach, and the thing's soul squirted out into his hand like red-black food coloring. He scrubbed and scrubbed at the sink, but the yellowish-reddish-purplish-orangey stuff just would not come off.

"It's true. No afterlife."

"Bullshit. I see signs of an afterlife every day. The energy, the- the whatever the fuck it is remains."

"You're only seeing our light."

There was more snickering.

Lisa turned around in his arms. Avery tried to stay comfortable, but as she turned, she covered more of their little single mattress, and there was no way that Avery could relax all of his muscles and not slide off. Still, it would look to a casual observer that Avery was having another one of his dream episodes. The snickering was still going on, and it also sounded like people were trying

461

to hold their breath.

"Yeah. See? It's just new to you. We're far enough along to know that there's no afterlife, or such a thing as karma, but telling people that they exist is a great way to keep them docile. It's like, 'hey- put up with oppression now, and later you'll have everything you want'. Can you imagine what would happen if everyone knew that the only chance they'll have to get what they want is right now? There wouldn't be enough for us!"

Just then there was a click, and a pop, and a new voice was on the line.

"How does it feel to be a slave, pussy-bitch?"

This was followed by a lot more snickering.

2:14 a.m.

"We did an experiment. We'd take the best thing going at the time, which was sort of like an Asian religious symbol for happiness and sunshine, and then turn it into a symbol meaning the exact opposite. Death and misery. Pretty much the worst thing going at the time. It became the symbol for your Adolf Hitler's Germany and there you have it. We say what the symbol means.

"'So what?' some said. 'People don't remember the good times. They better remember the bad. So to reprove our point, we invented a god with the face of an owl. We invented him as a vicious god, with insatiable bloodlust. Men were meant to fear him. He demanded sacrifices of their children. Sacrifices were made. Oh, stars! Were they made! And what do you have now? People putting up wooden likenesses of owls in their living room and kitchens like it's no big deal."

Avery had no idea how long the orator had been going on. It seemed as though he was catching the tail end of a lecture. Finally he had fallen asleep after the last one, and now another. He was just about to emit all sorts of nasty expletives, but before he could form them, mentally even, he thought of something better.

"That's nonsense. You would have had to start the second experiment before the first one ended. I've seen carved owls that pre-date World War II by a long shot. Besides, I'm reading shit that says that the owl god, Moloch, was actually a bull. You're obviously full of shit, man. Fuck off. Let me sleep."

It did appear, but only for a moment, that the lecturer would actually fuck off and let Avery sleep. Avery breathed relief. But, yeah. Only for a moment.

"Easy fix. We just changed a few websites."

"What the fuck ever. There's still the first thing. Your timeline is off. Scram."

"Go to a dimension that has time travel, travel in time, and change dimensions back to this one. We have dimension travel for that. Prick."

The more he listened to the static in his ear, the more it sounded like a dial-tone.

3:50 a.m.

"Crushed, subdued, stripped, razed, tyrannized, dominated, enslaved eternally, soulless, hopeless, helpless, mentally and physically and spiritually shackled, irrecoverably ignorant, a populace of upright sheep, bloodless, thoughtless, permanently astound, we will own you. You will know nothing but what we tell you. You will do nothing we cannot see, say nothing we cannot hear. You will love the hand that stays your food. You will revere the force that rules you. You..."

"For fuck's sake! Enough already! I just got back

463

to sleep, man! Fuck!"

"Humanity- all you so called little Gods, little animals, you'll be as malleable as a stick of hot butter. Hot wax. Uh, hot wax, like, flesh fat."

"Yeah, I've read that book already. And you're wrong. Orwell had no faith in the human spirit. I would never love Big Brother. Never."

"Orwell knew more than you know. Your future is written."

"As a work of fiction."

"As a work. It exists in your world, because of your world. It comes as surely as tomorrow morning."

"Fucking whatever. I'm not here in bed to debate with you. Let me sleep."

"Sleep? Let? Get used to this, monkey-boy. Get real used to it. The time is fast approaching where you will have no will of your own. You will live as our hands, survive as our property. Your days of slavery are near."

Avery sat bolt upright, not fooling himself into being tired anymore. He looked straight at the ceiling, because he didn't know where else to look. His tongue was bleeding from the side. At the rate his heart was going, he would have to wait a while for more sleep.

"I'll rip your throat out with my bare fucking hands, do you hear me? Fucking doomsayer- it'll be my boot stomping on your face for the rest of eternity. Not the other way around. My people will destroy you. My people always bear down oppression. You don't consider the long run. Orwell was dead wrong. I know that man will resist you because I know that I will."

"No love, no trust, no self, no hope, no emotion, no will, no passion, no devotion, no dreams, no humanity, no civility, no life, nothing other than how we choose to use you. You and everyone else. Trust the knowledge of a

464

superior being. I've been there. It happens. You will die. The individual will die. Your children will exist solely to lick the dirt from our boots. A generation of boot-lickers. A generation of cattle. No dignity, no worth, no cheer, no celebration, no energy... "

This shit was going to go on all night, Avery knew. Every asshole in the next dimension would have his number, and would be calling from here to Sunday, bragging about their ascendancy over humanity, laughing at their own jokes, rolling in their own self-confidences. It was far too much to bear. Avery closed his eyes once more. The creature was still going on, *no music, no art, no vision, no family,* and on and on and on.

3:53 a.m.

He concentrated. Felt his being push out like unflagging lungs at an air-mattress. This power was somewhere in him, all he had to do was locate it. Will it. Will a disconnection. Turn that part of him off. By and by will overcame, and the voice was gone. And Avery was left to himself to calm down and retreat back to relative nothingness, thinking all that while that he had won, and that the oppressors would do well not to underestimate the will of a challenged man.

CHAPTER 97

I don't know how to say what I'm thinking. I wish I could just plug you into me and skip all the words

465

and give you an exact account of what's going on. I wish you could just read my mind. You could fill me in. I guess I forgot to see you for the things you are. Somewhere along the way, I couldn't say where or when, some strain of complacency set it. I would think "Lisa" or "My Girlfriend" and stop there like it was enough. I know that you're the most caring and loyal person that times like ours can produce- you have rarely shown me anything other than selflessness, tenderness, and dare I say worship? I don't know how my appreciation for that could have waned. It wasn't on purpose. It wasn't... But I guess I stopped seeing that when I see you. I see brown hair, straight brown all to your neck, that nose of yours that looks better on you than it would on anyone else, I don't know why it stopped hitting me. Or at least why I developed a tolerance to it. I don't know why I see this like super-abridged version of you. It's like my love got fat and lazy. You are such a rich person, Lisa, and piece of shit I am, I've made you two-dimensional.

You gave me so many good times. What I'm going through right now, good or bad, I credit to you. I remember how magic it was when your uncle dropped us off and we left our bags in the hostile and went to get breakfast and you used your accent to get us our first tube tickets. Will you speak in the British voice forever, now that I've left? It makes me want to cry thinking about you using that accent with new people. A lot of things about this fucked up ending makes me want to cry. I guess now I know that I have the capacity for these emotions. Nobody's ever made me feel this before. I miss you so much. Barely gone and already I miss you so much. Have you done this before? How long until I'm back to normal? I want to come back. I would do anything that things were different and it was just me and you and nothing else to think about. But.. excuses, I know.

I hope that I remember things like they were. The memories I have of you- I want to verify them somehow. It isn't like a movie flashback, you know? Where recollection is perfect? Everything is congruent because there was somebody there whose job it was to keep everything the same and besides maybe minor variations in camera angles or editing the screen remains completely impartial... The smallest things are what get me. Remember that time in that cabin with your parents when we were arguing about apartments and you were opening the box of contact solution and were suddenly really happy that it came with a new contact case, and me being still bitter or challenging, I was like, "big deal" or "yeah, that's really fantastic" or something like that, and you said "I think it's pretty cool"? It was such a little thing but even then it broke my heart. How could I have been so callous? And so often? I'm sorry. I think that I'll know better now. There is so much I want to change. I want to let you rub the dirt off your hands, mysterious public transportation grime but yours, on YOUR hands, wherever you want. In my hair even. Lisa... fuck... I'm sorry.

It kills me to think that so much of what happened between us was my fault. But I guess in a way it doesn't. It makes me feel lucky too. Like, sometimes I think that I'm so righteous and competent but I'm humbled now. When Michael and I were growing up, there were a few occasions that I hit him too ruthlessly, or said some really harsh shit to him. I think back now, at this cute kid who was just so warm and all he really wanted was for me to love him like he loved me- what the fuck, man? What kind of a monster would want to fucking hurt a kid like that?

467

Why, Lisa? Why did I act that way to you and him? I mean- I don't with him anymore. But like you said, we'll always have each other. We're brothers while you and I were only related by choice. When you said you were jealous of him because we would always have each other I wanted to correct you. I thought that two people would always have each other as long as they both wanted it. I'm sure we still want it in some way but it's over isn't it? As we speak I'm off. As we speak. Every second there is more world between us. I don't like myself without you. I feel a failure without you.

I don't want to forget any of this. Isn't that selfish and unrealistic? Like how many times have I opened one of those juice boxes as a kid in elementary school? Hundreds of times, between 12:30 and 1:00 I'm opening juice boxes- do I remember? Yeah. I remember it as one big hazy ball of what was. I don't want to remember us like that. The little triangle mouths of those juice boxes and the squeaking sound they made when kids drank from them really fast. It all seems so meaningless. I really don't know what we're living for, Lisa. We had each other- I mean we did, right? It was that nice, wasn't it? We could hold our bodies as flat against each other as we could get and say I love you so much over and over and for a while nothing else was moving or happening in the world. It would just be us. Me and a girl who was every bit as significant as me and maybe more so. And this incredible girl- this gem- would spend the night in my bed while I was at work just to keep it warm for me when I got home. I would sit there at my machines and think about that, I would stand at the comparator and think about that or while I was checking finishes through a microscope.

Whatever happens, you'll always have a place in

me. I promise. I will always love you and I will always respect you. You have done more for me than anyone. Nobody knows me like you do. I won't keep telling you I'm sorry but I am. A big part of me is still you.

CHAPTER 98- In which Michael holds an unbelievable breath and a history of divine monks, whose lungs were at times equally inflatable, and whose magical feats were only disturbed by the shock of gunfire is told.

Michael pushed his fins alongside the bottom a reef, leaving a thin cloud of kicked up sand in his wake. It was a perfect day for snorkeling. The water temperature was peaked at seventy two degrees, clear as clear can be. There was about twelve feet of water above him, just enough to start to feel the pressure, and as Michael kept telling himself, just enough for most of the ocean's man eating monsters. It was fun to freak himself out. He imagined things popping out from under the rocks.

In what follows, it might be best to consider Northern China in the year 1898. Imagine peasants wandering the land aimless and hopeless. Floods leaving the countryside in ruins. Roman Catholic and Christian missionaries pouring over the nation as tendrils of Western Imperialism. Floods of water and foreign thought. Groups organizing in Shandong to fight what they espied a threat to their beloved culture. Fighters for the Society of Righteous and Harmonious Fists razing the countryside.

The 'Boxers' as they are called by Westerners. Supermen.

No. Wait. That might have come a bit early. It'll be important later, but it definitely came too soon.

Still elated by his earlier meeting with a Hawkbill turtle, Michael was swimming around all careless and daydreamy. Overlaying the actual light of the world, that rippled pattern of undisturbed sand, those ancient rocks holding steady amidst an ocean of movement, a few small, insipid fish living here and there, is Michael's imagination. In it, giant things erupt from holes in the Earth, mammoth sharks swim jaws-first into view. Suddenly, he screams a column of bubbles and muted sound.

Something giant actually *did* pop out of a hole, not four feet in front of him. It was a sudden shock that brought him back to actuality in an eye-blink. A Nurse Shark. Perhaps the largest he had ever seen, nearly six feet in length, had just decided to show itself. The panic didn't last. Michael knew that attacks from Nurse Sharks were extremely rare, just as long as he gave the thing a bit of space it shouldn't mind him much at all. Michael followed the critter as it swam a steady pace out to sea, into the blue and breathing.

Now China becomes a little more pertinent. Going from weak and hungry to strong and fast and healthy, one can imagine going from strong and fast and healthy to Godlike. Try to understand the liberation a man feels when he is a part of his people's fate. The founders of the Society of Righteous and Harmonious Fists taught men how to channel this under-refined sensation into a physical energy. With training and magic, it was enough to repel bamboo spears and dodge flying arrows. The Boxers, with all their martial potency, won the fear of the Qing Dynasty empress, who engaged the Imperial army with helping the Boxers cleanse China. Concentrate and try, one can do anything. Repel bullets. Hold your breath forever.

The sea was getting more serious. It was deep now, and where earlier it let the sunlight in without question, where it was just a lucent interface between land-life and gilled, it had taken on a color. And while earlier Michael could only sense outward vastness, ocean in front of him and the land an anchor not too far off, now enormity extends in all directions. He had been kicking with all his might after the big brown fish for some time now, perhaps for as long as fifteen minutes. At some point the floor fell completely out from under him, and he found himself hovering over a hole in the planet.

It went down much further than the light. A giant, diamond shaped hole, some seventy feet long and forty feet wide, down down down. Birth, knowledge, time, float, dark and infinity were the first words that came to Michael's mind, and he felt presently like a trinket among valuable things. Breathless, the abyss left him with nothing but lent worth- 'with me,' it seemed to say, 'is clarity.' Fins first, he sunk like a dead sailor, watching the cobalt waters dim. There were no noises or feelings beyond the desire to descend. And descend he did.

Christian, Protestant, and Catholic Missionaries-Chinese Christian, Protestant, and Catholic converts were by the thousands hacked to pieces. China burned. Beijing terrorized by its own inhabitants. Torture and fire rained upon the foreign virus.

International reaction was forthcoming. The Imperialist powers, seeing China as a valuable asset to world domination, could not allow such anti-foreign ideologies to take root. An Eight-Nation Alliance was formed by the United Kingdom, Russia, Japan, France,

Germany, Italy, the United States, and Austria-Hungary. Exotic troops and the modern contrivances of war aimed to present Western Peace to the Society of Righteous and Harmonious Fists, the Qing Empire, and the people of China. Gunfire.

The Boxers were slaughtered. The spirit army never descended to avail them of their purpose. Their magic failed to deter the foreign bullets. Their bodies proved vulnerable and, after all, only human.

Michael pushed eight bubbles from his nostrils, and they ascended to the ocean surface, where a small point of quivering sunlight swayed. Smaller and smaller, Michael down to who knows how deep, bubbles up, moving toward the light like a soul to over-excited cells in a dying visual cortex. This, for him, was the death of impossible, and he knew that something was up. Almost everything was up.

CHAPTER 99

Shocks came by the hour. Some hopeful, others demoralizing. Fact- layers exist for only you and everyone both, on top, beneath, and between your universe. Fact- neither science nor God are omnipotent. Speculation- the spectacular/disappointing life-force of the individual is tuned by the moon, or the stars, or the sky, or dead men, or nutrition, or chemicals, or chance, or tides, or fate, or the fates, or one D20 for toughness, intelligence, and charisma, or mother's touch, or any combination of these and other unforeseen factors. Fact-the seemingly infinite particles of the cosmos each and every one have something to do with it, definitely, and Michael's particular case was determined by one grain of cosmic dust, unnoticed by God, riding a ring of Saturn. But Avery could not know that. All Avery could know is that Michael's aura was big as all fuck.

"Ah! Avery! Hey," Michael said coming in. He walked over to grab his brother's hand and give him a hug. "What's the matter?"

A strong, quick inhale through the nostrils, half a step back, "Yeah, sorry. It's just really weird, you know? Some things are too much."

"Okay. But I'm afraid I don't know what you're seeing, exactly."

"I saw something like it on a bus, once," Avery started, not really knowing how to explain, feeling the sober ineptitude that all the drugs in the world couldn't worsen, feeling that drugs might actually be the answer- that the road to better understanding might actually be paved in drugs he wasn't on and didn't have, "but it was different. It wasn't as different as you. I don't know what it means."

To explain was obviously a daunting task. It was to quantify an abstraction. Avery hesitated for as long as possible, until Michael asked, "What did you see on the bus?"

"It's like a color, but kind of like a sound, a warmth. Sort of like those things. Everyone has something in them and I guess they're all a little bit different, but yours is like… really, I don't know. Weird. It's really powerful. Breathtaking. And I can tell it overlaps mine, but it doesn't swallow it or anything, I feel like it even helps. It's like black soil. It would be like walking outside, South Florida Summertime, two in the afternoon, wearing a thick sweat suit, sort of. No, not exactly but- it's hard. This is like giving a three hour Stephen Hawking lecture a half-assed listen and trying to tell someone what it was all about five days later. I don't know how to explain it," Avery said this, and other things, such as- "It's like taking an Eskimo to the Sahara and asking him to describe it to all the other Eskimos when he gets back. It's just, how could they really get it?" and- "Okay- this energy perception that I have, I can see energy everywhere. It's throughout everything. When female Copepods move through still waters, sometimes they leave a chemical trail behind. Human females do it too, but I think I'm the only one that can see it," and- "It all makes perfect sense. Here I get home and I finally think I have something, something that might make me as impressive of a person as you and here you are with this power that outshines mine like arc lamps to flashlights." There were more (believe it or not), less intelligible attempts to describe the Throughout that afternoon, though Michael insisted that he was getting the picture. The pair then went out to see Mr. Chase. Michael was very curious to hear about what caste life-force powered that man. And once Avery thought about it, he was very curious too.

Everything. An atom from every life; creation coursing through him. The thumbprint of God on his forehead. Morningstar scars, the flesh of his ghost. Protector. Guide. And of course, the tired cliché, the cap of angels, it alights itself above Mr. Chase's head.

"Hello, Michael. Avery. What a surprise to see you back," He greeted from the ground.

Michael nodded to Mr. Chase, looked to his brother, and said, "What's it like?"

"Huh? What are you talking about?"

"Try to describe what it's like," Michael pressed.

"Oh, come on. Put me on the spot like that?" Avery passed glances from Mr. Chase to his brother, back, and back, "Seriously, though? Now? You think?"

Mr. Chase had gone spacing out. As the conversation didn't pertain to him, he seemed completely unaware of it.

"It's pretty weird, too," Avery said casually, "It's almost like everything I've ever felt. There's really nothing there that's unfamiliar at all. Everything that exists is there in tiny pieces."

Avery started to explain that, no, of course he had yet to fully experience existence and everything might not be there, that he was only going with the first impression and could do no better than make awkward assumptions and describe them with miserable, paltry analogies, but Michael made a 'follow me' head nod and started to cross the street. Mr. Chase lifted two fingers, pointer and middle, as they left. He looked back to the clouds and whistled a vibrant note, striking Avery like a trumpet.

Michael pounded eight hard knocks against Mr. Thurbin's door. They were impatient knocks. Avery was thoroughly confounded by the immediacy and seriousness of Michael's behavior. So confounded, in fact, that he could do nothing other than allow himself to be driven about, a passenger on a bus in a foreign town, believing that the bus driver, who in this case seemed to command one of the most far reaching life-forces on the planet, knew the way better than he, the myopic tourist, ever could. "Don't worry," Michael said. It helped. His worry decreased. Michael knocked again. And again. And a roar erupted from behind the door.

"Aw, knock all that off and open up," Michael

yelled.

The deadbolt turned, the doorknob turned, and Mr. Thurbin stood before them looking extremely tense. Michael turned to Avery.

"What about this guy? What's his soul look like?"

But Avery's voice had wandered off. It was off in another aisle, probably looking frightened and wanting terribly to regroup. He wondered if Michael were just fucking with him at this point, if Michael just assumed he had cracked, and if his spirit was sufficiently weak to be led astray on a candid-camera goose chase. And when they finally found each other, Avery and his voice, his voice was still just a tad shaken.

"Nothing. It's like nothing's there at all."

"Alright. So. What do we know so far?" Michael asked, answering himself with, "We know that something is different about all three of- what do we call them? Souls? In my case, I'm telling you, it isn't what it looks like. There may be something strong there but it won't realize itself. I've always felt off,"

Avery stopped him. "No, man, listen- it's there. If you could see what I see you wouldn't be saying that. You have a life-force that could turn the world. It's terrifying."

"Could. Could turn the world. But I'm telling you, I've felt something off in me my whole life."

"Don't say that."

"There's something missing, trust me. Something happened that never should have or something never happened that should have. But forget about that. Mr. Chase- tell me more about him."

"I think he's seen God at some point. I mean that literally. Look, this is all just my interpretation. It could be that I'm applying my own limited experience to something that's much, much different. It's all outside my reality tunnel, and I have to fill in blanks and draw conclusions to make it fit, yeah? To make sense."

"Never mind all that. What about Mr. Thurbin?"

"He's an empty shell. It's as though he has no soul at all. Like he's a robot that no living thing has ever touched."

"Figures that you'd pin the robot thing on the wrong guy," Michael said, smiling. He walked over to the refrigerator and pulled out a box of Tupperware filled with watermelon wedges. It was hard for Avery not to feel struck when in his brother's presence. Anything Michael did- any human activity seemed beneath him. It was strange to see him eat, even. Strange that he didn't draw energy directly from the Sun, or that he'd need it at all. Avery's breathing became labored. His throat swelled.

"I wish you could see it for just a second," tears came into Avery's eyes now. "Christ, man. It's even more to be confused about. I don't know about anything but it's all there right in front of me."

Michael turned away from his brother, focusing on the cool lights and see-through surfaces of the refrigerator. He used his tongue to crush a sweet, juicy piece of watermelon against the roof of his mouth.

CHAPTER 100

There came a thin wailing, into Avery's ears,
Organic alarm-clock
Cradle-made, confusing for the count of no
Babies in the house, high noise.
The sound rouses him, and Avery is up and looking,
The room is exactly, as far as He can remember,
Just as he left it.
Black entertainment center, cheep wood with
Water worn circles like immature lunar craters,
Dusty television in the same place
Cattycorner,
A sewing machine where his desk used to be,
Darkness as before,
Lights all Off,
Even clothes on the floor, flowing to and from and
Over his suitcase,
Like Enki's semen Through the Garden of Eden.
More cries from outside,
Cries Of Stressed motors, drew his attention to the door,
And He noticed a red light Through The gap underneath,
The carpet touched and colored crimson.
He Glimpsed, by the Luck of instinct,
From the bottom of his DNA,
That the light was Hell's.
Avery shrinks, thousand years of flame, right here at
home. It made him hot, and He tried to move not at all,
As little care as possible,
No panic for knowing,
And Seeing,
That the city is real, and it is of and houses eternal torment.

And there he Was on his bed,
Sound asleep, he hovers over his body, inspects his form,
Decides The safest way out would be to go back to
His body, get in, and hope that sleep,
Death's fling, presented quieter pastimes
Elsewhere and elsetime.
A force rises beside him. He is back to body now,
Willing the specter disappear,
Thinking that if magic exists, he should use it too,
But fails.
Still beside him and Growing like a breaker to shore, evil.
Avery rips himself from sleep, turns, is
Saved, and shuts his eyes again.

The alleyway is lined with bricks and
Worn wooden fences, and walking down it
A lone man is wandering.
They are upon him straight away, the bodies, they
Seem to step from the very air, pale, pasty,
Flesh-eaters at the helpless.
As bodies Surround him another man takes form,
Taking over as the focus. He is the good-Savior.
The hero. Protector of the helpless from the
Bodies and the evils,
Baseball Bat wielding, he swings and
Cracks a hairless scalp, violence and blood splatter.
The body crumbles to the ground,
A death rattle is the last process.
More the hero Attacks, his bat swings
No mere warning shots,
The bodies are as dangerous, and
The game ends in curtains. A hard push away,
The end of his weapon against the
Cold cheek of a body, aim and swing, batter,

Another skull caves with sickening Death crush.
But something is happening to the other man in the alley.
The World is on him now, writhing on the ground,
Presided over by two bodies,
He Shakes,
And swords rip from his abdomen, trace lines down his
Legs, chest, arms, And head,
And he is opened, gory gift box.
A different body climbs from the Man,
Master of the other bodies.
A power much, much greater.
Over one of the wooden fences, the hero has
Made a quick and quiet retreat.
He Runs like hurricane winds down roads,
Over cars, through yards, crossing the man
Made lakes of gated communities in a single bound,
Burning the soles of his feet.
But the new body is with him.
Behind him and next to him,
Floating on the air, as If swept by Solomon's carpet.
There is no outrunning, no jumping that will
Stretch the space between them.
But for some reason the hero and his baseball
Bat are allowed to escape.
The master body slows, the bug scurries to safety, a
Single bug, bat or not,
Can hardly affect the super-magicians.

Never you mind the poor, hapless chap death-birthing
Master bodies, for here in The lap of luxury,
The rich fetch delight in Venetian yards,
Well dressed and bred.
They mingle and clutch their delicate glasses close
To their chests, waving them

Gently in crescent swings and they regale each other,
All merry. The rich standing
On the heads of the lesser. Higher up because
Of it, where view is better. In this Place, this
Mansion, high house on the hill, looking up only to
Olympus,
A pig Roasts over open fire.
Young ladies bite into chocolate covered strawberries.
Fine, fine stuff.
But as the night does caress the privileged,
As at the very moment time blows
Lovingly into their ears of ego, and of their gaiety,
There is a disturbance in the
Yard.
The damsels are suddenly in distress,
And the men scurry much the same.
Shock spreads over, as though it were a fire
Tearing outward into a dry field, and
Soon everyone knows the cause, the cause is
Upon everyone. They are ripping
Limbs and tasting flesh,
Herding a helpless rich and powerless center, to the swine
Roasting.
To the man- captured, tortured, the demons run
About and flaunt their Brand of hedonistic cruelty.
Let the lady loose her skin, and peel her hair back to
The very mind.
A young master is worn like a living coat on the back of
One demon, who slips his arms into the poor man's arms,
Chorus of screams, pain
Percussion. They are stricken and shake and shriek
Like the stings of a violin.
Madly they panic.
Madly the madness tremors.

Surrounded now, what strips of the living remain
Are rounded up and tied. The host looks on.
He is held by a Demon. The master demon.
Same as the master body.
Captive and captor Watch. Horror and
Fulfillment, in order. The guests, honored men and
Women, all their money and their positions flee,
They are no strong anchor in the moment of this ordeal.
They beg for mercy.
Plead for deliverance.
Squirm and wish themselves out of the Talons of Hell.
The host sees the first stroke of the file, which is
On each and every blurry gut.
His guests are cut to pieces.
Their abdomens are filed open. With each rough
Stroke there is less going back.
The damage is irrevocable. Death, then, at the
Hands of the Damned.
When finally the filing is finished, and the guests
Present their insides as outsides,
The Master demon sets their stomachs alight.
They burn BBQ ribcages, gray Kindling, the stomachs
And hearts roast.
The host is told to eat well. It wouldn't Do to waste.
He knows he is expected to eat the hearts of his peers.
Their eyes
On Him still, alive.
Suddenly he notices that he is unshackled, sprints
To the edge Of His yard, which overlooks a high cliff,
And dives over white plaster barriers.
He Is Head down plunging, ready for the fast
Death at the bottom, so much better
Than To Eat his own insides and play the favorite toy
To bitter angels.

He is Down, Down, Stopping, floating, floating forward,
Flying!,
Delivered at last by
Divine Intervention, saved by merciful Jove,
Free over the city and fast from Danger.
All the town is beneath him now, but as he floats
And rejoices, he sees. No hope Remains in his language.
Each and every house beneath him is his.
Looks just Like his. Oh, there is the library, but
It is built like his house,
With the same Windows and turrets, the same color paint.
And all the strip-malls and the middle
Class homes, the restaurants, all the gas-stations,
The airport, the storage facilities.
The guard gates, the condos, demonic facsimiles all,
The model-train land of
Hell,
And no matter where you stop,
No matter where you set-down,
You are sure to Dine In the house of demons.

Jarred from a sleep too desperate to bear, Avery
Turns his body hard and finds Himself free, bed
Sticky and wet underneath him.
The room seems to breathe, Alive,
Brought to life by power of his fear, still dreaming?
He wonders, sits up, his
Nostrils flare, he bites his jaws, sets his eyes to focus,
A hero before coming Ordeal.
There is a noise outside his room. A voice calls, a familiar
Articulation, His brother saying his name.
"Avery," it goes,
And along with a knock on his Door Goes again, "Avery".
This is the world he feels. The real one, physical,

Holding his body above a soft
Tool for sleeping, within a larger one for shelter,
Past moves back linear lines
From Present, always striving forward toward future.
The room looks like it did Before,
When he only thought he was waking up. But the
Light- the light of hell is
Still There, seeping in through the cracks of his sanctuary.
Michael is the bringer Of The Light.
His Throughout has changed.
It is coming out evil,
Oozing Outward Blood Red,
Like a puddle under a cracked head on the concrete.
And Here Michael rushes In,
As though the very sky were falling.

CHAPTER 101

There was Energy in the Tyler house that was something like wounds atop a body of water. Once destruction has run its course, once the solid thing has sunk to the bottom or burst from the top, once the wind has relented or the wave passes, once the water is left to its peaceful own, it begins healing its top to flatness. This kind of thing coursed through the house, and powerfully, and the Throughout crinkled, wanting a return to flatness. But Avery was too tired to notice. He was, in fact, still half asleep.

The chaos of his dream, violence of demons, faded into hazy memory, but there he was, standing on

484

his bed, like a man ready to embrace the impact of a fast oncoming car, looking at Michael, waiting to come to. He simply would not come to. He felt his body feel slowly, and with the same impatience as one that watches a lagging computer. He was slow, heavy, and dumb in waking.

Michael was talking, talking fast as though his target listener had already come to focus, had time for a hot shower and coffee. "Yeah, just…" Avery said, cutting his brother off and closing his eyes and raising a hand head-high, palm down. Here was a young man who felt like he was walking in a dream-city, with only strange, standoffish faces who already had friends and company and were hardly interested in helping him ward off loneliness. The Throughout poured into him relentlessly. It was on everything- like water on the courtyard after a hard storm. How else to describe Avery's lack of function, as he stood a weary slouch and looked about aimlessly? As a man in no frame of mind to solve problems or lead stronger men?

He was the visitor in a country guest house with a bathroom that hadn't seen visitors in ages, one that after a long shower throws a white bathrobe about his shoulders and ties it at the waist, feeling the dried, scratchy cotton and realizing it's rather yellow, isn't it? and noticing too that in some places the scratching is more severe, as though it can't be cotton, and looking to see what the problem is he sees that roaches, dried and dead, have been dying in that bathrobe probably for years, and it is their chitin carcasses and broken legs that scratched at his back and the backs of his thighs, and he is newly dirty. Or the old woman at the coffee shop, who was never particularly sharp or bright, feeling a vague sense of remorse at the existence she spent worshiping God, God as in the One True God, the humanoid all-powerful residing in the rolling and thunderous clouds, because now there was some vague skepticism- was there One God because One was the first number men learned to count to, and humanoid because man is egotistical?

Sounds were moving slow through the thickness of nighttime. Everything was, but confusingly so. Avery resented this reality, and dazed, like a man wondering how a culture such as his could transpire (such a one that seemed to thrive on the misery and discontent of all its inhabitants, sadness reigned, control allotted to the psychotic), stood like someone ready to defend against the rush of an enemy- with both knees slightly bent, weight distributed eighty-five percent or so to the rear foot, body forty-five degrees away from center (give or take), his front hand near his chin and the other beside his abdomen. He had completely forgotten the act of standing up, was a bit confused as to how he got there, figuring he must have been more or less asleep at the time, and was even more at a loss to consider what his brother was saying.

He finally, as though a bit of movement would get him together, stepped to the floor. He was just as trapped there. As trapped as a man in his life, with his work week and pointless entertainments, slave to a society of consumers, all their time to the construct of modern contrivances, while the resources owned by two percent of the population could provide for its whole and have the world living at leisure, leisure in luxury, the hungry fed and the working with all the free time in the world to indulge solely in passions, some of which would surely enhance the world and drive along utopia. A man puzzling over an answer that has eluded thousands of years worth of men and his bustling societies, knowing that the laws of law and ownership and hierarchy serve mostly to stifle freedom, that equality has throughout history been a figment of fool imagination. As trapped as that- as blind and weak as a race that could degrade itself in such a way. A race 97 percent dense and dim enough not to realize that it, as a race, would look more like a single hive from the outside, a caste system with workers and royalty, almost none of whom know where the queens rest and what they look like. Trapped like mankind, who blindly tolerate a thriving parasite.

There was energy in the Tyler house. The Throughout was blood red and bounced unnaturally off itself like the rush of three tides meeting on a single shore. Avery opened his eyes wide and shook his face. No help. He still felt ill prepared for anything at all. Still waking up. Like a man sitting on a toilet after a thirty minute night's sleep, allowing his eyes to shut for just a moment's more rest. Not ready for anything serious.

"Okay. Wait. What are you saying to me?"

"Dude!" Michael snapped, "Wake the fuck up already! How much of it didn't you get?" He walked over and began to shake Avery by the shoulders, repeating 'come on, come on,' while Avery scowled and frowned.

The reasons that Michael and Avery were freaking out were different. Avery is worthless because a nightmare had just ripped every vestige of hope he had for humanity from his very heart. Michael was worried that Mr. Thurbin was finally going to cross the street and smash Mr. Chase to death. They were talking in Mr. Thurbin's kitchen earlier, Michael and Mr. Thurbin, and the conversation ended with the following threat-

"I'll show you just how fucking neat that guy is. Watch."

487

Avery made no bones about the disheveled state of his awareness. "Everything's red, man. You're getting it all over my room."

Michael said that he felt red, or at least different, and red was about as good a description as any other since he himself couldn't at all describe the difference. He also reminded Avery that the world might be ending, just after asking Avery to really look around, and describe what he saw as accurately as possible.

It was highly interpretive, they knew. The Throughout was like the poetry of the Universe, of God, and what Avery saw was probably as much a reflection of his own intuitions and indoctrinations as it was actuality, like how everything was red now probably only because Michael was being intense. Still, he went on-

"It's reddish. But it's sort of transparent too. Almost like it isn't there yet but it's going to be. Like I'm seeing future energy. The only place where it's solid is in you. It looks sort of like a red star."

"Fuck," Michael said, "I don't know what that means."

CHAPTER 102

Not far away, a car that wasn't really built to be pushed to its limit was being pushed to its limit. This was all the day's boredom- red-lights, pennies and nickels at the bottom of the washing machine, setting the table with folded paper-towels, forks and knives, pep talk from the idiot employer, synchronized commercial blocks of all the area radio stations, wake-up call looming in the not far off enough distance of boring ass tomorrow morning, all of it weighing down the pedal of Luke's metal-blue sedan. Eventually a corner was taken, and the image of Avery and Michael at the edge of their driveway came sideways sliding through the windshield.

"What the fuck?" Michael yelled. Luke was getting out of the car and Michael was looking back and forth from Luke to Luke's car, eyes pissy.

"What?"

"What do you mean, 'what'? What is it?"

"What is it? What? What's all this 'what the fuck'?" But it was obvious that Luke knew. He knew that he'd been driving recklessly, and (evidently) figured that the best way to defend himself from a scolding was to feign ignorance. He was thinking that if he acted well enough like nothing, there was a good possibility that he himself could be the one doing the scolding, and convincingly accuse Michael of being hotheaded and uptight. This was not the plan originally. In fact, the thought had just occurred to him, just now.

Avery informed Luke that he was driving like a maniac, and Luke changed the subject with an impassioned- "When did you get into town? And why haven't you called me yet?"

"Just today, man. Sorry, I was going to call you. Shit's been weird lately."

"What if somebody had been walking their dog or something?" Michael asked. "As if we need that kind of thing tonight. Really think about that, Luke."

Luke glanced at Michael, sucked his lips back, turned back to Avery, rocked back on his feet, and said, "Don't worry about it. I got word from someone that you were back. I wish you would have called me, but it's cool.

489

How long for? For good?"

"Yeah. You look a little loopy."

Luke laughed and asked what the fuck that was supposed to mean.

"Ah, never mind. Hard to explain. But I'm glad you're here, man. Turns out you were right about a lot of stuff."

"What stuff?"

"Energy. Vibrations. Control. All that. Sorry. I know it's abrupt but I've been really wanting to tell you."

"This guy tells me I look loopy," Luke said to Michael, pointing at Avery with a thumb.

Michael launched into an explanation of how Avery had taken a nap, and was still, twenty minutes later, in the process of waking up. He was minutes into an analogy loosely involving dream-states, voodoo, Edgar Cayce, and tea kettles, when Avery stopped him.

"Stop," Avery said, and to Luke- "I'm serious, man. I have a lot to tell you about. I've been seeing the world a lot differently lately. I think that magic is real. I'm something like 99% sure. But there's more of it than we can possibly imagine. More of it than anyone can possibly take hold of."

"See, I used to think that, too," said Luke, interrupting, "But now I think that it was you that were on the right track, not me. All that shit is just disinformation. It's out there to distract us from the real picture," Luke was going into the mode, and so was Avery. It was a mode that Michael would usually bow out of, go look for something else to do, and come back an hour later once the two had exhausted their points or become sufficiently depressed over their dismal fantasy futures and a new, light subject had forced its way into their lives. This mode of conspiracy speak, it could happen any time, any place.

And one could tell Luke was going there. Something about the eyes. "If everyone is out there looking for ways to release trapped energy, or expose people trapping it, the elite could then do what their really doing and with less harassment. There's nothing mystical about it. It's a physical plan. Dumb down the population, increase the privacy of government, and increase the power of the governors. You were right, before. Not me. I see that now."

"Trust me," Avery said, "There's a lot you don't see. There's a whole other dimension on top of us. Most of it's pure and untapped. But there's oppressive influence there, too. I think you have an old spirit, Luke. It's something more people could probably see if they weren't too busy looking at themselves all the time. Remember when you said that you were a Roman General? That might be true."

"That's right!" The 'that's right!' didn't sound like 'I think you're right' but rather a 'that reminds me'. "That reminds me," and turning to Michael, "I do remember that conversation, and I remember that you kept trying to deny me my god-given right to believe that I'm the reincarnation of Lucius, umm," Luke was trying to remember the last name but gave up, quickly, hopefully before it became too obvious, "and I realized recently that reincarnation isn't about literally acquiring someone's spirit, but acquiring it *in* spirit. If a person's life has sufficient impact on you, you share their soul. They become you; or rather a part of you becomes them, just through their influence."

"And this guy," Michael started, "whose name you can't even remember, influenced you so?"

"Yeah, motherfucker." Luke removed a joint from his pocket, walked to the other side of his car and posted up against the passenger side door. He said, "Welcome back, Avery," and tipped the joint up with his lips, put his lighter to it and began to take the first few drags. He blew an arrow of thin, pale smoke and started to pass the joint to Avery, but decided instead to hang on to it a while longer while he talked. "It's just like all that magic-demon and Draconian shit. It's nonsense, of course. The people that say that shit only do it so that they can keep exposing *other* plots. Real ones. They have to sound crazy so they'll be allowed to keep talking. You understand, right? Imagine if they were only talking about the real shit. People would start listening and shit. Now, if a politician or like," he paused to inhale, "some big time company director or something gets called out and accused of being a ten foot lizard shape shifter, just because he isn't a ten foot lizard shape shifter doesn't mean it's all good. Whatever the other accusation is probably merits attention. But the lizard bit would have to get thrown in there. For other reasons, I mean. To make it less obvious. Or less offensive."

As Luke went on, Avery watched the blue-yellowish, red-purplish glow around him shrink. Its outer edges dissipated, grew hazy. Seemed to evaporate a bit. It was shrinking like the penis of a man taking his first freezing cold prison shower. Avery had more or less stopped listening, so scary was the loss of Luke's radiance.

"Are you stoned?" Avery asked, finally taking the smoke from Luke's fingers.

"Yeah, man. I got pretty high just now." He permitted a laugh but it was a semi-self-conscious one.

"It's zapping your energy. I can feel it. And look, I know, it's impossible to get the real picture. Everyone out there is pretending to know, adding a lot of speculation to a little truth, and even if something is absolute and profound to one person, that same realization might not fit into someone else's world. But what I can…"

Michael cut Avery off- "Is there something happening next door?"

It was like an evil wizard's cloud from a Walt Disney movie. Avery began to panic. "Dude, I don't know what the fuck that is. Come on, come on." He threw what was left of the joint in the grass, which Luke found terribly impolite, but the way Avery and Michael were walking away, something was obviously up. Someone across the street started to whistle.

"Where did you come from?" Michael demanded. He made a b-line towards Mr. Chase.

"Oh, good evening, Michael, Avery. I've been, oh…"

"Bullshit! You weren't out here a minute ago."

"Whoa, hey, man- chill," Avery said. Michael looked about as mad as he'd ever looked, which made no sense whatsoever. All Avery wanted to do was to put as much distance between everyone that that fiendish thundercloud energy thing as possible, and here was his brother, pissed off and stopping for no good reason.

"Chill? I'm fine. I feel great. Damn, I feel really together. With it. Like something just clicked in my psyche. Tell me about it, Avery."

But Avery was already trying to tell him. That cloud- death pepper, purse of bleeding bills and red hot razor blades, deaf cities, HIV in your aspirin, abomination and young guts in the gutter- it was raining on Michael and floating toward him like London morning fog.

"You're turning dark. Jesus Christ, please stop it. What the fuck's going on? I don't know what it means!"

But Michael was looking at his biceps and breathing in deeply. His nostrils flared and his lips turned

493

to cruel, serial rapist smile. Avery put his hands on his brother's shoulders.

"Stop! Whatever you're doing, fucking stop it!"

"I don't know what I'm doing," Michael said, speaking through his teeth.

Luke was lost and Mr. Chase started whistling again. Avery looked down, toward Mr. Chase, who, though he sounded as calm as a sleeping household, appeared rather worried.

"Do you know what's happening here?" Avery begged.

"Well, it's hard to say exactly. Your brother has seems to have something special about him. Is that what you're seeing? Perhaps it's in him to bring something to the world. Maybe he has the potential to be that influential. You'd get the wrong idea if I said Antichrist, but, well, maybe he could be the Antichrist. Would that explain it?"

Michael heard this, and looked down to respond. "Bring evil to the world?"

"Subjective, but sure."

"You've been cursing people!" Avery shouted. "The shit about the guy and his boat- that was you."

"Bring evil to the world?" Michael repeated himself, to himself. He was obviously uncertain if that's what he wanted.

"Of course, I would think that you'd have a say in the matter. I don't believe in fate. There's always some cosmic mistake that would allow an individual their own decisions. When it comes right down to it, the stars don't keep perfect track of themselves."

The garage door across the street began to thunder. Black continued to pour out. A vortex of consumption, slavery and abuse, unfairness and fear. It whirled around everything, and ended in Michael's chest. An engine was revving loudly.

"Then that's easy. I don't want it. No, thanks. I'd rather not be the Antichrist and bring evil upon anyone at all. I've kind of been making other plans," Michael said.

"That's a relief." Mr. Chase got up to stretch his legs.

Avery started crying a little, like someone who had once again been shown how little they have to do with the workings of the universe, and watched the storm of energy lighten and relax. In time with Michael's words, the world had become a different place.

The roaring engine stopped roaring, or rather, never started roaring at all. Mr. Thurbin's garage door was completely opened, and a tan Toyota Corolla pulled out. The man behind the wheel- a bookish, thirty-something man, steered the car with both hands out of the driveway and down the road. Somewhere, deep down, both Michael and Avery experienced the vaguest of sensations, and thought that Mr. Thurbin used to look a little different.

It was the first time that anyone had seen Mr. Chase leave his property. None of it was very clear, whether Mr. Chase had just been fucking with them about the whole Antichrist thing or what the negativity was that Avery felt or why it was there, but it all happened, fit together, was scary, and, thank God, seemed to be over. Avery was giddy now, and Michael said he still felt great, and Luke was looking really paranoid, trying to look like he would in a world where even though everyone was playing a big joke on him it was all nothing and the joke was on them, but he was failing miserably and looking in fact pretty scared.

"Going for a walk?" Avery asked Mr. Chase.

"I'm going, yes," he replied, nodding his head in the direction of a big, empty space behind their neighborhood. A new development was going up there, and it was all piles of dirt and a big, gaping hole in the Earth where the lake was going. A giant crane, black steel ladder as tall as any of them had ever seen stood proud against the horizon. As he began to walk, he said farewell to the three young men, and to himself he mumbled, "It is not climbable, therefore it cannot be climbed. It is not climbable, therefore it cannot be climbed. It is not climbable, therefore it cannot be climbed. It is not climbable, therefore it cannot be climbed. It is not climbable, therefore it cannot be climbed. It is not climbable, therefore it cannot be climbed. It is not climbable, therefore it cannot be climbed," until finally, once he got bored or figured something out (who could know?) said, "It is not climbable, therefore it must be climbed." Presumably, Mr. Chase then made his way to heaven, or someplace, presumably similar.

"This is for you," was what Michael said as he handed Avery a frosted mug of dark, thick red stuff.

It was getting into the hours of early morning, and Avery was making himself comfortable on a padded lawn chair in one of his world-wide favorite retreats, the garage.

"Is that what I think it is?"

"I made it for you earlier. My blood, with a dash of cinnamon and nutmeg. Now here's what I'm hoping-you say that my energy seems to outshine the energies around me, and if it's overbearing enough, maybe it can change you the way the other blood changed you. Maybe you can come back to normal."

To experience the Throughout made him

something other than human, Avery had all night been saying, and saying too, that he wished there were a way he could get rid of it. It was too confounding a thing to live with permanently. And who to ever connect with on that level? Reptiles? He wanted it gone, and kept saying so. It was not until he took his brother's blood in his hands that he thought, "Perhaps I'm being too hasty?

"A lot of things are obvious to me since this happened. It's like, now I know that humans aren't in charge of the world, and that everything in existence is comprised of different kinds of energy. The ability to feel that energy would be a great asset to, I hate to sound grandiose, but, mankind. Or at least I could live outside their influence myself.

"Maybe it's something that everyone would feel if they were only free of all their poisonous vices and addictions. Maybe I'm more human than most people for it, and once everyone is free they'll have the same perception," but even as he said this, Avery looked down, and swirled the blood against the cold glass. It was slow to drip down the sides.

"One thing, before I do this," Avery said. He wanted to talk once more with Lord Lilenthal. He tried unlocking his capacity for telepathy. He reached out with his life, searching, calling out with all his might, and felt it instantly devoured by an eternal vacuum. "I'm trying to talk to Lord Lilenthal. I've never done this before."

Michael offered that his presence might be a distraction, and went back into the kitchen.

"Fuck," Avery murmured. He wished that there were someone he could talk to about it. Someone to just say, 'oh it's simple, all you have to do is...' He leaned back in his chair and relaxed. Suddenly there came a voice.

Avery? Are you trying to reach me?

"Is that you?"

I believe I may be the 'you' you mean. How are you enjoying this new world of ours?

"It isn't yours. And it never will be. I just wanted to tell you that I'm getting rid of your gift. And that I'm going to do everything in my power to stop you and your kind. I'll never cooperate."

Well, if you insist. You'll be shown no mercy at the end of the world, just so you know, It sounded like sarcasm, like someone who was enjoying a role forced upon them by someone who took that role a lot more seriously.

"Wouldn't dream of it. I'm taking myself off the grid, now. Goodbye."

Wait, just wait a minute, Avery. I find your determination, shall we say, admirable? but I have to stress- this version of humanity that you hold so dear, the virtuous humanity of limitless potential- it's a fallacy. Something that you, in your dreams, wishfully entertain. The strong of your race will always push the weak, and the smart always trick the stupid. They are not the angels you envision them to be. Trust me, I know them. They are a race that cannot win. Who of them will help you?

"I have friends. And I have family. Now, if you'll excuse me."

And with that, Avery hung up the line, unplugged from the net, hoped that the whole discourse wasn't just part of his imagination, and drank deeply of his brother's blood.

CHAPTER 103

1. How exactly does one go about saving the world?

2. Who is mad enough to think themselves qualified to save it?

He wrote these questions down and stared blankly at an otherwise blank sheet of paper for some time. He sat there, flat gaze, wishing that God would just intervene already- not by saving the world, of course, but at least by morphing the pen strokes into pages of colorful answers and encouragement. God spoke through the Throughout all the time. Avery drew a pentagram in the middle of the page, which made the paper warm, a reaction that Avery didn't confidently know the cause of.

When Avery went downstairs, he found Michael leaning against the kitchen counter, eating an apple. His left arm was crossed over his abdomen, and his right arm hung in front of him at half of a right angle. He looked at Avery and chewed, reaping an unfair amount of pleasure from it, as though each time he clenched his jaws his spirit embarked on some sort of manic tear through a blossoming universe.

"Good morning. You feeling okay?"

"Feeling great. But more importantly, what about you?" 'Are you still seeing energy' was what Michael was really asking. Avery nodded, said right after that he was okay with it. Their conversation was topical, 'what do you feel like doing's and 'eh, I don't know's. When Avery walked back up the stairs to his room, he sat down with a notebook on his lap and began writing.

The first chapter of Avery's novel started out very much like one that already existed as a first chapter in somebody else's novel- as if the story had already been taking place long before he thought to record it.

Michael was eating everything that he could get his hands on. He thought suddenly of the genius psychologist living across the street. The words that man spoke, thinking of them now, didn't seem terribly significant, but what a world of impact they had at that moment! An impact that lasted at least longer than a night of sleep, longer than apples and cashews and a half-bowl of chickpeas. But something else threw Michael into greater awe- had he made the opposite decision and embraced the chance, brilliantly coined 'antichristhood', would he not have felt a little off his whole life? Did this particular instance speak fully, finally, for the non-linear nature of time? Empirical evidence of this magnitude had strange effects on him. It made him hungry, and feel as though he needed to take a walk. Halfway down the driveway, he heard Avery's window open.

"Where are you going?" Avery yelled down.

"Just for a walk. Care to join me?"

"Yeah, sure. Just a second."

Avery slipped into his shoes and started for the door. On his way out he noticed that the page he had written on earlier, the two chicken-scratch questions and pentagram were gone. Now it said something different. Letters of colors that bent to Avery's fancy. And once again it was to suggest that the Throughout came from him, that mankind was magic, that his will was written somewhere within the world. Writing, and it went thusly-

'We will be like the first spectators to lend our applause. Just me- clapping. You- clapping. And soon clapping next to us and across from us, followed by more- clapping and yelling, all different rhythms and varying strengths. An entire stadium can roar. And many may have had it in mind to clap. But there will always be someone, bless their soul, that starts clapping first.'

Epilogue

A bronzed man walked through the middle of a parking lot. He stepped over smooth, shining parking curbs, which were completely straight and anchored on each side, each and every one. The asphalt was the darkest black, and the lines marked upon it were brand new, bright, bright white.

Anyone watching the man walk would have noticed, and wondered, why he was bothering so much with his sunglasses. He would remove them from his face and position them on the top of his head, drop them back onto his nose, take them off, fold them, carry them, wear them again, then hang them from his collar, put them back on, and had been carrying on like that all day. They were very hip sunglasses, and everyone had been telling him that he looked good in them. Still, he wasn't sure they were *him*, and he was a little insecure about wearing them. But this was a trifling matter. Guy Weeks, though hardly starving artist ever, was in tune with fortune again, thinking of his fully loaded strip mall and smiling.

The pristine parking lot led to a building that was new enough to be mostly empty. It was a pretty typical building, as far as all the other new buildings in South Florida went- a kind of safe, cheap art-deco, with the sparse ornamentation and unfinished ceilings serving to save money and, luckily, achieve a modern aesthetic. Guy wasn't in the market for a new condo, or for that matter a bicycle, lunch, or pornography. He didn't need his dog groomed and he didn't want to pay for a massage. He received an anonymous tip earlier that he knew to be from Avery, 'Get yourself to 302 Euclid Drive by four o'clock this afternoon. Later if you're busy. It doesn't really matter what time you get there. 302 Euclid Drive.' So here he was, on the corner of Euclid and Mary, looking at a small row of ground level shops, and when he read their neon and printed signs, he could easily admit to feeling emotional.

They served Vietnamese food at 'Just say Pho', sold bicycles at 'Wheelin and Dealin', pornography and adult toys and costumes at 'Red, White, and Screwed', gave dogs haircuts at 'Give a Dog a Comb', and people massages at 'Red Handed'. It was a perfect homage to an artistic presence. It was imitation. It was a sight enough to choke Guy up and make him forget about his sunglasses.

He nodded his head absently, and in a private voice that didn't come off at all contrived, said, "Far out, man. Far out."